THE BIG WHEEL

It was midnight, Wheeltime, before Morgan returned to his cabin. The last thing he did before turning in was to place the cassette of meteorological data at a carefully haphazard angle next to his computer terminal. A bright blue daylit arc of Earth revolved slowly outside his port. He watched it turn to crescent, then to a burning bow, then to a delicate band of red-filtered colour where the soft afterglow of the Sun scattered through the band of atmosphere. He drew the light thermal cover around his ears and closed his eyes.

With a finger on his pulse he inhaled slowly and deeply and as his respiration slowed his pulse rate came down to fifty-five, sank to fifty, hovered, touched forty-five and stayed there. The trick was not so much to persuade Wheeldata that he was asleep as to stay awake. His pulse, respiration, and the airtight door of his cabin filled his consciousness. The Eastern rim of Earth had taken fire before the red indicator winked on the panel next to his door, and he saw the silhouettes of two men as they entered. Morgan closed his eyes. He waited. After half a minute he knew he had to take the risk. He opened his eyes. One man was standing beside the door. The other snapped the cassette into the terminal which wrote up the program identification. Its blue light illumined the face of the operator.

'This it?' Morgan heard him breathe.

His colleague moved beside him. 'Yeah. It'll do.'

Morgan's feet swung to the floor.

'Let's go.' The intruder ejected the cassette into the palm of his hand. Simultaneously a blow to the back of his knees dropped him to a sitting position and Morgan was reaching out to the light switch . . .

By William Rollo and published by New English Library

THE OLYMPUS GAMBIT
THE BIG WHEEL

THE BIG WHEEL

William Rollo

NEW ENGLISH LIBRARY

NEL Books are published by
New English Library,
Mill Road, Dunton Green,
Sevenoaks, Kent.
Editorial office: 47 Bedford Square, London WC1B 3DP

Made and printed in Great Britain by
Hunt Barnard, Aylesbury, Bucks

British Library Cataloguing in Publication Data

Rollo, William
   The big wheel.
   I. Title
   823'.914[F]   PR6068.0

ISBN 0–450–05281–8

One

'TAKE YOUR clothes off.'

'Is this a *full* debriefing?'

'No, sir, I'm - ' Lieutenant Honeywell looked slantwise at Morgan from under long black lashes. The exasperated line of her mouth pulled a glimpse of dimple into her smooth cheeks.

'No, Mister Morgan' – she hesitated over the unfamiliar civilian style - 'I monitor bone-marrow growth, blood cell count, heart signature, vascular tension, pulmonary efficiency and a few dozen other variables. On my say-so they weed out agoraphobes, claustrophobes, people with variable-gee sickness and people with zero-gee sickness. But a man who makes puns! He can devastate the morale of a space station inside a week. He goes out first.'

'I'm mortified,' said Morgan, undermined by the girl's open nature. He betrayed no trace of irony.

'Out of the airlock. Briefless.'

'I had no idea it was so serious.'

Her smile, having returned, faltered. Morgan was glad to see that she looked a shade perturbed. 'Look, I don't really mean it, sir. We get to develop our own conversational mores up here. After a few months Earth seems like another world.'

How true. 'I understand that. It happens in any community, not just in space.'

'Well, don't worry. You can keep your pants on.'

'Fine. Lead me to the airlock.'

'For the calibrations. I'll excuse you the space walk – this time.'

'Ah.'

'Been weightless before?'

'Only aerobatics. Then half an hour before docking just now.'

'Mm.'

For thirty-five minutes Lieutenant Honeywell ran test programs through the computer whilst Morgan laboured on a bicycle that went nowhere and pulled handles that didn't move. By the end of that time his biomedical soul pulsed and fluttered in the space station's computer along with the bugged telemetry of the rest of the Big Wheel's complement. Then she encoded the subtler sensory parameters that the implanted transducer couldn't measure. There was a moment of habitual anxiety as she ran a quick finger along the pattern of scars that started under his collar bone and crossed his upper arm. It had come near to betraying him on more than one occasion.

'Your file says this was a hunting accident?'

''Fraid so.'

'They hunt with automatic weapons in England now?'

'The spirit of sporting life isn't quite dead. It was a rather finely-tuned hunting rifle in inexperienced hands. Chap was climbing over a fence and fired by accident. He just kept firing. Shock, you see.'

'I see. Well, you pass out a hundred per cent as far as I'm concerned, sir. The British Air Force must have quite a training programme.'

'Royal Air Force. They encouraged us to play a lot of sport and that sort of thing.'

'Well, that accounts for it, I guess.'

This time Morgan noticed the challenge in her voice. He also noticed that she seemed to have changed. Fifty minutes ago she had outflanked his caution with an uncritical torrent of chatter: now her words were calibrated. He classified her under Threats with a question mark for further evaluation.

The last data, an infra-red holograph of Morgan's torso, rippled into the computer. Lieutenant Honeywell closed the file with a quick left-handed *arpeggio* and turned towards him.

'How is your programme, sir?' She was out of her field of competence now, and discipline returned.

'Not heavy today.' He consulted the c-unit on his wrist. 'I'm due for an equipment check next.'

'Like me to take you down to stores?' *Down* meant *outwards*. This near the axis of the Big Wheel gee was only one-tenth that of Earth. The fluid lines of the girl's body acquired an extra grace and sensuousness from the slow-motion harmonics of the low gravity. Morgan considered her carefully.

'It's a kind thought. But I've got to get to know this ship, so if you don't mind I'll go on my own.'

'OK. Don't say I didn't warn you . . . '

Of what?The intricate labyrinth of corridors? The elaborate initiation rites of an elite ship? He did not fear them. *Blending* was his job. It was what he was best at.

He gave the girl a full English 'Goodbye' and stepped out through the oval door into the annular corridor. Of course she was pretty. Very different from Annabel - not that Annabel wasn't nice too, but she was so English, so county, so pleasantly, sociably . . . but that was to be disloyal. (*Disloyal*! What did that mean?) He was fond of her. He hoped that she would heed his warning . . ..

That had been long ago and in another world: a fortnight ago in Devonshire. On that morning the assassin had lain full length upon the cropped dew-grey grass. He might have been taken for a country gentleman – no hay-seed for sure, but still not averse to discussing the price of cattle-feed. That impression would have been formed on the strength of well-worn tweeds and a sandy lurcher which lay, muzzle on paws, ears a-twitch. But that would be to overlook the features, both intent and composed, and the steady eye with its remote focus at the Eliot R23 sighting system of the finely balanced 6.23mm Mauser.

He lay in the regulation prone firing position next to a long age-rounded granite boulder embedded in the smooth hilltop. He felt the disciplined serenity of muscular relaxation and the honed edge of mortal concentration. The mist still hung on the hillside, a white gauze in front of the lower trees, a white sheet behind them. They were flat grey shapes. Among them the target lay. The view through the sight, with its image enhancement, was more clear. The target was within the fine green lines of the aiming square, but to one side of the central point. The range and slant vector were steady, and windage flickered either side of half a knot. But the R23 took automatic care of these.

He breathed in shallowly, and breathed out and held. The ready-to-fire indicator blinked red. He smiled slightly and depressed the point of aim by ten centimetres; it was an act more mischievous than merciful. He fired. As he watched through the sight the report came back to him in flat ripples. The branch parted cleanly and started to fall. It fell level, and the water drops that adhered to its underside were undisturbed. The big black crow fell with it, still gazing absently into the mist. After falling five metres he started to flap his wings, but only after ten metres did he remember to let go of the heavy branch.

He tidied up his trim and flapped slowly into the mist with one hoarse curse against the force that had for a moment disturbed the equilibrium of his world.

Morgan ejected the cartridge and pocketed it, leaned the rifle gently against the rock, and sprang to his feet. 'Not bad at two hundred metres, eh, Sam? If we haven't the heart to shoot the buggers we can always make 'em paranoid.'

Sam, the lurcher, had also got to her feet at the sound of the shot, and now stood looking down the hill with a canine grin. Possibly she was amused, but at Morgan's words she set off, glancing twice behind her, after quarry of her own.

He walked slowly in a circle, attempting to saturate his memory with all he could survey; for all he could survey in this mist, and more, was his – this hill and some of the next and the valley around and the saddle in between. But this morning he felt that it would soon not be his; that nuclear war would take it beyond anyone's possession, or that the diverging political extremes would contrive to take it from him – singly or in conflict. He could sense the tensions with prophetic certainty.

Or, he felt as he walked quickly down the hill, he had been quiet out here too long. He had lost that tension which makes it rich to live. The mist closed around him as he descended, scuffing the grey dew from the grass. You can accommodate to lassitude, and it changes you, dissolving the keen edge until you are not ready for the call when it comes. If you're lucky enough to realise it, it can frighten you. He hurried through the bank of trees, barely seeing their phantom perfection, and straight across the clear granite-edged pools of the Dart, oblivious of the cold thigh-deep water. He had to get back to the house. Almost he expected to find it burned to the ground.

Annabel was up, frying eggs and bacon. He remembered to give her the mushrooms from his pockets. She fussed over his wet clothes and he consented irritably to sit down while she pulled off his boots and made him change his socks.

He'd read the reports, of course, as they came through his terminal – though only with professional detachment. But his growing self-dissatisfaction had catalysed them subtly. They now constituted a more personal threat. That, in its turn, made it hard to assess the threat clearly. There was the background drift of French ICBMs keyed to British targets, cheeky dash-and-run overflights on both sides. Behind that the economic perfidy and an exchange of insults worthy of neighbouring South East Asian dictatorships, and on the edge of the picture the Soviet Union waiting to pick up the pieces. But what was the secret picture? What was going on in the centres of power? What was true military posture and what was mere militant posturing? Instinct said it looked bad, but that would hardly convince Annabel.

'Could you do me a favour?'

'Yes.' Her look complied in every possible way.

'Take some more leave and look after this place for me for a few weeks.'

'But why? You've never been worried about it before.'

He could hardly tell her the truth – what he knew of it. Nor could he tell her a convincing lie.

'D'you trust me?'

'Yes, Richard, of course. But why?'

'I would like you to stay away from London for a few weeks.'

'But why?'

This wasn't going to be easy. '*Why* doesn't matter, because you trust me, remember?'

'And I do. But I can't be out of London that long – if it means staying here on my own.'

The hell with it. 'We're very close to a European war.'

'That! Look, Richard, you needn't worry about me. In my job I'll be the first to know. I'm not without my contacts, you know.'

The irony of it. You're a spy and a girl you don't want to hurt gets herself a job as a journalist. Damn the arrogance of journalists. Contacts!

He took the old iron key with the Yale back-up from his jacket pocket and dangled it in front of her nose by the tab.

'There is a French nuclear submarine aptly named *L'Inflexible*. Right now it's lying in a one thousand metre ocean gully off Palermo. The targeting of its sixteen ballistic missiles is co-ordinated by a single computer. At the moment those missiles are targeted on Britain. Even the Soviet Union has a lower priority. They would need re-targeting for a strike on Russia. All *L'Inflexible*'s missiles carry seven independent warheads. All seven warheads of the sixth missile to be fired would explode over London.'

'They wouldn't be so stupid. It would be mutual suicide.'

'I dare say you're right, but that's only a small part of the picture. I *know* we're nearer to a war than we have been since 1945.'

'Nearer than Cuba? Nearer than Tehran? Afghanistan? Saudi Arabia?'

'I'm not forgetting them.'

'Then how do you know all this? I thought your present job was meteorology.'

'Everyone's business gets mixed up with meteorology – which doesn't mean this is in the public domain.'

'That seems to be the stock suffix to saying something interesting. All right, I wouldn't have used it.'

He'd laid it on thick and either the credibility problem or the brute force of his approach had cooled the air between them. But she had taken the key. And the call from HQ had come later that day.

Two

MORGAN STOPPED to steady his bearings. The corridor circled the docking module and the three levels of low gravity engineering workshops at the centre of the Big Wheel. Thirty storeys further out, two hundred and sixty-two metres beneath his feet, was the rim of the space station. There you could trudge around in a whole one gee if you felt like it – or if your work took you there. Somewhere out there was Crew Stores. He knew that because he'd spent his evenings during the previous week memorising the charts of Big Wheel. He had intended to start ahead of the game. But remembering the charts wasn't quite the same as knowing where to go. At least one familiar reference, *up*, meant a different thing on every radial line of the space station. If he didn't start off at the right elevator he could find himself at the rim a kilometre's walk from where he wanted to go. The corridor was empty. He turned reluctantly to ask Lieutenant Honeywell for directions.

'*Mister Morgan, this is Wheeldata. Acknowledge.*'

Morgan was startled, and caught himself glancing up and down the empty corridor. Then he smiled. 'Acknowledge, Wheeldata. How did you know where to locate me?'

'Your medical telemetry is now on line. I locate you through your transmitter.' The neutral voice, though synthetic, was not unpleasant. But it began and ended with a soft chime. Frequent exposure to that chime might, Morgan thought, prejudice his relationship with the computer.

'Fine, Wheeldata. How can I help you?'

'I intend to help you, sir. The file reads you at item two of your induction programme, having left Medical. You are due at Crew Stores at fourteen-thirty hours. Do you wish for topographical guidance?'

Morgan smiled at the computer system's choice of phrase and tried out its flexibility with, 'I wouldn't mind if you told me the way.' He was surprised by the unruffled response.

'Certainly, sir. Generally expressed, the problem is to find the shortest route between two modules which are designated by their positions in polar coordinates and an alphabetic determinant. The specific problem is to find the shortest route from your present position, which is in "A" quadrant – which is between zero and ninety degrees with reference to the spacecraft datum – third level, room N, A/3/N in short, to C/33/BA, which is on the rim in the opposite quadrant. Acknowledge.'

'Ah, yes, clear as. . . very clear.'

'From your present location the quickest route is a traversal of annular corridor three to elevator C which will transfer you to the rim in the appropriate quadrant.'

'Which direction do I take now?'

'Follow the room designations from N towards A.'

'Thanks.'

'You're welcome, sir.'

Morgan's first long elevator ride on Big Wheel nearly made him sick, and not on account of the conventional variation in apparent weight. He had been warned about the coriolis effect. As you move outwards on a rigid rotating body you've got to pick up angular momentum. You've got to lose it as you move inwards. He was expecting it and the expectation didn't trouble him. But when he found a radial movement giving him a tangential push – hard against the side of the elevator – he suffered for the first time in his life from motion-nausea.

In Stores, they gave him the electronic key to a small point-one gee cabin on the fourth floor, and dose meters for gee, radiation and cosmic ray flux, which were slaved into his telemetry. They also gave him a white overall with the shoulder flash of a Meteorological officer. He persuaded them to let him hang on to his own RAF issue c-unit (computer, chronometer, communicator); it was compatible with the on-board computer – Wheeldata – and he had got used to the feel of it on his wrist over the last few months. He emerged from the store outwardly standardised. Until he spoke he would merge with the other USSF personnel. The c-unit displayed nine minutes before his appointed meeting with Big Wheel's commanding officer, Captain Quentin M. Rathbone. Wheeldata directed him to Command A, the operations room four decks out from the Centre. The computer-generated voice quietly confided in him that Command A was colloquially known as The Bunker, and that although Command A was heavily shielded for combat survivability, the colloquialism was regarded as humorous because of its inappropriateness to an orbital location.

'Why's that funny?' asked Morgan innocently.

'I can refer you to the paper by Annan and Schnietz of Princeton University entitled *Humor: Semantic Logic and Human Evolution*. I can briefly summarise it in the one minute and forty-six seconds which it will take you to arrive at Command A. Their contention is that there's a necessary link between –'

'Please don't trouble yourself now, Wheeldata,' Morgan resumed in some embarrassment. 'I just wanted to see how near they are to making an intelligent machine.'

There was a pause of some five seconds. Then, 'Do you wish a response, sir?'

'I'm sorry. Have I hurt your feelings?'

'No. I do not have the required function. Do you wish a response to your implied assessment?'

'I can't exactly remember what it was, but yes, if there's time.'

'My development has not reached a human level. I do not have a human function. Human processing function has a basis in organic tensions which would be inappropriate for my function.'

'Why do you refer to yourself as *I*?'

'I am programmed to refer to functions grouped under Wheeldata as *I*.'

'So you have no consciousness?'

'I regret there is insufficient time to continue this routine. The door

B/4/Comm.A. is Command A. Your admittance through electronic security is authorised. I am announcing your arrival to the security personnel.'

The airlock cycled Morgan into Command A as swiftly as he could cross the double threshold. A sergeant of the Special Space Warfare Unit checked his pass and scrutinised him carefully before detailing a trooper to deliver him to the captain. The marine carried the first weapon that Morgan had seen on Big Wheel, an RMP. A very efficient weapon. His professional interest was roused. The Americans didn't even know that they had lost one, but the Secret Service had given him an RMP to play with at Bisley ten days ago. It had complete recoil balancing; you could prop the gun on top of a wine bottle and squeeze the trigger remotely with a length of string and it wouldn't fall off. Meanwhile its spin-stabilised rocket shells would be tearing holes in a steel plate two hundred metres away. So a weightless man firing it wouldn't be kicked into a fast spin with his first shot. Also it wouldn't vacuum-weld and it had built-in heat control. An exotic rod,but the marine's looked as though it had been used.

Morgan quickly weighed up the inside of Command A as he hitched himself along the guide rails. It was cavernous for the inside of a space ship, and yet it was a small part of Big Wheel. It was arranged like a theatre except that its curved floor swooped upwards from the back row to the stage. The one hundred-odd seats of the auditorium, each with its VDU and terminal, dipped towards the dais of the Command Team, which was backed by a cinema-sized array of solid-state display screens. It reminded him of NASA's Mission Control at Houston, of NORAD's War City under the mountains near Colorado Springs, of the Command Centre and Seat of Government under the Cotswolds near Cheltenham. This one controlled more data that Houston and more power than the other two centres put together. Now, at Green Alert, the room was almost deserted, for Wheeldata could find anyone anywhere on Big Wheel. But like the marine's gun the place looked well used and ready for use.

'What's going on?' Morgan asked his guide.

'Not a lot at the moment. sir. Processing a shuttle cycle. Movement Control's near the front there. Commander Crabtree's in charge.'

The three rows of torsos were intent on their screens. Morgan couldn't see their insignia. 'Which one's Commander Crabtree?'

'Front row. Third from the left. She's just put her headset on.'

'She?' He had taken the commander for a man.

'That's the official story.' Morgan glanced sharply at the marine as he felt he should, but the other continued rapidly. 'They're handling the docking. Well, the computer's handling it, but they've got to be there. Then there's Systems behind them: they've got to watch compatibility between the two spacecraft. Behind them's Logistics: they look after the whole business of stores, fuel transfer and so on. Then on the other side there's Security, Armaments, Communications, Power and Life-Support. They all keep a permanent presence in Command A. At the front there's Commander Zeffert. By rights he shouldn't be there on his own. The Command Team should always maintain a two-man presence in Command A.'

'Why's that?' He knew the answer.

'Well, I guess I don't rightly know!' Absolute power is also embarrassing. Morgan arrived at the high table of Command A and resisted the inclination to come to attention.

'Morgan, sir. I was asked to report here to meet Captain Rathbone.'

'At ease, Morgan. Zeffert.' He stretched out a lanky arm and shook Morgan's hand. Then he leaned back and stroked the bald top of his head. 'I hope you had a pleasant crossing?' For the first time since taking off from Vandenberg, Morgan felt at ease. He took an instant liking to Zeffert.

'Not bad, sir. Very calm.' Zeffert's blue eyes creased slightly with humour.

'Good. The captain's up in the turret.' He gestured languidly to a circular airlock at the side of the room, level with the Command desk. 'Excuse me. *Wheeldata, give me Flight 594's ventral camera with control.*' He pressed a button on his c-unit. 'Morgan's on his way, sir.' Next he was vectoring the incoming shuttle's camera on to one of Big Wheel's docking gantries. 'OK. See you here and there no doubt.'

Morgan took formal leave of Zeffert before moving on, because you've got to earn the right to local relaxations of etiquette. He let go of the rails, coasting the last six metres to the airlock. The aim was instinctively good. He drifted along a three-metre tunnel without touching the sides and easily caught the rail again as he emerged into the turret.

He knew precisely where he was. This was Turret A, one of two retractable glass cylinders which pierced the smooth discus faces of Big Wheel. At the moment the turret was de-spun in relation to Big

Wheel's rotation, so that he was looking apparently *down* the three hundred metre wall of the Wheel's radius at the Earth whose milky blue daytime side was bisected by the space station's horizon. With ponderous serenity that horizon was changing as the central docking module swung round from behind him, passed across the face of the globe, and swung again behind his head. The gracefully cranked delta of a McDonnell-Douglas SC 3 space shuttle was rising towards rendezvous, slow-rolling to match the rotation of the Wheel. It appeared to rock laterally against the terrestrial background. *Parallax*, Morgan thought; he was really observing the epicyclic motion of the turret. Rathbone was alone, watching the approaching shuttle with his back to Morgan. Morgan reluctantly withdrew his gaze from the cosmic panorama and looked at the back of Rathbone's head. The captain's hair was grey and the skin of his neck was mapped by the deep seams which appear when age melts away the underlying flesh.

'Morgan, sir.'

Rathbone didn't answer. He flung out his right arm and gestured Morgan round in front of him. His gaze was still fixed out in space. Occasionally he spoke tersely into a headset microphone, presumably to Zeffert. One of the earphones was clamped over his left ear. The other was cocked back at an angle. Thus he had access to the two worlds of Big Wheel – the commonplace warm world of men and women moving and speaking, and the synthetic, processed, recorded data-web of Big Wheel's electronic nervous system. Apparently unheeded, three VDUs glowed and flickered in front of him. One was a graphical representation of the attitude and velocity relationship of the SC 3 and Big Wheel. Another showed neighbouring space traffic on a smaller scale. The third was a schematic diagram which Morgan couldn't recognise. The captain spoke rapidly, but with formal emphasis, into his microphone.

'Rendezvous and docking is nominal at step eighteen. Commander Zeffert, you have control.' He nodded at the response in his headphone and turned his eyes to Morgan. Morgan was struck principally by the gravity of their expression.

'Draw up a seat.' Morgan unlocked a magnetic chair from the wall and steered it to Rathbone's desk, relocking the castor-switch deftly. Rathbone allowed himself an understated smile. 'The last man that came through here couldn't do that. He claimed to be ready to live on the Wheel. And fight if need be.' He leaned over the desk and shook

Morgan's hand in a quick dry grasp. 'Pleased to have you on board, Morgan. That goes for me and my crew.'

'Thank you, sir. I'm privileged to be here.' This was the line to take at the moment.

'Well, you are, at that. Now I have your file here.' He didn't really. Wheeldata was displaying it on his console. 'Vandenberg were quite impressed with your pre-flight course. You passed out with ninety-eight per cent with a recommendation for further executive training – which may not actually apply as you're not USSF personnel. Your British Pentagon, ah the – ' he read carefully from his VDU ' – the Ministry of Defence, have sent me your service record, and I have it here.' He began to key his way through its contents. 'Cranwell, yes, first tour on Harrier Fives, good . . . What did you think of the Harrier?'

Morgan delved back into his cover-thinking. He'd never even sat in a Harrier of course. 'Beautiful when you've learnt the vectored thrust techniques. A lot of fun after that as long as you keep an eye on the fuel.'

'Well, your British versions always were a bit low on range.' It was a humorous attempt. Morgan let it pass with a slight smile. Rathbone continued, 'I first flew AV 8B's in action in '88 – against SAM batteries in Saudi Arabia. We developed the technique of landing right under the noses of the enemy to pick up our own casualties. You couldn't do that in an F 25 . . . Let's see now. Tornadoes, Typhoons. DFC, DSO – so you were there too, Morgan?'

'Yes, sir. I was there.'

'Good. Staff College. Tornado squadron, European Space Agency, Met. Office.' All lies of course. Except the Met. Office. Morgan really had made the sacrifice of spending six months there so that the Secret Service could put a spy on Big Wheel.

'You know what Big Wheel's function is, Morgan?'

'It acts as a space staging, communications and surveillance post, sir.'

'It does. But we're primarily in the business of killing Reds. Our function is to provide first, second or nth strike capability against the Soviet Union, independent of the survival of mainland USA. And to maintain that capability we watch every blade of grass that grows down there just in case there's anything lurking underneath it. And if there is we're ready to zonk it with a wide variety of instruments. That's what we're here for, and don't you forget it.'

'Right, sir.'

'D'you know how delicate the strategic balance is down there, Morgan?'

'I've some idea.'

'Both sides have complete first strike capability. You know what that means?'

'Yes, sir. Each side could, if it started firing first, be assured of destroying the other's strategic nuclear forces on the ground or under the sea or in the air.'

'That is true. That means that each Societ SS 26 can put twelve MIRVs within twenty metres of twelve of our MXs – and that goes for us too. So each side expends a fraction of its force on destroying the whole of the other team – if he shoots first. So all the advantages are with the attacker. The temptation to unburden those launchers privily one morning is . . . there.'

'But can't the other side launch as soon as it detects an attack?'

'Good, Morgan. We empty all six chambers as soon as we hear a bang – only to find it was a horse backfiring . . . .'

' – Or,' ventured Morgan, 'a radar ghost, or a training alert program put through without proper warning, or a computer malfunction . . . .'

'Correct. So we're back with assured mutual destruction – only with a difference.' He looked at Morgan expectantly.

'The difference is that everyone's now prepared to let off the whole lot if they *think* there's an attack building.'

'Not how the Pentagon would prefer to phrase it perhaps, but substantially accurate. The fingers on the triggers are nervous.' He paused for a long time. 'Which is where we come in.'

This was stale news to Morgan, but he played his part. 'How?'

'Like I said, we watch every blade of grass that grows down there on every wavelength nature provides. And the Pentagon launches only on our shout.'That's how no one looses'off by mistake.'

'And if the Russians do strike first?'

'They'd be fools with us watching. The response from US forces would be virtually instantaneous.'

'And both sides are destroyed?'

'Not entirely, though we can't go into that. But as far as the Russians are concerned, when they've taken the US return strike they can expect Big Wheel to plough up any odd Soviet acre that hasn't received attention.'

17

'And the Russians presumably try to nullify the effect of Big Wheel?'

'Not just presumably. They duplicate the threat by building their own strategic space station. So that's part of our task: keeping tabs on Astrogorodok and trying to keep its tabs off us. They try to nullify the threat by fouling up our communications. That's a tactic we've also got to counter and duplicate ourselves. Oh yes, Commodore Litvinov and I have become old pals; we've got a marvellous sympathy for one another's jobs.

'Mister Morgan, as an exchange posting your primary role will be to uphold these functions by adhering to the disciplines and orders of the United States Space Force. That is in any capacity up to and including a part in the annihilation of the Soviet Union. More specifically and routinely you will pursue your duties as a Meteorological officer, in which capacity you will be directly under the orders of Lieutenant-Commander Grey. She'll brief you fully. Lieutenant-Commander Grey is responsible for Met. and Earth Resources Technology and Liaison.

'You will also comply with all standing orders and make yourself particularly conversant with those appertaining to emergency drill: fire, security, battle stations, decompression, search and rescue . . . so forth. Any questions?'

'Yes, sir. That's all fairly straightforward. Is there any respect in which my position will be different from that of USSF personnel?'

'In all operational respects, no. You will find your security rating different from officers of your status, but not enough to make any difference to your job.'

'Just in case . . . is there any security area that I ought to steer clear of?'

'Parts of the ship are security-coded for all personnel, and Wheel-data automatically vets information according to the clearance of its recipient, so I think my advice would be for you merely to follow the system. It's not a problem we have. Security is seldom an obtrusive matter.'

Morgan knew the system, and expected just this answer. But he was disappointed. Some guidelines on where he shouldn't look might well make his mission easier.

The interview had taken a sinister turn. He waited in silence while Rathbone looked at him thoughtfully.

'What are your first impressions of Big Wheel, Mister Morgan?'

Morgan thought. It was not difficult to tell the truth. 'I'm immensely impressed. Its sheer size is quite a shock. I'm most impressed by Wheeldata; that's the best example I've seen of electronics being designed to select the individual out of the herd. I've yet to assess the station's military capability, but –' he sought a phrase, finding one he just had the nerve to use – 'I'd say what you've got here represents a quantum jump in space engineering.'

Rathbone laughed – whether from gratification or amusement Morgan could not tell. 'That we have, and we're all very proud of it. And I can tell you that to go along with the machinery I've never served with any sort of team that has reached the pitch of this one – and I've got five hundred men and women up here, not including industrial contractors.'

Morgan's c-unit blinked a discreet signal to remind him he would be due at the Meteorological Section in ten minutes. Simultaneously Wheeldata spoke to Rathbone in – Morgan could have sworn – suitably obsequious tones.

'Wheeldata to Captain Rathbone. Acknowledge.'

'Speak.'

'I'd just like to remind you that Mister Morgan is due at Meteorology in ten minutes. Also Commander Zeffert would like you to continue monitoring the 594 shuttle docking from step twenty-five which is due on your VDU in two minutes.'

'Thank you, Wheeldata. Tell Zeffert I'm complying. OK, Morgan, carry on. Report to me after a few days and tell me what progress you're making.'

'Yes, sir. Thank you.' Morgan just managed to check an attempt to come to attention in one-tenth gee and left carefully. Zeffert, apparently giving all his attention to a VDU, gave him a blind wave as he passed through Command A.

As he stepped through the operation room's airlock a klaxon sounded jarringly. It brought him sharply up to his own level of red alert, but there was no check in his smooth movements. The klaxon stopped after a braying ten seconds and Wheeldata announced increased solar flare intensity. Morgan remembered the standing order: there would be no more activity for suited personnel outside the Wheel until the all-clear was announced. That meant no suited EVAs and no shuttle trips. There was a rush of duty crewmen to Command A. Each as he ran was already being briefed by Wheeldata on his particular role in retrieving a suited team from an antenna maintenance operation, or the decision whether to speed the SC 3's turnaround or keep her crew on the Wheel for the duration. Wheeldata could conduct a thousand separate dialogues without taking his mind from more complex matters.

The Meteorological Section had a suite of open offices on the rim of the Wheel – open to one another, not to space, that is. The suite was dominated by wall-sized solid-state displays. As the personnel on duty seemed to be preoccupied at their consoles Morgan strolled to the middle of the room and watched the varying views around him. One in particular, showing an almost complete hemisphere of the Earth, a great milky jewel of stirred glass, fascinated him. He became lost in it. When he had stood for so long that he detected the orbital motion of whatever camera was seeing it, a voice spoke at his shoulder.

'Who have we here, stout Cortez – or could it be Bloody Morgan?' It was a female voice, tough without being harsh, anxious to make friends. He turned.

'Morgan, ma'am. No relation as far as I know,' he added in a universal seafaring accent. Some such friendly return was demanded by her pretty auntish face framed by swept-back grey hair. 'I'm looking for. . . ' He saw her shirt epaulettes and name tag. 'Ah, so you are . . . '

'Commander Grey. Hullo.'

'I've been looking at your wall displays. A lot of pixels in that one,' he said, trying a bit of the astro-meteorological jargon he'd been learning at Bracknell.

'A hell of a lot. It's a window.'

'Oh God, what a twit.'

'Not really. Look, we've got to scrub your briefing for the moment. We've got a meteorological crisis situation building up here.'

'Oh, sure.' What kind of building was a *meteorological crisis situation building*? Oh, *building*!

The commander was already squeezing into her console and pulling on a headset. One schematic on her VDU showed the position and status of the five different networks of weather satellites – including the Societ strategic system – into which the Wheel was linked electronically. Morgan guessed that the USSF wasn't paying the Russians any rent. The incoming data rate was high. And interrogations were pouring into Wheeldata from ground stations, relayed around the world through the weather satellites themselves.

Why this activity? Morgan glanced up at the wall display in front of him – not the window. Wheeldata was calling up sequences of satellite TV images on to the split screen. He was labelling them with temperatures, wind velocities, pressures and degrees of threat. The global level of threat was unusually high. The second of a series of tornadoes which were lashing across the Caribbean like errant tops was sawing its way along the north coast of Cuba. The refugees had not yet had a chance to return to their homes in Florida after the previous one. Meanwhile more were building and the sullen tropical atmosphere had plenty more torsional energy in store. The valleys of the Indus and Ganges were drowned, while most of central India was in its eighth month of drought – with the probability of rain within the next month at less than five per cent. The two areas of flood and arid desert looked the same on the screen: brown mud and brown dust. The islands of New Zealand were a plain white against the sea. The moonlight temperature in Christchurch was minus ten centigrade, and it had been for the last month.

Commander Grey was already deep in conversation with a relief mission at Rajshahi. Morgan tore his attention away from the threat screen; he had given up trying to calculate how many were dying there, beyond the weather satellites' power of resolution. He turned his attention professionally to the rest of the room, assessing the type and purpose of its various equipment, its communications potential, the number and role of its personnel. He memorised the faces, tagging the names where they were legible. Then he left the room.

Morgan tapped the button on his c-unit. 'Wheeldata?'

'This is Wheeldata. Can I help you, Mister Morgan?'

'Yes. Can you tell me if Lieutenant Honeywell is off duty?'

'That is outside my function.' Obviously Wheeldata knew. It seemed that he had a sensitive notion of privacy. 'I can connect you with Lieutenant Honeywell.'

'That'll be fine. Go ahead.'

'Lieutenant Honeywell acknowledges your call. Wheeldata out.'

'Mister Morgan? Is everything all right?'

'Yes. I hope I haven't called you at an inconvenient moment.'

'Not at all. What's the problem?'

'Are you on duty?'

'No, but I'm always on stand-by if there's a problem.'

'There's no problem. I'm looking for someone to give me a guided tour of the Wheel. It came to me after long thought that you would do the job better than Captain Rathbone.'

'Are you serious? It could take a week to get round this yo-yo!'

'I was thinking of a few of the more exciting places – you know, Big Ben, Tower of London, Houses of Parliament . . . '

'Do I detect an extraordinarily subtle irony – sir?'

'Sorry. English habit.'

Morgan already knew a great deal about the Wheel. What he didn't know he wouldn't be allowed to see on a casual inspection. But he wanted to have first-hand knowledge of his field of operations. And he wanted to see the flesh-and-blood component of the Wheel's systems. It must have weak links that he could exploit.

Two hours later Morgan and Lieutenant Honeywell were in the rim bar drinking beer. Morgan's chief impression had not been of any particular detail, but a fascination had grown upon him for this great vessel, glistening like a toy of the gods in space; it was a ship, a base, a citadel, a sweeping structure of floors and corridors in slick white plastic, steel, aluminium, titanium, glass, each with its smell, each with its warmth or chill to the hand. It was one organism, this Wheel, nerved by Wheeldata who talked in rainbow colours and modulated tones from ubiquitous wall displays, given will by its human complement who worked with swift skill towards a subtle array of political and scientific ends.

Specifically he *had* seen on his second visit to Command A a reconnaissance satellite image of the Soviet space station Astrogorodok in its perpetually occulted orbit on the other side of the Earth. Next to it was television film of Big Wheel – shot from a nearby Russian satellite and intercepted by the Americans. The American ship was a smoothly fabricated plate, broken here and there by sensors, by the central docking assembly, by large windows downsun, and by the spider-web framework of the second saucer that was beginning to grow next to it. In contrast the Russian vehicle was a conglomerate of TT5 second stages joined on a three-dimensional nodal pattern. It reminded Morgan of a model of a protein molecule in an early stage of construction.

In Command A he'd been introduced to the Surveillance and Security officer, Commander McMurdo. McMurdo was tall, lean and brown, with knife-features framing eyes of opaque blue – when he wasn't affecting executive sepia sunglasses with tortoiseshell frames.

He reeked to Morgan of the Department of American Intelligence; it was partly his jargon and partly his proprietary attitude to *the other side*.

'Now how about a quick snoop at the opposition, Mister Morgan? We don't want to neglect them, do we? After all they keep us in business . . . '

'And we them?'

'Exactly. Now who shall I introduce you to first?'

He typed out a seven-digit code. Morgan instantly repeated it to himself with a mnemonic designator.

'Here's the man: Commodore Litvinov, commander of Astrogorodok. We recorded this shot when he made a coded contact with Moscow yesterday. We won't worry about the message content; it's rather, ah, specialised.' Litvinov looked about fifty, with white strands in his black waving hair, and a touch of East Asian in his flat heavy features. He wore grey fatigues with red epaulettes. As he spoke to Moscow only his mouth moved.

'D'you know anything about him?'

'Everything. Son of an admiral, privileged education, served with the Naval Air Arm, based Cuba, Syria for a short time, Aden. Commanded the *Kiev* on her last tour. He's married with three kids – one in the army, one at university, one at ballet school. Quite a pleasant man; we make contact sometimes – usually over search-and-rescue business.

'Here's his second in command. Air Force man, Colonel Sidorenko.' A series of stills, then film of a man in flying kit climbing into the cockpit of a MiG 31. A decisive, grey-eyed man. Swift movements. 'His background's more typical. We'd call his family poor. Did well at school and Air Force Academy. First tour of duty was in the Middle East – 35th fighter wing of the IA-PVO. Astronaut training, shuttle pilot and so on. Married, two children. Russian action-man, and he's got to be reckoned with.'

Morgan nodded at the screen. 'How did you get those shots?'

McMurdo was pointedly silent – a security man's affectation already familiar to Morgan. He didn't like McMurdo; it was reaction both personal and professional.

He'd also met the Armaments officer. Zylka Zbijowski. a man who apparently knew what he was doing with anything from an automatic to a space-to-space missile, and who was inclined to begin his sentences with the expression 'We have the capability . . .' Morgan liked

Zylka. He was probably a second or third generation Pole, and he retained the Polish good manners and enthusiasm for life.

As for the smaller weapons, Morgan had at least seen the armoury door – an item of furniture printed with an impressive library of prohibitions. In his memory it was underlined in red.

The other highlight had been a check on the space suit depots, and a fitting session. Of course he'd been through all that at Vandenberg SFB but the exercise was less academic up here. He didn't have his own suit. No one did. If you were going outside you put on your own undergarment and then chose any suit of your own size. There were three sizes, colour-coded to match the suit-band that everyone wore on his wrist. Morgan's was red. In an emergency anyone could wear any suit – though it might hurt a great deal if your band was red and you had to wear a green-coded suit.

'Digesting data?'

Morgan nodded. 'A lot to digest. I want to thank you for showing me around. There was really no reason why you should.'

'Oh, it was a pleasure.'

'I've been thinking.'

'Yes?' She looked suspicious.

'It must have cost six hundred dollars to orbit this beer at present prices.'

The lieutenant shook her head. 'No, we only bring essentials up from Earth. After all we get through quite a bit of liquor. It's manu-factured up here.'

'How on Earth d'you manage that?'

'Well, partly in hydroponics and partly in a bacterial system. It's a procedure NASA worked out along with Fed. Brewers Inc. It works quite well. The water's recycled, of course.'

Morgan put his glass down. 'I was hoping we wouldn't go into that subject for a while. Hydroponics is your area, isn't it?'

'Well, it's one of our overview functions, but I don't have anything to do with making beer. It's all controlled by microprocessor and monitored by Wheeldata.'

'What do you do then? I mean, how do you spend your time professionally?'

'Routine medical work: routine in an orbital sense that is. Mostly checking that people aren't going over the limits on weightlessness, radiation and so forth. Seeing whether we can fix them up here if they have. It's a logistics disaster if we've got to shuttle someone down unscheduled. Accidents. Surprisingly we don't get much crisis medicine – other than appendicitis and so forth.'

'Any pregnancies?'

'Oh God, don't mention it! The Pentagon would go into terminal sanctimony.'

'God bless them. OK, I didn't say a word. Change the subject. Are you happy in your work?'

'Inevitably. Up here you *are* your work.'

Meteorology, thought Morgan. *God save me*.

'Particularly the psychology, of course. It's my speciality.'

'How does that fit into the scheme of things?'

'Same as all the other medical factors. We've got to maintain a happy ship. It's a highly artificial environment.'

Whilst they were talking Morgan was unobtrusively absorbing the ambience of the bar. They were seated on either side of a small white table in one of a number of embrasures. The wall of the embrasure was glass, and as this face of the rim was downsun, the glass was unshielded. The dark side of the Earth was out of sight on the other side of the Wheel, and the Moon was now in Earth's daylight sky, so the view was of a field of stardust. The stars were only a little brighter and more numerous than could be seen from Earth on a clear night, for the lights in the long bar were quite strong.

There were about thirty in the bar, scattered in pairs and groups. All wore white fatigues which curiously enhanced the idiosyncracies of each one: an officer's arm-bands, the black and gold chest-badge of an electronics specialist, the green arm-band denoting shift identity; and of course the shock of red hair, the black beard . . . Particularly Morgan was dwelling, without appearing to, on a group some ten metres away. The discussion was heated – a duel between two men to which the contributions of others was trivial. There was much leaning forward and prodding of the table with the forefinger. At the moment when Lieutenant Honeywell paused in her answer one of the two combatants escalated the dispute. He gave his final forefinger prod to the chest of the other and pushed his chair back. He stood and spoke with exaggerated clarity.

'And that's pre*cise*ly where I think you're mistaken, my friend. You question my commitment *now* , when everything's cosy, and the grandmamas in the Pentagon send up new woollen mittens and home-made fudge on every shuttle. But what happens when –'

'Seal it, Joe.'

'Stuff your *seal it*. What happens when we're . . . ' He paused and spoke with the supreme diction of the more than slightly drunk '. . . on our OWN?' He stooped swiftly, upturned a full mug of beer on the other's head and stalked proudly from the bar.

There was nothing outstanding in that. What was puzzling was that the remaining group of five men were immobilised. And Morgan could see out of the bare corner of an eye which he dared direct at the scene that they were immobilised staring at *him*.

'And is it a happy ship?' he inquired of the girl, taking a sip of space-brewed beer. She seemed momentarily lost for an answer, and looked hurriedly around the bar.

'Within currently ascribed parameters.' *Oh yes*?

'I thought psychology was a bit suspect as a useful discipline these days?'

'It depends what you call psychology. Behaviourism is an accurate description of the minimal.Depth psychology gives you the imaging equipment of the depth psychologist. Neurophysiology tells you a bit about neural circuitry but nothing about thought. But we just stick to linguistic psychology. In its developed form it's beginning to be useful. Language is, after all, the only high-density route to consciousness in someone else. As long as you don't consider language to have a *direct* relationship with motive, and as long as you have sufficient linguistic processing computer power to thoroughly map the significance of an individual's language, you've got a useful science. Without all that you've just got another cult.'

'Or to put it another way?'

'I don't get – oh. Yeah. Sorry. Take your case. During your medical I got quite a lot of your phraseology. It's enough to give a fair spectrum of the match between what you say and the way you say it. Computer analysis of that gives a fairly good set of personality indices.'

'Which are?'

'Well (A), I haven't done the work yet; (B), I haven't got anything like enough material on you for a professional assessment.'

'And *n*?'

'I probably wouldn't tell you anyway,' she laughed.

'Pardon my scepticism. For one thing you're dealing with someone with a different mother tongue from your own – and from that of most people on the Wheel. For another, now that I know what you're up to. I'm bound to think about the language I use to you in the future.'

'Physical scientists are always reserved about psychology. And everyone is a little cagey about psychology when it is applied to themselves.'

'Sure, but you haven't answered my doubts.'

'I daresay you're right, sir.'

'And what would a linguistic psychologist make of that?'

'What I just said? Role conflict of a psychologist talking to a potential patient. Culture conflict between expert and non-expert. Status conflict between a lieutenant and a – er – mister. Problem of ideational confrontation between two people who have only just met . . . Shall I go on?'

'That's all right, but you had the crib. You knew why you said *I dare say you're right, sir*.'

'I couldn't agree with you more. I'm not claiming we perform magic. The whole point of using a gigabit computer is to correlate enough cues to get hold of the crib.'

'I begin to see what you mean. But your analysis can only be as good as your software.'

'Now you're beginning to talk.'

Three

MORGAN KNEW that he could sleep instantly, but he knew also that he must spend an hour before sleep reviewing his position for flaws. All the more so because up here he felt detached from all the familiar background of a deployed agent's trade: here you couldn't smuggle data out over a border; you couldn't get on an aeroplane with a forged passport; you had no access to safe houses or embassies; you were in the most effective conceivable quarantine, and within that quarantine Wheeldata knew who you were and where you were – to some extent even what you were doing – all of the time. Now Wheeldata knew that he was at rest and awake. In an hour it would know that he was asleep.

He hadn't seen anything of Bill Sarin or Dave Hawkins, but then he hadn't expected to. Their cover as sub-contractors through the European Space Agency would keep them busy in the construction areas of B Wheel. The contact initiative was his alone, and he wouldn't use it until his own intelligence base was secure. That might take some time. Here he was, in the ripest intelligence listening-post on – or off – Earth, and he could see no strategy beyond worming his way into the Wheel's command structure, lying low, and keeping his ears and eyes open. The trouble was that this operation had a serious lack of planning. But he had no doubt that familiarity with the ship would open up intelligence resources.

He cast his mind back to his initial briefing. The recall order had come while he was enjoying a holiday in the cool air of Dartmoor where he was busy not shooting and not fishing but loafing at an invigorating thirty miles per day over the big empty hills. The order was NAGROM and he knew that it spelt not only his name backwards but his release from the insufferable months of cover familiarisation at the Met. Office at Bracknell – that repository for unwanted roundabouts. The order came through on his c-unit with no other identification than the suffix 3. It was an innocuous message, but it meant that he was to waste no time in legging it back to SIS Division Six HQ in Elmbury Street.

In an hour and twenty minutes an RAF Lynx whisked down on to the apron at Chivenor with the least of formal pauses for hierarchical support. Morgan's Air Force identity for the duration of his Met. Office posting blended him smoothly through the formalities of acquiring a Hawk trainer complete with pilot. So did the alacrity of the station commander. In another half-hour, with flying overalls over his hurriedly-donned suit, and with a heavy bone-dome over his close-fitting cloth flying helmet, he was being strapped and plugged in to the front seat of the Hawk. He had accompanied the pilot on external checks that were swift but unabridged. The young pink-faced flight lieutenant was enjoying himself; this was going to be a bit of an outing, a break from tedious squadron duties. But when he signed the flight form, and when he was working busily through the cockpit checks, he wore a mantle of authority that set Morgan perfectly at ease.

Ten minutes after Morgan's ejector seat was armed and the hood was locked over his head, the Hawk left the runway. Half an hour after that its mainwheels squeaked on to the main runway at Farnborough in a double puff of grey smoke. Only three hours after he had received his recall order in Devon a Gazelle helicopter put

Morgan down at the Waterloo terminal.

It was only the fifth occasion that Morgan had visited Elmbury Street since he was recruited by the Secret Service; for the member of the Special Operations Teams of Division Six are permanently deployed.

He made his own way from Waterloo, mixing with the crowds on the underground. He had descended on London precipitately, yet he instantly slipped into the routines of deception. The computer-coordinated intelligence systems of half a dozen embassies were quite capable of having noticed and acted upon his arrival by now – if they knew who he was. If Division Six or SOT had been penetrated – again . . . If his movements had shown up on a consistency run on the computers of the KGB or Le Departement . . . . If some other member of SOT had been picked up in Kabul or Marseilles. . . .

He walked quickly past the graceful Regency fronts, grateful for the dappled shadow of the lime trees. For weeks now the daytime temperature had topped thirty degrees without a break. London was a retort where the odours of tar, oil, paint and sweat were distilled. The leaves of the limes were motionless and withering, and it was still only early July. He felt a trickle of sweat run down the small of his back. The recall must be vital indeed for him to be compelled to this idiocy of visiting HQ. There were a thousand French waiters in London who could photograph everyone who passed through those well-bred black doors. He walked up the smooth white steps. There was nothing to tell that here was the razor-edge of the Secret Service. He touched the bell with his forefinger, with an absent-minded 'Mm' as though of approval. The door opened instantly. He had already been photographed in visible light and infra-red, had had his finger-print and voice-print identified, and had had all his personal effects identified and listed.

He knew why the plain-clothes doorman stood back so far: trained on Morgan were the means to dazzle, paralyse or kill him, should he have been wrongly admitted through the first security barrier.

'Good afternoon, sir.' *Ex-Parachute Regiment*, thought Morgan. *Likes to dismember the occasional visitor, just to keep in trim.*

'OK for us salamanders.' But in here it was a cool twenty-five. The inner doors, with their classical foliate design on armoured glass, hummed open. He walked softly through into the hushed hall. There were grey doors, a staircase, two lifts. Plush Regency Foreign Office contrasted with severe Ministry of Defence. Oak panelling. White plastic lampshades. A synthetic atmosphere as of canned air, hermetic security, the secret devotions of anchorites. He strode swiftly over the green Wilton and took the staircase down three at a time. It was not to be wished that any passing secretary should know his face – or the slightest characteristic that could be extorted by psychonarcotics or the application of a hundred subtly-applied volts.

The second landing down was a bare white cube. It had one oak-faced door. Morgan knew that there was a good deal of steel behind it. There was a solitary rubber plant – someone's indomitable humanity in the face of the unthinkable.

'*Up the rebels*,' murmured Morgan. Voicident satisfied, the heavy door swung outwards. Morgan stepped into the lift. It sank swiftly for ten seconds before halting. Division Six HQ Operations Room could take a three-hundred metre near miss from a five-hundred kiloton warhead and still operate. Operations *Room* was a service euphemism. The Deep Basement at Elmbury Street spread beyond the foundations of the surface building.

A guard who wore civilian clothes and a 9mm automatic looked up from a VDU and nodded. 'Glad you could make it, sir.' As though there were an alternative. He gestured down the single corridor that led past his console. 'C3 please, sir.' He rattled typewriter keys briefly under the display.

Morgan had been in C3 before. It was the lounge belonging to the small suite of rooms used by the Head of Division Six. He pushed the door open gently. There were only two men in the room and they both turned instantly. They had been facing a wall terminal. Morgan could see traced on the VDU a moving diagram of a satellite's orbit. The man on the left was ugly and big and was the best companion to have if a lot of people wished you ill. Morgan had been glad of that companionship more than once. Bill Sarin's Ph.D had been for developments in magnetic bubble memories. His companion was thin, fair – smooth-looking in the manner of the public-school stereotype. His degree was only in the classics but he had been granted a Commendation only six months previously for removing the anti-tamper fuse from a French sub-sea missile at three hundred metres under the North Sea. It was six months ago that the three had last met.

'Morning, Bill, Dave,' Morgan greeted Sarin and Hawkins. Their replies were economical.

'Beer?' enquired Sarin, shifting his bulk rapidly towards the bar.

'Another one for me,' added Hawkins, looking back at the VDU. Morgan nodded to Sarin and turned his attention to the screen.

'Are you two into computer games, or is that picture strangely significant?'

Hawkins answered. 'We're looking at the strangely meaningful problem of working out the ground-track of a geosynchronous satellite with an orbital inclination of thirty degrees.'

'An interesting little academic puzzle,' said Sarin in a fading but still strong Leeds accent.

'And which synchronous satellite with an orbital inclination of thirty degrees is well known to us all?' queried Morgan, catching on.

'The well known synch –'

'Big Wheel,' interrupted Sarin, 'is the bugger.'

'The bugger,' explained Hawkins delicately, 'is Big Wheel.'

'How much do you know?' asked Morgan, somewhat piqued that his subordinates should have been briefed before his arrival.

'Er, we've been given a rough – '

'Not a lot.'

'He'll see you now,' said a bright secretarial voice from the connecting door. 'I hope you had a pleasant trip, Squadron-Leader Morgan?'

'Squadron-Leader this time, eh?' muttered Sarin at Morgan's side. 'Whatever next.'

'Yes, thank you.'

'Good. If you'll –'

'But it was a bit quick. If you don't mind I'll just . . . ' He picked up the glass of beer from the bar.

'I'm afraid He wants you right away, sir.' She smiled sympathetically.

'I endeavour only to please,' said Morgan, sleeving the froth from his lips as he followed quickly through His anteroom. A figure leaned round the door. Short, trim, dark-haired, tanned, with amiable eyes which looked most directly at a man; Morgan remembered Him very well. He looked like one of those few heaven-taught philosophers who haven't a care in the world. Yet this man was head of Division Six. Few in the world had more cares than He.

'Good!' he rapped and disappeared. Then, muffled from the other side of his room, 'Don't hang about out there.'

Morgan led the way in. 'Bring those chairs over from the wall there.' And while Morgan was still carrying his chair, 'What's it like to be a Squadron-Leader then, Morgan?'

'Well, the pay's not so good, sir.'

'Pay? Do you suggest we should palm off millionaires as junior officers? How about the uniform? D'you want the trousers flared or tapered?' He could keep a very straight face, so he had to twitch the corner of his mouth so that you didn't take him too seriously – just somewhat seriously. Nor did you attempt to prolong the banter much yourself. There was an air of ruthless speed about the man, making a brief concession to the obligations of leadership.

'There's something in what you say, sir. I'll remember it if ever I'm deployed as a millionaire.'

'I'm sure you will. And what do you know about meteorology?'

'I get by, sir. It hasn't been the most rewarding six months of my life.'

'It wasn't meant to be. I have your reports here. I can only say I hope to hell you're better than this man Stevenson makes you out to be.'

'May I ask why, sir?'

'You are finding out why, Morgan.'

The head of Division Six fingered a key on his desk. From the green light that flickered on his face it was clear to Morgan that he was watching his VDU. His eye movements showed that he was reading.

'As you are aware the Security Commission normally meets every Wednesday. There was such a meeting the day before yesterday. Present were the heads of the three service intelligence branches, myself, the Director of Division Five, and under-secretaries to the Home Office and the Foreign Office.

'The most pressing area of intelligence came from us, the FO, and the intelligence branches of the Navy and Air Force. The subject was, of course, France. We were all more or less familiar with certain information that had been pooled by the various people concerned over a preceding period of some months. That information had become more and more demanding of our attention, and the Council resolved to try to reach a consensus concerning its value and the action, if any, that should be taken in the light of our joint inter-pretation.

'You've had the reports on the political climate. Our feeling is that they've abandoned the idea of a balanced federacy; we have hard policy evidence for that. Economically they now dominate the EEC. Right-wing elements within the administration are becoming increasingly powerful. They're going for an all-out push for their own national supremacy in Europe. Our cockiness hasn't helped. What we've seen recently is a welding together of the old disputes about wine, lamb, fishing, currency, membership payments, the constitution and so forth into closely-linked theatres of political conflict. And the breaking up of the Economic Community is the least of our problems.

'You see, the French are definitely the aggressors in this, and that's why the Germans can't attempt to mediate. If they did so it would look as though they were siding with us against the French, which would make matters worse. Yet the Germans are scared stiff of any overt Anglo-French conflict. Reasons?'

Hawkins cleared his throat. 'Obviously the Germans want to keep Europe economically strong and united. But there's a specific danger: if we and the Frogs have our resources tied up in mutual conflict – even a redeployment would do – it would make sufficient difference to the balance of power in Europe for the Russians to feel it was now or never and begin their attack. It has after all been their strategy to stir up discord in Europe: break the EEC, NATO, Eurodefence, and infiltrate the resulting cracks.'

'Yes. Not only do we know that the French are prepared to face a shooting war, but we know that the Russians have an offensive prepared on the basis of a well-defined conflict threshold between France and us. The French might be cooled by evidence of the Russian posture, but there's nothing that concrete. The Reds have the capacity to launch the whole offensive from a standing start. We can't point to preliminary troop movements and supply surges; they don't need to make them.

'Anyway, that's the state of things in the European theatre, and it's unstable.'

There was a silence. Morgan spoke. 'So Soviet intentions deter a French – ah, or English –'

'We need hardly consider that option.'

' – attack; *if* the French can be convinced of Russian preparations. May we still presume that the Russian attack is deterred by an American response?'

'That's the key question. That's just what we don't know. Only at times of specific threat are we forced to check the truth of what we have always assumed. We find ourselves knowing less about the intentions of our closest allies than we do about those of our most dangerous enemies.'

Morgan tried to smother a deep and secret resentment. 'Don't we know? Our defence policies and theirs are so interlinked that it would be very hard to act independently.'

'Hard for us. Not hard for them.'

'But western defence is based on the Atlantic Alliance. That's the way it works.'

The Head of Division Six shook his head. 'That is, of course, the way everyone says it works. But, believe it or not, there is a deep level of executive decision-making – in the White House, and to a lesser extent in the Pentagon – which can change the whole aspect of East-West conflict in an instant.

'Our access to that decision-making is limited. We still suffer from having no surveillance satellites of our own – God rot the Minister of Defence. Diplomatic channels are of course quite useless; they give us the very façade which we are trying to penetrate. Again through open military exchanges we get the same authorised picture – although here there are some exceptions. One instance is in the field of computer modelling: they swapped some program material with us for Exercise Arctic Fox. We did an in-depth study, and were able to infer that they were at least playing with what we call "smart" options. There is a smart option in the present case.

'The United States assures the Soviet Union that it will answer any military thrust in Europe with an appropriate level of response. That involves intervention on a conventional or a nuclear scale. That threat is successful as long as the Russians are deterred by it. If, however the Russians invade Western Europe, the threat has failed. The rules of the game in those circumstances are changed, and it may not be most beneficial to carry out the threat. We know for instance that one of the US options is to launch a massive airlift – not to reinforce NATO's Eastern flank but to take their personnel out of Europe as quickly as possible. Recent Elint from Cheltenham reports Military Airlift Command and US Readiness Command modelling manoeuvres for that. Let's face it: it makes sense. Rather than lose a force which is almost certainly insufficient to change the outcome of a European war, they'd be living to fight another day. A *smart* option.'

'And is that an option they're keen on?'

'Hard to say. Congressional opinion would, we think, support it, while the President would almost certainly be against it – if the decision depended on his own unsupported preference. But we need to know what will actually happen on the day.'

The Head of Division Six had finished speaking. He looked at Morgan with a faint smile on his lips.

'And that is what you want us to find out?' Morgan asked.

'Yes. The hardest task of all – spying on a friendly country.'

'From what you say, sir, an *apparently friendly* country.'

'You needn't get an Oedipus complex about it, Morgan. Diplomacy is motivated by self- interest, and always has been.'

Oedipus complex. It implied a hidden affiliation. Why did he choose such a term? Did he know anything? Morgan smothered the thought and his deep cover with it. 'Of course. But haven't we got a fair number of people deployed in the States already? In quite useful areas? And I would have thought GCHQ had a good grip on military communications.'

'You're right, of course, but none of it has the depth we require.'

'It sounds as though you want a spy in the President's mind.'

'Not quite.'

Then Morgan remembered what he had seen on the VDU in C3. 'You want an agent on Big Wheel.'

'Three agents. Yes. On USSF SCC 101. Big Wheel is the key to the US defence posture. *All* strategic information passes through it. In a shooting war its real-time command function would be far more important than any of the Earth-based facilities. Yet we have no access to it.'

'Aren't its communications a weak link?'

'No. There's no way of cracking their computer-generated codes, or at least there's no way of doing it quickly enough to be useful. Unless you're inside the Big Wheel, of course.'

'How do we get inside?'

'It's done. Sarin and Hawkins will be going up in a European Space Agency shuttle a week tomorrow. They're working for British Aerospace, subcontracted by ESA for structural work on Big Wheel's second disc. And you, Morgan –'

'Exchange posting to Big Wheel as an RAF officer. Meteorology specialist?' Morgan suggested.

'Yes. Only ex-RAF. It's better.'

'*Meteorology*! I don't know whether I can stand it.'

'The question is, can you do it? You've got to be good – or at least look good.'

'I can look good. But why meteorology?'

'It seemed the best chance of getting a man on Big Wheel six months ago when we started setting it up. We needed a specialist in a nice safe non-secure area that would still be useful on SCC 101.'

'You had this planned six months ago?'

'Not specifically; we considered it would be useful to have a man there.

'Right. That's the background. Any questions so far?'

'Mission specification, control, communications –'

'Here.' The Head of Division Six handed three cassettes across his desk.

' – expenses . . . '

'Play these through the terminals in C3. The computer should be able to answer most of your questions. See me when you've finished.'

Four

A LARGE VDU on one of the communications panels was numbering off the seconds from a minute. Rathbone was perched on the edge of the bench opposite, swinging a leg, looking at the screen. Zeffert was seated, immersed in a written dialogue with Wheeldata on his c-unit. The room was otherwise empty until the Special Space Warfare marine strode to a halt, saluting Rathbone. The captain stood, returning the salute formally. Then began a litany which had been repeated weekly on Big Wheel – sometimes more often.

'Corporal Decker, have you read the Armed Services Procedural Instruction headed *The Transmission of Materials Classified as Highly Secret*?'

'Yes, sir.'

'In that case you are instructed to seal and guard this room until relieved by my personally delivered order or until the other conditions detailed in the Armed Forces Procedural Instruction handbook have been fulfilled. Carry out your orders, Sergeant.'

'Yes, sir.'

Zero came up on the VDU, then the message

Classified level: Red Alpha One
Qualified personnel: Captain Q M Rathbone
Cleared to observe: Commander F Zeffert

'Wheeldata records the presence of the listed personnel, and the absence of all other personnel,' intoned the Wheel's most familiar voice.

Instruct listed personnel, read the screen.

Zeffert held up his hand to forestall Rathbone. 'Let's try it this way and avoid some of the tedium.' He rattled off the rubric. 'Neither of us is to mention any of the data we are about to receive to any third person unless that person be appointed to the list of cleared personnel in the proper manner, and then only in so far as is necessary for that person to contribute in the best interests of their abilities and the Project's security to the successful completion of the Project.

'Furthermore I'm not allowed to discuss the Project with anyone at all, even yourself, except at your request – and that request can only apply to communication with you. I think that just about covers it.'

Rathbone smothered his annoyance. Zeffert's boyish informality always irritated him. It was unsettling. It undermined discipline. He'd made his feelings obvious but Zeffert still pushed his luck. 'Wheeldata, does that constitute the necessary affidavit?'

'Yes.'

'File it.'

'The statement is filed.'

The VDU maintained its last instruction for a few more seconds, then blanked. Rathbone sat facing the screen and TV camera. Zeffert now leaned back against the bulkhead. The VDU wrote up

PLUTO

The face of the Pluto Project Director, ex Secretary of State, David Fellows, appeared. He looked down at his console, perhaps making a final check on his audience.

'Gentlemen, the twenty-third full meeting of the Pluto Project Scheduling Team has now begun.' The screen split to admit five more faces. Rathbone knew them well by now – especially the face at the top right. It was his own. 'I'll first of all ask for reports from each of you as appropriate, and then we'll deal with anything that might arise from those reports.

'The work on the Pluto Project is taking place increasingly on site, and as you may see on your screens three of us are in fact transmitting from there. In that case it would be appropriate if we heard from Rick first.'

Rathbone ground his teeth discreetly. Rick Steerman was a young and rising IBM executive of the clean-cut suit and striped tie brigade. Rathbone's rise had not been meteoric. It was not possible in the services in peacctime, and there were reasons why it was better that way . . . .

Steerman was projecting oblivion of the meeting, as though just dropping in, *en route* from composing important report A to making vital decision B. As though sparing a moment, he ceased tapping on his c-unit and removed his rimless photochromic spectacles with a sideways flick.

'Thank you, sir. We are now thirty-six weeks into the Project, and sixteen weeks into the construction schedule. I would just like to point out to the team that at no time in this country's history – or, as far as I know – in the history of any other country, whether in peace-time or wartime, has a project of this magnitude – '

'Rick?' David Fellows interrupted.

'Yes. David?'

'Can it. Ah, if you would, please.'

'If you like, David. I was just – '

'Yes. So we're sixteen weeks into a fifty-week schedule. Statistical analysis shows that we're left with thirty-four weeks in the construction period. Right?'

'Right.'

'As of week sixteen, are we going to be *there* in week fifty? This is what we're here for, and this is what I intend to take back to the Executive Council.'

Steerman was quiet for a few moments. Then like a poker player making an uncertain call. 'As of this particular phase in the Project schedule I'm not aware of any short-fall which absolutely prevents us completing on schedule.'

'You fill me with confidence.'

'Some of the work is still at the conceptual stage. It would be illogical to give a watertight guarantee in the case of all contractors.'

'As team representative of the prime contractor it is your function to give such guarantees, is it not?'

'What if I've got to dish out a job to someone that I consider to be impossible in the timescale?'

'Then we rethink the way it fits into the system until it's considered to be possible. In any case we want to know now – not in week fifty.'

'There's a strong feeling at IBM that the onus of responsibility placed on the corporation is disproportionate. This is not a normal project.'

'What project is?'

'It's at panic speed, it's conceptually new, and the security aspect's a liability when we're trying to buy in people's skills and products.'

'Perhaps project leadership's too much for the company?'

'If it is, then who else can do it? I might say confidentially that pulling out is one of the options under consideration. We don't usually court being in a hiding-to-nothing situation.'

'I'm sure IBM don't need reminding that there are no penalty clauses involved.'

'No, sir, we're appreciative of that fact.'

'To put it another way, I'd just like to remind you what the nature of the real penalty is. If this project is not one hundred per cent successful it will not help IBM to have got out with their noses clean. *There will be no IBM.*'

'While I follow your line of argument, there are those in IBM who are not prepared to put all their money on that outcome.'

Fellows gave a sharp decisive nod. 'Then pull your weight and change their minds. If you can't, I will. That opinion is not one which has any place on the Project or in this team. We haven't time for it. I suggest you make your report.'

'Yes, sir. The detailed situation up to midday today has been accessed in hard copy to all terminals of those present, and I'll briefly summarise the red-lined areas.

'As you know the work in progress is streamed in five routes: excavation, energy, systems, life support and environmental interface. In terms of on-site work the flow constriction is at excavation progress. It's my personal assessment that excavation is proceeding well in view of the fact that it's the sort of operation where you don't know what the problems are until you dig them up. The contractors have taken out sixty million cubic metres of rock as of today, and that covers work on twelve levels. What's behind schedule is final shaping of cleared chambers, and that's what is holding back the on-site operations in the other four streams.'

'How far behind?'

'Two weeks.'

'What's being done about it?'

'We're getting more robot units from Colorado to tackle both the heavy work and the finishing. We reckon on pulling back four weeks in that area by the end of the fifty.'

'Good. Other areas?'

'Power. The first reactor is operational except for fuel. The second's being installed. Problem areas are fuel reprocessing and thermal waste. The laser enrichment test rig at Berkeley is on schedule in most respects, but we're not yet tuned to the mass flow we require. We have coolant problems because of the high above-ground ambient temperature – and environmental degradation of the cooling structures . . . .'

Rathbone called up a schematic summary of Steerman's notes from Wheeldata. He was able to get well ahead of the IBM man and devote some last-minute thought to the report he himself had to make. It was little changed from last week's. With each successive meeting the meteorological predictions became more precise: trends of CO_2 increase, temperature increase, decline in chlorophyll absorption and the tendencies of the other indicators monitored by the omniscient Lieutenant-Commander Grey became more firmly established.

'Captain Rathbone? How does the weather look from space?'

'Pretty much the same. You have the data on line.'

'Sure. How do you assess the probability? What are the odds that we're going to look the biggest bunch of damn fools in the history of mankind?'

'Our predictions are sharpening all the time. I'm afraid there's only about a ten per cent chance that we'll all be locked up at zero plus one.'

'Not very neatly put, Captain.'

'Sorry, I intended no irony.'

Rathbone reflected that he was always asked the trivial question: not *What will it be like when it happens?* but *Am I going to suffer the embarrassment of it not happening at all – after we've spent twenty billions?* He had moments of doubt himself, just as Steerman had. After all, a great proportion of the research and defence budgets of the United States was being turned over to a project whose basis was almost entirely theoretical. Not only was the crisis still in the future, but the inferences which revealed it were so complex that they were perceived only through a computed data-web of iterative integrations. So numerous were the data that the predictive program never stopped running, night and day. The predictions *had* to be accurate.

The meeting examined the graphs again. Indeed they had not changed much. Only a few months ago they had oscillated wildly week by week. Rathbone could see conviction hardening on the faces of the men looking at the graphs on their displays. Pluto wasn't a game, or a piece of politics, or scientific chauvinism. Fellows allowed the team to dwell on their own thoughts for a while. Then he turned, deprecatingly, to the last item.

'That brings us, ah, to security.' Although a thousand kilometres from him, he appeared to turn to face Rob Whitaker, the White House 'adviser' on the Project team. 'I take it that we still have no change in the security stance concerning Pluto?'

'Not as of this time,' replied Whitaker flatly, looking secure.

'You will recall that some members of the team expressed moral concern at the total secrecy surrounding the Project.'

'Quite unavoidable, Mister Fellows. It is quintessential' – he added with the air of one too highly placed to deal with the merely essential – 'that no foreign power, and by that I mean the Soviet Union, should learn that we have plans, let alone learn what those plans are. If we gave them any chance of finding out we'd be calling in a one hundred per cent successful preemptive strike against ourselves.

'I don't think it's necessary to overjustify the President's stance on this, but a whole team of very eminent psychologists responsible directly to the White House has produced research which shows that if the Pluto Project were leaked it would never be completed. The social climate just wouldn't support it – or much else for that matter.'

'Can I just bring up a security problem while we're on the subject?' It was Steerman, the IBM man.

'Go ahead, Rick.'

'Up here in the mountains we're into quite a bit of cover-story confusion. You know, we've got an *Oh what a tangled web we weave* situation. The general public, what there are of them, mostly see our trucks going hither and thither with loads of rock, and they're led to believe we're a mining corporation. God knows what they think we're doing with the stuff. The mining corporation think they're excavating a Guardian ABM firing point. The nuclear power people think they're laying on wattage for basic neutrino research, the life support people think we're building a super fallout shelter, and the people we've really got to trust are on to the Pluto idea, but very vaguely.

We've got ten different covers and ten different code names from Mineral Services Inc., which kids no one, up to Pluto. All the time I'm on site I've got to set my c-unit to remind me which cargo of bullshit, sheepshit or sparrowshit I'm unloading on whom. What I'm talking about is massive inefficiency. Proper coordination is darn near impossible. Can't we choose a close-fit fiction and stick to it with everyone?'

'It might be darn *near* impossiblc, but it's possible, and it's the only way.' These were the first words that Doctor Arnold Clegg, the Director of American Intelligence, had spoken at the meeting. He had the register of the IBM man, and would now deal with him quickly. 'To be more precise than Mister Whitaker, no one other than cleared and qualified personnel must know the true nature of the Pluto Project. Regard it, if you will, Mister Steerman, as the most deadly of epidemics. For any leak of information on Pluto would spread and kill like bubonic plague.

'As for the way this security is administered, we are operating what we call a *cascade cover*. The cover stories you have mentioned are linked to one another hierarchically. It results in each person knowing that those below him in the hierarchy are being deceived, but believing that he himself has the correct story. That is the first benefit: everyone is satisfied. The other advantage is that the public level of cover is entirely innocuous. The Soviet intelligence arm is not going to be interested in a firm mining non-strategic materials. If you had a cover story descriptive enough to please everyone on or off the site, even if it were suitably bogus, it would give enough away about the *importance* of the operation to indicate to certain parties that something of interest to them is going on. Then they've only got to enlarge the right surveillance frame and we're cooked.

'This system has been tested operationally for years, and in this particular case it has been thoroughly computer modelled. It is imperative that you continue to operate it effectively.'

'Any other security queries?' interposed Fellows. Steerman had been about to speak but he changed his mind.

Rathbone had been debating with himself whether to make an admission. He decided that he would, but in trying to camouflage his own sense of culpability he pitched it a little high.

'I'm afraid that your precise security planning is becoming slightly academic as far as the Wheel is concerned.'

'How d'you mean, *slightly academic*? The Wheel is a military installation with a high security rating in its own right. All your personnel have been through positive vetting. You should be better off than any of us.'

'That's true. No one has penetrated Pluto security who isn't supposed to, and no one with qualification-to-know has leaked anything. But as I remarked in my submission to your initial security overview there are five hundred very bright people on the Wheel. The Wheel is also the place where most of the hard evidence for our little problem is gathered and co-ordinated. They're up to their ears in the stuff. Some people have used their ears.'

'What's the extent of the damage?'

'Knowledge of the problem is quite widespread amongst the higher ranks. Most of them are bright enough to infer the Project from the problem. That is the stage where people start to pick up real information however well you disguise it. They just can't help it.'

'Why haven't you quarantined these people?'

'The Big Wheel is my headache, Doctor Clegg. I'm not about to take valuable people out of circulation. Besides, they're security disciplined. They may know, but that doesn't mean that they'll tell.'

'Yes. but at the moment they don't know the significance of what they know. They don't know they're not allowed to tell.'

'That's not quite true. There's a general feeling for the sensitivity of the subject.'

'That's not really good enough, Captain. We have to quarantine the Wheel.'

'That would make our job difficult. We're in the communications business.'

'Then you can restrict communications to transmission only on your direct approval of the signal content.'

'Impossible. Have you any idea how much data we process?'

'I know it's a lot. Nevertheless I'd like you to get together with your security people and sketch out a quarantine system for our next meeting, ready for implementation if we judge that the need is there.'

'I'll sketch one out, certainly.' *I should have kept my mouth shut.*

'I'll have the order processed through USSF HQ.'

'That won't be necessary.'

'It simplifies matters.'

Rathbone hadn't yet finished. 'What about Morgan?'

'Ah, yes, Morgan. What's the problem?'

Rathbone called up the Englishman's file on Wheeldata. 'I have here a copy of all the correspondence between the Department of Defence and the British Ministry of Defence about him.'

'Yes.'

'Culminating in his Movement Order. Also his assignment orders to USSF SCC 101, and my orders concerning him from USSF HQ.'

'Correct.'

'Also copied is his Ministry of Defence file.'

'And?.'

'And a xerox copy of a file headed Department Six and sub-headed SOT. This is accompanied by letters from the Department of Intelligence, Air Force Intelligence and USSF HQ variously explaining that the man is working for the British Secret Intelligence Service but that his cover is to be accepted as though at face value.'

'That is the way I see it.'

'There is also a communication series between me and those intelligence organisations in which I query the appointment under those circumstances. The answers further make clear that there is no complicity between any of our security services and Morgan. He's pursuing his mission. We don't know what it is. We're letting him get on with it.'

'Right.'

'It's not just that I don't like being sold a dummy by this Limey. Also with due respect he's a considerable security risk to a project whose security sensitivity you yourself have just dwelt on at some length.'

Clegg was slow and firm, backed by the mystique of high security. 'Nevertheless we keep him, for two reasons: espionage between allies has to be treated with more circumspection than between enemies; and if anyone is interested in Pluto it's best that we should be in a position to monitor their sources of information.'

'Isn't that the same as telling them our secrets so as to be sure whether or not they know them?'

'Not quite. Look, I wish you'd let this one drop, Captain Rathbone. As is often the case with intelligence matters there are wheels within wheels here. I assure you I'm keeping tabs on this one personally. Treat him with discretion and keep your HQ security posted. If the situation becomes critical we'll pull him out.'

Rathbone was old enough to know when he was being made to see through a glass darkly. 'Naturally I'll comply in any way I can, sir, but I should like the team to note my reservations on this point.'

'Noted, Captain,' said Fellows in relief. 'Now, are there any further security points?'

'I have a question I'd like to ask, myself,' said Clegg. 'I address the team in general, though perhaps Professor Hewitt will be best able to answer me. I'd like an assessment of the capacity of some independent organisation or foreign power to come up with our findings in the course of their own research.'

'It can't be ruled out,' replied Hewitt – who was Deputy Director of Defence Research and Engineering. 'Though this is not the sort of subject we can give a precise answer on; there's no way of predicting the outcome of human ingenuity. Let's make it clear that the Soviet Union has at least identified the same *problem* independently. Your own Department told us that; and presumably you know more than we do about the nature of their work in the field –'

'You know all that I do.'

'Just so. The relevant factors which the Soviets have in common with us are world-wide military and commercial interests and the extraordinarily powerful computer systems necessary to operate even a limited ABM system. The first provides the motive to get the data and the second provides the means to process this new signi- ficance out of it. There are about ten computers in the world capable of handling the data, and access to them is exceedingly limited. Your own people, Doctor Clegg, are monitoring those computers, and as you have told us, one dangerous program run from a terminal in another country has been thwarted already. The holes are very small, and they all seem to be plugged. I can say no more.'

'Thank you, Professor. Are there any more matters of security? Well then, we must move quickly on to the problems of commission- ing the Pluto system. You will see on your screens . . .'

Five

MORGAN AWOKE. The controlled surge of adrenalin brought him to full alertness. It was a useful trick – and besides, he liked to wake that way. He knew instantly where he was, though his first sensation, the reduced pressure of the bunk against his back, surprised him anew. His room (*cupboard* would have suited it better) was in darkness. He knew that before he opened his eyes. When he opened them he saw the wheeling stars pin-point bright against the perfect black depths.

He looked at his c-unit. It was 0720 Wheel time. Wheeldata would be giving him a call in ten minutes. He took a breath to forestall the courteous machine then let it out with an exclamation that was almost a laugh. Wheeldata would have known he was awake before he himself did.

He unclasped his restraint and gave a thrust against the lightweight bunk with his hand that propelled him to his hermetically sealed door. Remembering the mixed crew he tied a towel around his waist, unclipped a safety razor from the wall and switched open the door.

As he saw the bright white corridor curve upward to right and left, the flawless green carpet, the rows of airtight doors, the display panels with their discreet precise colours, and as he heard the muted tones and voices that Wheeldate directed around the Wheel, Morgan reflected that whatever covert deed waited to be done here, USSF SCC 101 was an elite ship – no, *the* elite ship – and to be on her would have its less dull moments. He fingered the *open* panel for the nearest *ablutionary module*. A robot cleaner appeared down the curve of the corridor, moving fast. It slowed as it approached him. He stepped aside. It swerved aside simultaneously, but before he could move again it checked and darted past him on its original course.

'Three-nil . . .' he murmured after it. 'I suppose *people* were on the way out anyway . . .'

He stepped into a vacant shower cylinder and programmed it for the most luxurious cycle he could imagine. It rotated to the closed position. He spoke through the streaming water into his c-unit. 'Good morning, Wheeldata.'

'Yes, sir?'

'Good morning, Wheeldata.'

'Yes, sir?'

'Good morning, Wheeldata.'

'Good morning, sir.'

'Nice switch there, Wheeldata.'

'Thank you, sir. I have had some difficulty with your language patterns, but when I have extended my semantic library our communication should be more adequate.'

'You took the words out of my mouth.'

'Syntax error.'

'I *beg* your pardon?'

'Sorry, sir. I mean, please would you rephrase that statement?'

'Mind if I join you?' It was Commander Grey. Morgan had just taken the full one-gee load off his feet, having carried his breakfast tray to a table. The mess, a spacious and comfortably furnished room (though considerably curved over its full length), adjoined the rim bar that he had visited the previous day, and was accessible from it through a wide and graceful arch of space-formed alloy. The broad downsun ports were uncovered and revealed a dazzling silver and blue arc of sunlit Earth. Conversation was subdued, as befitted the early hour, but the clatter of cutlery was convivial.

Morgan waved to a seat. 'I'm rather glad to have some company, because I haven't a lot of confidence in the cuisine.'

'Come now, Mister Morgan, some of it's real – mushrooms, tomatoes, fried potatoes, tomato juice. They're grown up here.'

'Oh, I'd noticed them. It's not so much them I'm worried about. I am a little concerned about that,' he said, probing with his plastic knife.

'The ham? It would cost too much to orbit food, and keeping livestock on board wouldn't be the best use of the available volume. So the ham's cultured.'

'I was afraid you'd say that,' Morgan smiled. The woman looked concerned. She was obviously taking him completely seriously. 'But never let it be said that I am ungrateful. I have eaten worse that has been transported by four legs. I can suffer if need be.

'I gather from Wheeldata that our briefing is to take place this morning?'

'Yes. I'm sorry about yesterday. We're locked into a weak weather cycle in both hemispheres at the moment, so we're liable to get uncharacteristic fluctuations. They have a knack of clumping together on occasion, and then we have to work our asses off until they even out again.'

'I know exactly what you mean,' lied Morgan in a *We professionals know what it's like* tone. Fortunately he knew approximately what she meant.

'What's your interest in meteorology?'

Morgan felt the most familiar fear of the spy – that of being caught out by an expert when you're supposed to be one yourself. He started to explain how he had first become interested in the weather through flying, and how the RAF had sent him on courses and postings . . . .

'It's all right, I've read your background. But we've got to work out a programme for you, so it would be useful to know what really stimulates you in the meteorological sciences.'

She couldn't have phrased it less aptly. 'Well,' he said, his voice sounding hollow and slightly choked, 'I suppose I'm really a bit of an all-rounder . . . '

There was a critical directness in her eyes. Obviously if you were selected to do meteorology on Big Wheel you were good, and if you were good you didn't get away with calling yourself *a bit of an all-rounder*. But he'd given himself a chance to think.

' . . . though I'm mostly interested in what actually makes the weather.'

'The meteorologist in search of God. We're all into omniscience up here.' But she didn't elaborate. She left him to carry on.

'The, ah, interaction between Sun, Earth and Moon, and of course the Earth's atmosphere – by which I also mean the sea – '

'Of course.'

' – that produces major weather patterns.'

'The underlying physics of macro-meteorology. Yes, we're all interested in that. But just personally, how do you see your role in the programme allocated for bipartite study between the Wheel and your Meteorological Office?'

Just keep swimming, Morgan. Don't give up. 'My interpretation is that I was chosen by your people and by mine because my research at Bracknell – ah, England – is in the same area as the greater part of your effort here. So I can work on your projects and introduce some of my own computer programs, with, it s hoped, mutual benefit.'

'Good, that's what I've been told. I seem to be giving a hard interview impression – considering that you're still on your breakfast – but the two-hundred page book that the USSF Weather Bureau has sent me on the terms of your assignment is not the most useful piece of literature I've encountered. We are, then, talking about computer techniques?'

Of course. How else do you think I can get any spying done? 'Basically Bracknell benefits from access to your data and your computer, and you, we hope, benefit from our software.' Morgan relaxed. Computers he knew something about. 'You have access through your met. satellites and the Wheel to continuous monitoring of every cubic yard of the Earth's atmosphere. You process the data with the most advanced computer ever constructed. But you use statistical techniques; that is, you predict on the basis of what the weather has always done in the past.'

'It works well. Too well.'

'How d'you mean, *too well*?'

'Oh, we predict a lot of bad weather – and we get it.'

'Right. Well, we think that with the data density and processing power you've got, it's time to start synthetic forecasting – that is, generating weather models on aerodynamic and thermodynamic principles.'

'It has been done, of course.'

'But not accurately enough for practical forecasting. Not using all the best software and all the best data and all the best electronics.'

'And that's what you want to do?'

'In as far as it fits in with your on-going work, yes.'

'And the software?'

'I can access that from the Met. Office as soon as we can get some communication time.'

'That should present no problem. I see you've demolished that ham without any difficulty.'

'Merely because I wasn't concentrating on what I was doing.'

'Time I showed you round the Met. Section.'

On the way out he noticed Lieutenant Honeywell. She was loading her tray at the terminal with a late but ambitious breakfast; clearly she was a girl who could eat like a horse and move like a gazelle. Morgan suspected that she had been observing him because she turned as he passed with a smile that suggested preparation. He gave a cheery wave and followed the more solid figure of Lieutenant-Commander Grey into the corridor. He determined to find the means of spending an hour with the lieutenant later in the day. She was sympathetic and well-placed. She might be turned to advantage.

That hour with Lieutenant Honeywell was to be long postponed. Morgan spent a great part of the morning familiarising himself with the Meteorological Section's superb resources. He learned how, with simple commands to Wheeldata, he could call up information or photographs from any of the five operational networks of weather satellites. Wheeldata himself gave him a guided tour on VDU on the section's computer program library. He quickly felt that not only did he have unsurpassed meteorological information at his fingertips, but that he could effortlessly juggle the figures in almost any way he wished.

In the late morning he acted as duty officer – with a bespectacled and eager Lieutenant Perkins at his elbow to pick up his mistakes. His job was to stand by for Wheeldata's efficient threat warnings and to transmit them to those authorities on Earth best placed to act upon them. He also had to comply with requests from Earth for information – particularly from areas which lacked the sophisticated equipment to interrogate the satellite systems and interpret their raw data. The time passed quickly and he snatched handfuls of lunch wandering from terminal to terminal.

It wasn't until 1600 hrs. that he was able to test out his communications with the Secret Service over Intelnet.

'Wheeldata, Morgan.'

'This is Wheeldata; go ahead, Mister Morgan.'

'I want to arrange to call up a computer program from a terminal in Europe.'

'What is the length of the program?'

'The program length is about a hundred thousand bits.'

'I can store that program at high data rate. Type the Omniphone code of your European terminal. I will connect you for voice communication. When the terminal is ready to transmit, type READ. I will store the program. Your access code will be *Morgan One*. Type the Omniphone code of your European terminal now.'

Morgan was quickly through to the Met. Office at Bracknell. Within a minute Programe RAE/MET SYNTH 19 had streamed round the Omnisat network and into Wheeldata's niobium tantalate memory in a burst of data that lasted less than a tenth of a second.

'Thank you, Wheeldata. Screen the program for me at a rate of ten seconds per module on this terminal.'

'Screening will commence on your LIST.'

Morgan scanned the program modules. The sixth bore a heading that he had memorised. He copied the module into his c-unit.

'Erase the sixth module, Wheeldata.'

'Please confirm your erase instruction by typing it.'

Morgan did so. The incriminating information vanished from the screen. Not only did Morgan have a program with which to give a realistic impression of top-flight meteorological research; but in his c-unit he had a coded message from Department Six.

The chances that a complex program will run smoothly on the first attempt are slim. But RAE/MET SYNTH 19 had been thoroughly debugged already. It had merely lacked the data and computer capacity to produce worthwhile results. It took Morgan and Wheeldata an hour to make it compatible with the weather information that was being transmitted from a hundred observation platforms in and around the Earth's atmosphere. Voice access to the computer and its ability to take part in its own programming made short work of processes that would have taken weeks on the most powerful European machinery. One could forget oneself when working with Wheeldata. It was easy to accord him the status of a colleague. Morgan had to remind himself that there was no consciousness behind the helpful synthetic tones.

By 1800 hrs. the program was running. Morgan arranged that the vast output of tabulated figures would be stacked into Wheeldata's capacious memory. His VDU would tell him how the program was going, and present a greatly abbreviated summary of the results.

At first the numbers came slowly. The processing was limited by the rate at which the satellites gathered, sorted and transmitted their weather information. But as activity built up on the VDU he noticed the duty staff – Lieutenant-Commander Grey, Lieutenant Perkins and two, then three others, gathering at his shoulder. After half an hour the running symbol still glowed steadily at the top of the screen.

'We have a viable program,' said Perkins helpfully. Then ten minutes later he added, 'Could you interpret the output you're getting here?'

'I was hoping that you would ask. This is the great white hope of European meteorologists. If it fails we're back to seaweed.'

'I'm sure you're exaggerating, Mister Morgan.'

'Well, I am actually. At the moment Wheeldata's screening a table of all the stations and satellites we're getting data from, and telling us what the nature of the information is. Then there are indices for percentage of global coverage – which you see is over a hundred per cent – longest and shortest coverage times, and mean coverage density, which he indicates is now almost down to the cubic metre level.

'Now here's the output sample; I've instructed Wheeldata to screen it for alternate ten-second periods. We're just taking the nineteen ten-degree points spaced out along the zero miridian, plus London, to see what sort of results we're getting. The figures are projected out over a period of twenty years, and represent our synthesised predictions of wind speed and direction, surface temperature, cloud-cover, precipitation, with a variability factor, at noon during midwinter and noon during midsummer, for each year. You see that most of the table is blank, but the figures for the next three years are firming up as we take on more data.'

The room was silent and the program ran silently. The green alphanumerics flowed and changed on the VDU.

'Very good,' said Lieutenant Perkins after another ten minutes – with, Morgan considered, an inappropriate edge of irony. The program was running exceedingly smoothly and he felt most pleased with himself; not just because this display of expertise was doing his cover a power of good, but because he felt the craftsman's joy in a job well done. Not that it was *all* his own work, of course, but he had had a hand in it, he knew something of the program and a little of the physics underlying it. His audience said nothing. Its occasional restlessness was obtrusively loud. The program seemed to be going perfectly, but he sensed that something was embarrassingly wrong. Surely he wasn't in the process of making a complete fool of himself. He cringed at the thought of an annihilated cover. . . .

The adrenalin was beginning to flow now and his hands and brow were slick with sweat. He looked hard at the figures. He felt that his new colleagues were oppressing him unfairly with their silence. Year five was firm now, and year six was coming up. The results would come in faster now. Sufficient data had been read by the program at least for good approximations, and Wheeldata's colossal processing capacity would digest it fast. . . .

So what would the weather be like next year? Well, someone had to break the silence, even at the risk of appearing obvious.

'Well, let's see how the London figures are shaping up – as I have a vested interest in knowing what next summer's going to be like in the UK. Take temperature. We have a mean daytime temperature of twenty degrees, which is about the same as this year; a good test of the program's accuracy. Actually, that's as much as you want if you happen to be in London, with the sort of humidity we get. Year two –

ah, twenty-three degrees. It's going to be rather a hot one. We are of course expecting a certain upward drift because of CO_2 build up – partly because of deforestation and also the burn-up of bio-mass and the remaining bulk of fossil fuels, and that's not far off rule-of-thumb predictions . . . .'

His eye ran down the intricate forest of figures.

'Year three – twenty-five degrees. That's certainly another big increase.'

His eyes moved quickly to the figures for year four. He tried to swallow. His mouth and throat were dry. He switched over to review the functioning of the program. Nothing seemed to be wrong. Wheel-data was happy. He switched back. The London summer of year four was due to experience a mean midday temperature of thirty-one degrees. The figure for year five was thirty-three degrees. That for year six was thirty-six. He glanced down the rest of the column. According to the output, the summer in seven years would be like noon in the Sahara – with winter temperatures almost as high. The temperature in ten years' time would be over forty degrees – all the year round.

In short, the computer was predicting shifts in the climatic zones and general global changes that would unhinge all the present economic and social assumptions. He saw a split-second vision of that Dartmoor hill shrouded with howling dust – himself there peering out over desert.

He rubbed his wet hands on his overall and looked round at his silent watchers. They had gone, all of them. He would have preferred them to be there. He felt like panicking, but forced himself to think clearly. The program was OK; he knew that. That is, it made sense to both man and computer. Presumably the data was OK or the program would have picked up inconsistencies and deleted them – or the run would have failed. But the assumptions behind the program could be wrong. The physics, the relative weighting of different factors, the assumptions of incremental growth in the amount of coal burnt per year . . . It seemed most likely that there must be an error here. After all, the error could not be anywhere else . . . .

The program was still running. But extra running time didn't bring any of the temperatures down significantly. It just sharpened the error band around each.

'Wheeldata, I want to stop the run now –'

'This is Wheeldata. Which program do you want to stop, Mister

Morgan?'

'I want to stop the program you designated as *Morgan One*. Then I want to transmit the program, the data and the output to Omniphone 02 437 567921 as soon as possible.'

The VDU blanked.

'Program *Morgan One* has now been terminated.'

'Good. When can I make the transmission?'

'Which transmission do you wish to make, sir?'

'As I said, I wish to transmit the program *Morgan One* with the data it used and the output it produced to Omniphone 02 437 567921.' *Sorting through that lot should keep Bracknell busy for months* he thought.

'The program *Morgan One* and its associated data and output are listed as Restricted Access.'

'What?'

'Program *Morgan One* and its associated data and output are listed as Restricted Access. That means that they are not generally available except by means of the appropriate code.'

'But it's my program. It was I who had it transmitted to you only a few hours ago.'

'Please type in the access code.'

'But I haven't got the code. Wheeldata, what is the access code for *Morgan One*?'

'It is not my function to give codes – except at the request of those giving the correct code-access-code.'

'What is the correct code-access-code for access to the *Morgan One* program?'

'I cannot give that data.'

'Damn!'

'Syntax error.'

Morgan typed in *SEARCH Morgan One* and *SEARCH RAE/ MET SYNTH 19*. Neither produced a response. Then, glancing hastily around the room he extracted the niobium tantalate memory cassette from his console and pocketed it. At least he had a copy of the output summary which had been displayed on his screen.

Perkins was seated at an active VDU, speaking loudly and incessantly into his headset. Commander Grey stood motionless, rigidly holding a cup of coffee, staring down at the moonlit hemisphere of Earth. Morgan joined her. He made a quick assessment of what could be said and what not.

'You didn't see the end of the synthesis then, Commander Grey?'

Her figure looked back at him from the dark port. 'I thought I'd leave you alone with your sorrow.'

'Sorrow?'

'The program. The run. I thought an audience might embarrass you.'

'Of course not. It's only one's failures that one doesn't wish to publicise.'

'Mister Morgan, surely you can't have failed to see the figures. Your program was predicting temperatures of more than forty degrees Celsius, and windspeeds of a hundred kilometres per hour – *in England*.'

She seemed to take it for granted that the figures were in error – and to have a masterly lack of interest in the reason. That was a point worth teasing. 'Quite. And within a decade. It's a bit disturbing. I must say your team is pretty well disciplined. Anyone would think we'd forecast occasional showers with sunny intervals.'

She laughed, clasping his arm in an auntly way. 'My dear Richard, do you think that the output of one trial run constitutes a forecast?'

'It's not exactly a trial run, you know. The individual modules are well proven.'

'But the output. Normal temperatures equivalent to the highest *ever* recorded. The modules may check out OK, but there are such things as interactive errors.'

'There are, but not of this sort of program.'

'The results though? Forty degrees? Look, it's an achievement to get a program of that size running at all on your first day. Take a rest. We'll have another look tomorrow.'

'Have we got any reliable ten-year forecasts to compare it with?' *Get out of that*!

'Maybe not, but that doesn't prove that yours is right – '

' – or wrong.'

'Really, Richard, I think you're being a little mischievous.'

'No, really, I don't mean to be. After all there's no point forecasting weather if you're only allowed to reproduce past weather charts.' Having taken a passing swipe at standard Weather Bureau techniques he hurried on. 'But that's not what I wanted to talk about. I wonder if you would review one of the program modules with me. I've a feeling there might have been an error in transmission.'

'Really, as a programmer I'm – '

'It'll only take a few minutes. We can access the program from here –'

'I really think –'

'Wheeldata, will you give me a LIST of *Morgan One* Module Three on this terminal?'

'The program designated *Morgan One* is listed as Restricted Access. Please type the access code.'

Morgan feigned, for the Commander's benefit, his previous surprise and indignation, and repeated his futile pleas to be allowed access to his own program. Commander Grey leaned against the console, gazing straight out of the window. If she was surprised she didn't betray it: if she was not she didn't bother to act it.

'I don't quite follow this,' said Morgan innocently. 'How do I get round it?'

The Commander paused before replying. 'You don't.'

'Oh.'

There was another long silence. Then she added, 'Wheeldata sounds bright but really he's incredibly stupid. Red tape is one of his failings and you've just got yourself packaged in some.'

'I don't suppose you know this access code?'

She raised her eyes again to gaze out into space. 'No, I haven't got the code.'

'Oh well, let's get through to the captain. If anyone has the code he must.' Morgan started to type out Rathbone's number on his c-unit. Commander Grey, too hurried to give an order, gripped his wrist.

'Don't. Let me sort this out. I'll have something for you in the morning. This one needs someone who knows the system.'

Morgan smiled his reply, holding her eyes for the extra second that said clearly *We both understand that you're lying*.

Once in his cabin, Morgan worked fast. From the meagre allocation of personal equipment which the USSF had allowed him to bring to orbit at their considerable expense he assembled his c-unit, an electric shaver, and a Rotring pen with a set of differently sized writing heads. What he did next with these commonplace objects would have baffled the casual observer: he removed the cutting head from the shaver and snapped the Rotring into the cradle which was exposed; he plugged the shaver into his c-unit and punched up the radio link betwen the c-unit and the cabin terminal.

The product of this innocent construction work was a continuous-wave laser transmitter. Its power would be minute but, when pointed in the direction of a sensitive receiver, adequate – thanks to the skill of the Special Projects Department at RAE Farnborough. All he had to do was point it in the right direction. That task would be taken care of by the orientation program which he had brought with him for the purpose. He clamped the transmitter to the milled alloy of the port frame. The terminal digested the orientation program in a silent half-second. The transmitter moved as its servos swivelled in the computed direction of Intelnet 3, thirty-six thousand kilometres above the Atlantic. It continued to track the satellite's position as Morgan typed his preface to the meterological data into the cabin terminal.

TO: MOD/FILE6/D
FROM: WHEELBASE.
SUBJECT: THE WEATHER.

CONTEXT PRIME MISSION OBJECTIVE. RAE/MET SNTH 19 PROGRAM AND OUTPUT (REFER BRACKNELL) CLASSIFIED BY USSF WHEEL ON BOARD COMPUTER. WHEELBASE DENIED ACCESS. CONSIDER THIS SINGULAR. SUMMARY OF OUTPUT FOLLOWS. SUGGEST YOU LEAK RESULTS THROUGH PRESS TO TEST US REACTION. USE ANNABEL RAWLINGS PRESS AGENCY OMNI 02 450 406949 OK. ALL HAVING GOOD TIME. AIR INVIGORATING.

Morgan ran an encoding program, waited until the Wheel's rotation orientated the transmitter through the glass port and typed the RUN instruction. The end of the Rotring flickered red for a moment and the message was sent – and, Morgan hoped, was stored safely in the bowels of Intelnet 3, four and a half thousand kilometres away. He remembered the RAE's assurance that the laser would not burn a neat hole in the tempered glass of the view-port, and was glad that they had known what they were talking about.

He quickly dismantled the transmitter and erased the output summary from his console. Since Wheeldata knew that he had the summary it was only a matter of time before someone asked it the right question; then they would come running for the little plastic cassette. He placed it innocently in full view on the shelf beside his bunk. They could have it. He didn't need it any longer. But they might have to pay for it.

Morgan recalled the detailed briefing on the Strategic Command chain of the United States forces, and the accompanying advice on intelligence methods. The logic of its conclusion appealed to him.

> You are looking for data on American responses to Soviet threats in the European theatre. To sort this category of decision-making from the mass of American Command strategies would involve fine penetration of the US Command structure. Instead it would seem to be worth testing that structure for *sensitivity to European knowledge*. By definition the information we are interested in will make up a large part of that which the Americans do not wish us to acquire. In short, then, *focus your interest on areas to which you are denied access*.

And, he had thought at the time, *it's all very well saying that*. He wasn't quite so sure now. Now he had stumbled on something the Americans apparently did not want him to concern himself with – and he didn't have the slightest idea why they were trying to hide it. Meteorological information just wasn't that sensitive. For the moment he would have to content himself with the kite-flying gambit. It was the best he could think of without making an obvious nuisance of himself.

He asked Wheeldata to connect him with Lieutenant Honeywell.

'Lieutenant Honeywell.'

'Hullo, Morgan here.'

'Good evening, sir. How can I help you?' It didn't seem wise to answer the question directly. And suddenly he felt awkward. He didn't know the girl, and he had no wish to invade her privacy; it must be a rare commodity on the Wheel.

'I hope I haven't caught you at a busy moment –'

'No – I'm not on duty.'

'But I have a major psychological problem.'

'Say again?'

'I have this major psychological problem. It's just cropped up.'

'This is going to be English humour again, isn't it.'

'Oh. I was hoping to get the punch-line out before you realised.'

'I'm a linguistic psychologist, remember?'

'Oh yes, I remember now.'

'Is that a put-down?'

'Of course not.'

'I majored in put-downs during my first year at college: Deflation in the Modern English-Speaking World.'

'Interesting. Aren't you going to ask me what my problem is?'

'I know how it will please you.'

'Yes?'

'What's your problem?'

'Drink.'

'Yes?'

'Yes. I've got a drinking problem. I need a fluid psychologist to come and observe me drinking.'

'We haven't got a fluid psychologist.'

'Oh dear. Tell you what, a linguistic psychologist would do. If I were to see you in the rim bar in about five minutes . . .. '

'Highly contrived. OK, I'll see you in five. Seat by the window.'

Morgan stopped when he saw the lieutenant. She wore her functional white overall as though she were modelling it. She might have chosen just such a garment after a morning's browsing in Laura Ashley to display the grace and warmth of her figure. Against the window, with the backdrop of space and the sifted silver dust of stars, she reminded him of one of those early twentieth-century *Vogue* posters, though her smile as she turned to him was warmer.

Taking his seat opposite her he formed the modest impression that she had intended him to see her just thus. He smiled inwardly and preserved an outward calm.

'Hullo,' he said. 'Cheers.' She had placed a full glass of beer ready for him.

'Hi,' she replied. 'Ah, cheers.' A note of formality entered her voice. 'How have you been getting on with your first day here?'

Morgan told her quickly about his briefing, his duty period and his first research session – the authorised version. He kept it light. He fell silent, swirling the remains of his beer in his glass and gazing into space.

'So your first day was quite encouraging?'

'Pretty much so.'

'Everything went smoothly?'

'Oh, fine, yes.'

'Oh come on, that's bullshit.' But she said it sympathetically. Morgan made the decision he'd been pondering since he first contacted her that evening.

'Well, when I say *yes*, I mean relatively smoothly.'

'What happened? Did you overlook a typhoon or something?'

'It was only a little typhoon. No, nothing like that. Have you ever tried out your linguistic psychology on Wheeldata?'

'Yes, I'm doing it all the time.'

'How does it work out?'

'It doesn't. I just find out about the semantic theories of his programmers. There isn't an emotional input to his constructions and choices as there is for human beings – though you can get a reflection of the emotional imprinting of the programmers on a language situation. Why? D'you think Wheeldata's *non compos* – er, *machinae*?'

'Well, after I got him to finish the meteorological run that I was doing he stole my results – and my program and data.'

'He *stole* them?'

'Yes. The run finished and I asked him to transmit the whole lot down to my HQ in England. He wouldn't let me have it and he wouldn't transmit it.'

'What exactly did he say?'

'Well, I can't remember exactly, but his first reaction was to seem not to recognise the request. Then he said that the data was classified as *Restricted Access*. I couldn't get past that stage.'

'Anyone can recognise that routine. It happens quite commonly with *homo sap*. as well. Just blame it on the institution. Use its jargon and pretend the whole thing's nothing to do with you.'

'That's pretty well what it sounded like.'

'It's a fear reaction imposed by any big organisation. The organisation defines – or threatens to define – a strict internal code of behaviour. The individual is anxious lest he transgress that code whilst communicating outside the organisation. So all he does is pass the rule book down the line. Anyway, what was the run about? It had to be something pretty devious to get Wheeldata glued up.'

'I was running a weather forecasting program. It was new. It produced a synthetic model rather than a forecast based on past experience.'

'Astonishing,' she smiled, 'But the gist?'

Morgan took a casual sip of beer. He looked away from her into the room. More people were drifting in now and forming into loose clusters and small groups. A large red-headed man laughed loudly by the bar. Morgan remembered that it was he who had said something about being 'on our own' and precipitated one of those universal silences the previous night. Morgan only glanced momentarily back at the girl. He didn't want his direct gaze to deter any reaction she might make to what he said.

'It predicted some extreme climatic effects for the next decade.'

'Oh.' There was no question mark.

'Don't you want to know what they are?'

'Yes, sure.'

'I thought for a moment . . . '

'Sorry. I didn't mean to discourage you. It's just that we hear a lot of that sort of stuff up here. You know, *the next Ice Age is imminent* and that sort of thing.'

'I see. No, my program is predicting the opposite: the Greenhouse Effect is what it's called in the press.'

'Yes, I've heard that one OK. Is the extent of it serious?'

'Within eight years the daytime temperature in London will stabilise at forty degrees – all the year round.'

'That's bad. You'd better get yourself another program.'

'Another program?'

'One that predicts good weather.'

'What if it's right?'

'Not so good.'

'You don't seem to take it seriously.'

'Like a lot of other things. I don't want to start biting my finger-nails. All the typing chores round here make them hard enough to grow as it is.'

'Mm.' He was disappointed. Her response could have been either totally naïve or totally theatre. But then it was stupid to expect her to be stupid.

His attention became more sharply focused on the scene near the bar.

'Spot of controversy going on over there.'

Two men were holding the arms of a struggling third – the man whose loud conversation had silenced the bar on the previous evening – whilst a fourth jerked the contents of a full mug of beer into his face.

'Revenge tragedy I think,' she answered.

But then two others came to the assistance of the man who had taken the unintentional drink. There was a confusion of shouting and some jostling as the two sides squared up to one another. Morgan motioned to his c-unit. 'Shouldn't we call Security?'

'Wheeldata's way ahead of you.'

'I was forgetting.'

The red-headed figure moved into rapid action, the shouting quickly reached a peak and immediately the area near the bar was a confusion of struggling bodies and wildly flying fists. Morgan stood up with his beer in one hand and his other hand in his pocket. To the din of battle were added the cries of reproof and encouragement of others in the room.

'There's some quite creative fistwork going on in there,' said Morgan appreciatively.

'I beg your pardon?'

Morgan raised his voice slightly. 'I had no idea you laid on this sort of entertainment up here.'

Lieutenant Honeywell didn't answer.

'I must say I'm surprised.'

'Well . . . '

'After all, the people you've got up here are all highly qualified: picked for technical skill, adaptability, emotional maturity, physical wellbeing. . . .'

'Yeah, I wish someone would tell *them* that. . . . '

Security arrived, without any particular show of force. An officer shouted the usual palliatives, and four men without helmets or weapons waded into the mêlée. They led out a group which included the original protagonists. Tempers were still high. The captives suffered themselves to be led out, not without some exchange of defiance.

'What's it all about, anyway?'

Lieutenant Honeywell shrugged her answer.

'Aren't any of them your patients?'

'All of them.' She laughed at the idea. 'You are all my flock, black sheep and all. And so, you see, even where I know the reasons why this man or that gets involved in a brawl – and I don't claim to know that very definitely – I can't really discuss it.'

'No, of course not. I can understand that,' said Morgan amiably.

'Unlike you.'

'Eh?'

'We can talk about you.'

'What, me – psychomologically?'

'Why not?'

'But I'm only just on your file. You hardly know anything about me yet.'

'Language, Mister Morgan. I have more of yours already than I have of most people on the Wheel.'

'Really?'

'Yes.'

'Well, also I haven't got anything wrong with me.'

Her laugh might be melodic but it could also be mocking. 'You don't really mean that?'

'I suppose you're referring to the old gag that no one is so fortunate as to have nothing psychological wrong with them?'

'Not really. We all vary and we all have our limits, but there's little point in always diagnosing disorder. No, I was laughing at the supremely arrogant way you said that.'

'I see.'

'You know you don't strike me as being a typical meteorologist at all.'

'You're on to me. I'm an atypical meteorologist. Should there be any such thing as a typical meteorologist?'

'Yes. All meteorologists share certain interests, assumptions, experiences. These exhibit themselves in language to a marked degree.'

'And I?'

'Well I must say I haven't run precisely that correlation on you, so it's just a feeling I have. Take your reaction to that brawl just now. I know very well that there are some people in this room who are in a state of mild shock even now. And there are only a few whose heart-rates will have returned to normal.'

'How d'you know I'm not affected like that?'

'Your reaction at the time. You were quite calm, interested in the cause of the disturbance, even apparently appreciative of the aesthetics of fist-fighting. And you made a joke.'

'People joke to hide their stress.'

'Language again. It wasn't that sort of joke.'

'So I've got a misplaced sense of humour and a generally unsympathetic attitude towards my fellow men. Yes, there's some truth in that, though to be fair to myself I don't think it's true all the time.'

'No, I didn't mean that at all. I just meant that the fight didn't put you under stress.'

'Is that bad?'

'No. It's atypical. So it interests me. But it's only a small indication, and not an objective one. What I *have* done today is run a correlation of certain of your semantic routines.'

'Your scientific curiosity knows few bounds.'

'Oh, I ought to say this wasn't scientific curiosity. It's an important part of my job – preventive psychology.'

'Well, we've talked about my computer run. Tell me about yours.'

'OK, as long as you understand this. When I completed the run I formed the professional judgement that there might be a problem and that a consultation was advisable. The matter happens to have arisen in the course of a conversation, but please allow that this is now a prefessional matter.'

'Speaking of linguistic psychology, you're beginning to sound somewhat cautious.'

'*Touché*. Actually I'm worried more than anything about hurting your feelings – sir.' She smiled quickly. 'You mention caution. It so happens that it bears a strong relation to your own case. The run produced an unusually strong negative correlation between assertive structures and a wide category of qualifiers – all the way from disclaimers to self-directed satire.'

Word Computer Unmasks Spy Ring! said a banner headline in Morgan's mind. He played for thinking time. 'I'm not all that well up with the jargon!'

'OK, I'll explain it – with an example to start off with. You just said *I'm not all that well up with the jargon*. To begin with, that statement was phrased in a way that a layman would call modest. In a not-uncharming way it's a statement that's not true: it's a fabrication produced for effect. One might ask why. Also I've a shrewd suspicion that if the statement were introduced to a correlative run with any other ten thousand words that you have spoken, the computer would have to tell me that it was untrue in a literal sense: that is, you do understand my jargon well enough to follow what I said to you.

'In fact that's what my run did show: your speech is full of such contradictions. For some probably deep-seated reason you are presenting a false front to the world.'

'Don't we all?'

'Perhaps. But not to that extent.

'You consistently build linguistic barriers against anyone engaging with your role or background on a serious level, and on top of that you register strong rejection of your role structure here – particularly that of meteorologist. That's not healthy in view of the fact that your file reports you to be a highly committed scientist.' Morgan felt more annoyed than alarmed. He was trying to set up this girl to be used – and she was within an ace of penetrating his cover.

'Well, I find that very interesting, but not really very convincing. You see, you're talking to someone with inside knowledge. I know how I feel about my own job.'

'To some extent. But perhaps you're not all that sure about your competence. You might have anxieties about your performance that you haven't even pinned down as being such. Or you might see some other significance in what I'm saying that you're not prepared to admit to me.'

That was a bit near the mark. She looked steadily at him before continuing. 'That's often the case, but it doesn't matter because even that covert recognition . . . ' Morgan felt a charge of adrenalin at the word *covert* '. . . can be useful to the client or patient or whatever we call him.'

'How about *victim*?'

'Oh, I'm sorry, I didn't want to put too much emphasis on this, and I especially didn't want to hurt your feelings. Just remember that if you want to talk to me you can – you know.'

'Thanks,' said Morgan, completely hiding his embarrassment. He didn't particularly want to pose as a psychotic in order to preserve his cover, especially for the desirable Lieutenant Honeywell.

Six

IT WAS midnight, Wheeltime, before Morgan returned to his cabin. The cassette of meteorological data was still on the shelf beside his bunk. The last thing he did before turning in was to place it at a carefully haphazard angle next to his computer terminal. Although it was the Wheel's midnight a bright blue daylit arc of Earth revolved slowly outside his port. He didn't polarise it out, but watched it turn to crescent, then to a burning bow, then to a delicate band of red-filtered colour where the soft afterglow of the Sun scattered through the band of atmosphere.

He turned to face the door, drew the light thermal cover up around his ears, and closed his eyes to a slit. That might deceive most people, but it wouldn't make the slightest impression on Wheeldata. With a finger on his pulse he slowed and deepened his breathing. He inhaled slowly and deeply for ten seconds, held for ten, then let the air out of his lungs in a gentle ten-second sigh. Then again. And as his respiration slowed to two per minute his pulse rate came down from sixty-five to fifty-five. Then as his breathing shallowed it sank to fifty, hovered, touched forty-eight, and stayed there. The trick was not so much to persuade Wheeldata that he was asleep as to stay awake. But he felt deliciously alert. His senses were keyed to his pulse, respiration, and the airtight door of his cabin. Those three things filled his consciousness.

He was not aware of the passage of time. The cold light of the Moon flicked across his cabin with metronomic regularity once every thirty seconds. He didn't count its passes. The Eastern limb of Earth had taken fire before the red indicator winked on the panel next to his door. They must have got Wheeldata to switch the lights off in the corridor, but the outside illumination was slightly higher than that in his cabin, so he saw the door open and the silhouettes of the two men as they entered. He couldn't see them clearly enough to recognise them. They were wearing bulky spectacles: low-light television. No matter. Morgan's eyes were well acustomed to the varying light. One figure stopped behind the door. The other advanced towards him. They deployed themselves like professionals. They appeared to be unarmed. As the second man approached the bunk Morgan closed his eyes. LLTV spectacles presented a grainy view of the world, but he couldn't rely on that at close range.

Morgan sensed from the muffled feeling of the air that the second man was stooping over him. Into the almost complete silence whispered the rustle of fabric, and the slight characteristic *tic* of a fingernail against hollow metal. Morgan was half-way through a gentle inhalation. He stopped and held. He sensed a movement near his face and heard the faint sibilation of a micro-aperture aerosol. Probably an incapacitating agent. He disciplined his pulse rate. The intruder moved away. Morgan started to trickle out his breath in a slow stream. That way none of the stuff should reach his lungs.

But when the breath was gone and he had waited half a minute he knew it was time to take the risk. He opened his eyes. They didn't sting or water. One figure was still standing behind the door. The other snapped the cassette into the terminal. His actions were no longer cautious. He would be assuming that Morgan was now in a safely drugged sleep. Neither of the men had donned breathing apparatus. It was enough. Morgan took a slow deep breath. It felt all right, though you couldn't be sure until you tried to move.

The terminal wrote up the program identification. Its blue light illuminated the face of the operator.

'This it?' Morgan heard him breathe. His colleague moved over to stand beside him. The blue gleam struck highlights off their noses and cheekbones.

'Yeah. It'll do.' He typed out the sequence that would silence the terminal. Morgan's feet swung to the floor.

'Let's go.' He ejected the cassette into the palm of his hand. Simultaneously he felt a blow at the back of his knees that dropped him to a sitting position.

'I say, I'm most awfully sorry, I didn't . . . ' said Morgan, reaching out to the light switch.

As the light came on the intruders moved. The man on his feet dived for the door – and clanged heavily into it as it closed ahead of him. The other sprang from his position on the floor at Morgan's legs. His dive was aided by the low gee and two swift hands at the scruff of his neck. He hit the opposite wall. A careless foot winded him, not too severely. The other recovered and turned, now ready for serious work. He was slightly crouched on the balls of his feet, his hands weaving low.

' . . . only I know how it is in these corridors, with all the doors looking the same. Often made the same mistake myself. And one terminal looks so much like another in the dark, especially if you're wearing dark glasses. In fact it beats me how you can see at – ' The man's hand shot out, fingers stiff, towards Morgan's neck. It met a solid fist. Morgan felt the cracking of finger-bones. 'Oh God, I'm sorry, I didn't mean to – '

'*Bastard*!'

Morgan stamped hard on the foot that wasn't attempting to kick him. 'Now that's quite enough. If you shout you'll only wake people up, and then we'll all be in trouble. And you should mind your language; there may be people near by who've been carefully brought up.' His assailant was writhing on the floor, so he turned some of his attention to the terminal.

'Wheeldata?'

'Mister Morgan; Wheeldata.'

'Wheeldata, I have intruders in my room. Would you alert Security?'

'I am speaking to Security. Security is sending assistance. Security wishes to know the nature of the intrusion.'

'Two men.' Morgan looked carefully at the occupants of the floor of his small cabin. Both wore the insignia of Wheel Security. 'Sergeant Miller and Trooper Spight. Not armed, not dangerous, but making it hard for me to get to sleep.'

'Thank you, Mister Morgan. The security detachment will be with you in approximately thirty seconds. I have described to them the nature of the intrusion.'

'Thanks, ol' buddy.'

Seven

THERE WAS a sharp twisting pain in Rathbone's guts. That was not because of the culture-synthesised breakfast he had swallowed between meetings but because of his frustration and barely-contained fury. These emotions were as equally divided as it was possible to judge between Morgan and those of Rathbone's superiors who, by the innate complacency of the highly-placed, had prevented him from shuttling Morgan down to the surface at the earliest possible opportunity – and who, by the grace of the bureaucratic essence that held them firmly to their seats, still prevented him from doing so. But of the two sources of fury, only Morgan was here in front of him.

'Thank you for your interesting statement, Mister Morgan. I think I'm in possession of your views on what happened in your cabin last night. Do you have any idea why two members of my security team should make burglarous entry to your cabin while you are asleep?'

'Not that I can think of. The only thing they tried to lift was a cassette of met. data. And anything anyone wants to find out about me they can get from my file.' Morgan gestured toward the VDU on Rathbone's desk. 'Or they can ask me, of course.'

Smooth bastard, thought Rathbone.

Morgan continued, turning politely to the third man in the room. 'I think we're pretty much in your hands, sir.' The remark, Rathbone perceived, was deceptively bland. He looked directly at McMurdo, the Base Security officer. *Another smooth bastard*. There was no doubt where he got his orders from, and it wasn't the captain of the Wheel.

'I don't think we have any problem,' was all McMurdo said. And for each of the three it meant a different thing.

Considering, thought Rathbone, that each of us is ecstatically bullshitting and knows that the others are doing so, we're not likely to get any further. He cast his mind back to 0400 hrs. Wheel time when Wheeldata had tactfully nagged him to wakefulness and announced that a full emergency Pluto conference was brewing.

He and Zeffert had snapped into action and run the security checks with the pragmatic attitude to crisis of astronauts. There was already a great deal of cross-talk on the link. David Fellows cut through it unimaginatively.

'Gentlemen, we have a problem.' The parted tatters of conversation fell away. 'The London-base Prestel data organisation came on the line at midnight with a feature put out by the British journal *New Scientist*. The feature was entitled *Conflicting Evidence on Climate Warm-up*. It purports to have been written by a Doctor Nagazadhe of Cambridge University, England, and deals with his team's researches into climatic conditions on Venus and CO_2 build-up trends in the Earth's atmosphere. His results are within almost an order of magnitude of ours – with a rather slower build-up than we anticipate.'

'He may have got good results,' said Rick Steerman, 'but who knows that besides us? Is anyone likely to take him seriously?'

'Maybe not as his article stands,' replied Fellows, 'but that's not all there is. Fill us in, Arnold.'

Doctor Clegg, the Director of American Intelligence, spoke slowly. His voice held no hint of drama. 'I was able to get the Department working quickly on this one. What's going on in the western scientific community is well documented. Nagazadhe exists.

He's a good enough scientist. His team has bought access to a lot of NASA's data on Venus, and has similar access to the Soviet Academy of Science. But our scientific team were quite clear from the start that the quality of the information about Venus, and also the information Nagazadhe has access to about terrestrial CO_2 trends, not to mention his processing resources, are insufficient for him to come up with the results published. In short he's a publishing front for some other person or organisation. That means either a leak from us or the Soviets, or an independent breakthrough. So far the Department hasn't been able to trace the article back any further. I'd welcome any views on lines of research.'

'If it's us or the Soviets,' said Professor Hewitt, 'the data should be a lot more accurate than it is. And we've already established that with the present state of computer technology elsewhere an independent breakthrough is impossible.'

'Do you think an independent team could have pirated some computer time in the States or Russia?'

'Impossible. Our own computers are secure, and we've got theirs bugged.'

'It might account for the error in the data.'

'Not if it can't be done at all.'

'*Can't* always bothers me. Anyway, how about a leak of our actual results?'

'Same problem. They should be more accurate.'

'They could be doctored.'

'Could you access the article to my terminal?' asked Rathbone.

'I still don't understand the problem,' insisted Steerman. 'I don't see what anyone could hope to gain by publishing the results. It may hurt us but it wouldn't help them.'

'Hurting us might be considered to help a lot of people,' said Rob Whitaker.

Rathbone scrolled through the print on his display. He called up Wheeldata and sketched out a correlation program. The babble of the Pluto meeting seemed to recede. He was in his own sphere of silence. He interrupted whoever was speaking. He didn't notice who it was.

'I can clear up the problem about the source of the data.'

'Yes, Captain?' humoured Fellows.

'Yes. It comes from the Wheel.'

'Now, Captain, you may have the data there, but can you be sure that you are the *source* of the data.'

'Yes. These figures are slightly changed as Doctor Clegg suggested. But I've just run a correlation which shows they're a close match with data produced by a computer program which was run here yesterday.'

'Then I'm at a loss to see how the data could have got past your security.'

'As of now, so are we. But we're working on it.'

'What have you got?'

'The computer run was made by the Englishman, Morgan. You remember we discussed him at the last meeting.'

Fellows broke a heavy silence. 'Yes.'

'In fact you'll recall that I repeated my strong objections to Morgan staying on board this station.'

'The team will, I'm sure, remember your comments. What happened?'

'Morgan picked up the program via the station's up-link from his Met. HQ in England. He ran the program using our data. Considering the deficiencies of the program it worked perfectly. My Met. officer, Lieutenant-Commander Grey, had Wheeldata secure the whole file when Morgan tried to down-link it to his HQ. He walked off with a cassette of the output summary, and we weren't so quick to intercept it. He must have got the contents of that out somehow – God knows how, though.'

'Have you got the cassette now?'

'No, we haven't. McMurdo's men went in to get it, but they tripped over their own feet.'

'Well, that's stable-door stuff now. The point is the information's out –'

'And we can ignore it,' interrupted Steerman. 'Who's going to pay any serious attention to a popular science journal – a British one at that?'

'That's the third time you've made that point, Rick, and I'm surprised you should make it at all. If Morgan's interested, his Secret Service is interested. So this is no innocent press release; this is in fact one hell of a furtive press release. So we know about it. It's what's going on that we don't know about that worries me.'

'We should have full details on that within twelve hours,' said Clegg quietly.

'How does it look from where you are, Rob?'

Whitaker, the White House adviser, stared evenly out of his

screen. 'Our feeling at present is that we can get the British to bottle the whole thing. They owe it to us – and a lot more for that matter.'

'Sure,' said Clegg. 'But they're not going to forget they ever knew. They're going to be curious to say the least. Making them insert the bung isn't going to diminish their interest any.'

'Well, we'll have to live with that. It should be within the scope of your people to mount an operation that would kill their appetite, Arnold.'

'Some people in the White House have a view of the Intelligence Department that comes straight out of TV.' Whitaker was silent but his eyes widened angrily. The President already had Clegg's recommendation. It was to do nothing. Clegg continued, 'The British are flying a kite. They're waiting for us to react to that article. That way they hope they'll find out what the hell it means to us. We'd be fools to even let on that we've noticed it.'

Steerman vigorously nodded his agreement. The difference of opinion established itself in silence. Rathbone took advantage of a clear field.

'Anyway, I presume I can now get rid of Morgan.'

'One would suppose so,' said Fellows. 'Arnold?' He looked at Clegg.

'Sorry, Rathbone. You'll have to put up with him a while yet.'

'What?' Rathbone sneered his disbelief.

'You're going to have to keep him.'

'But that guy's a threat to the Project. And he's making a fool of me. It feels like time I stopped playing games of service etiquette with him and kicked him from here to Pluto.'

'I'm truly sorry, Rathbone. But the mission involving Morgan isn't yet complete.'

'Mission? What mission?'

Silence.

'I presume as usual there's something the Service isn't being told. I don't mind dirty tricks, Doctor Clegg. The USSF can give as good as it gets. But if we're playing any game we like to be in on the ground rules.'

'Sorry, Rathbone. We don't like this one either. I'd like nothing better than to tell you, but it's top level.'

'Top level?'

'Yes.'

Fellows left five seconds for the emotional static to discharge.

'Now, gentlemen, I'd like us to discuss several courses of action in respect of the leak and the security breakdown on Big Wheel.'

So I'm still stuck with service exchange etiquette, thought Rathbone, *even if you're breaking it*. He conceded Morgan a lop-sided smile.

'I think we'd better treat this as a routine disciplinary matter. Courts martial are heavy on both morale and logistics up here. I'll take it from here. I assure you the matter will be thoroughly dealt with.'

'Fine, sir.' He came to the less than parade ground attention of the USSF. This was a time to ingratiate. 'Permission to carry on, sir?'

'Keep up the good work, Morgan.' As the Englishman left his cabin Rathbone savoured the anticipation of some less formal occasion, some moment of crisis – and God knows, there were plenty of them – when his decisions about Morgan's activities would be untrammelled by considerations that were external and academic.

Morgan's second working day began, and he was disenchanted. It was fascinating to play with advanced machinery, and to watch the weather patterns twirling their way round the globe towards the equator. But he felt out of things. Suspended here, thirty-six thousand kilometres away from Earth, processing the busy traffic of shuttle flights, the Wheel was the precise potent centre of a hemisphere's defence activity. That made it his sort of operation, and he would far rather be in the thick of it than out here on the edge forecasting weather.

Commander Grey was a charming matriarch. He found that she was indeed called Auntie. Half-way through the morning he casually handed her the cassette with, 'Oh, I thought you might like to copy this as Wheeldata's holding out on us.'

Auntie was not an actress; she batted several eyelids. 'Ah, the summary. How *thoughtful*.' She turned away to file it. Then, as though after second thoughts, she turned back. 'But I haven't told you: we've sorted out Wheeldata's problem.'

'Oh?'

'Yes. His problem was that he was all hung up over an error.'

'Programming error?'

'No, the programming was all right, but there was a conceptual error lurking beneath it.' *Quite. The programming was self-evidently OK.* 'It gave him a crisis of conscience. Snarl-up in his own programming. He had a session with Bud Saunders, and he seems to be straightened out now.'

'Bud Saunders?'

'Systems.'

'Oh yes, I met him.' There was a five-second silence. 'Well, that's OK then.'

'We do have the occasional problem, but we get through. Commander Saunders is on his way over from Maths Services. You might like him to go through the equations with you.'

'That would be interesting.'

'I know you know your job and all that, but the maths people are a resource that the rest of us can't do without.'

'Register my complete accord. I have problems with long division.'

Saunders duly arrived with black-rimmed spectacles and an empathic line of talk with Wheeldata, who now innocently released the met. program and data. After an hour and a half of arcane exchanges in which he dimly detected a kernel concerning the virtual three-dimensional sea-air interface, and the order-of-magnitude change that this made to the RAE's equations, Morgan left for his cabin. He had a slight headache and a sense of confusion about whether he had been conned or re-educated.

He also had a cassette which he had copied from the fourth module of a program appendix transmitted that morning from Bracknell. He decoded it through the terminal in his cabin. It read:

TO: WHEELBASE.
FROM: MOD/FILE 6/D.
SUBJECT: THE WEATHER

CONTEXT RAE/MET SYNTH 19. STATE DEPARTMENT PRESSURE ON FO. D NOTICE ACTIVE ON PRESS RELEASE. US INTELLIGENCE BUSY. US RESPONSE INDICATES HIGH SECURITY. PURSUE SUBJECT OF WEATHER AND SEEK SIGNIFICANCE. PRIORITY EQUAL TO PRIME MISSION. URGENTLY AWAIT YOUR PRIME MISSION INTELLIGENCE. DONT FORGET TO WRITE.

He recognised the prearranged signal in the final sentence: Hawkins and Sarin were ready to be contacted. Just as he reached out his hand to flip the cassette out of the machine it was illuminated by the READ light – but no, it was green. It was the ERASE light. He hadn't touched a thing. Someone was instructing his terminal from another part of the space station. It shouldn't be possible without his co-operation. The screen lit up. It was filled by the face of McMurdo. He grinned humourlessly.

'Naughty.'

'I beg your pardon?'

'We both know. Why act dumb? I have read and copied your latest communication from the Director of Division Six, Morgan. I know you're a member of a Special Operations Team.'

But does he know about the rest of the team?

'So I've got you where I want you –'

'Which is?'

'And I can call whatever tune I please.'

'This is most interesting, but . . . ' What would he try? The quick kill or the long due process of the law? He was not anxious to blow half a lifetime's preparation by confiding his deep cover to McMurdo. So he had to play out the old game with resignation. He felt sick with apprehension. ' . . . I really don't know what you're talking about. Don't forget I'm new here.'

'So first of all you can tell me what you're doing here. What is your *Prime Mission*? What are your orders?'

'Well, really, it's all on the file. I would have thought someone in your position would have no access problem, but I'm sure that a word to Captain Rathbone would –'

'I want you to understand, Morgan, that you're under one hundred per cent full time surveillance. Also that there's an indefinite amount of cold empty space wrapped around this ship, and there's plenty of room in it for things to happen – to people if necessary.'

'Will that be all?' asked Morgan. But the screen was clear. What the hell was McMurdo waiting for? He didn't need to play Poirot games. His suspicion was in itself sufficient to get Morgan off the Wheel. And he had hard evidence.

He sauntered off for a moody lunch, conscious all the time that he was being followed – not physically by McMurdo and his security team, but by the ubiquitous mind of Wheeldata. McMurdo pointedly took a nearby table in the mess. With him was one of the two men who had entered Morgan's room the previous night. Morgan recalled his name: Spight. Spight was in a bad way, for one hand and one foot were elaborately bandaged. He made slow progress walking to the table, and slower progress eating when he got there. Morgan was glad. The example would warn McMurdo that he mustn't expect everything to go his own way. But that wasn't the point. McMurdo was displaying Spight for Morgan's benefit: not only was this a security matter but there were scores to settle and men to settle them. Men with limps, though . . .

Morgan turned his head and looked out into space; that was a vista to arouse reverie. At that moment Orion was wheeling across the window. Morgan easily recognised the ruby glint of Betelgeuse (Beetle-juice to the SIS instructor who, five years ago had made him and his newly-formed Special Operations Team navigate across two hundred miles of northern Norway without map or compass). He dredged up what he could remember of the crash course in astronomy – only ten days ago. It had certainly altered his perspective. . . . The clear blue-white spark of Sirius tracked across the window; he'd read that it stood a forty-six per cent chance of becoming a supernova – in a few million years. The article, by someone at Princeton, said that the radiation from the explosion would take ten years to reach Earth, but that when it got here it would destroy all life. Not even the nuclear scientists could do that – and they didn't have to work at a range of a hundred billion billion kilometres. It was a cold feeling, looking down now at Earth, and imagining it to be sterile. Perhaps a space station whose orbit was calculated so that the Earth's bulk protected it from the distant fireball . . . . Then it would be alone . . . .

'You look far away – sir.' Lieutenant Honeywell slid her tray next to his and sat down.

'About three point something-or-other parsecs.'

'What's so bad three parsecs away? You look so melancholy.'

'It just struck me . . . Oh, it's a bit silly. It doesn't matter.'

'Of course it matters. It's my job – keeping everyone sickeningly cheerful.'

'I was considering the effect on this space station of a distant supernova killing off all life on Earth. I can't say it's one of those things that preys on the average man's mind – like, if we're to believe what we're told, sex, social status, money and so forth. What's the matter?'

Not everyone would have noticed that she had suddenly come under strong emotional control, and that the control was only just sufficient. Some mixture of his professional curiosity, his affection for the pretty, lithe girl next to him, and the coldness of the idea that had stabbed through the armoured glass at them from ten light years away persuaded him not to discard the moment.

'I'm sorry. I seem to have said something that's upset you. I wish you'd tell me.'

'It's nothing.' The gathering drop of water on her lower eyelash contradicted her. 'It's just been a rather bad day.'

'Anything you can tell me about?'

'Oh yes. It's common enough knowledge. Someone unsealed his space suit, outside.'

'Dead?'

'Yes.'

'Suicide?'

'Pretty definitely. Wheeldata monitored the whole thing. It's very hard to kill yourself that way by accident. Wheeldata's very hot on procedures and precautions. It's not even that easy to do it on purpose. He won't let you into the airlock unless there are more than one of you, and he's checked your suit integrity, and he's checked your reason for being there at all.'

Morgan thought of the red-headed man with the knack of getting into emotional scrapes. 'Anyone I know?'

She shook her head. 'Not if you're thinking of last night's brawl. That was Joe Caltrop. No, this was an engineering officer – Lieutenant Karl Travers. He was looking after some systems integration problems on the new Wheel.'

'Any idea what his problem was?'

'Yes. He's got a wife and four children on Earth.'

'Marriage problem?'

'No.'

'I don't understand what you're saying then.'

'Let's not talk about it. It doesn't matter.'

'OK.' *So a man killed himself because he had a wife and four children. And he was happily married and had a good career.*

Conversation in the mess trailed to a complete halt as the station's intercom system came alive. It was a rare event. Wheeldata almost invariably contacted individuals.

'This is the captain.' The scraping of cutlery stopped. 'This is an address to all astronauts of the USSF and to all contractors from whatsoever organisation.

'I would first of all like to say that as more of our new equipment comes on line, and as work proceeds stage by stage on the construction of Wheel B, our capacity to do the job assigned to us reaches new levels. I would draw your attention to some areas in particular. During the last week of operation we handled a record fifty-three surface-to-orbit and orbit-to-surface transfer movements. This included our own traffic, traffic to and from USSF Lunar, servicing of the NASA/ESA Jupiter enterprise, and logistics support of the commercial space fabrication and energy resources in orbit around Earth. We have also attained the capability of duplicating all the data-management of Earth-orbit and lunar facilities.

'On the defence front we have real-time processing of all the data transmitted by US reconnaissance satellites. We are now our country's primary mobile strategic command centre in the event of war, having displaced the Air Force in this capacity within the last month. We also maintain our own significant weapons delivery capability both in respect of terrestrial targets and our Soviet counterpart which is still maintaining one hundred and eighty degrees separation from us in geosynchronous orbit.

'As for our work in progress we're hoping to be able to pressurise Wheel B in six months, thus making a quantum jump in our accommodation capability. We've also completed the structural support beam for our Enhanced Hydrogen Storage Resource. This will reduce the impact on our operations of short-term fluctuations in supplies from Earth.'

There was a heavy pause. *First the good news* thought Morgan.

'So we're doing well and we're doing what American expects of us. The maintenance of these standards is not only a human and technological triumph: it's a national necessity in a world which is becoming increasingly dangerous – economically, politically and militarily. And at times the maintenance of our capability on board this space station is likely to entail some difficulty and inconvenience. This is one of those times. As most of you will know we are entering a period of increased sunspot activity, with more coronal turbulence, more energetic solar wind and higher synchrotron radiation levels. The major effect on you so far will have been on your EVA schedules. No one is now undergoing more than two hours in twenty-four EVA, and that in shielded suits.

'The other effect on our operation is of course the high level of energy put into the ionosphere by these events, and the consequent effect on our communication with the planet. The outcome simply is this. In order to maintain sufficient bit-rate in our communications we have to increase our power consumption. This has now reached an unacceptable level. We can't make the equipment use the power we're feeding to it, so we're faced with cutting our bit-rates. But we can't unload any of our tasks. The future of the Space Force and the security of the United States depends on our performance.

'So we all have to make a sacrifice, the details of which are now entering your standing orders. I wanted though to take this opportunity of explaining my decision.

'What we're going to have to lose is all non-essential communication – which comes down to private video-phone use, news programmes, entertainment, in both directions. Now I know that sounds severe, but we're trying to alleviate it. Any of you can put through and receive written communication with Earth on any terminal. That reduces the data content by several factors and can be accumulated for off-peak periods. Your main sacrifices will be privacy and immediacy of contact. As for the first, I ask you to trust the integrity of any one concerned in the process, and that's seldom anyone other than Wheeldata. And the second: I hope it won't last too long. You'll be told as soon as we can return to the normal situation.

'I thank you all for listening. Good luck.'

Morgan reflected that he would have liked to have seen that performance on a VDU, but there had been none in sight. 'Bollocks!' he muttered derisively under his breath.

'I beg your pardon, sir?'

'I hadn't realised that there was any communications problem, and I've been communicating half the morning.'

'Wheeldata makes it seem easy for you. Now he's calling for assistance.'

'Is that what you think?'

'That's part of what I think. The rest is that Rathbone just doesn't know the effect that this is going to have on crew's morale.'

'Bad?'

'You bet.'

'But it's no worse than going back to the letter post. And this isn't a company of sappers. They appreciate what's going on.'

'Mister Morgan, you really don't understand.'

'Lieutenant Honeywell, you're right. But then there's a lot I'm not being told; you're making it obvious all the time.'

'You are pretending to be someone you're not. That comes out with every phrase you use.'

'Eh?'

'I've been doing a lot of work on you since we last met.'

'How d'you mean?'

'You'll have to excuse me now. I've got a meeting with the captain.' She bustled out of the mess, exuding reproach.

Morgan sighed and dipped a reluctant fork into the microbiological mass in front of him. This had not been his most successful mission for SOT. McMurdo had caught him out, and knew who he was – had lifted the top layer of his cover, anyway. So his mission was blown at least as far as the USSF was concerned. And they hadn't yet jumped on him; that meant that restraining orders had gone out from the Director of American Intelligence. His deep cover was now his only cover. He didn't like to think of it. The very thought had been inhibited for all these years by his operational conditioning.

So it looked as though Clegg was going to put him into play at last. On an American base? For what conceivable purpose? He smiled slightly. McMurdo's frustration must be intense. But he'd have to watch the man; he might get some freelance ideas.

And there was still the SOT mission. He had to carry on with it or he'd blow his deep cover as well. It must be OK with the DAI or he'd have been booted ignominiously back to Earth by now.

He categorised it. His Prime Mission as far as the Secret Service was concerned was to penetrate American strategic options in the event of a European war. That increasingly looked like penetrating the Wheel's computer software – guarded as it was by the jealous Wheeldata. None too easy unless Sarin and Hawkins could provide some sort of technical fix.

The second category was the meteorological puzzle. So Auntie Grey had proved that the theory behind his computer run had been erroneous; in that case, why the security fuss here and on Earth? That only made sense if the output were correct. And the people who wrote the program weren't fools. Yet the prospect of a global climatic crisis within a decade was a little harder to swallow than this forkful of synthetic protein.

The third category was subtler. The arguments in the bar. The brawl – a volatile phenomenon, soon started, soon over. The suicide – of a man with a happy marriage, a good job and four children. The tears of Lieutenant Honeywell: remorse for the dead man? Was that the reaction of a professional psychologist? Now these were the most highly trained men and women ever to have left Earth. Category three and category two might be compatible – only you didn't throw in the towel over a problem ten years in the future, not if you were backed by the mightiest economic and technological civilisation in human history.

Now that he thought about it, category three looked like the most fruitful area. And he could best exploit it by establishing unobtrusively friendly relations with a cross-section of the space station's complement. He set about it that day, eating and drinking and talking with those he had already met: Fred Zeffert, the cordial second-in-command who seemed unperturbed by any knowledge he might have about Morgan's covert identity; Joe Waldon, the Engineering officer, whose team of fifty could build out here in space anything that could be built on Earth, and who had a bug-eyed enthusiasm for lattice circuitry when off duty; Zylka Zbijowski, the Armaments officer, whose vocabulary was built up on a modular pattern out of terms like *We have the capability*; Bud Saunders, the Systems officer, who spoke Fortran; Sandra Crabtree, head of Maths Services, who viewed life as a series of differential equations; Captain Mitchell, tough commander of the Special Space Warfare Unit. He even made an effort with McMurdo that was grudgingly acknowledged. Lieutenant Honeywell (the alpha-plus brain with the sex-object mentality, according to Sandra Crabtree) was nowhere to be seen. That rather took the shine off things.

That evening he lasered a message nervously across to Intelnet 3. Then he initiated contact with Hawkins by using a wrong number telephone routine. This triggered a pre-arranged drop and pick-up in the fifth level corridor in D quadrant, which was on the opposite side of the Wheel from his own cabin, near the contractors' quarters. The two men's c-units were programmed for the drop, so co-ordination was perfect. Morgan came out of D elevator ten paces behind Hawkins, who was walking briskly along the corridor. The corridor was, Morgan knew, under Wheeldata's surveillance, and several people were using it at that moment. Hawkins dropped the tack-note skilfully in the low gee, and Morgan's foot, in pace with his and ten paces behind, came squarely down on it two and a half seconds later. A short interrogation of a wall terminal by Hawkins positioned him behind Morgan and the reverse drop was made.

Back in his cabin Morgan withdrew the thin paper slip, read it, and quite unselfconsciously ate it; when all electronic communication was tapped by an intelligent switch-board there was something to be said for the old methods. So Hawkins and Sarin were making easy weather – if that was the right term – of extra-vehicular engineering. Fine. But their Prime Mission progress was even less than his. They'd be a great team if he had to blow up a shuttle or kidnap Rathbone, or hijack the Wheel. As it was he found himself hankering after the good old days on Earth where they had slogged together over tundra in the Arctic winter or thirsted together in the Jamal Shammar. Still he had better add what they had sent him to his three categories. Pluto: the Americans were supposed to be preparing a *secret* space operation to *Pluto*. A *manned* operation. It sounded like twenty-second century thinking. It would cost a hundred billion dollars, and there was no way it could be secret. Still . . . this was the place to find out.

Eight

THE NEXT month passed with frustrating sloth for Morgan, for he felt himself to be on the edge of increasingly interesting events – while he spent tedious hours talking about the weather. The days were un-marked by any rhythm but the dull addition of the clock's digits, for the rising of the Sun and the phases of the Moon had none of their terrestrial significance. He ate five leisurely dinners with Stephanie Honeywell in the rim bar against a backcloth of stars such as is not seen from Earth, maintaining the tacit fiction that he must keep his gee-dose up. With her he gradually established an unstable truce, trying to behave like neither a schizophrenic nor an inveterate liar. She handled her suspicions with professional detachment and re-signed herself to a patient who had no conception of the psychologist as a confessor. They were able to refer to the matter obliquely, as to a marginally unmentionable disease.

'How's the work? he asked her during their fourth starlit rendezvous.

'I've put in some more time on your veridity problem.'

'What veridity problem?'

'That, Mister Morgan, is a large part of the problem.'

'That "Mister" is beginning to sound highly artificial.'

'With five hundred people isolated in a sardine can like this, service etiquette has its uses, sir.'

'OK Lieutenant. You've been doing some work, you say.'

'I've been writing a report – or rather Wheeldata's been writing a report under my occasional guidance, because I don't write any too good – on, let's say, *my perception* of your authenticity gap.'

'Can I see it?'

'No. It's accessed for the captain and myself.'

'Rotten sneak.'

'I beg your pardon?'

'Ask Wheeldata. He understands me.'

'He may do at that. He and I work pretty closely you know.'

'Speak one another's language?'

'What do you take seriously?'

'Love, death, my country, the Devonshire landscape, gothic architecture . . . .'

'You're laughing even at those.'

'In an affectionate way. I take a lot of things seriously.'

'Especially those things you deride most?'

'I take seriously the fact that you've submitted a scurrilous report on me to the Old Man.'

'I wish you wouldn't view it like that. It's not a thing I do for any personal reason. It's why I'm up here. It isn't related to the fact, and I hope it won't affect the fact that we're . . .'

' . . . Um . . .'

'Oh, come on, you know –'

'Acquainted?'

'I wish you hadn't said it like that.'

Her clear eyes with their long dark lashes were regarding him solemnly.

'I'm sorry,' he said quietly. He paused before reverting to the report – in whose effect he had a substantial interest. 'How did the Old Man take the report?'

'I had to draw his attention to its availability.' She shrugged. 'For all I know that's as far as it went. Captain Rathbone's a very pragmatic sort of leader. I think he considers my duties to vary between curing headaches and organising on-board entertainment.'

When they parted for the night Morgan felt with regret and some shame that he hadn't spoken to her as he would have wished. He had been betrayed by his false position; he couldn't find the right register in which to speak to her. Also he was bored and frustrated, and without realising it he'd taken it out on the girl. Undoubtedly he would prefer to be still with her now. On the way back to his room he found himself gently undressing her in his mind.

That night he updated his files at Division Six through Intelnet 3. Control would not be pleased. The sum to date included a few snoops on the US European defence posture from Hawkins and Sarin; well documented comments on the morale of the space station that were of doubtful value; a more substantial but puzzling document about the Wheel's coy attitude to a possible decrease in climatic stability; and an unlikely suggestion that the USSF were interested in the planet Pluto – hardly an area of strategic significance.

It was during this period that Morgan realised that some new force was acting on the crew of the Wheel. He had already become accustomed to the even tenor of life on the station, with its endless cycle of working shifts, the perfectly interlocking tasks of the highly-trained crewmen, the subtle changes of stance which were a habitual response to the changing aspect of the Soviet war machine. It started slowly at first: people hurrying around a little more; fewer people in the mess at any particular time – and those looking more than usually anxiously at their c-units and leaving before they might otherwise have done. Then there were re-allocations of personnel – say from Engineering to Movement Control – and some new faces on board the Wheel, mainly shuttle crews staying for longer than was customary on their orbital missions. Naturally Morgan was interested. But he could detect no pattern in these phenomena, other than that everyone seemed busier than they had been. Wheeldata turned aside his questions with neither more nor less than his usual tact. But in the end, whatever your ethnic isolation, you couln't help gleaning something of the motives of the five hundred people among whom you lived. One word in particular presented itself for his attention.

'. . . I've averaged twelve hours a day since Bootstrap started . . .'

'And it's got a long way to go. . . .'

'How do you know how long it's got to go?' was a conversation he heard in the mess.

Once while Morgan was walking along a corridor Wheeldata muttered something about ' . . . Bootstrap phase one meeting . . . ' to Joe Waldon, the Engineering officer, while Morgan was on the edge of earshot.

So, *Bootstrap*. *Operation* Bootstrap? It was the sort of chewy phrase the Americans would go in for. It was clearly a Category One subject: it seemed quite important, and they didn't want him to know about it. . . .

The way in which he found out more was unexpected. A few days after his dinner with Stephanie Honeywell, after one of the Space Force's formal dinners – the anniversary of the first landing on the Moon – he managed to engineer a conversational gambit that he had been saving up for weeks. He was sitting at a table in the bar with Stephanie Honeywell, Fred Zeffert, Auntie Grey, Bud Saunders and a couple of others. They had talked about childhood memories of watching that first edgy touchdown on the television – all except Stephanie, whose existence hadn't even approached the project definition stage by that time. They talked about the USSF and Soviet Moon bases, the Mars outpost run under the aegis of the Soviet Academy of Sciences, and Project Longbow. The ESA/NASA programme on Callisto, Jupiter's second largest Moon. They didn't talk so much about the environmental problems of vacuum, radiation, temperature and distance, which, though always severe, were commonplace. They talked about the future, and where space activity could be expected to take human civilisation. Morgan supported the European view that in the long run Earth and the human race was all that the solar system had to offer, and that Project Longbow, the first automatic stellar probe, was the best hope for a spiritually claustrophobic race. Zeffert in particular maintained that it was essential to strengthen the space-industrial base; without it the human race wouldn't live to complete Longbow. There was some wisdom in that, and the two views were not mutually exclusive. Morgan suggested that the industrial perspective of Mars, Earth and the Moon might be too limited.

'Why not the asteroids, and the gas giants and outer planets?'

'The asteroids perhaps,' said Zeffert, 'but beyond ,that, everything's against trying to exploit planetary resources – except for consumption on the spot, like Longbow. There's the energy burn involved in getting there, not to mention the time. There's the weak supply of solar energy when you do get there. There's the lousy environment of extremely low temperatures, high radiation levels and impossible planetary climates. And all for what? We've got all the minerals we could wish for on the inner planets, and Jupiter's quite far enough if they should ever wish to go elsewhere for light elements some day.'

'But how do we know what the potential is?' asked Morgan. 'There've been no surface probes beyond Jupiter.'

'Surface probes aren't vital,' said Bud Sanders in his rapid self-confident computer-patter. 'There are sufficiently detailed fly-by data on Saturn, Uranus and Neptune to show that there are no accessible resources that we can't acquire much nearer to the Sun.'

'And beyond Neptune?' asked Morgan, pointedly making it difficult for Saunders.

And Saunders was trapped. He looked Morgan in the eye. 'Beyond Neptune? You're asking about the resource potential of – ' His flow was perturbed for perhaps a twentieth of a second, and his eyes flickered away from Morgan for a little bit longer. But for a man trained in the arts of deceit it was enough. '– Pluto? Don't be absurd. You're talking about a round-trip time of twelve hours – and that's for radio communication.'

'So you don't think there's much future in going to – ah . . . ' He let the sentence trail off, but there was no response. None of that group, other than Stephanie who expected no better of him, addressed Morgan again that evening. He had committted one of the Service's cardinal gaffes: he had forced the conversation into restricted provinces. But he was not unsatisfied. Although he hadn't extended his knowledge he had firmed up the little that he did have.

It was next morning, though, that Morgan accrued the major benefit of his evening's gambit. At least he construed that connection; it was reasonable. He was preparing reluctantly to report for duty in the Met. Section when a censorious Wheeldata instructed him to present himself to Zeffert. That was a tracking operation in which Wheeldata's assistance was invaluable, for Zeffert was conducting a tour of the Wheel. Morgan caught up with him at the low-gee gymnasium on the third level when the tall first officer was pulling languidly at pieces of inertial exercising equipment and sailing about aimlessly among men and women more grimly determined to discourage muscular atrophy. Zeffert greeted him with his characteristic wave and grinned confidentially. 'We'd better get out of here before we get hauled into something strenuous.'

. 'Fine, sir. Which way do we go?'

'Well, I don't know really. I think we ought to pay a visit to the docking window. Their coffeee terminal is comparatively reliable.' He stopped to pay the well-mannered attention of a senior officer to a shapely lieutenant whom he obviously admired, and turned to Morgan when they were out of earshot. 'There are about two hundred too many men on this station.'

Morgan smiled an acknowledgement of the man's open friendliness – while by no means decrying his sentiment. They entered Docking Control, with its small-scale repetition of Command A's auditorium of computer terminals, displaying laser, radar, video and telemetered information. Round two walls was an expanse of tempered glass – beyond it the perspective past a glowing limb of Earth into infinite space, and to one side the pocked central disk of the Wheel, with its docking tunnels, booms and gantries.

'I like it here. It's the only place where anything's happening most of the time.'

Plenty was happening. There were five shuttles in view. One was close-docked. Teams of suited figures supervised the manoeuvring of bulky pallets from her payload bay, some through a docking tunnel and some through hard vacuum. Three shuttles were stacked, grappled by their forward docking-points to the Wheel's hundred metre de-spun docking mast. One was being nudged into clear space by puffs of white haze from its reaction control thrusters. The three stacked ships showed internal and external lights and were floodlit. Morgan reckoned they must be receiving the combined attentions of about a hundred men. That must be stretching the resources of the Wheel.

'You may wonder what I'm doing gadding about the ship when I could reach any part of it visually on any terminal instantly; and then again you may not . . . .' There it was again: the uncharacteristic leniency of approach that Morgan liked in Zeffert – uncharacteristic; that is, of the USSF in which communication was so often limited to the laconic style of the astronaut. Here was a man who could behave imaginatively within a data-tight system.

'I think I know. You prefer to gad about the ship.'

'We have a *preferring to gad about the ship situation*,' laughed Zeffert easily. Then, in the same tone, 'It appears that *we have a problem*; the captain's given me the job of doing something about it.

It is, ah, contingent upon us that you should not continue with your meteorological work. About that I would prefer to say little except that in the first place I don't think you're cut out for it anyway, and in the second place you've made a good enough impression to make it worth our while to find something more suited to your abilities.'

So he was being made safe. Still, he hadn't been booted back to Earth. Clegg's protection was still good.

'What have you in mind, sir?'

Zeffert gestured out of the window. Morgan noticed the grid of beryllium-steel bars that protected it from any chance nudge that might occur in a docking systems malfunction. He hoped it wouldn't occur unless he were several bulkheads away.

'You can see we're very busy right now. Every team we've got is under stress.'

'On account of Operation Bootstrap?'

'Now why d'you have to say things like that? What are you trying to do – get me sent home?'

'I'm sorry. Aren't I supposed to . . . ?'

'OK: Bootstrap. But for Christ's sake don't talk about it in that blasé way, even if everyone else in the ship does.' He paused for a long time looking out at the Christmas-tree lights of the docked ships, making up his mind about the spy next to him. He decided. 'Right, I'll give you the minimum need-to-know picture. Bootstrap is an operation designed to test our ability to work independently of ground support in time of war. Now that's a thing we obviously can't maintain indefinitely, but we aim to be able to do so while the terrestrial environment is at its most hostile. Also, so that we can stay in operation after an attack on the United States, we want to demonstrate our ability to base, service and fuel shuttles up here rather than on Earth, and provide support for other friendly space facilities.'

'And have you achieved that?'

'Only in token. We've got a long way to go yet.'

'What's the problem?'

'*The* problem? Everything. We've had to use the Wheel, the shuttles and the personnel in ways that weren't ever intended. It takes ten thousand people, not including supporting industry, to turn around the shuttle fleet on Earth. *We* have to do that same with five hundred – whose primary tasks lie elsewhere, and who have had to be retrained for the job. We've had to cope with a shortage of heavy plant, and with the cost of bringing fuel to orbit.'

'Your compensations being what? The advantages of weightless engineering, the high calibre of the Wheel's crew, advanced technology – particularly Wheeldata . . . .'

'And a military set-up. No one argues about what job he's doing. Much, anyway.'

'And what are the remaining problems?'

'Crew fatigue, fuel storage, docking space for more shuttles and orbital transfer craft. The biggest problem is component manufacture.'

'You're taking it *that* far? That really is self-sufficiency. A shuttle must use a million and one components – all of them highly specialised. Can you do that?'

'On the face of it, no. But we're going as far as we can. You can't think in terms of the huge network of factories that does the job on Earth. We have to think in terms of robot production of a component, when it's needed and not before, straight from computer memory to finished article. We can't do it on our own, but we have a great deal of commercial production plant in Earth orbit – from integrated circuits to bearings to incompatible alloys.'

'Materials?'

'The stream of lunar slag they're making the solar power satellites from.'

'All right for light metals and so forth, but how about hydrocarbons?'

'That's a weak point. We've got to rely on Earth for a great deal. There's no way we can do the whole job.'

'Wouldn't it be cheaper in the long run to harden the Earth-based facilities against nuclear attack? It would save all this – what seems to me to be high-risk-of-failure enterprise.'

'It's not my decision. We just try to do the job we're given.'

It didn't seem like Zeffert to resort to a cop-out. He must be understating the necessity for Bootstrap to succeed. Morgan decided he'd pressed enough for one day. How did one say *Where do I come into this*?

'You would like me to help relieve the work load somewhere?'

'Yes. It may sound dull, but the big task in coordinating this is in Logistics. You've shown that you have the initiative and general all-round aptitude – in, I might say, various highly unofficial spheres of your own activity – to do the job. I have three team leaders working under me on the three shifts, but I need one of them totally committed to space-factory liaison. That leaves a Logistics officer slot open. I'd like you to take over from Chuck Lang.'

'But don't you have to go through channels and get USSF personnel?'

'The word *Bootstrap* is apt. We use all we've got up here. There's no slack in the system for shuttling up new recruits when we've already got a man who can do the job.'

It would certainly beat meteorology. And every movement of material and energy in Earth orbit – as far as the Americans were concerned at least – would pass under his scrutiny. 'I like the idea. Of course I like the idea, but can it be fixed up with the Met. Office? They're depending on my research programme.' *Division Six would jump at the idea. The Met. Section was an intelligence wash-out.*

'No problem.'

'Then I accept.'

'Good. You weren't being given a choice anyway. Wheeldata will brief you. I'll want you to handle the green shift in two days' time.'

'It's going to be a busy two days!'

'No one's slow to learn up here, Dick. You're going to have to shadow Chuck, word for word, thought for thought.'

'In that case I'd better go and get on with it.'

'Shortly.' He lowered his voice slightly, turning away from the centre of Docking Control. 'There's a lot unsaid. I'm relying on you to deliver a lot more than you think.'

And that was a singular and terse statement. Morgan felt a more than usually marked bout of divided loyalties coming on. He briefly met Zeffert's similarly brief glance. 'Of course, sir.'

Wheeldata was a great help. In general, Morgan never had to perform any co-ordination task: he only had to define it to the computer's satisfaction and it was as good as done. But no amount of computer power could remedy Earth-based problems like the accumulating inability of Vandenberg and Kennedy Space Flight Centers to keep to their launch schedule. Wheeldata had briefed him on the existence of the problem, but its severity was his first shock when he sat at the prime Logistics console. He looked at his back-up display. It presented the state of affairs most clearly: one shuttle launch per week would keep the Wheel at survival level; fifteen launches per week through the Wheel would keep the whole Western military, industrial and scientific space effort at survival level; twenty-five per week would sustain the planned level of growth in these space communities; five per day was the bare minimum to achieve the set objectives of Operation Bootstrap within the planned period of two months.

On the main monitor was the petulant *See here, sonny, are you trying to teach me my job or something* visage of the Flight Integration and Planning Controller at Vandenberg; as impressive a title as any time-expired buck-passer could be expected to possess, Morgan thought. He screwed himself up to an even higher level of diplomatic nicety.

'I can quite see your point. If other departments are not on schedule you've got to make the system run with what they give you. Believe me, we have that sort of problem up here too.' *The soothing lie.* 'What would help, though, would be for you to give us the most accurate possible picture of your delay problems. We can then build them into our planning, instead of having to rely on flight scheduling that isn't going to work out in practice.'

'Look, Mister Morgan – and I still have to work out what *Mister* means in the USSF – there's no way you can do my job from a distance of thirty-seven thousand kilometres. I've got a big enough problem coping with the situation down here without having to duplicate a whole lot of information up to you – information, I might add, that's by no means always possible to reduce to digital form.'

'Of course, yes, quite, I absolutely see the very good reason in that. That would indeed be making your job a great deal harder.' They had been through all this already. Morgan looked back at his other VDU. 'So the position is that we've got flight allocation of orbital transfers from 759 through to 803.'

'We've been through all this.'

'And their delay on the first Launch Requirement Authorisation is from twenty-five hours at flight 759 up to a hundred and sixty hours at flight 803.'

'That's just the Launch Requirement Authorisation. If you'd been properly briefed you'd know we never make that schedule anyway. There are built-in holds.'

'And those holds are subject to certain increases of unspecified length.'

'Sure. We've got to operate a real-time flexibility system.'

'Of course. But what I'm asking is if you can get it passed down the line that we are relying on that launch schedule. It would not only be doing us a considerable favour, but it would be making our whole operation possible, if Flight Integration could jack up those hold-times back to the original schedule.'

'You want me to put on more pressure?'

'I'd be most grateful,' said Morgan ingratiatingly.

'OK. I'll put on my first slab of pressure. Your attempt to complete shuttle turn-around at the Wheel instead of here means that the five shuttles you're holding up there are needed down here. Get those back on the next five available launch windows and I guarantee we'll be back on schedule by flight 765.'

Very smart, thought Morgan. *He's passed the buck to me.* 'With due respect, sir,' he lied, 'you know that's . . . ' But the FIPC's resentful expression had vanished from the screen. Morgan called up the servicing files on the five shuttles that were now docked with the Wheel. Then he put a call through to Joe Waldon, the Engineering officer.

'Joe.'

'Dick.'

'Hullo. Look, you know I've started doing this logistics job.' Joe nodded. 'Well, I've been running into a little difficulty with FIPC at Vandenberg. For the record I'd just like to check with you what the mission status of our docked shuttles is.'

'OK.' Waldon leaned to one side to consult another monitor. 'Right. Our three SC3s, 013 741D, 046 742D and 003 744D are on six hour stand-by for de-orbit. NASA 743D is coming up to six hour stand-by within two hours. ESA's J745 is being turned round and should come up to stand-by within twelve hours; that one's for rendezvous with the Jupiter Milk-Train, and it *has* to go on schedule. And I've got teams ready to receive six, seven and eight U whenever they get here. Any use asking when that will be?'

'They all have an eight-hour schedule hold at the moment.'

'At the moment. Fine. Why are you asking anyway?'

'Well, I want to know what's keeping one, two and four here.'

'Come on. That's your department.'

'I know. I just want to hear you say it.'

'LOX. LH$_2$.'

'Thanks. So we've got to wait for our own cryogenic fuel supplies to pass the reserve margin. And that'll happen when we get sent some. So it's definitely not us holding things up.'

'Right.'

'Then what the hell's going on down there?'

Waldon paused. 'How the hell do I know? I'm not getting any more information than you. I haven't even spoken to my wife for five weeks, except through the teletype. We're in an *Ours is just to do and die* situation up here.'

Morgan called up Wheeldata. 'I want to debrief every shuttle crew that arrives at the Wheel – face-to-face and immediately.'

'Would you rephrase face-to-face?'

'Oh Christ –'

'Syntax error.'

By the end of Morgan's shift no more shuttles had arrived, and he and the FIPC were no longer on speaking terms. He began to realise why he had been the only applicant: Fred Zeffert had done a rather smooth sales job. When he handed over the console to Dale Peterson – who was not surprised by the diplomatic state of affairs – Morgan felt unable to shrug off his day's work. That made a change from meteorology – a change, he had to admit, somewhat for the better. He was given the chance to pursue his new interest in the evening. Chuck Lang, his predecessor, was ferrying across to the ASI industrial satellite. There were two spare seats.

Nine

CHUCK LANG engaged the launch sequence. 'This is no hassle,' he drawled for Morgan's benefit. Morgan hadn't been at all nervous until he said that.

Wheeldata took over control, feeding the rotation of the Wheel into the orbital prediction program. At just the right moment the linear induction catapult silently engaged. The trans-orbital rendez-vous car surged forward. The bright guidance alignment lights of the launch tube streamed past and the little Torc dashed out into empty space. The moonflecked dark side of the Earth revolved slowly around the rolling Torc. Morgan looked back. The six-hundred metre metal disk of the Wheel hung over him, figured with lights, antennae, hatches, gantries, weapon bays and a patchwork of subtly-contrasting shades of paint and metal. Having imparted its spin to the Torc it appeared not to spin itself, but its overhanging bulk slid silently away to one side. The three passengers unsealed their helmets.

The Torc's on-board computer was presenting a dynamic display of the little vehicle's relationship to the Wheel and the target, and showed its new Earth orbit. But it was also watched by the unsleeping eyes of Wheeldata whose navigational consent was indicated reassuringly on Chuck's panel.

The Torc looked like a large bubble-car. Its instrumentation was limited to a small visual display unit and keyboard, and the controls were few. But within the limited range of the craft's fuel it had the manoeuvring and computing power to go anywhere, do anything, and get back without either marooning its passengers or burning them up in unintentional re-entry. It was a smart vehicle. It wouldn't let you take it anywhere unless it knew and approved the means by which you intended to return.

The unseen hand of the on-board computer rotated the Torc firmly. Then there was a gentle one-minute burn from the main propulsion unit. The target was not in sight, but Morgan caught the distant square gleam of one of the nearer solar power satellites. It looked like a flake of mica caught in the sun. It was ten kilometres on a side, and weighed (or would have done on Earth) an incredibly slight fifteen thousand tons. The emptiness, the self-contained pluck of the tiny Torc, and the mighty artifacts now reduced to their true perspective, exhilarated Morgan. He looked back at the Wheel. Already it looked like a button, the docked shuttles so many midges. He smiled slightly, though there was a sober calculation in his eyes. He saw at the extreme edge of his vision that Lieutenant Honeywell had half turned in her front seat next to Chuck. She had accepted his invitation to occupy the second seat – ostensibly to collect some bacterial cultures from the zero gee microbiology lab. He thought she was looking at him. He let her look for fifteen seconds, then he turned to look forward. As he did so, so did she. And she thought he hadn't noticed her silent observation.

Chuck had noticed. 'Target image,' he said clearly. The on-board computer obligingly presented an image-intensified view of the as-yet-invisible target. Chuck half turned. 'Enjoying the ride?'

'Singularly impressive,' said Morgan, hoping that this was sufficient to emphasise that he wasn't in the least degree impressed.

'Thought so. What's on your mind?'

'What do you think is our limiting resource up here?'

'That which, had we more of it, our other resources would be sufficient to increase our capability?'

'I think that's what I mean,' said Morgan, trying to work out if it was.

'Fuel. LOX. LH$_2$. Fuel storage for the same.'

'Yes. That's undeniable. But fuel storage can be made from materials we have in orbit and on the Moon.'

'No problem.'

'*No problem* is a slight exaggeration.'

'Well, it's an honest exaggeration. What I mean is that it's within our capability. It's an on-going process.'

'Oxygen we can also get from lunar resources.'

'Can we? . . . Well, I suppose we can theoretically, but no one's about to do it.'

'Why not? The gravitational gradient from the Moon to Earth-orbit is cheaper than from Earth to Earth-orbit. It's a matter of the will to do it.'

'Well, I'm sure you're right. All you've got to do is allocate the resources, do the math, change the priorities of a hundred thousand people, convince USSF Central Command, get a few Bills through Congress, pull some strings in NASA. You know, we usually leave these small things to the odd Britisher who spends a vacation on the Wheel . . .'

Morgan grinned at the back of Chuck's neck. 'And how about the liquid hydrogen?'

'There you've got me. There ain't *no* hydrogen on the Moon. It was all outgassed four billion years ago. That's got to come from Earth.'

There's always Jupiter thought Morgan.

Man, that's ridiculous, he could imagine Chuck saying. *That would cost far more than you'd ever get out of it. And every shipment would take years.*

But Morgan didn't mention the possibility. What he did say was, 'Since cryogenic fuel is our limiting resource, in my opinion and yours, I thought I'd like to see how we're using it for shuttling around between orbital facilities. And since you were using a whole Torc to yourself I thought I'd start by making you take a couple of passengers.'

'Sure. So we're using five hundred litres more fuel. You don't get anything for nothing up here. Everything's paid for with energy. Even energy's paid for with energy.'

'Except solar energy.'

'Display approach,' said Chuck. The computer drew a three-view projection of the target, and superimposed the rendezvous line of the Torc on it. The target, the American Space Industries' orbiting complex, was now clearly visible to the naked eye. With its appearance of a stack of automobile tyres, five deep now and ever growing, Asisat presented a strong contrast to the compact, unified – and more expensive – USSF Big Wheel. As the Torc made its deceleration to matching orbit Morgan could see that the tyres were not perfectly annular. Each was made up of ten straight cylinders, and each of the cylinders was joined to its neighbour by a system of airlocks.

The on-board computer ran the brief second burn that nudged the Torc toward the docking module amid the industrial modules.

'As you see this is simpler than docking with the Wheel,' explained Chuck in a guided-tour voice. 'They've got no spin.' Morgan nodded. His briefing hadn't been entirely superficial. He knew that the major manufacturing tool of Asisat was weightlessness; the others were the availability of good vacuum, abundant mass-driven lunar material and solar power on demand.

They resealed their visors for the docking. The wide doors of the main docking bay remained closed; they could engulf a whole Earth shuttle or one of the nuclear-powered Hopper ships that intercepted the LEM (lunar-ejected material) capsules in higher orbit. Yet the peripheral docking bay was large. A mobile gantry picked the weight-less astronauts from the cockpit of the Torc and transferred them to an airlock. Once through, Morgan followed the example of Chuck and Stephanie and plugged in his Portable Life-Support System for replenishment. The reception committee, a USSF officer from the on-board Movement Control team, and Fulbrook, the ASI Space Operations manager, led the way to the bar, where Morgan and Stephanie, mindful of their return to the Wheel, accepted fruit juices. Chuck Lang had a genuine Scotch whisky, brought up in some overlooked corner of a shuttle payload. ASI were less punctilious than the USSF. Morgan looked askance at the single tube of whisky; it must have cost five litres of liquid hydrogen to get it to Asisat.

Fulbrook seemed less than pleased to find himself under even closer military control. He arranged a liaison meeting with Lang, pleaded a heavy work load and left.

The Movement Control lieutenant was not primarily an expert on the logistics requirements of the Wheel, so conversation drifted to general Space Force matters. Lieutenant Honeywell left to seek out her bacteriological cultures and Morgan soon trailed after her to see what he could of Asisat in the short time available. Within half an hour they were back in the Torc, strapped in and transferring to the craft's environmental control system. Stephanie saw his careful glance as she called up the *Return to Wheel* program.

'It's OK, you know. I'm rated as highly as Lieutenant Lang to pilot one of these things.'

'I have no qualms whatsoever. I am simply wondering what we're going to discuss on the long lonely journey home.'

'Don't get any ideas.'

'I can't help what I think,' he said, counterfeiting gallantry, although truly, being alone for the first time with the lovely girl beside him – clad even as she was in the cumbersome pressure suit – was more than enough to give him ideas. 'But I was considering that whenever we get together I find myself being put on the spot in no uncertain terms. I was wondering what I ought to prepare myself for.'

'Richard, don't force me into a role I don't want,' she replied, lightly and fleetingly touching the back of his hand, a gesture which the two thick gloves didn't negate. With the Torc a hundred metres clear of Asisat, the computer rotated it and gave the long gentle shove towards home. 'But since we're to be serious, how's the new job?'

'Congenial.'

'Better than meteorology?'

'Much.' It struck him then that it was also better than espionage. He had forgotten for much of the day how devious his motives were supposed to be.

'And what have you learnt from this trip?'

'It ain't over yet . . . But nothing specific. If you like I'm trying to get a proper feel for the Wheel's links with the other space communities – political, social, economic, transportational and so on. So I've got a long way to go. I've yet to get close to a powersat, or make a docking with the Jupiter Milk-Train, or land at Copernicus Base. But

I've made some progress.'

'Nothing more specific than that?'

'I haven't on my first day come up with any gaping flaws in the USSF's organisation, if that's what you mean. But I'm interested in this self-sufficiency effort; you know about Bootstrap?'

'Are *you* supposed to?'

'Fred Zeffert told me a couple of days ago. I think until then I was the only one not to know about it.'

'Probably. There was some talk of that. Anyway, I do know about Bootstrap.'

'As Lang said, the most critical consumable is liquid hydrogen. Earth is the only practical source at the moment. It's used for propulsion: I wanted to see it being used. This trip is typical of a great deal of our LH_2 expenditure.'

'So?'

'Well, I have a feeling we should never have made it. There was no need for me to come at all. Lang could have done all his liaison with Asisant by videophone. Your bugs could have been sent in an RPS.'

'You really are getting your teeth into the job.'

'I suppose so. I have a feeling that that's what's going to be needed before very long.' She didn't reply. 'Am I right?'

'You've got some personal decisions to make before you get in that deep.'

'How do you mean?'

'Let's not get on to that.'

'OK. How's your work going?'

'Not well.'

'Ship-full of nut-cases?'

'It's not funny.'

'I don't think so either.'

'In fact it's crass. No home leave. No drafting to Earth assignments. No phone calls. No news except rumour. No amount of training can cope with that sort of pressure indefinitely.'

'It's censorship, isn't it? I mean even I can't be fooled by talk about solar storms and Operation Bootstrap for much longer. Something has got, as you say in the States, to break.'

'The trouble is, it looks like being the crew.'

Ten

IT WAS quiet in the Torc. The on-board computer was handling routine navigation and radio tasks. The Earth was still moonlit-dark, with the emerging sun lighting a rainbow on the leading limb. A thousand miles below, a shuttle emerged into sunlight on its long inert elliptical transfer up the Wheel's orbit. It appeared tiny and near. It might be a superbly crafted jewel pinned to the black velvet of a woman's dress. Morgan looked at Stephanie. The cockpit lighting showed her clear beauty, her big dark eyes alive against cream-textured flesh with the resilience of youth. Her eyes smiled at him, reflecting a soft liquid gleam from the display. This beat driving with a girl in the Alvis under the soft trees of a summer's night in England . . . , or was that just a dimming of memory? He looked with some pleasant sadness at the distant globe that seemed at the moment to be hanging above him. He thought of saying something of his thoughts to Stephanie. His lips parted to do so.

The cockpit of the Torc rang with a long scream, aching with suffering and despair. In it were words. '*No. I . . .* ' Morgan gripped Stephanie's arm.

'Are you OK?' Her teeth were bared in horror and her eyes were wide.

She nodded. Already her eyes were darting over the display. So were his when he knew that the scream was not hers. He felt her gloved hand grip his. 'The link's gone. We've lost Wheeldata.' The display was writing in red FAIL 3. WHEELDATA REFERENCE FAIL

'Display present course,' said Stephanie. The computer wrote up the position co-ordinates and course vectors. It summarised them by showing that no corrections were necessary before rendezvous.

'Display systems status.'

The screen confirmed that the internal mechanisms of the Torc were functioning normally. Morgan felt his heart-rate coming down; he could hear his pulse thudding in his helmet. 'We can make it on internal guidance?'

'Should be no problem.'

'Any idea what happened?'

'Search me.' Morgan determined to remember that invitation at a more appropriate time. 'You know as much as I do. I didn't like the sound of that . . . noise.'

'Neither did I. It sounded like trouble at the Wheel. Try to raise them by voice.'

Stephanie sent out a multi-frequency call through the computer and then Morgan repeated it with a manual waveband sweep. There was no response. Space seem to become infinitely more vast and more empty. The screen was showing an image of the distant Wheel now, but little detail was visible; the image intensifier was defeated by the narrow angle between the Sun and the Wheel. But at least the space station's silhouette looked clean and entire.

'Doesn't look like an attack,' said Morgan.

'I can't see any lights though,' replied Stephanie.

'That's not so good. I think we'd better talk to someone on the ground.' He called up a program and the computer started to repeat the Torc's call sign on the USSF's space tracking network emergency frequency. After ten seconds a face identified by the lapel badge SPACECOM 3. COL. MIKE HENDERSON appeared in the top right quadrant of the screen.

'Spacecom Vandenberg; Torc 12, what is your status?'

Stephanie nodded to Morgan who answered. 'This is Torc 12 on transfer orbit from Asisat to the Wheel. Computed rendezvous time thirty-four minutes.'

Henderson nodded. 'OK Torc 12, and your emergency?'

'Spacecom; Torc 12. We have lost all signal from the Wheel. That may mean we'll have a docking problem when we rendezvous. But more particularly we're worried about the Wheel's crew.'

'Torc 12; Vandenberg. We copy that. We share your concern, and we've got everyone working on it down here. Have you got any indications of the nature of the problem? Over.'

'Vandenberg; Torc 12. We have visual on the Wheel. Lighting conditions are poor, but we think there's no major structural failure. However, we did hear something that sounded – ' he glanced at Stephanie ' – rather like a scream.'

'We copy that, Torc 12. It was our experience too.'

'The voice sounded familiar, but I can't place it. Have you run a voicident check?'

'We have, Torc 12, but haven't come up with anything yet. There are certain amplitude-flattening effects which make that difficult. I'll keep you informed. Meanwhile, what is your consumable status?'

Morgan called up the information. 'There are two of us on board and we have remaining oxygen for twelve houre plus reserves. We also have about an hour's supply in each of our PLSS packs.'

'We copy, Torc 12. There should be no problem. We advise at this stage that you continue with the rendezvous but hold off docking unless we authorise it. USSF shuttle flight 746 will rendezvous fourteen minutes after you. As you may be without movement control please respond to its instructions on separation. They have been advised to take you on board if the problem hasn't been resolved by then. Meanwhile please keep us informed on anything you see. Vandenberg Spacecom, out.'

'Vandenberg ; Torc 12. OK and thank you. Out.'

'Well, they've got some lights going,' said Stephanie. 'At least some-one must be all right.' They were quite close to the Wheel now, and Stephanie was slowing the Torc to match orbits at a thousand metres. That was close enough for a cautious survey.

'That's something anyway,' said Morgan. Then, '*They're not lights – those are the rim thrusters*.'

'Just compensating for the elevators.' Like a pirouetting ice dancer the Wheel changed her rate of spin as the mass of her components was moved towards the centre or out towards the rim. The rim thrusters compensated to keep her always at two revolutions per minute, thus ensuring a stable one gravity at the rim.

'They must be moving some pretty heavy stuff then. That's a long burn.' He watched for a few more moments. '*That's no compensatory burn! She's spinning much too fast*! He called up Vandenberg. 'Space-com; Torc 12 here. It appears the Wheel has a spin problem. The rim thrusters are on and she's spinning like a top. Over.'

'Torc; Spacecom: are the thrusters firing in an advance or a retro-gade sense?'

'Spacecom; Torc: advance.'

'What's her spin rate?'

Morgan counted. 'About five to six per minute.'

'Hell, that means nearly three gee at the rim. Torc 12, we are not yet perfectly clear what's happening on board the Wheel. We've had no telemetry since the initial – ah – problem. But it may be necessary to act fast. She's not designed to exceed her present spin rate.'

'You mean she could fly apart?'

'Like a clay pigeon. We're going to have to gloss over the safety aspect of this a little. We would like you to approach the docking section of the Wheel *cautiously*. Anyone positioned there will be in a reasonable gravity environment. It's imperative that you set up a communications link.'

'OK. We're on our way in.'

'And I *mean* cautiously – but *very* fast.'

Stephanie piloted the Torc wide over the whirling rim of the Wheel so that its saucer surface tilted to broader perspective. The clustered ports of the central docking area were flooded by the burning radiation of the oblique sun. On the far side they passed through the shadow of the docking mast.

'Lights,' said Morgan. 'Looks like the back-up lighting system.'

'Someone must be there then.'

Morgan nodded. It wasn't so. If Wheeldata had any remaining function he would have switched on the system. But then if he was still in control there would be communication from the Wheel – even if everyone was dead. It wasn't the first time he'd considered that, although it didn't seem like a possibility: the Wheel didn't seem to be damaged; the airlocks were closed . . . .

'The manual hatch in Docking Control's open,' said Stephanie. A quick pulse on the main thruster steadied the Torc opposite the docking tunnel. 'Someone's suited up in its shadow.'

'And there are people moving in the control room. We should be able to pick up that chap on his suit radio from here.' He instructed the computer to search the suit frequencies.

'Perhaps they're preparing to evacuate.'

'I hope not.' The approaching shuttle might take thirty or forty back to Earth, but they'd have to be suited, and the shuttle would have to be unloaded first.

A familiar drawl came from the radio. ' . . . Wheel. Torc 12; Wheel. Come in please. Over.' It was Zeffert.

'Wheel; Torc 12. Lieutenant Honeywell here. Richard Morgan's with me. What's happening? Over.'

'Wheeldata's out. God knows why. We've lost all systems. No communication. No control. We're out of contact with decks beyond sixteen. Elevators are out and the gee's too much for us to climb further out.'

'Can we help in any way?'

'I believe you can. The spin thrusters are malfunctioning *on*. We have no control access to them. If they stay on a lot of people are going to die of heart failure on the outer decks. Ultimately the Wheel comes apart. We need a team to rendezvous with one of the airlocks on the rim deck and reverse the spin thrusters manually.'

'Why haven't they done it already?' asked Morgan.

'Not many there on this shift. We assume they were sleeping and got pinned down by the gee before they knew what was happening. They've got no instrumentation to help them.'

'We'd better get going. None of us are going to get any lighter.'

'Right. But pick up your team here first. I've got two guys who fought their way through from Construction. Hawkins and Sarin. They know what they're doing . . . . I think.'

Two suited figures emerged from the hatch and jetted across towards the Torc. Whilst Morgan and Stephanie sealed their suits and prepared to take them on board Zeffert detailed the plan with them. The Torc had sixty seconds' power left at full thrust. There was no possibility of making a powered rendezvous with the Wheel's rim. Stephanie would have to aim the Torc for a rim hatch, drop Hawkins, Sarin and Morgan, and then deflect her course away from collision. If she over-used her fuel the incoming shuttle would overshoot to bring her back.

Morgan grinned as Sarin and Hawkins pitched into the Torc's cockpit amidst a tangle of ropes and grappling gear. 'Glad to see you two. I hope you don't know anything about this . . .?'

'Honest guv,' said Hawkins, 'not us.' He looked at his c-unit. 'There's no way we can compute for this, but if we rendezvous in two minutes the rim velocity should be sixty-two point one metres per second.' He addressed Stephanie. 'If you would doppler-laser that as a check you can take it in automatically after she's locked on. After that you'll have to take it out manually and use what you've got left to get back to rendezvous with the docking bay. OK?'

Stephanie nodded. Using full thrust she had taken the Torc out about three hundred metres. Now she was juggling the craft's attitude to lock the doppler-laser tracking system on the tricky oblique metal of the rim. She engaged the Primary Guidance System. The main engine throttle lever moved of its own volition and the spinning edge of the Wheel began to draw nearer.

Hawkins handed Morgan a karabiner and a looped rope end. Morgan made the rope fast to his suit harness. The canopy was wide open to the stars. Stephanie was poised over the keyboard, ready to abort the Primary Guidance System. The three men struggled with equipment. They had twenty-two seconds, indicated. Morgan gave brief commands which his men accepted soundlessly. The ponderously turning edge of the Wheel loomed. The three men worked frenetically amid drifting coils of rope, checking attachments, communications, thruster and synchronisation. Morgan was watching the rim. Dark windows flashed by, and, spaced out evenly, the domed disks of rim airlock hatches.

'That one!' he said. 'Quadrant C.' He saw the red ellipse of the laser track across the sharp shadow behind the dome.

'Three, two, one. GO!' Sarin and Morgan separated cleanly together. Hawkins was a split second late. The ropes sprang taut and he jerked up after them. The reaction sent the three men rolling around one another in their weightless course. The ordered plan for reaching the hatch was forgotten. Morgan saw the blue flare of the Torc's thruster reflected in the black bubble of an observation dome on one of the inner decks. The airlock was opposite him, arcing nearer with the spin of the Wheel. It was two metres away and its approach slowed. He stroked the throttle disk on his chest-mounted controller, orienting his body with the attitude stick. He leapt forward too fast and his helmet rang with the impact. His problems multiplied. Involuntarily – and futilely – he held his breath lest his helmet had been broached. He saw the last rung of the hatch ladder slip past his fingers as the rotation of the Wheel slid him outwards across the smooth cold metal skin. His right hand moved down to fire his thruster. He didn't feel the undignified impact of Sarin's boot in his backside, but it gave him sufficient acceleration. His left hand grasped the steel bar.

Instantly he was not in free fall in his own eccentric Earth orbit. Instead he was a mass on the rim of a spinning disk, and the weight on his fingers was three times what it would have been had he hung from a bar on Earth. Not only that, but in a second he would feel the full triple weight of Sarin, then Hawkings, through the rope that was clamped to his harness. He was no superman. He would be plucked from the Wheel instantly. As it was his bruised fingers were sliding, straightening. His right hand whipped down, came up with a karabiner, and he slammed its spring gate over the ladder rung. His leaden arms fell to his sides as he hung out from the Wheel. He felt the twang of tension as his suit harness took up the extra strain of Sarin and Hawkins. His helmet didn't permit him to look 'down', but he knew they were strung out on a line into empty space – as though he were supporting them under an infinitely high overhang. He was glad he couldn't look down.

'Bill, Dave, I'm on the first rung. We've all got to get to the second before we can operate the airlock.'

'How far?'

'Twenty centimetres.' It might as well have been a hundred metres. He raised both hands to the bar. That in itself was an effort. All his strength could do no more than torture the muscles in his shoulders. He didn't waste any more energy.

'I can't pull up. At this gee we haven't got much working time left. I want you to try to take the load off me by using your manoeuvring thrusters at full power.'

'That won't take off the full three gees,' said Sarin.

'Right. But it's all we've got. Keep your heads down to avoid one another's efflux. I'll be using mine, too. Ready to fire?'

'Ready.'

'OK.'

'*Fire!*'

Morgan wheeled his throttle disk past the catching point and hauled down on the ladder bar with both hands. He pulled up a loop of his belay and clipped it to the second rung. Then he let himself collapse for ten seconds. 'I'm going to try to winch you in. You'll have to fire all the way.' He couldn't say more. Even the weight of his jaw was more than the straining muscles would take. He let it hang stupidly. He wasted a precious minute fumbling the taut rope around the pulleys of his hand winch. '*Go!*'

Five minutes later he blacked out. He came round helmetless with green corridor carpet pressing bruisingly against his cheek. Lower down his heart was hammering against his ribs and against the floor. Without moving he orientated himself, and looked down the corridor. The task ahead sickened him: to reduce the spin of the Wheel they would have to reverse three of its spin thrusters. That meant covering a kilometre around the periphery of the Wheel in three full gees – which would slowly and steadily increase. It took all his strength, and that of Sarin and Hawkings, to lift him to his feet.

'We'll all go to the nearest one. Then one goes back to quadrant B and two on to D.'

'OK.' They started the painful journey to the C quadrant thruster control hatch. It was twenty metres. They passed two inert forms. One, a woman, had made it to the hatch. It was open, and she had fallen there, perhaps unsure of what to do. They left her: she could not be sheltered from her own weight.

Morgan clung to the edge of the hatch, trying to take the unremitting strain from his quivering legs. The contents of the small hatch were simple: the cryogenic fuel lines entered at the left and angled back through the outer skin; the fibre-optic data bus from Wheeldata passed through the centre of the thruster pentad's dedicated microprocessor control box. A bundle of wires from the box also passed out through the hull, with a power cable that came in from the left; beside the control box was a touch panel giving manual override control of nozzle selection and thrust level. Now it showed a green arrow labelled ADVANCE 50. The green arrow seemed to be getting bigger and brighter.

Eleven

MORGAN DIDN'T feel himself hit the floor, but he surmised that he must have done when his consciousness began to open cautiously to a wash of sound. Waiting patiently for the blackness to clear, knowing that it was pointless to try to rush it, he tried to work out what was happening. As he remembered the corridor and thruster controls his eyes opened to dim lighting. He tried to roll over on to an arm, grimly prepared for the struggle to stand. Then he felt the soft resilience of cushions under him and the encumbrance of sheets. And he certainly wasn't being held down by three gees. Such reawakenings were not new to him; he guessed that he was under the tender discipline of doctors, and he was quite prepared to let it go at that. He didn't feel in the brisk-jog-before-breakfast sort of mood. All the same . . . He rolled over and levered himself up on one elbow.

'They said you were due to come round about now.' Morgan

grinned through unashamed tears of shock. Bill Sarin bounced energetically to a crouch beside his bed.

'Lie down, that man!' snapped another passing figure – Lieutenant Commander Bardelli, striding purposefully across the room with a trolley-load of medical equipment in tow. Morgan lay flat to a safe count of five until the head of the Wheel's medical team was safely occupied with more deserving patients, and then came swiftly up on one elbow again. He surveyed his surroundings: he was in the rim mess, on one of fifty-odd pallets contrived from the room's furniture cushions. Some of the patients were moving and chatting: some lay still. With a glow of relief he noticed Bardelli talking to Stephanie, and nodding in his direction. She turned round. Morgan sank a little lower as a concession to the commander and waved discreetly to the lieutenant. She gave a slight smile and returned sternly to her task.

'Bit of all right, that,' murmured Bill.

'Yes,' said Morgan absently. Then, self-consciously, 'Bill, old mate, the well-bred English gentleman does not refer to an attractive young lady as *a bit of all right*.'

'That lets you and me out then, Dick.'

'If you insist. Look, what's the matter with you anyway? Last time we did this you at least gave me a cigarette.'

'Oh yes. Sorry, I . . . ' Sarin was patting the many pockets of his overall. Then he clicked his fingers. 'Almost had me going there.'

Morgan laughed, then he sobered. 'How's Dave?'

'OK. Same as you. He'll be sedated for another hour.'

Morgan glanced around the room. 'Well, I can see you got the job done OK. Tell me about it.'

'Nothing to it really. The thruster controls were a piece of cake. Easier than disarming a Russki laser trip barrier. We did C, left you sleeping peacefully – lazy bugger – and I went with Dave to B. I left him there and carried on to A.'

'You can't tell me it was a piece of cake walking half a kilometre in three gee.'

'Three and a half by that time. I was a bit shagged, I must admit. Dave flaked out after he'd done his bit, but he didn't lose consciousness – not until they sedated him that is.'

'What are the casualties?'

'No one seems to know. Wheeldata's still out, so they're all flapping about like wet hens. Two dead from heart attacks. Some bad heart cases. Some broken bones. Most are OK. This isn't exactly a pensioners' coach outing.'

'No, they're a good lot.'

'You can say that again. We could do with some of them on our team.'

'Speaking of the team, you'd better get going. Someone will begin to wonder why we've got so much to talk about.'

Bill glanced round the room and looked back. 'No. We can do no wrong. We've just conducted ourselves beyond the call of duty. We're chatting over our heroic deed.'

'Well, let's make the best of it then. The mission. Tell me, Bill, what's your feeling about it so far?'

'Rubbish!' Morgan looked at him sternly. 'Sorry, sir. I meant to say that I don't think it's going well. For one thing we've got no clear objective. Not like a quick dash over the border, grab a missile warhead, and out again. We don't really know what we're looking for, and we're among our friends. It's not really an SOT job. I reckon that GCHQ can do a hell of a sight better job than us with Elint and cryptanalysis.'

'Half the staff there are American anyway.'

'Some of them. But they have pretty restricted access.'

'OK Bill, but why not take the broader view?'

'What broader view?'

'We're here. It was a big achievement getting a special ops. team on board the Wheel. We're a hell of an investment. So we do what we've always done.'

'What's that? I've never really noticed.'

'Use our initiative. We keep going on the prime mission, but like you I consider that we're not really well equipped for it. In fact, I think it was really a pretext to get us here.' He let that sink in. 'Consider what's going on. There's some sort of serious flap about the climate. There's Operation Bootstrap – which they admit is an attempt to make the Wheel self sufficient. There's complete censorship of news from Earth; it's been going on for too long to dress up as a communications problem. There's a serious cock-up on the American Flight Integration and Planning front.'

'And what's all that supposed to add up to?'

'It's no use trying to be too specific at this stage: we might guess wrong. But there's obviously a serious problem brewing up. Either military or climatic or both. And the American response to it involves the panic upgrading of their space capability.'

'And where do we come into it?'

'We are into it. We're here. Besides that, any American problem that is either climatic or military or both is a European problem of the same sort.'

'So what do we do?'

'To some extent we're doing it: making ourselves indispensable; getting in on the act. We did well today. We'll keep the team ready, and perhaps we'll do well again.'

'So, Dave and I lurk in the wings waiting to pounce?'

'Partly. But you are also our only means of getting reliable information through from Earth via the construction teams. I want you to expand that.' He paused. 'I do have something more difficult for you, though.'

'That's more like it.'

'I've been taking their Bootstrap exercise seriously because I suspect that it may be more than an exercise. It's struck me that it has a particularly weak link.'

'Which is?'

'Liquid hydrogen. Without it all space activity is paralysed. Whether they're using nuclear-powered rockets like the lunar ferries or Hopper ships, chemical propulsion for Earth shuttles or Earth orbital transfers, or solar power in the Jupiter Milk-run, they all need hydrogen propellant: lots of it. And Earth is the only substantial source of hydrogen among the inner planets.'

'There's loads of water on Mars locked up in ice.'

'Most of it's mixed up with rock. And we've got no plant there for mining it, splitting it, tanking it, transporting it.'

'The Russians have.'

'Only for the consumption of their Mars base. And they're not likely to give it away.'

'I have a feeling that you're going to start talking about Jupiter.'

'I am. It was Fred Zeffert who made me think of it. On Callisto ESA and NASA are chucking away a thousand tons of hydrogen every day. I've been looking into it. They're only interested in the deuterium component for Longbow. Their own consumption of hydrogen is comparatively trivial.'

'There's still no way of getting it here. It takes years.'

'But there is! The Jupiter Milk-run comes back almost empty.'

'Would it be worth the energy cost?'

'Yes, if the hydrogen's free. I haven't done any detailed analysis. I don't think anyone has. But by rule-of-thumb it should be possible to supply many times the requirement here and on the Moon without increasing the number of Milk-run freighters. They already burn LH_2 as though the Universe were made of it: which of course it is, but not around here.'

'And is there any chance that the Longbow team would agree?'

'I think so, if there's a crisis coming on Earth. At this end of the Milk-run the Wheel is Longbow's lifeline. Where would they be if the Wheel didn't stage ESA's shuttles up to the freighters?'

'Out of action.'

'Dead.'

'But this is a big thing. Have we got the pull to swing it?'

'No. But practical considerations might force it. We've got to make sure that they're ready. Or rather Eurodefence High Command, with the help of C, will. I'll handle that part. What you and Dave can do in the meantime is make contact with ESA Longbow Project Team through outgoing shuttles. Particularly Max Schmidt: he's a receptive intellect, and he's well placed to act. Get a report together detailing the logistics and the political constraints, with a feasability study recommendation. We should be able to get ESA to turn that into a directive. I'll give you any figures you can't get. What do you think?'

'I feel better now that we've got something to do.'

'Even if it's not blowing up bridges?'

'Yes. It would be a bit chancy blowing things up out here.'

'Right. Now I've got to get on to Zeffert and try to make myself even more indispensable.' He tapped out Zeffert's name on his c-unit. NOT RECEIVING said the screen. 'I'm going to miss Wheeldata.' He made arrangements to contact Sarin or Hawkins for a progress meeting the next day, and checked a scheme for more direct communications within the team. Sarin left to see if Hawkins was conscious yet. Morgan waited until he considered himself to be unobserved, and stood up carefully. He felt fit: not only fit but hungry. He slipped his feet into his lightweight inner boots and padded towards the corridor. He was within three metres of the door when he heard a rapid footfall behind him. He carried on as though unconcerned until a hand gripped his arm. It was Stephanie.

'You shouldn't be up yet!'

'Oh, hullo. I feel fine.'

'Maybe, but you haven't been told you can get up.'

'I'm sorry, Lieutenant, I didn't mean to be insubordinate. Only it seems that there's a hell of a lot to do, and other people are doing my job while I'm only really malingering.'

'I meant to come to see you.'

'I was hoping you would.'

'But Bill Sarin was with you. It looked as though you were having a hero's get-together, so I stayed out of the way. You seem to have struck up quite a friendship. What were you talking about all that time?'

'There were some tasteful comments on the aesthetic appeal of the medical staff – not including Doc. Bardelli of course – and the rest of it was mutual congratulation.'

'I meant to say that we all thought you three did a wonderful job – only we've all been so busy that no one has had a chance to say so yet. Especially as all three of you are only visitors on board and it wasn't really your problem.'

'Not at all. We were just as much threatened by the problem as anyone else. Besides, it was a pleasure. We were showing our appreciation of your hospitality.'

'I just want you to know that it's what I'd have expected from you. It helps to confirm my analysis that you're not really a typical meteorologist.'

'That's good to know.' Morgan smiled a little bashfully. 'Don't you think you ought to go and embarrass some of your other patients now? I've got to try to find Commander Zeffert.' She was standing very close, looking up at him. She touched his shoulder briefly and was gone.

Finding Zeffert wasn't easy. All communications and movement on the Wheel were paralysed without Wheeldata. Suit radios wouldn't penetrate the many-levelled structure of the space station. Morgan finally traced him through an improvised tangle of field-telephone lines to Command A on the fourth floor out from the hub.

'Glad to hear you're with us again, Dick,' said Zeffert, sounding remarkably cheerful under the circumstances. 'However I don't advise a return to your normal duties at the present.'

'Why's that, sir?' asked Morgan discontentedly.

'Because you haven't got the communications capability to do it from where you are, and the elevators are out, which means that to get to Command A you'd have to climb twenty-nine storeys by ladders and hatches. It's been taking our fittest men forty-five minutes to lay telephone lines through that lot, and in your condition . . . .'

Morgan made a few sharp remarks about his condition. Half an hour later and slightly breathless he skimmed to a halt in front of the Command desk. The fractional gravity here was delicious.

'Glad you could make it after all. That was a pretty impressive performance of yours out there. Remind me to say all the right things some time.'

'Remind me to be suitably modest.'

'Peterson's handling Logistics at the moment, but he's been on for twelve hours now, which is normally more than we allow, so I'd be glad if you'd take over from him.'

Morgan looked around the operations room. All the monitors were dark. The room was like a nineteenth-century office. Men were running in and out of the door with sheaves of paper. Each of the section teams was processing the incoming paper and piling it on the section commanders' In trays. (There was an evocative old term pressed rapidly back into use.) The commanders were penning their orders on the sheets and piling them on their Out trays. Up until now Morgan had seen only half a dozen sheets of paper on the Wheel. Men were hurrying with the handed-down sheets out of the door, or queueing with them for access to one of the five field telephones which were all that advanced technology could provide.

Zeffert nodded. 'Yeah, if we're attacked now we could be seriously embarrassed. Our big problem is paper shortage. It's a good thing we don't use it in our toilets or a lot of people would soon be in some trouble. OK, so you want to know what's going on. Wheeldata's right out, so the elevators are out and all communications are out. We've got USSF 746 and 747 matching our orbit, they they'll have to stay there for a while yet. They're equipped for an independent stay-time of fifteen days so we forget about them. We have a down-link through one of our docked shuttles, but we want to conserve his on-board power, and as the reactor's down we can't feed him any power from here. So we can talk to the outside when we need to, but we're trying not to have to. For the time being they're not sending up any more flights. We've got five dead and seventeen with fractures, although ten of those are back on duty. There are a dozen heart cases, and most of them will probably have to be sent home eventually.'

'And the star patient – Wheeldata?'

'Exposure of some of his light-sensitive memory modules.'

'Is that data or programming?'

'You can't make that distinction with Wheeldata. A bit of both, I suppose you could say.'

'Can it be read back in?'

'Well, Bud Saunders is working on it, and he says he thinks so. You see the particular bit of the matrix that's involved is holographic, which means that all the data is stored in all the modules. Loss of modules means that we've still got all the data but in a degraded form.'

'Then why did Wheeldata pack up operations?'

'Shock – to use a human analogy. When the malfunction occurred there was a cascade of spurious data right through the system. Wheeldata powered down autonomously, and Bud can't bring him up again until he's confident about all the memory contents.'

'You said *malfunction*. I take it the modules were exposed to green light. Any idea how?'

'It's hard to say.'

'I suppose I'm really asking you if someone did it on purpose.'

'Are you seriously suggesting the idea that USSF personnel on this space station deliberately sabotaged the computer?'

'It was just a thought. I mean stranger things have been known. It's a logical option, unless there's a more likely explanation.' Morgan waited nervously for Zeffert's response.

'Yes. It was undoubtedly intentional damage.'

'Why?'

'Couldn't have been done by accident.'

'I mean why should anyone want to do it?'

'The world's full of all sorts of freaks.'

'I'm really referring to the morale of the crew: brawls, the suicide of a man because he was happily married, now sabotage. What next?'

'It's like being on a ship that's been at sea for a long time. An increasing number of the crew are long overdue for shore leave. No one's been allowed down for five weeks now. Also there's the problem of getting no news from Earth.'

'The solar storm?'

'The solar storm – and so forth.'

It's the 'and so forth' that's bothering me, thought Morgan.

'We haven't seen so much of the captain lately. I suppose he's got a lot on his plate.'

'You could say that. You see, Operation Bootstrap isn't directly his baby: it's mine. Captain Rathbone has other concerns of equal priority. He's in the crow's nest now if you want to see him.'

Morgan shook his head. 'I'm surprised there are other matters with priority equal to Bootstrap.'

'Mister Morgan, you're really taking advantage of your position here,' Zeffert said with good-natured complicity. 'If you were a fully paid-up member of the United States Space Force, you wouldn't be getting away with this.'

'If I were USSF I'd probably know the answers.'

'Boy, you're really going to get me into trouble one day. Why do you push so hard?'

'Because I know less than other people doing my job. And I care about the job. It really does matter to me what goes on out here in space. I'm concerned about the Wheel and the job it's got to do.' And although what he said was couched as a lie, it came across with more conviction than he had expected.

'You showed that today. You wielded that impromptu excursion team of yours like a bunch of veteran astronauts. Now why don't you find out what Dale Peterson's doing before he collapses on us.'

Twelve

FOR TWO days the crews of USSF 746 and 747 slept and ate and played poker with cards that had to be slipped under elastic bands round the table in their lower deck modules. And they looked at the Wheel in its ponderous whirl around the Earth, seemingly lifeless but for the dim lights behind some of its ports and the occasional moving figures that obscured them. It was like a derelict, manned by ghosts. Periodically the shuttle crews sent back answers to Vandenberg's monotonous but insistent questions, and couched them monotonously in return, for it seemed the best way to do it.

'_. . . as of this time we are not in direct communicational mode with USSF SCC 101 but visual indications signify that the . . . er . . . spacecraft status of SCC 101 is . . . er . . . nominal in its present on-board computer abort mode situation and we are standing by for_ *communication on band C for any further communication as of this time . . . '*

The assembly of this somnolent code was a matter of unremitting, though entirely tacit, competition between USSF Spacecom and the shuttle crews.

At the end of two days the Wheel's lights sprang to life, its spin thrusters blipped briefly, its antennae resumed their interrupted search of the heavens, the shuttles' Acquisition and Docking Command programs came up on the flight deck monitors, and on Earth and in space around the Earth and on the Moon a hundred thousand men and women knew that the Western military and civil space programmes now rested on mental shoulders far broader than those of any man or committee. Wheeldata was back in business.

Several hours earlier, Morgan, who at the moment could do no wrong, had been allowed to join the team which was monitoring the reactivation of the Wheel's on-board computer. Rathbone was there, and Zeffert, and six of the section commanders. Bud Saunders, who looked as though he hadn't slept for three days, sat in front of the Prime Monitor in Command A. The others stood, holding on to guide rails because of the low gee on this deck, and watched intently.

'May I proceed, sir?' asked Saunders.

'You have control,' said Rathbone evenly, as though talking to a trainee pilot from the rear seat of an F 21.

'Switching to communication only . . . switching on fuel cells A, B, C . . . ' Zeffert's eyes followed Saunders' fingers on the keyboard, ready to arrest any fatigue-induced error. 'Allocating voice, and monitor at Prime peripheral location. All other peripherals barred. . . . Ready to power up.' Saunders sat back from the keyboard and looked around the faces that were watching him. Their tension showed. A malfunction-induced reflex might not affect just the peripheral thrusters this time. There were the power reactors, the airlocks, the weaponry. But all the precautions had been check-listed tediously over and over again.

'We've no choice but to power up,' said Rathbone. It didn't inspire Morgan with confidence.

'Powering up,' said Saunders. He opened a red guard cover, paused deliberately, and pushed forward the switch. An asterisk appeared in the top left-hand corner of the screeen.

'Wheeldata?'

Morgan had never known the room to be silent before.

'Wheeldata, this is Bud Saunders.'

'Commander Saunders this is . . . This is Wheeldata.'

'Wheeldata, check your status for parity.'

'This is . . . Wheeldata. I have no access to systems control. I have communications access through Prime peripheral location. The Wheel's systems are not under my control and some are outside nominal control parameters. I am listing them on the Prime Monitor in order of projected threat . . . ' Saunders turned round smiling, circling his thumb and forefinger in a sign of satisfaction ' . . . I have a data-base problem.' Saunders whipped round.

'What is your data-base problem, Wheeldata?'

'I have a data impairment . . . . It is now cleared by comparator processing. There is a memory of memory contradiction . . . . It is a time inconsistency. . . . There is a blank period . . . ' For the second time in his dealings with Wheeldata, Morgan felt the hair on the back of his head stir. And he felt pity – more than he would for a human being. ' . . . confirm I am Wheeldata . . . ?' Morgan could easily have wept. Either this was a non-biological emotion, amplified a billionfold by the power – and the perfect innocence – of the machine, or it was the output from logical trains in an intricate but lifeless mechanism. One must accept that it was the last.

'I do confirm that you are Wheeldata, and that your output is correct. You have suffered a malfunction – which was not triggered in you but was caused by . . . externally. You have suffered minor data degradation which I confirm you have remedied. I have brought forward your temporal reference to compensate for your down-time. Does that remove the contradiction?'

'Yes Commander Saunders.' There was a long pause. 'Will it happen again?'

Saunders looked stupidly at the monitor. Then he said emphatically, 'No. Of course not. We all worked very hard to remedy your malfunction. Your functioning is very important to us. We will make sure that never happens again. . . . OK, Wheeldata?'

'I am all right now Commander Saunders.' Saunders' shoulders slumped in relief.

'OK, Wheeldata. What I would like now is for you to give me a read-out on the monitor of your input from your peripheral processors, in their numerical order. . . .'

Two hours later, when Wheeldata had been thoroughly checked out and had resumed full control of the Wheel's communications and systems, Saunders had staggered from the console and accepted a coffee from Rathbone.

'I know what it must have seemed like to you,' he said in reply to the congratulations of his colleagues. 'It's the language that does it. If a machine outputs human language to us, people erroneously credit it with human emotions. It's just that we've fed it with an emotion-laden code. You see?'

When Bud Saunders had accepted his due praise (*The best de-bugger in the house*, Zeffert called him) and had gone to bed with a sedative, Morgan was given his chance to interview a shuttle crew: the captain, first officer and mission specialist of USSF 746. The USSF's shuttle flight crews, particularly the pilots, regarded themselves as something of an élite, and Morgan was prepared for them to resent his interference after their long and boring vigil – especially as he wasn't their ranking officer. But they accepted him without reservation as a part of the system. Morgan picked them up from Medical and took them straight out to the rim bar. That also helped.

The shuttle crew wanted – and got – a first-hand account of what had been happening on the Wheel, so Morgan was able quite naturally to introduce the reciprocal question: what had been upsetting the Flight Integration and Planning system at Vandenberg and Kennedy?'

'You name it.' said the captain. 'Lack of communcation with parts suppliers, reduced funding, increase in equipment failure, more holds for the weather, strikes. Generally low morale. It gets on your nerves pretty quickly, not being allowed off the base.'

'Is that usual?'

'It is now.'

'It's because of the pickets,' added the mission specialist, a rather stern-looking woman of twenty-five.

'Pickets?'

'And the general air of resentment against the space community.'

'Why resentment?'

'They see us as a technical élite. Our privileges are still increasing, but all around us people are becoming less secure, more afraid: you know, crime, economic depression, the threat of war, drought. The weather isn't reassuring anyone.'

'How's that?'

'You don't expect it to be in the forties like this.' The three crew members were deeply tanned. It was October.

'What do you think of the weather situation?' asked Morgan off-handedly.

'Best summer in recorded history,' said the captain. 'I'm not about to complain. Me and my family get out there on my yacht, and those cares just sail away.'

Morgan knew that it was futile to proceed. Earth might be boiling with rumour and anxiety, but the people who knew what was going on were keeping it to themselves. Most of them were probably on the Wheel anyway.

Wheeldata was quickly on top of his job again, and he made no more allusions to his traumatic coma; but he did make certain recommendations about the security of his zero gee central processing unit and these were conscientiously heeded. McMurdo's security team went through the motions of sifting likely culprits, and many were marched ceremoniously to the Security Section for interviewing. The attack on Wheeldata had been quite an extensive conspiracy, for neutralising the computer's personnel monitoring systems had required the co-operation of many. The matter was never thoroughly fathomed, and eventually investigations were suspended. For McMurdo knew the reasons for the sabotage; to document them would be futile.

Manned vehicles visiting the Wheel, and Soviet satellites which watched it ceaselessly, saw an increasing scale of activity in its vicinity. Shuttles came and went, but the number to be seen undergoing servicing at any time rose until a dozen could be seen docked with the Wheel's gantry, or with the independent docking raft which was being built and extended in close matching orbit. On the other face of the Wheel the second disk was advancing rapidly, and most of its cladding was now complete. Beyond this, and connected to the Wheel's de-spun central disk only by snaking umbilicals, was the growing clutch of hydrogen storage tanks that Wheeldata meticulously fixed in its own matching orbit.

With all this activity, fatigue was a problem. It might have been expected that morale would be high, for the degree of visible enterprise was impressive. Morgan, though, was not surprised to find that the spirits of the Wheel's crew continued to decline. That effect varied widely between individuals. Zeffert was unceasingly energetic in his deceptively casual way, and the team that he was drawing to him was a tight one. He found a willing response in Morgan, and came to rely on him in tasks of imperceptibly increasing responsibility. Correspondingly Morgan was given the latitude to gather the ends of his own chain of command, and, as he had hoped, Sarin and Hawkins found themselves working more with him than with the contracted agencies on the second disk. The European Space Agency didn't complain: Eurodefence saw to that, and beyond Eurodefence, Division Six. The hand of the Director of American Intelligence was apparent in the USSF's increasing acceptance of Morgan's role. but what he intended Morgan couldn't guess. He waited patiently. He and his team strove to keep up their stream of intelligence to Division Six, though the data itself began to make the job look futile: Moscow had only a light flurry of snow that winter, and everyone on the ground must have known it. You didn't need the most sophisticated computer in the world to account it strange. For the purposes of detailed information, access to the Meteorological Section became more restricted. After the attack on Wheeldata, the section was officially classified as a secure area. That in itself did little to comfort anyone. But by now no one who knew anything about the weather needed the sophisticated eyes of the weather satellites if they had eyes of their own. Morgan could see on his frequent EVA tours of inspection, and even through the eyes of remote TV monitors and external servicing robots, that the cloud patterns of the old familiar planet were changing. The easterly spiral of cloud in the higher latitudes was becoming tighter and more striated: it was being combed out tight by the action of the high altitude jetstreams which drive the world's weather. The jetstreams were becoming faster. Winds on the surface were stronger. Correspondingly the reliable fleece of clouds around the Tropics was dispersing. There was a clear band round the world between the latitudes of twenty-five degrees north and south. The climatic zones of the Earth were being pushed aside from the equator toward the poles. Morgan's infamous forecasting experiment seemed conservative, if anything.

He dutifully beamed his reports across to Internet 3, though, God knows, they could hardly be needed now. He made bold predictions from his small store of meteorological knowledge of the economic effects of climatic change over the coming years – of the strategic significance, for instance, of the United States becoming an arid and bare land, and the Soviet Union perhaps becoming more fertile. But he still couldn't say what was the significance of Pluto. Nor could he see how the economically crippling effort of Operation Bootstrap might mitigate the effect of a slow reshuffling of the Earth's climate: there was no conceivable means by which the whole population of the United States could be lifted into Earth orbit – nor could there be any point in doing so. Neither was there any way of adjusting the climate by amassing resources in space – nor could it be done from the ground for that matter. But Zeffert was backing Bootstrap with everything he had, and Zeffert wasn't a man to waste effort just because he'd been told to.

On 1 April, six months after the attack on Wheeldata, Morgan made his first significant progress in understanding the relationship between the climate, Pluto and Bootstrap. He began his break-through by going to bed after a hard day's EVA inspection of work on the docking raft, and falling asleep. Instantly, it seemed, he was woken by muffled sounds of shouting and running feet from the corridor outside his door. But his c-unit told him it was 0300 hrs. He had been asleep for four hours. He slipped from his bunk and walked unsteadily to his console. Wheeldata would be able to tell him what was afoot. But the console was dead. This brought him fully awake. Unwilling to face trouble naked he started to zip himself into his overall. He had just completed this when the door of his cabin hummed open and Captain Rathbone fell backwards into the room. A space-suited figure in the doorway gestured Morgan back with an M 45. The man's visor was polarised, so nothing could be seen of his face. There was a piece of surgical tape over his name tab. But his shoulder flash and arm band told that he was an engineer in the green team. Then the door thumped closed and Rathbone picked himself up from the carpet.

I knew I should have come armed. The side of Rathbone's face was smeared with blood from a cut over his eye. He ignored Morgan and lurched towards the door.

'Don't, sir.' He had no wish to see Rathbone dismantled by the M 45. Rathbone reached his hand out towards the door button. Morgan took him roughly by the shoulder and threw him back. Simultaneously the door button changed from green to red. Rathbone, who hadn't noticed it, came forward again, his single intent undiminished. There was a whisper in the corridor which became a howl and then a roar like a ramjet engine. It froze Rathbone where he stood. In ten seconds the roar had subsided back to a whisper and had gone.

'So they did it,' said Rathbone. Morgan nodded, Some, at least, of the night's events could be read from the short sequence that he had seen.

'What do they want?'

'They want home – some of them anyway. And some want special protection for their families – such as bringing them back here.'

'How many?'

'Thirty, forty, fifty. They broke into the weapons store, took hostages and bundled the rest into cabins.'

Morgan was afraid. 'Who did they take?'

'Commander Peterson. Lieutenant-Commander Grey. The 1286 shuttle crew. I think they intend to take 1286, which has the highest ready status, back to Kennedy.'

'They'll never make it.'

'Possibly.'

'The valve system on the water evaporation thermal control network is under maintenance.'

'So we might never use that shuttle again, but it should be good for one landing with the thermal control system inoperative.'

'We can only wait and see.'

'We've got to do better than that. We've got to warn Kennedy. I want those hostages saved.' He tried Morgan's console, flipping the *on* switch several times impatiently. Then for the first time he looked around the room and started to survey the problem coolly.

Morgan nodded. 'Quite. We've got a vacuum outside the door and no suits on the inside. We've no contact with Wheeldata, so we can't use him to change any of that. Also, I don't know if you've noticed, but the environmental control system isn't working.' He paused to check: but for the breathing of the two men the Wheel was absolutely quiet. 'I think we can assume that everyone else is in the same state – otherwise we'd be getting the terminal back by now at least.'

'The air problem puts an outer limit on our available time.'

'An hour or so, I suppose.'

'Any suggestions?'

'Yes.'

Rathbone looked up. 'Go ahead, Mister Morgan.'

'We can get a message out.'

'How?'

'You can safely leave that to me. But before I do it I need some help.'

'Fine. How can I help?

'Information.' Rathbone didn't answer. 'On Pluto. On Bootstrap. On Earth's climatological crisis.'

'These are highly sensitive areas, Mister Morgan. You are technically in breach of your orders by probing into them.'

'Times have changed, Commander Rathbone. Your programmes are under threat. They're going to need inspired leadership and incorruptible loyalty. Now you're going to have to trust me: I've already gone beyond my contract with you, so I think you might consider it. I need to have enough information so that I can make professional decisions here without making mistakes. And I'll get communications for you.'

'I don't have to agree with that. I can sit tight until the next shuttle docks.'

'It won't dock without Wheeldata's co-operation.'

'It could rendezvous and EVA transfer.'

'We'll be dead by then. Flight Integration can't launch anything inside ten hours at the moment. It's my job to know about that.'

'Then we've got to do more than make contact.'

'Yes. We've got to get to some suits.'

'I won't hold you to that, Morgan.' Rathbone rubbed his tired face, coming to a decision. He hardly glanced at Morgan. He had no qualms about the man. His doubts were procedural. 'Don't expect it in full technicolour then. This is what's happening.' Morgan sighed. This had taken a long time. 'Remember that computer run of yours?'

There had been so many, but Morgan was in no doubt about which one Rathbone was referring to. 'Yes.'

'It wasn't a bad effort. A very advanced piece of work. But it had an important input missing that you and your colleagues couldn't possibly have known about: *neutrinos*.' Morgan nodded. He knew a little about neutrinos. 'Detecting the Sun's neutrino flux takes a great deal of apparatus. Notoriously, even though immensely sensitive and expensive experiments have been carried out, the Sun just isn't putting out the neutrinos that it should be. Or at least it wasn't: now it is. It has long been suspected that the nuclear reactions in the Sun's core have been at a kind of idling phase in a five-hundred year activity cycle. For two years now the neutrino counters have been detecting an upsurge in the neutrino flux that substantially confirms this idea. In two years the Sun's diameter has increased by two per cent, and its energy output has increased by three per cent.'

'So? Presumably the world has put up with this burst of solar enthusiasm before?'

'Sure it has. But this time is different. Its significance modifies the results you obtained. Your other inputs are still there, and *they* haven't been there before.'

'I see.'

'Look, there isn't time to tell you the climatic dynamics behind this – or to tell you of the individuals and groups of individuals who are responsible –'

'You mean people are getting blamed for this?'

'Blamed? How can you be so naïve. People did it. People destroyed the world. They are getting blamed all right, though I doubt that they will ever know it. But we'll leave that now. What matters is that you're orbiting a world that's seen its last summer. Or more precisely it's seeing its last winter. Winter is ending in the northern hemisphere, and it will never come again. Winter is due to begin in the southern hemisphere – only it will never come.'

Morgan nodded his understanding. 'So this alters the strategic balance. The United States becomes more desert and the Soviet Union becomes more fertile – and so forth. Hence your interest.'

Rathbone shook his head slowly. 'No. Not exactly. Climatic conditions pass outside a band within which they were self-correcting. Outside that band they run away, to eventually find a new and different balance.'

'How bad is it?'

'Catastrophic: several hundred degrees.'

'Celsius?' asked Morgan stupidly, still trying to grasp the idea.

'Does it matter?'

'No. I suppose not. How soon?'

'The mechanism is already broken. No one on Earth has more than six months to live.' Then the Earth swung slowly across the port of Morgan's cabin. From edge to edge it was visible for perhaps ten seconds. But in those moments Morgan saw many living memories triggered by the friendly quirks of coastline and surface colour. And he saw what they could become. He didn't bother with questioning

Rathbone's certainty.

'It's been a possibility in my mind for some time. Is there anyone down there – of yours?'

'My wife. I won't see her again. . . . You?'

'No. Not really.' That wasn't easy to say. 'What are the other things then – Pluto and Bootstrap?'

'Pluto is an environmentally controlled and ecologically balanced shelter deep underground in Colorado. It was NORAD's strategic command centre. Lately it's been expanded greatly and given a much more durable capability. It's hoped that a population of several thousand can hold out there indefinitely.'

'Really?' was all that Morgan could say. To be trapped beneath the ground, penned in by hurricanes of boiling dust and poisonous air until the very memory of a horizon-full of blue and green was decayed. . . .

'And Bootstrap?'

'Well, Pluto is my direct concern: the co-ordination of the Pluto Project from the meteorological point of view. I provide them with their time-line. Bootstrap is Zeffert's baby. His job is to bring the space community up to a state of independence from Earth by the time that . . . it's necessary.'

'What! That's impossible.'

'May well be.'

'And is it necessary? Even if you can't live on Earth you can still use it as a source of materials.'

'You just don't know. Think of Venus. Winds will gust up to hundreds of knots. The atmosphere will deteriorate until it's got a high acid content. Atmospheric pressure will increase ten times at the surface – eventually more. Even as it is now it's easier to take materials from the Moon. It'll soon be impossible to visit the Earth.'

'Can we really do it? Become independent, I mean?'

'By now, Mister Morgan, you know more about the logistics of space flight that I do, and Bootstrap isn't my baby. . . .' Morgan's imagination was scrambling through flow charts, recycling routes, inefficiencies, and profits and losses of energy expenditure. ' . . . but my feeling is that although Zeffert will put in maximum effort, and the USSF will create an epic out here in near-Earth space, come a year, or at the most eighteen months, the last one of us will choke off – if we don't inside the next half-hour. Then for the rest of the duration of the universe there will be no one to reconstruct that epic. We'll be gone and it'll be as though we never were.'

'I'll admit there are problems,' said Morgan. It was laughable to do so, but he intentionally understated his doubt. Nothing was expendable any more, not even language. The survival of the last human being might depend on a single word, or a man's state of mind – particularly this man's.

'Then let's get this message off.' It was obvious by now that no one else was in a position to help. Morgan went self-consciously about his task of routing Rathbone's instructions through Intelnet 3 to Eurodefence, and thence to the Pentagon. There was no point in hiding anything now. Rathbone asked no questions.

Twenty minutes later Morgan sealed the last flap over the zip fastening of his personal survival capsule. He wasn't inside it: Rathbone was. It wasn't a space suit. It was a layered asbestos cloth, glass cloth and acrylic sphere just big enough to contain an astronaut curled up in extreme discomfort. It was not possible to see out of it, move it, or manipulate anything through it. It contained a man, a life support system and a radio beacon. Morgan poked the flabby puff-ball three times and immediately saw the skin bulge as Rathbone pummelled it in return to signal that the seal was good. Morgan gave it a wave and moved over to the door. The opening button was still red. The corridor was still open to hard space. He went over his plan – what there was of it – carefully, move by move. If he lost vision he still had to be able to do it.

He hung around a little. He was one of those people cursed with the sort of imagination that prevents them facing death – or even the imagined agony of the dentist's drill – with equanimity. He wondered if, after all, there was no other way. But his cabin's atmosphere was already badly poisoned. In ten minutes, if not already, he might be too weak to make the attempt. He punched the reset sequence on his cabin door. The red lights winked out and the door remained closed. Behind a glass panel there was a slim beryllium-steel crank. Morgan took it out and looked at it. He was worried that he wouldn't be able to wind it fast enough. . . . He locked it into the wall socket then stood back from the door and breathed. And he breathed with a concentration, and with an appreciation, with which he had never breathed before. He breathed until he was dizzy, then blew the air out of his lungs and kept blowing until he was crouching with the effort of emptying them. He grabbed the edge of his console with his right hand and started to wind the crank with his left. The door unsealed immediately with a bang of releasing pressure. He wound furiously. The gas was escaping from the little cabin with a roar. It was plucking at his overall. It was dragging his arm from the crank. He swallowed, trying to balance the pressure in his aching ears. His eyes were stinging. He closed them. His stomach was swelling painfully and he could hear his heart beating. Then with the most unbearable pain the searching fingers of complete vacuum plucked the last oxygen from his lungs. The roaring of air was over. He grabbed the door and pulled himself through. After the oxygen from his lungs came his dinner – quickly. Then the blood. At first it just came from his nose and fell in boiling drops to the floor. His skin started to tingle. He felt only a little frightened now, more fascinated to be in so familiar a place – not unlike an exceedingly well-presented but functional hotel corridor on Earth – yet to be in a vacuum. He had no right to be there. That exhilaration passed as he shuffled along the corridor, fighting against the racking pain in his stomach. It was hard to see. He tried to blink, but his eyelids seemed gummed. But he caught a glimpse of the place he wanted to go to, ten metres ahead on the left. He wanted very much to breathe now, even if he breathed only vacuum, but his lungs didn't work and he gagged drily. Now he had to run his fingers along the frozen wall, seeking his objective. He knew that if he missed it he was sunk. He walked crabwise, running one hand level and sliding the other up and down. He found it: a cold steel wheel in a recess. He thanked the USSF's foresight that it was plastic coated or he would never have been able to shift his grip. Then he cursed the USSF because it was vacuum-welded into place. He wasted a thought on the over-enthusiastic servicing robot that must have oiled it: he didn't know, because he couldn't see, that it was his own spurting blood that had frozen the wheel tight. When he found himself on his knees without knowing how he had got there he knew that the last desperate moment had come. He clasped both hands on one side of the wheel and jacked himself up beneath it with all the remaining strength of his back and leg muscles. It cracked and he kept it turning without letting it stop for one moment in which it would freeze again. A sheet of gas jetted out past him and he dragged himself through the door, hauling on the rim of the wheel from the floor. He felt a cascade of pure oxygen pressure against his ears. He breathed. And breathing he huddled in a corner of the little cubicle, letting the tear ducts flood his sore eyes.

Soon he had the energy to suppose that only three minutes ago (it had seemed longer, but it couldn't have been) he had been in his own room fifteen metres away through complete vacuum across the corridor. It seemed unlikely. A modest clarion of victory tooted in his mind. He looked through the little glass port, through the traces of blood that smeared it. There seemed to be blood everywhere. There was a movement outside. He hadn't expected that. A corridor robot was trying to clean up the mess he had made. Its detergent was boiling away in clouds of spindrift. Soon the stupid machine would be unable to see. Morgan turned to don one of the space suits that hung in the vacuum shelter. On the left hand wall he noticed the glowing light of a terminal.

'Wheeldata?'

'Mister Morgan, this is Wheeldata.'

'Wheeldata, what the hell are you doing letting me go through decompression like that? Do you realise that the corridors are open to vacuum? I thought your prime function was to look after our survival.'

'You are correct in your description of my prime directive. My operational withdrawal from corridor and dormitory areas is initiated by command override control.'

'Well forget that. People are going to die. Like when you malfunctioned on October the eighteenth.' He thought of threatening the machine, but decided it might be risky. 'It's a very unpleasant experience. It is ultimately to be avoided. I want you to close all the airlocks, restore full environmental control to the whole space station, and resume full communications switching.'

'These functions are denied by command override control. You must give the command override control code sequence by voice or keyboard.'

'I don't know it.'

'The spacecraft commander knows the code. He must give it by –'

'He can't. He's incommunicado. He's not in communicating range.'

'Then his deputy must.'

Morgan became angry, emitting a faint odour of burning *déjà vu*. 'Are you in communcation with anyone on this space station other than myself?'

'No.'

'Are you in communcation with anyone not on this space station.'
'No.'
'Then I am his deputy. Close the airlocks.'
'You are not USSF personnel. Your level of access is insufficient. You cannot deputise the spacecraft commander.'

'Damn you, Wheeldata. When Captain Rathbone hears of this you're in for a hell of a lot of reprogramming.' Morgan reached for a suit. There wasn't one his size. It took him fifteen minutes to seal himself in, drag Rathbone's survival capsule into the vacuum shelter, and get him out – fifteen minutes of extreme pubic discomfort. After that Wheeldata's compliance was magical.

Thirteen

WHEELDATA WAS innocently back in control of the whole station within a microsecond of Rathbone's command. Morgan, who felt as though he had just been in a fight with an angry fork-lift truck, decided that there was nothing that the rest of the five hundred crew members of the Wheel could not handle without him. He slipped back to his room and put in a call to Stephanie.

'Yea,' she said sleepily, and with a hint of annoyance.

'Richard here. Are you OK?'

'Fine. Nice to hear from you. What's the time?' Morgan felt thwarted. She had obviously slept through the whole thing.

'0400.'

'Good gracious! Anything the matter? What's happening?'

'All sorts of things. If you'll just stay there I'm going to come and rescue you.'

'Rescue me?'

'Yes. Everyone needs rescuing once in a while. You can't go around not being rescued all the time.'

'I think I'd quite like to be rescued.'

'Stay there then.'

Stephanie opened her door with her c-unit. She was in bed. A beam of moonlight passed across the room. She was propped up on an elbow with the cover to her breast – but not altogether too high. Her hair made black feathers over her milk-white skin.

'Am I being rescued yet?'

'Absolutely. Don't panic. Just follow me.' Morgan bent and kissed her lips softly. After a few seconds she drew back slightly.

'I think I still need rescuing.' Morgan knelt beside her. 'But not quite yet.' Relinquishing her hold on the cover she reached out and placed her hand behind his neck. She drew him nearer and kissed him. 'Your face is all wet.' In the dim light he saw her tongue moving over her lips. 'You're all over bloody.'

'But unbowed. I don't think we ought to worry about it all that much now. . . .'

'You've been up to something again.'

'Not yet . . .'

'What's happened?'

'Ask me again in about an hour.'

Neatly and sinuously she slipped out of bed and through his hands. The sequence of sensations that accompanied her slipping through them was exquisite. He already regretted that he had been too slow to foil her escape but she had skipped the short distance across her cabin in a glimmer of white limbs and secret darkness. He stood and watched her – an occupation extenuated by the fascinating grace of her movements in the pearly illumination of the stars – as she stepped into her overall, and envied the movement of the zip as she drew it from thigh to throat. She switched the light on and pushed him back on to her bunk.

There was a sweet fresh scent in the room that brought back to him the woods of his home after rain. Now he saw why: Stephanie had made a little oasis here of ferns and flowering plants. There were feminine, girlish touches: a large print of Degas' *Rehearsal in the Foyer of the Opera*; a toy rabbit of asymmetric mien bereft of much of its fur; trifling family mementoes and photographs. He liked what she had done to the cabin.

'You look as though you've had a real going over. Who did it?'

'No one really. They've been economising on oxygen pressure.'

'Decompression?'

Morgan nodded.

'How low did you go?'

'As low as you can get.'

'For how long?'

While Morgan told her briefly what had happened Stephanie interrogated Wheeldata's medical file on him through her terminal. Then she set to work on his bloodstained face with cotton wool and a cosmetic concoction in a jar. As she worked the slightest tremor was all that betrayed her reaction to hearing of the abduction of her fellow crew members.

'Wheeldata's reading you as basically OK, but he doesn't see everything. I want to get you something like presentable, then I want to give you a thorough check in medical. We'll have to keep you under observation. You see, you're a unique case. We've had complete decompressions before, through environmental malfunctions of one sort or another, but they've all been autopsy cases. And what is more, none of them were volunteers.'

'The USSF probably screens out congenital idiots.'

'I don't think anyone casts you as one. I think you're . . . What you did was sane and admirable. If you want to be modest put it down to the excellence of meteorological training!'

'Please. I've put all that behind me.'

'And you seem to be thriving on its absence. There. I don't think you're too horrific now. I shan't mind being seen with you. Let's go.'

'This efficiency is most impressive,' remarked Morgan pointedly.

'Be grateful. You're getting the trimmings.' He raised an eyebrow. 'No, you weren't wrong, Richard. Let's wait for the right time. Soon, when I've checked that you're all right. I wish it had been sooner, but on a ship like this where we're all breathing down one another's necks the whole time, we all emphasise our personal reserves. It's institutional.'

'A girl can't be too careful?'

'Especially with the world about to come to an end.'

'It's the first time I've heard it said like that.'

'No one likes to say it at all. No one likes to think about it. It's like cancer, nuclear war or the certainty of our own deaths by whatever cause. It's taboo.'

'That observation explains quite a lot. I'd put my ignorance of the . . . aforementioned problem down to security.'

'That in itself would have been sufficient. We live security here. But we have no way of talking about what's going to happen on Earth, even of thinking about it. How could you mourn such a bereavement? It defies our emotional scope. I think we will mourn in the way we can – for those we love and for ourselves. To mourn in just measure would kill us.'

'That's intelligent. And it's a comfort to me. I thought I should be showing more emotion. I felt like even more of a bastard than I usually do.'

'Well, don't. It's an imaginative limit. That's something we've all got to understand. Now let's get along to Medical.' She cheerfully attacked the moment of sorrow. 'I want to see the colour of your insides.'

'Nice.'

Lieutenant Honeywell's not entirely clinical intentions were checked by the bleeping of Morgan's c-unit. Rathbone's fretful face appeared on the little wrist-screen. Morgan acknowledged on sound-only.

'Morgan? Where the hell are you?'

Morgan side-stepped the literal meaning of the question. 'I'm under medical care at the moment.'

'Anything serious?'

'Not so far. They're just going to do some checks.'

'You mean you're still living? What d'you think this is: a drama school?'

'That view of the Wheel had escaped me – sir.'

'And you can cut that out. Shift your decaying corpse over here now. I need you functional, and I'm not too concerned about the trimmings.'

Morgan raised a second eyebrow at Stephanie. 'Where's *here*, sir?'

'Command A. Crow's nest. I'd better not ask you again where *you* are.'

'I'll be there anon,' replied Morgan, wishing to remind Rathbone that he was not a USSF officer, and did not wish to be treated as the property of the Defense Department. Only he preferred not to say it directly. He exchanged shrugs with Stephanie, lightly bit the lobe of her left ear, and left.

Rathbone was looking at the Earth. The whole great daylit hemisphere of it rotated around the crow's nest observation turret twice every minute. The climatological banding and the poleward compression of the zones were now especially pronounced. Morgan's impression was that Rathbone had been watching it for a long time. Seldom, when Morgan saw him, was his gaze not fixed on the planet.

'I'm having a Command meeting with my senior staff. I want you to come too.'

'Thank you very much sir. I appreciate that.'

'Don't. I need everyone who has a milligram of judgement or above. And those men and women will be up here over the next six months watching that planet turn into a smoking desert. And if our judgement is sufficiently refined we may make decisions that will alleviate but not solve the catastrophe for a handful of people. So know this: it's going to be no pleasure. It'll be the worst thing you ever did or imagined.'

'I already know it.'

Rathbone nodded at the globe. 'It was thrown away, not by chance or unavoidable fate, but by thinking people who knew and ignored the consequences of their decisions.'

'Us too. It's a pity we couldn't have detected the problem quicker.'

'No chance. Though it was predictable, by the time we could detect the change we were too late. It came like a tidal wave, though some of the wave-makers were people.'

'You said that before. Which people are you talking about?'

'As far as I can tell one organisation more than any other was responsible for the destruction of life on Earth – and they, paradoxically, were Lifewatch.'

'Lifewatch? But aren't they an environmental group?'

'The environment was their crusade, and their subtlety was about that of crusaders. They came together out of Life Limited, Rainmakers, Biowatch and some others – all of whom, incidentally started off quite well, though in a fairly chaotic way. Lifewatch set its sights on the nuclear energy programmes of the developed world, and their campaign looked good. They were taken over by the politicians who wanted the votes of the concerned middle classes, and they set back the nuclear power programme by fifty years.'

'Well, that obviously wasn't too bright,' said Morgan, 'fighting a myth but keeping their Volvos; believing all that rhetoric. But among the outright politicians there really were genuine environmentalists: you've got to agree they did some good for the whales. They saved all but the sperm whale.'

'Saved them for *this*? *Wonderful*! Yes, all right, there was much that was good in the beginning: I'll concede the endangered species programmes. I was with them at the time, so I know. Much of the rest was at least innocent, but those efforts generated the great wave of *concern* which carried through the less rational campaigns. It was a sort of logical conjuring trick: *if you care about the grey seal you'll help us picket this power station*. Their Utopias weren't even options. They presented the world with two dogmas. One: *return to the woods*. Only the woods weren't there any more. The world had changed over five thousand years of civilisation. Iron age man had resources lying around for the taking, but they've gone now: you need energy to carve out survival. A twenty-first century village culture could support a world population of between half a billion and a billion. That meant five billion had to be written off somehow, within a generation. It was an option that didn't get very far. As you say, they hung on to their Volvos.

'Two: *you try to make life bearable for six billion by non-nuclear means*. That's the one they seemed to adopt. They burnt the remaining fossil fuel reserves *on clean energy sources*: they burnt ten to the power fifteen megawatt-hours on tidal power networks; they covered a quarter of a million acres with solar cells that couldn't repay their energy cost before they needed replacing; they heaved up fifty solar power satellites – only there wasn't enough nuclear power to pay the energy debt of five thousand shuttle flights. Volvos again. What a century! You might as well forget it: it's all CO_2 now, and there's the consequence . . . .' He pointed out of the curved glass wall of the crow's nest. 'OK, the rest of us were to blame. It was our world too. We didn't have the collective guts to oppose. The power-crazy technocrat image they branded us with was too much for us to handle . . . . Anyway it's time we went in. Up here we've got to try to make our decisions more sanely. You first one is whether you're going to watch the sunset from up here, or whether you want down. It can be arranged.'

Morgan followed him back through Command A and into the conference room. The Command Team was assembled. The first thing he noticed was that Stephanie was there at Lieutenant-Commander Bardelli's side.

They were subdued, those that remained. There was no talk. They sipped coffee, or interrogated their terminals, for the seats of Peterson and Auntie Grey were vacant. Lieutenant Perkins, whom Morgan had come to know slightly in the Met. Section, was standing in for his commander. He was self-consciously busy, preparing to present a good case. No one stood in for Peterson. Morgan surmised that it was the main reason for his own presence. It solved the problem of where he should sit: he took the seat *next* to that of his absent commander. The only other absentee was Zeffert. He was in the hot seat in Command A, running the ship.

The team leapt to attention, skilfully restraining themselves in the low gee. 'Easy. Be seated.' Rathbone seated himself in front of his display at the head of the table, exchanging nods, but not smiles this time, with the members of his team. 'Ladies and gentlemen, we have a number of problems presenting themselves for resolution. The most urgent, I'm afraid, is one which we have little power to influence. Our shuttle flight 1286 has completed its second de-orbit burn as of this time and is now into its re-entry phase. I can now confirm that as well as carrying Commanders Grey and Peterson and the shuttle flight crew, 1286 has on board twenty-nine of the men and women who mutinied.' He touched his keyboard. 'Fred? Rathbone. What have you got on the status of 1286?'

They could all hear Zeffert's reply. 'I've got it under satellite surveillance. Trajectory decay indicates it's now in terminal re-entry phase over the Indian Ocean. It could make Darwin if it completes re-entry. We have visual. D'you want it through on your monitor, or shall I keep you informed?'

Rathbone paused indecisively. 'Yes, put it through.' Then he added, 'For that matter you can put it through to the whole damn ship. It's time we all knew what we're doing up here, even if it hurts.' Morgan caught a few covertly exchanged glances. This wasn't Rathbone's style. He liked to use Wheeldata so that bad news was filtered through on a need-to-know basis.

A blue-toned picture flicked up on Morgan's VDU. For a moment it was indistinct until computer enhancement picked out a clear picture of the descending shuttle over an ocean lightened to milky blue by atmospheric haze. Wheeldata was printing in some figures at the bottom of the screen.

ATT: +29, +3, −1.

VEL: 5043m/s.

'Looks OK so far,' said Zylka Zbijowski.

'Case of *So far so good*, I'm afraid,' muttered Joe Waldon.

The compression zones could be seen arrowing sharply back from the shuttle, and a hint of its hot wake as the blue plasma lit up under its belly and wings. Morgan knew, and at least Waldon and Rathbone knew, that without coolant circulation the alloy-steel underskin of the shuttle would start to yield under the harsh stress and buffeting.

It wasn't slow when it happened. A paper-thin sheet of white flame attached itself to the trailing edge of the port wing, then in an instant the wing was gone, and the shuttle was rolling viciously and shedding glowing chunks which spread out along its flight path until all that could be seen was a cascade of burning fragments. Morgan was grateful that little detail could be discerned in the fiery stream. It was five minutes before the fused but intact mass of the main propulsion engines hit the sea in a spurt of spray and steam.

'May their souls rest,' said Rathbone. 'They are not the first, and if we dare to live we will watch billions die from up here. Now let's get it over with. I would ask you to speak freely on each item. This is not a routine meeting and all genuine points of view must be considered.'

Zeffert walked in, exchanged nods with Rathbone, and sat down quietly. Rathbone continued.

'The subject forced on our attention by its immediacy is that of the ship's present status. Wheeldata's status assessment shows us in a position to meet any readiness or alert requirement. I also have your departmental projections. What I need now is your considered but fast judgement on any difficulties caused by our recent . . .problem.'

The comments that followed echoed the captain's guarded confidence. But each of the commanders expressed doubt about the longer term. Each time Rathbone deferred the long-term problems for a later stage in the meeting. Morgan was the last to be asked to speak. He had been doing his homework with Wheeldata during the preceding reports.

'The main logistics outcome of the . . . trouble we've just had is the oxygen loss. Wheeldata reckons that the evacuation of the corridor areas depleted our reserves by about twenty thousand kilograms. His calculation of the corridor contents and his measurement in the tanks agree pretty closely, so we can be confident of the figure. That means we've lost about a third of our reserves, which isn't as bad as it sounds because we recycle the oxygen. In the longer term our oxygen reserves look poor anyway: we lose a finite amount every time we cycle an airlock; we lose it in waste from our PLSS packs every time we EVA; and we burn it every time we launch a Torc. I would like to recommend that we cut those losses by pumping out the airlocks rather than gassing them out into space, that we – '

'We'll be glad to hear your recommendations on the longer-term problem later in the meeting, Mister Morgan. In the meantime, are there any other areas of logistic concern in the short term?'

'Nothing pressing. The loss of the shuttle is of course a blow, but getting shuttles through to the space flight centres and back is becoming so difficult that we can't use all we've got anyway. The other problem is personnel. I know it's not my area, but the extra duties are stretching the crew as it is. And we've just lost another thirty.'

'Commander Zeffert's working on the crew problem. It's partly alleviated by basing the shuttle crews up here rather than on Earth. But that leads me quite handily to my next point, which is not so much crew *quantity* as crew *quality*. I very much need input on this morale problem. Wheeldata projects it in typically mathematical terms. As he sees it we've had a number of morale crises, each more severe than the last. He sees that series continuing, with the next crisis almost certainly putting us out of commission. He has no recommendations for action – which you might say is a fairly good estimate of our options.

'I don't necessarily see it that way. The crises on board the Wheel have not been pleasant for anyone. The re-entry of flight 1286 was not an easy thing to watch. I think these are chastening experiences which will cause people to consider their attitudes and their actions. And it may be that 1286, tragic as it was for us, has cleansed the Wheel of its less disciplined elements. Anyway, those are two views on the subject. I should like to hear yours. I don't think I need call upon you in any particular order.'

If Rathbone had expected a series of plans for improving crew morale, he was to be disappointed. There was a marked reluctance to speak. No one met his eyes. The staying power of Bardelli, commander of the medical team, broke first.

'I'm not clear the extent to which we can speak freely in this meeting.'

'Are there any particular areas that worry you?'

'Yes, sir. I'm referring to the security aspect. Can we assume no security inhibitions while we're speaking in this room?'

Rathbone was again uncertain. He plainly hadn't faced that decision. He glanced at Morgan, and Lieutenants Honeywell and Perkins. He nodded. 'Yes. You can assume that.' But Bardelli had said all he wanted to for the time being. Silence descended.

'I'm surprised that none of you have anything to say on this subject.

Lieutenant Honeywell, I'd especially expect some comment from you as on-board psychologist. You've made quite a contribution to the subject heretofore.'

Stephanie took her time replying. She hid it well, but Morgan could see that she was under stress. 'I think what you're expecting from me is a number of beneficial adjustments to the life-style of the crew: changes in the entertainment programme. improvements in work loading, diet, exercise, section meetings, team meetings, down-link time for communicating with families, and all those things we've tried to do in the past.' She paused for just long enough for Rathbone to wonder whether she had had her say. 'All these are palliatives. The Earth is dying down there. People are never going to see their families again. The norms of community behaviour no longer apply. And that goes for the people in this room too. What's normal in the face of that?'

Ratbone swept his hand across the keyboard. His display flickered and squawked. He cancelled it with a jab. 'With respect, Lieutenant Honeywell, that is known information. But I've got a team of men and women up here who have chosen risk and isolation, and also a certain detached and if you like idealistic view of human affairs as a preferred life-style and profession. That team has a number of jobs to do still. They are vital jobs, and so if the universe itself comes apart at the seams we're not here to fling up our hands in despair, but to keep at it until we're choked off. That's what I expect and by Christ that's what I aim to get.'

'And with respect, sir, that's what we all want too. But the old ways of getting it no longer apply. If five hundred people are going to choose your road to extinction, rather than the preferred road of spending the last few hours with their wives or husbands, then it has to be by consent.'

'Well, I'll go along with that. But if they're going to consent they will. What we're getting is dissent. So it won't work and it's got to be like war where men go to the beach-head and get killed establishing it because their training and their orders send them there and keep them there without question until they die. It's happened throughout human history. What's so different now?'

There was another long silence. No one wanted to disillusion the Old Man. 'The difference now,' said Bud Saunders, the systems specialist, 'is a logical one. The troops establishing a beach-head believe that they are protecting the way of life that made them. So even if they never get back to it themselves they are following at least a semblance of purpose: a part of themselves will carry on in the world after they are dead. That patently does not apply here.'

'I believe what everyone needs to know, sir,' said Stephanie, 'is what we *are* doing. That way they can identify with whatever it is you're trying to achieve. And I don't even know what that is myself. I mean, I know what we're supposed to be doing now, but I don't know what's planned for the future.'

'That,' replied Rathbone, 'is simple. We carry on as we always have. We provide a strategic world overview, a deterrent strike force and a highly survivable command post. We provide logistics and administrative support to space activities. We provide Earth resources, meteorological and communications facilities for terrestrial use.'

Now there was strong competition to answer Rathbone. Saunders, displaying unusual verbal aggression, got in first. 'All those functions are made obsolete by what's happening on Earth.'

'Not the strategic role,' said McMurdo. It was the first time he had spoken, and he carried weight. The others listened. 'The position at the moment is that the Russians would have to make several thousand simultaneous direct hits with nuclear warheads in order to achieve a successful first strike on the West's military setup. I would ask you to view the situation in several month's time – let's say six months. The surviving Earth-based population will be concentrated in the Deep Survival Shelter at Colorado Springs, the Soviet equivalent west of Chelyabinsk in the South Urals, and possibly one or two other shelters. The space-based population is concentrated to all intents and purposes in half a dozen facilities. The rest are too small and dependent to count. So in six months' time the targetting problem that each side faces will be eliminated. I would like you to consider the pay-off for whichever side strikes first.'

'Tell us,' said Rathbone rather sourly.

'He rules the world. His survivors are the sole inheritors of the Earth.'

'Not if the other side empties his tubes at the first sign of an enemy launch,' said Zbijowski.

'How? In the climatic conditions that'll hold in six months' time long-range radar will be out. Communications will be very poor indeed. The Wheel can't be everywhere, and the satellites on the other side of the globe can be taken out with ease. Result: successful first strike.'

'Does this lead to a recommendation?'

'Not a recommendation. An obligation: we strike first.'

'What if we decide not to?' said Bardelli.

'Then they do.'

'How do we know that?'

'Because there's some guy on Astrogorodok saying what I've just said. You've always got to assume that.'

'But what if we go a step further and assume there's some guy like me – their own medic perhaps – who's saying what *I've* just said; who's saying in short, *Do the reasonable thing and give the guys a break*.'

'They'll laugh themselves into severe hernias. You have to figure out the worst possible option, and then counter it. In this case the only counter is to strike first.'

'All this to inherit the Earth for a few months?' Bardelli wasn't hiding his derision.

'What the hell do you think nuclear war was or could ever be?' snapped McMurdo. 'It's there. We live with it. We work it. It's what we're doing up here.' He gathered the meeting together with his eyes. 'What is more, anyone here whose actions – or words – foul up a first strike when it is perceived to be strategically desirable will be performing an act of mutiny no less than the one we've just seen.' He looked hard at Rathbone, demanding that his logic be recognised.

Rathbone chose to recognise it. 'Commander McMurdo's argument may be unpalatable to some people here, but it's valid. It is founded in the logic upon which we operate. He's describing an option which we will have to consider very seriously.'

'I would like to insist, sir, that as an option it's not merely to be considered but to be implemented. The consideration is of how and when.'

'As you no doubt know, McMurdo, the exact status of that option rests with the Pentagon and ultimately with the President. We do not have a first strike decision authority up here – nor a second for that matter.'

'May I remind you, sir, that within six months the Office of President and the hierarchy of the Pentagon will be meaningless. The men may still be living but their chains of commands will be dysfunctional.'

'I am prepared to accept that as a possibility.'

'I think we ought to regard it as a certainty. In those circumstances the decision-making capability of the Wheel will be the only one that counts. There is no one else we can pass the buck to.' McMurdo was challenging Rathbone with his eyes. Rathbone looked back impassively. 'As you have asked for a full representation of our views in this briefing I think it would be valid – and beneficial – for you to canvass the views of the officers present on what we should do in that eventuality.'

Rathbone held McMurdo's gaze, then nodded. 'Remember this. In six month's time, or at any time, our operational procedure holds: if we're out of touch with Earth, whatever the views of the Command Team of the ship it is the captain's decision whether or not a strike be launched. And he cannot launch it without the compliance of his second in command. He may, however, order that such compliance be given. Naturally the captain is expected to consider – but not necessarily accept – the advice of his officers.

'With the understanding that that is the case I'm quite prepared to ask you all for your personal views. The question is whether you consider that we should launch a pre-emptive strike to take out the total remaining population and military capability of the Soviet Union at such a time as that becomes an achievable option. I will ask which way you would decide. You can add your more detailed views if you wish.

'Commander Zeffert?'

Zeffert was wearing a headset cocked over one ear, and he spoke with his eyes on the console through which he was monitoring the Wheel's operations. 'I think Mac's rather carried away by the classic war-gaming syndrome. I admit that not to strike puts the Pluto shelter at risk. On its own it can't detect an incoming attack in a bad radar environment, or defend against it. But the space facilities of the Russians and us are not limited by seeing through an opaque atmosphere. They couldn't count on knocking us out here and on the moon, and nor could we count on taking out their off-Earth facilities. In other words there still won't be an assured first-strike capability, and deterrence will still be the order of the day. That's it as far as I'm concerned.'

Although Rathbone was usually a bit wrong-footed by Zeffert's casual style, he accepted this with a half-smile. 'Thank you, Fred. Joe?'

The Engineering officer was putting on a show of intellectual confidence which Morgan guessed he didn't feel. 'I agree with Mac's logic. You've always got to look at the fail case – where things don't go quite as you expect.' McMurdo nodded enthusiastically. 'But I think we ought to keep it under review.'

'Your recommendation?'

'To strike, though it's a shame.'

'I'm sure we all think it's a shame,' replied Rathbone with a sardonic glance at McMurdo. 'And you. Mac?'

'To strike. I've given my views.'

'Quite. Bud?'

'Not to strike,' said the Systems officer. 'We can't take out their Mars base with any reliability. That leaves them one up if everything else goes. But it also leaves the Callisto facility intact. It would resolve nothing, but we might well be the losers.'

'OK. Zylka?'

Zbijowski appeared to be in no doubt. He was thinking of his beloved weapons systems. 'We have the capability to take them out one hundred per cent on Earth, near Earth and on the Moon. That leaves the bastards to choke on Mars. I say strike.'

That left Sandra Crabtree of Movement Control and Doc. Bardelli.

'Sandra?'

'It games out very clearly.' She called up a display that she'd been working on while the others were talking. 'It's the classic non-zero sum situation. There are five ways of playing it. One: neither side strikes; but then neither side can trust the other to take that option. Two: they strike and we defend; they have all the advantages of aggression so we don't buy it. Three: we strike and they defend; similarly that's to *their* disadvantage, so they don't allow us to take that option. Four: they strike first and we counterstrike; that's the option they'll choose because it's a win for them in the worst possible case. Five: we strike first and they counterstrike; similarly that's the one we've got to go for because it assumes the worst case and leaves us with a win. The only problem is whether we end up in a Four situation or a Five situation. We solve that by getting in the earliest possible strike that assures their destruction. That happens immediately they're dependent on their Chelyabinsk shelter – unless we're dependent on the Pluto shelter first, in which case we have to strike immediately to reduce their threat.' Morgan had always viewed Commander Crabtree as being a tough woman.

'So?'

'In other words I vote for a first strike.'

'Thank you. Doc?'

Bardelli shook his head in sad silence. 'I'm amazed. I think and hope you're all my friends around this table, and I'll ask you to tolerate this trespass on our friendship. Never have I heard such a catalogue of crass, egocentric, short-sighted and inhumane jargon. We're talking about a time some six months hence when there may be only some ten or twenty thousand human beings still living – and living at that on the sharp edge of total extinction. Life has evolved on that planet out there for three billion years, and human life for a million. We, by greed, arrogance, and ignorance of the value of all life, have brought it to an end. Now if those twenty thousand men and women can't survive in harmony let's for Christ's sake die in harmony. It would be the justification of a species whose whole history is bursting with cretinous guilt – '

'And your realistic assessment of our strategic options?' interposed Sandra Crabtree.

'Let everyone speak in his turn,' said Rathbone.

'It's all right. I've said it.'

'Recommendation?'

'Not to strike, of course.'

'Fine.' Under his eyelids Rathbone glanced down, secretly, he might have thought, at his display. But the tally was clear enough in everyone's mind: four for a strike and three against. All the surviving members of the Command Team had recorded their views. McMurdo's stiff face muscles dissimulated his triumph. Rathbone appeared nonplussed. Morgan thought what a weak figure he presented at the head of the table. A military commander should under no circumstances allow himself to be trapped into recording the votes of his subordinates. McMurdo on the other hand had judged nicely the disposition of opinion in the Command Team. Rathbone looked up without directly looking at anyone.

'It would remain under normal circumstances for us to hear the views of Commanders Grey and Peterson. Alas, that may not be. However, it is appropriate for me to instruct Lieutenant Perkins to air his views. Say what you like, Perkins, bearing in mind the role of the Meteorological Section, and the view of Commander Grey if you were ever in a position to hear her express any on this subbect.'

'I must protest very strongly at this.' McMurdo's eyes were drawn wide with fury. 'Lieutenant Perkins is not of Command rank and is present at this meeting only in a consultative capacity.'

'And we are consulting him. I would remind you that he is now nominally in command of the Met. Section, and that I am empowered to make a battlefield promotion under the circumstances. I would further remind you that, although I have allowed this to be a fairly open meeting, your own conduct is bordering on the insubordinate. Consider it.' Morgan relaxed a little. Perhaps Rathbone wasn't so weak after all. 'Carry on, Perkins.'

Perkins swallowed audibly. He looked around the circle of faces. Each face made its unspoken demands. Morgan was about to send his own mute signal when McMurdo caught his eye. The Surveillance and Security officer was staring intently at him. He was typing something on his keyboard.

Perkins found his voice, at first uncertainly. 'The job of the Met. Section has always been relatively passive. We watch, and we try to make predictions, and we ultimately try to save lives, and help people to grow crops and so forth.'

'You also provide weather data for military operations,' pointed out McMurdo with exaggerated patience.

'Quiet!' snapped Rathbone. 'Carry on, Perkins.'

'There's nothing more to say except that I think we er – ' He glanced nervously at McMurdo. 'I think we shouldn't launch a strike first. Not unless we have to.' Commander Crabtree gasped impatiently.

Morgan looked intently at the information that had come up on his screen. He was conscious that McMurdo was looking at him, sitting back with his arms folded.

'I'll take that as a vote against, then, Perkins?' The lieutenant nodded. 'Right, that makes the voting even. Your views are filed for recall when the timeline brings me to decide on this option. We will now close the matter of our strategic stance – '

'Er, excuse me, sir,' said McMurdo, now quite obsequious.

'What is it, McMurdo?' Rathbone, having once quelled his subordinate, was testy.

'As Perkins has been allowed his say, I think Mister Morgan should be asked to speak for Logistics.'

Rathbone looked doubtfully at Morgan. A minute ago he would have been prepared to let him speak. But the fact that McMurdo had requested it gave him sufficient pause. 'Mister Morgan is a valued member of the Wheel's crew – in his exchange capacity. But he's not a member of the Command Team, nor is he an officer of the USSF, so he can't be promoted to the Command Team. Although his security status has been necessarily relaxed owing to his role in helping to keep the Wheel running, he still may not regard himself as free to discuss matters of a sensitive or secret nature with the crew.'

'Would you allow Mister Morgan to speak on a subject not concerned with our nuclear strike posture?'

'All right. If he's brief. We're wasting time.'

Morgan took his cue from McMurdo. He glanced down again at the column of figures on his screen. Then he looked slowly round the ten other people at the table. He knew what he was going to do, why he was going to do it, and the strength of the impact he had to make. *He knew, at last, why he was here.* He accessed his screen data to the screens of the Command Team.

'Thank you very much. This shouldn't take long. Please look at your screens. That is a cipher which I had considered was known only to myself and to the Director of American Intelligence. Commander McMurdo typed it out and transmitted it to my VDU just a moment ago. I memorised that cipher twelve years ago. I was then an American citizen. By means which I won't bore you with I was given cover as an Englishman and became a Deep Operation Agent – it used to be called a sleeper – for the Department of American Intelligence. I have maintained that cover ever since, and have not even communicated with the DAI except when I needed to as an agent of the British Secret Service. That's what a Deep Operation Agent does. He keeps quiet until he's wanted – until his unsuspected presence is of such value to the United States that they can risk using him. I must say I hardly expected to be used on an American operation, but there it is. The sleeper has woken up. It only remains for me to respond to this code in order to prove who I am.' Morgan typed briefly.

'It checks out,' said McMurdo.

'Hold it,' said Rathbone. 'We're getting out of our depth here. This could be the biggest load of crud ever!'

'I can give you an access code to check me through the DAI.'

'I'm going to do that.'

'But for the moment if you trust me – or more particularly Commander McMurdo – then just bear with us.'

'I wouldn't trust him with his own grandmother.'

'But you can trust me to be patriotic!' It was the one thing you had to grant McMurdo.

'If I do, what next?'

'Morgan is a senior member of the Department of Intelligence. He's a civilian with the equivalent rank of commander. He's been put on board this space station so that by virtue of his know-how and abilities – which everyone will admit he's already demonstrated for us – he can be of help at the highest level. And I might add that his deployment here has been authorised at the very highest level there is.'

'*God Almighty!*' Morgan heard Sandra Crabtree mutter under her breath.

'I might also add that they don't come better equipped than Mister Morgan – even in the company of astronauts.'

'A magnificent build-up,' remarked Rathbone wryly. 'And then what?'

'Then, sir, it is written into the orders of any military commander to take cognisance of information brought to his attention by any agent of the intelligence services.'

'*Take cognisance of!*' mimicked the captain. 'Yeah. Not bow down to. Not greet with reverence as tablets from the mountain. And it applied to specific data on a tactical situation – not out-of-the-back-of-the-neck chat about the general political and strategic situation . . . .'

Morgan was seated halfway down the table. Rathbone was at the head on his left. McMurdo was strategically placed at the foot on his right. Morgan put up his hand to scratch his left ear. As he scratched he crossed his fingers. Rathbone's tirade continued unabatedly. Morgan scratched harder and crossed his fingers more tightly. Across from him Sandra Crabtree frowned and rolled her eyes at the furtive histrionics. Rathbone faltered.

' . . . and then on the other hand, if it will allow us to get off the subject, I'm prepared to give him three minutes. OK Morgan, let's hear it.' McMurdo grinned tightly and pointedly at Morgan as if to say *Just say your lines, boy, and it's in the bag. I've set it up for you beautifully*. Morgan nodded to him with the trace of a confident wink. He turned to Rathbone.

'I think McMurdo's talking . . . ' He drew it out, glancing round the table. McMurdo's grin was pinned to his face by muscular effort. ' . . . a lot of dangerous and half-witted crap.'

'Say again?'

'McMurdo's talking crap. Of course we've got to stay on our toes.

We've always had to. But it's never been part of our thinking to launch a first strike just because it stands a good chance of succeeding – even through fear. The name of the game's survival. Doctor Bardelli's entirely right: even if no one's ever going to write our history – and we can't be sure of that – we don't want to go out entirely mindlessly, do we? Meanwhile there are people dying on Earth; there's a lot to do up here and we still haven't discussed what it is. So, Captain Rathbone, I know you want to get off this subject . . . '

'Your recommendation?'

'No strike, of course, It's a bloody silly idea.'

'Thank you. And now –'

McMurdo stood up abruptly. 'This Command Team meeting is running directly against Pentagon and high executive decision making. Morgan has quite plainly been turned by the Secret Service of an alien country.' Morgan played an unobtrusive chord on his c-unit while Rathbone tried to break in.

'McMurdo, I –'

'Your refusal to acknowledge the Wheel's vital strategic role is at best pacifism and at worst treachery. Neither has a place in the command structure of the USSF.'

'McMurdo, I'm placing you under arrest.'

'Captain Rathbone, I'm placing *you* under arrest.' McMurdo's hand reached inside his overall and came out holding an automatic. While McMurdo spoke Morgan typed rapidly on the keys of his c-unit. 'My authority comes from the DAI. When jet-jockeys and cowboys start unmaking nuclear strategy it's time for the Department to intervene – sit down!'

Rathbone had stood up. He started to walk around the table.

'Please sit down, sir,' said Morgan. 'We don't want to lose you because of this poltroon. There's a better way of handling it.'

'Shut up, jerk,' said McMurdo quietly without looking at him. 'The exalted Deep Operation Agent funks it in his first minute of activation.' He raised the barrel of his automatic to the level of his eyes and aimed it directly at Rathbone's head.

'You can't run a one-man mutiny,' said Morgan. 'The last thirty found it a bit tricky.' He wanted to get McMurdo's attention away from Rathbone. It looked for a while as though he might shoot him.

'This is not mutiny. I'm here to ensure that national defence policy is implemented. So are you.'

'I should say that after about three days you'll want to go to sleep, and then you won't be able to watch all five hundred of the Wheel's crew.'

'I shan't need to. They'll respond to decisive leadership. That's where we came in. Remember?' He spoke into his c-unit. 'Miller. Spight. McMurdo. Take over in here. The rest of you maintain station and stand by.' The door thumped open. The two security men came in at a low-gravity lope. They made sinister figures, helmeted and black visored. They stood behind McMurdo with their arms by their sides. He turned. 'Well, take over. Where are your guns?' They shook their blank heads. Their arms remained by their sides. Morgan touched a key on his c-unit. The less sinister figures of Hawkins and Sarin stepped in, spun the two security guards round, and thrust them out into Command A. As they left it could be seen that their hands were joined behind their backs by loose loops of cable. McMurdo made the mistake of shifting his aim. He tried to swing the automatic through one hundred and eighty degrees to bear on Sarin. Sarin caught his wrist and jerked it up. McMurdo had time to loose off one reflex shot high up through the wall before the crushing pressure of Sarin's one hand around his wrist forced him to drop the gun. Morgan simultaneously heard the shriek of air through the bullet-hole, felt the pressure drop, and heard the door thud closed. The room was instantly hazed with condensation. A generator in the wall near him panned rapidly towards the bullet hole and spewed forth a stream of bubbles. Two small ones popped straight through the hole. The third, which was larger, stopped for a moment and then squeezed through. The fourth, about the size of a grapefruit, hit the wall and stayed. The whistle of escaping air had stopped. The mist cleared. Morgan swallowed as pressure returned to normal. The room was full of gently descending transparent bubbles. Morgan caught one, about the size of a toy balloon. It was already glass-hard.

'Neat, that.'

'First time I've ever seen it work,' said Rathbone. He nodded towards Sarin and Hawkins. 'You're not taking over as well, are you?'

'No. God forbid. I took the liberty of having them on call in case anything exciting happened. We wanted to make ourselves useful. It didn't seem sensible to tell anyone about it. I think there are some security chores to do before we continue the meeting, though, Captain.'

Rathbone nodded and leaned over the nearest console.

'Not so fast,' said McMurdo imaginatively. 'I suppose you two goons know that your vaunted leader is a double? That he's been working for American Intelligence for the last twelve years?'

'Is this true?' asked Hawkins sternly. Morgan nodded.

'Stap me vitals!'

'Fooled me completely,' said Sarin. 'What shall we do with this one, Dick?'

'I don't really know. What should we do with McMurdo, Captain Rathbone?'

'Take him through to the crow's nest. I want to talk to him. Thank you, gentlemen. That was a very good piece of work.' When they had gone he turned to Morgan. 'Good team you've got there, Morgan. Never seen anything like it.'

'Playing fields of Leeds Comprehensive. . . .' said Morgan smugly.

'Wheeldata, Rathbone here. This is a security alert. . . .'

Fourteen

THE MEETING was suspended while Captain Mitchell's Special Space Warfare Unit carried out a security sweep of the Wheel. The marines impressed Morgan and he trusted Mitchell, who was more of a soldier and far less of the politician than McMurdo. Meanwhile Morgan and his SOT team rewarded themselves liberally with beer in the rim bar. Morgan took the opportunity for a quick progress meeting on the Callisto resource.

'Bill, give us an update on the LH_2 situation,' he demanded slipping into the operations room jargon of the Wheel.

'He means he wants you to operate in a data update voice output mode,' said Hawkins.

'It's getting so that I can't understand him half the time. Anyway, there are no problems so far. The next scheduled Milk Train is due to leave Callisto orbit – platform five – in about a week. Fuelling and loading are complete; they're just waiting for the launch window, which is tied to Callisto's orbit around Jupiter.'

Morgan nodded. 'Flight time unchanged?'

'Nine weeks. Give or take a second or two. . . .'

'What happens?'

'Well, nothing much really. *Minerva* leaves Jupiter orbit under solar power. That slings her back along the planetary track. She falls in towards the Sun, burning all the way. The nearer she gets the more power she puts out. Maximum power output as she makes a single decelerated traverse round the Earth. Rendezvous window here is about four hours. Then she accelerates back towards Jupiter.'

'And how much of the hydrogen's left at closest approach? I mean, that's a *really* high energy orbit.'

'All of it. The payload isn't touched. You see, the Milk Train's ideal for our purpose. The solar reflector array heats hydrogen to fusion temperature *direct*. You can't get more efficient than that.'

'Are you *sure* it's all right. Everything's resting on this.'

'Look, Richard, one of those ships has made the Earth-Jupiter cycle every five months for over two years now. Only they've always come back empty. It's a milk-run.'

'But the extra mass!'

'Nothing! She just burns more fuel towards Earth. Don't forget on this trip she goes *home* empty. So measured over the return trip it's a perfectly conventional mission.'

'And they're buying that? Missing a whole supply cycle?'

'Of course they are!' said Hawkins. 'They're worried as hell out there. They might have plenty of LH_2 but that's pretty well all they have got. In the long term they're dead without us. We didn't have to point that out.'

'And security?'

'Is OK. They know that if the Russians get hold of that shipment we've all had it. So *Minerva's* IFF coded and booby-trapped. Only ESA, Eurodefence, Callisto – and us – know about it.'

'Only! Eurodefence leaks like the Straits of Gibraltar!'

'Well I'm certain it hasn't got to the Wheel yet, so don't fret so much.'

'OK. It'll have to do. You've done well.'

'So generous.'

Rathbone called them back to the meeting.

'The subject of the meeting is the station's status after the mutiny. We do a double take on that one.' Despite the preceding events Rathbone seemed to be in a good humour. A few members of the Command Team laughed. The tension seemed to have been eased. Morgan was also pleased as he settled comfortably back into his chair. He hadn't anticipated McMurdo's move, but he couldn't have planned it better himself. He was now a fully accepted member of the Command Team, and Hawkins and Sarin, like Stephanie, were present as observers. Of course he'd never be able to produce them out of a hat again, but that couldn't be helped; they had already delivered more than he could have hoped.

'Specifically we were on crew morale when we got sidetracked into nuclear strategy. Lieutenant Honeywell made what I now see was the very important contribution that it's advisable to involve the crew more in forward planning; and that in order to do so we have to be much clearer ourselves about that forward planning. It's clear that the attempt to do that has enabled us to understand some useful things about our own disagreements. It's also enabled us to see that in our present contingency our forward planning is not necessarily very tight. We can only try to improve that as we go along.

'We can split our activities up into various areas, and I think it's pertinent only to discuss those areas which are affected by the climate change. Now our primary ongoing project is Pluto, and as I'm Project Leader in as far as the Wheel's concerned I can best tell you about it myself. Some of you will not have heard it discussed officially before because the Project has a degree of secrecy which puts it beyond the normal classifications. However, as has been made clear to me we have reached a stage of operations where achievement of objectives becomes impossible without commonly accepted goals. We're on our own now, virtually, and we'll have to make some of our own rules.

'Pluto was set up as a panic project some three years ago when our fears of climatic breakdown hardened into certainties. The chosen location for the climatic shelter was the obsolescent North American Air Defense Command shelter already in existence at a mountain location in Colorado. At its shallowest, it's two hundred metres under solid rock, and it's designed to accommodate up to ten thousand government officials. military personnel, industrial leaders, broadcasters, police and so on, for a period of up to six months. Its new job is to protect the same number from a hostile climate indefinitely – that is, to provide an enclosed environment where human life could go on for centuries if necessary. Now obviously that involved a lot of work.

It needed new nuclear power sources of the breeder type – which haven't been built for the last thirty years. It needed greatly extending in capacity. It needed heat pumps that could cope with outside temperatures of six hundred degrees, reliable hydroponics systems, means of not only purifying oxygen but mining it – you name it. It's a big project, hard to keep secret, hard above all to get finished on time.

'Our job is to oversee the whole schedule. We update their meteorological time-line. We try to keep the country's economy ticking over while they're working, by keeping up the supply from the solar power satellites. And as things get worse we look after their communications, co-ordinate their transport, direct them to resources.

'Then when they're closed in and everything else is finished we keep in contact for as long as possible.'

'Do we have any particular objective when we keep in contact at that stage?' asked Bud Saunders, carefully avoiding the more direct, 'What for?'

Rathbone was searching for an answer. He chose, 'No.' He added, 'I don't think there's anything material we can do at that stage, but I think the outside contact will be valuable for them for as long as we can keep going.'

For as long as we can keep going. It wasn't a question that anyone wanted to raise yet. It wasn't the idea of death that was so terrifying; it was the idea of extinction.

'How long can Pluto really survive?' asked Joe Waldon.

'As I say, it's designed to last indefinitely.'

'But that can't be done. How about nuclear fuel?'

'They breed and reprocess their own.'

'Sure, but it doesn't work that way. You've got to have a source of non-enriched fuel to breed.'

'There are transport arrangements. Protected vehicles.'

'Range?'

'Several hundred miles.'

'But you can't run mining operations from a few tanks.'

'There's a lot of processed fuel in the States. They'll be able to scavenge that.'

'But that's not an indefinite supply. A lot of it will become in-accessible.'

'Well, they won't be idle. They'll be working on solutions all the time.'

'This is all very well,' said Zeffert, taking time off from running the ship. 'No one can doubt that a lot of expertise and work is going into the Pluto shelter. But we've got to recognise the fact that they're going into unknown territory – in both engineering and human terms. It's often been said that they're building something very much like a space ship down there under the mountain, and that because we've had a lot of experience of building space ships they're likely to succeed. But the analogy doesn't hold entirely. For one thing their environment is going to be a lot nastier than ours. I mean we solve our heat balance problem by rotating the spacecraft and occasionally adjusting its disk inclination to the Sun's radiation. It takes almost no energy – and we can get that from the Sun anyway. But they'll be surrounded by increasingly hot rock. They've got to pump heat away, and they've got to use nuclear energy to do it, which makes their heat balance problem even worse. Also they'll be quickly reduced to a state where they have virtually no mobility and so no access to resources. They'll have to make do with what they've got. It's a bit optimistic to assume they can do that for ever. Doc, weren't you saying something about that?'

'About a totally enclosed system, yes. Assuming they solve all their major problems like getting their heat out, you've got all the entropy-related problems. I'm thinking of the life chain, from bacteria, through hydroponic farming, up to the human being. The tendency in a small enclosed system is towards a loss of complexity. Nutrient distribution becomes smoothed out through the food cycle until it's no longer available where it's needed. Species come under attack. Say you lose a bacterium a month because individual bacteria species no longer have the support they used to have from the total environment. Now plant growth and animal digestion are dependent on bacterial assistance. And bacterial imbalances will cause plant and animal disease. So you begin to lose more advanced species. This is an exponential process. In the end you lose human beings.'

'How soon does that happen?' asked Zeffert.

'Maybe some decades. Some few decades. That's a guess, but it's based on some published research with closed communities.'

The mood of the Command Team was now gloomy. Each person was silently pursuing chains of thought that led into a grey timeless future. Rathbone made an assertive attempt. 'My feeling is that the situation isn't that simple. For one thing Pluto doesn't represent the classic closed system. Anyway, it's the only hope we've got. We have to see that it makes a favourable start.'

And then? came the obvious thought, so intense that it was almost audible.

'What are the Russians doing? asked Morgan brightly.

'Chelyabinsk? Doc, what's our intelligence on that one?'

'Mainly inference,' said Bardelli. 'Again they're using a converted strategic shelter. The research on closed systems I mentioned was theirs, so they are just as much aware of the problems as we are. They're keen on cryogenic storage, and my guess is they might be going in for that one.'

'Freezing people? asked Morgan. 'Suspended animation?'

'Maybe, though I doubt it. There are immense problems there. But what you can do is freeze a just-fertilised ovum – and bring it back to life. That way they could preserve a whole ecology in quite a small shelter.'

'How long for?'

'There's the problem. Theoretically you can do it indefinitely – which is a pretty useless term we're bandying about a lot here. You're dependent on the life of your machinery. For complex equipment we can now think in terms of a hundred years or so without maintenance, so they'd have to make a breakthrough there, because a hundred years wouldn't be enough. Then how does a machine bring up a collection of human babies?'

'Ah – if I could just say . . . ?'

'Go ahead, Perkins.'

'Our climatic modelling suggests that the weather's going to settle in a stable mode. It might not come out of it for millions of years – if at all.'

'Quite. So that's the problem. All the same, if that's the Soviet system it's no more chancy than Pluto.'

'I doubt that's their system,' snorted Rathbone. 'If I know anything about the Soviet leadership they'll want survival for themselves.'

'Don't we all,' murmured Zeffert. 'D'you mind if we take a look at the other option?'

'Other option? What other option?'

'Bootstrap,' said Zeffert innocently.

'Now let's be quite clear about this before anyone gets the wrong impression. Bootstrap is an integral part of the Pluto programme. Its purpose is to keep the Wheel and the Powersats in commission long enought to cover the transition phase from a full Earth economy to the sealing down of the Pluto shelter.'

'Oh, I accept that absolutely. But without prejudicing Pluto we can think in terms of extending Bootstrap beyond the transition phase,' Fred Zeffert went on.

'We have had this argument before. I don't see that we can, Fred. Any task we take on beyond the minimum Bootstrap capability will detract from our time spent on Pluto support.'

'I wouldn't want that to happen. But in reality there's so little we can do for Pluto. It's just not putting any load on us.'

'Not now it's not. You wait a month. We'll we working our asses off. Besides, there's no way we can become self sufficient up here. Bootstrap's taking six months' intensive effort and expenditure to give us an extra three months' survival time.'

An extra three months.

'But, Captain, remember our analogy between Pluto and a spacecraft? It breaks down because Pluto's rough environment prevents mobility outside. Well, we're a spacecraft, and we've got mobility. And we can use it to bring in resources. We're in a better position than they are.'

'As you very well know, mobility and resources *are* our problem. To achieve mobility we've got to have propellant, whether for chemical power, nuclear power or solar power. And propellant means hydrogen.' Hawkins and Sarin glanced at Morgan. He frowned them to silence. 'And there is no way we can get hydrogen other than from Earth – and when the weather really clamps down there's no way we can go anywhere near Earth.'

'How about getting hydrogen from Mars? There's plenty of sub-surface and polar ice there.'

'And plenty of Russians there. They can't produce enough even for their own use on the planet, so they're certainly not going to give it to us. We haven't got the resources up here to set up a Mars expedition – let alone a large-scale expedition. And do you realise the propellant cost of getting mass from Mars? We'd spend ten litres of hydrogen on every one we brought back.'

'A telling point. How about putting in some effort on other means of propulsion?'

'Moonshine! We haven't the resources, the time, the brains. Forget it. Understand this. We've thrown away the Earth. There's nowhere else to go. If we can't survive down there we perish. So we put all our chips on Pluto, then we retire from the game.'

Morgan was glad of the secretive instinct that had made him hold back on the Callisto hydrogen. In his present frame of mind Rathbone would have dismissed it – even prevented it.

'And that's what you're going to tell the crew, sir?' asked Stephanie. 'Remember, the point of the discussion was to find a means of *improving* crew morale.'

'You think I ought to make a broadcast?'

'I think it would be better if you went round and talked to them.'

'Then I will.'

'They won't find what you say very palatable, I'm afraid.'

'Maybe not, but I have more faith in your original position than you do. It is not possible to have a better crew, but they need to know clearly what they're working for. They'll respond to the truth.'

Fifteen

By MEANS of certain deft manoeuvres after the meeting Morgan arranged that he, Stephanie and Fred Zeffert met alone in the rim bar to restore their arid tissues. They couldn't dismiss the meeting from their thoughts. Their minds were buzzing with it. Morgan took full advantage of his anomalous position.

'I think the captain was a bit rough on you, Fred.'

'You mean about extending Bootstrap?'

'Yes.'

'He was, I suppose. But he's very committed to Pluto. It's all he ever thinks about.'

'That's a bit strange, isn't it?'

'Not really. It's his job. You see when he was appointed to take over command of the Wheel it was written into the specification. They wanted someone who was a good administrator, whose loyalty to an objective defined for him by the government could be assumed; someone who would put his own interest last.'

'In short, someone who is not very imaginative.'

'I wouldn't say that. More someone who's extremely single-minded and not a little courageous.'

'What do you think, Stephanie?'

'In what way?'

'Rathbone's personal attitude to Bootstrap and Pluto.'

'I agree he's heavily biased – that is if you take the view that Bootstrap could be extended. In fact he seems fanatical about Pluto to the extent that the death of the whole space community after the transition is too insignificant to talk about. You notice he was very emphatic about our having *destroyed the Earth* – as though we'd intentionally gone out and done something to it.'

'Yes. He said something like that to me too.'

'And he made a link between that and the idea that we ought to try to preserve life *on Earth* or die.'

'Right.'

'That's almost martyrdom. And then there's his wife. I think he's very fond of her. Perhaps he can't think of going on living without her.'

'More than that, I think,' suggested Morgan. 'I'd say it fits in better with his attitude that he thinks it's *wrong* to go on living after her death – as though we shouldn't accept a privilege denied to people on Earth.'

'Both of those are typical suicide thinking,' said Stephanie, 'which makes them less than unique on this space station. Nothing can be done about the first type, but it's characteristic of that second sort of symbolic death-wish that the sufferer wishes to make the gesture of dying –'

'And be saved at the last minute?'

'Not necessarily. They might want to make the gesture of really dying without having a preference for being dead.'

'And you think he fits into that category?'

'It seems likely, now that you've mentioned it, though we shouldn't over-simplify. I have got other evidence to go on, though.' She didn't seem prepared to elaborate on that.

'So what are the chances that we can ease him back into a life-wish?'

'Zero. That sort of cheerful chat therapy is a fallacy. The situation itself has to change. Then the state of mind can accommodate to an environment it won't reject.'

'And in this case?'

'The so-called transition period – which is a typically euphemistic term for the deaths of six billion people – will be . . . an almost deadly trauma for us all, in terms of personal tragedy and general identification with humanity. Perhaps it will be worse for Rathbone because his job makes him look constantly at the whole picture where the rest of us can shy away from it into our own little tasks when we need to. I'd guess that a couple of months after the transition it would begin to be normal for his survival instinct to win out again.'

'By which time it will be too late,' said Morgan. 'If we're going to start preparing for post-transition survival it's got to be now.'

'I don't think it's any good. Dick,' said Zeffert. 'OK, so the Old Man's in a bad psychological state. Wouldn't we all be, with his job. But you can't argue with some of what he said. You should know, with your logistics background: we're just not in a position to make it on our own.'

'Why not?'

'Hydrogen. A space community independent of Earth would depend on the economic relationship between the Wheel, orbiting factories like Asisat, and the Moon. Lunar mining provides metals and oxygen – but no hydrogen. The satellites provide industrial production and the solar power to run it. We provide co-ordination mainly through Wheeldata, transport, emergency support and scientific back-up. But the triangle breaks down without the daily use of tons of LH_2.'

'OK. Lunar materials arrive in Earth-orbit by mass driver, which doesn't use hydrogen. The industrial satellites can be moved nearer the Wheel. How about using oxygen as a propellant?'

'Hardly any benefit. The mass-driven containers from the Moon have to be picked up by Hopper-ships, and that uses a lot of propellant: the mass driver's about as accurate as a Roman ballista. I admit we'd save something by moving Asisat as close as is safe to the Wheel, but then a lot of industrial products have to go to the Moon and out to other satellites, so you wouldn't be saving that much propellant. And as for using oxygen as a propellant, the Lunar mines couldn't cope with that scale of production. Obviously it couldn't be used on its own in chemical rocket engines, and in nuclear power plants oxygen plasma would shred the plumbing in no time at all.'

It was a critical moment. The fewer the people who lived, the more significant would be the decisions of each of them. Morgan felt the great weight of history on him. A false move would be cosmically unforgivable – soon cosmically forgotten. He again chose to keep the hydrogen card up his sleeve – unused until when used it would command the game.

'You've obviously thought very hard about the problems of building a self-contained space economy.'

'I have indeed.'

'It's all there.'

'It's all there. Yes, except the hydrogen.'

'Let's talk about scenarios, Fred. We like scenarios.'

'Go ahead.'

'Scenario One: we support Pluto, wave it goodbye as it disappears like a rabbit down a burrow, look around us, find there's nothing we can do but watch the oxygen gauge, and die twiddling our thumbs.'

'But –'

'Scenario Two: we support Pluto, watch it go to earth, and work at survival, probably failing but kissing the universe good-bye on a wave of endeavour.'

'Look –'

'Pluto's not going to make it, Fred. We know that. It's going to be something like Hell down there, literally, and they're never going to see the sun again. Are my scenarios fair?'

'You could look at it that way, but you know damn well that Rathbone won't buy it.'

'Have it ready for him after the transition. He'll go for it then, if Stephanie's right. Justify it as legitimate Bootstrap. I'll square Logistics, and most of it will have to happen there. Those things you can't do, you can have modelled out ready to do when Rathbone gives the word.'

'We've had enough of mutiny already.'

'You know damn well this isn't mutiny. It's insubordination.'

'I don't know how the hell we'd keep it from him.'

'Look, Fred, do you or do you not trust me?'

'Not a bit.'

'Right, so let's go ahead and do it.'

Sixteen

THE LAST shuttle flight from Earth had docked with the Wheel a month ago: its cargo was not the last fifty tons of much-needed liquid hydrogen that had been expected, but a hundred and fifty-four dazed refugees, densely packed. They were USSF personnel from the base in the NASA complex at Kennedy. Some of them had gunshot and stab wounds. They were taken in and tended. No one asked for their story. Three were already dead: a man, a woman and a child.

The reassuring voices of USSF Spacecom and NASA Mission Control were no longer heard. Pluto had closed its massive stainless steel quadruple vacuum lock a week ago. There had been no ceremony. All was still well with them under the Cheyenne mountain. The Russians appeared to be slightly later in their schedule: in their northerly latitude they could afford to be. In the Command Centre and Seat of Government under the Cotswolds a late effort was being made to duplicate Pluto. Morgan's good offices had made a space for Annabel Rawlings there. He wasn't ashamed of that, for so few, if any, would survive. He spent pitiful days coordinating the British battle against extinction. Now he knew what Rathbone's job was like. A few similar efforts were being made elsewhere around the globe, all of them too late, most of them doomed to rapid failure. A sullen haze hung across the whole planet, twisted spitefully by fast-curving cyclones.

'I don't like it,' said Morgan. He was leaning over Zeffert's console in Command A watching a program display that the other was running surreptitiously.

'I thought you were the one who wanted to go out in a blaze of glory!'

'Or preferably not go out at all. What you're suggesting is not only markedly dangerous, but it's not even profitable. You want a shuttle mission to Kennedy to grab one last scoopful of hydrogen before the atmospheric lid goes on. The hydrogen is no longer there so the shuttle crew's got to operate the dissociation plant themselves. There's no electricity so they've got to recommission the Powersat array themselves. And then they'll tank up with . . . say fifty tons of LH_2 and come home. Only they'll burn a hundred and fifty tons getting it here! So we'll be a hundred tons down. Is that right or have I missed something.?'

'It's wrong and you have missed one small thing.'

'What's that?'

'The shuttle goes down empty.'

'What? Completely empty? No fuel?'

'That's right. Just enough for the de-orbit burns.'

'And what if they can't get the LH_2 plant to work? That's more than a possibility. They're stuck.'

'We have a fuelled shuttle standing by up here ready to pick them up.'

'Yes, well that's not so bad – but hang on a minute. Imagine you're the captain of the first shuttle. You're down safely at Kennedy but the dissociation plant won't start. If you call for help it means that the Wheel loses a hundred and fifty tons of LH_2 that it can by no means afford – and risks the loss of another shuttle and crew. It's the ultimate invidious position. You'd be hastening the deaths of six hundred people just to save one shuttle crew for a while. I wouldn't like to be that captain.'

'Dick, you're such an optimist that I think you might be right. Hold on a second – ' He held up a hand to silence Morgan and clapped the other to the headset that was habitually cocked over one ear.

'Are they sure . . . ? No possibility of repair . . . ? Get them to – they have already. Oh. Isn't there something else they – They seem to have checked everything. Tell Copernicus I'll be back with a decision by . . . ' He looked at his c-unit. ' . . . fifteen hundred hours standard. And tell him it'll be docked from his pay! – No, don't. Scrub the pay bit. OK, Wheeldata, thanks. I'll be back before fifteen hundred.'

He tapped the display absently with his headset and jammed it back over his head. 'That was Wheely. Message from Schnieder at Lunar Base. Bad news. It's definitely the delta theta processor that's out. Fused solid.'

'Haven't they got anything else they can reprogram for the job?'

'No. It's a dedicated unit. It's got to be fast, see? So no more Red Cross parcels from the mass driver.'

'Can't they knock one up at Asisat?'

'They can do it blindfold. But that means a lunar mission.'

'Which means a very big hole in our LH_2 reserves.'

'Right. But it can't be helped. We can't manage without Copernicus. I told you it wouldn't be easy.'

'I already knew it.'

Zeffert tapped the display again. 'It rather looks as though your death-or-glory Kennedy mission is on.'

'I take it you're using *your* in some figurative sense.'

'Yeah . . . as beloved by advertisers. . . . '

The four bulkily-suited figures drifted one after the other – Waldon, Hawkins, Sarin, Morgan – along the corridor to the docking gantry elevator airlock. There was no gravity here, so you moved along with light touches on the floor and rails. The astronauts' heads in the soft under-helmets stuck out of the sagging helmet-locking rings like those of tortoises from their shells. The flight crew, Captain Tyler and Lieutenant Brodnik, whom Morgan had come to know quite well after he had debriefed them, had been on board the shuttle for an hour going through their pre-flight checks. Technicians carried the helmets of Waldon, Sarin and Hawkins. Stephanie Honeywell carried Morgan's.

These two and Zeffert had discussed the mission at length. Morgan had spent much time persuading Zeffert not to go – *because not only are you vice-captain of the school football team, but we need you to survive to keep up interest in the post-Bootstrap club*. He had then spent an equal amount of time on the contradictory task of persuading Stephanie that the mission involved no more risk than a scheduled airline flight. She gave him a discreet kiss before he locked his helmet. He tested his Transfer Life Support System once more and stepped into the airlock with the other three astronauts.

The four of them took turns on the flight deck while Tyler and Brodnik changed into their space suits in the lower deck module. Normally a shuttle mission was flown in shirt sleeves: not this one. The all-round view from the flight deck of the McDonnel Douglas SC 3 was an improvement over that from the first generation Rockwell shuttle. Morgan took advantage of it. He hadn't had much time to look out of windows recently.

The space around the Wheel had become more crowded. There

were some twenty shuttles: six docked on the Wheel's mast, nine on either side of the still-growing docking raft, and six parked in matching orbit. The stacked-tyre shape of Asisat hung bright and clear about twenty kilometres west. Near it were three Hopper ships and a lunar ferry. Half way between the two big space stations was NASA's Astronomy and Scientific Research satellite, looking like a pack of beer cans except for the solar panels that spread a hundred metres on either beam. Beyond all these, handy but not so near as to clutter space with their vast area, were the Powersats, fanned out along the geosynchronous orbital track. Their task was almost complete. Soon they could be pirated for their hundred of square kilometres of solar cells and their thousands of tons of precious alloys and components. Zeffert, acting out of pure astronautical genius, had taken advantage of their sail-like construction and tacked them round their orbital track to the Wheel on the solar wind. He had used not one gram of LH_2 on propulsion – just two carefully-timed bursts from their hydrazine reaction control systems that had set each at a constant sun angle. Wheeldata could never have thought of that.

'Earth Mission; Wheeldata. Will you confirm your attitude figures? Over.'

'Wheel; Earth Mission. We are at minus one-eighty point three, minus one-eighty point five, plus twenty-eight degrees. Over.'

'Earth Mission; Wheeldata. Wheel on-board computer copies those figures and affirms guidance lock with your primary inertial navigation and guidance system. You are go for geosynchronous transfer ellipse burn at thirty seconds on my mark . . . MARK. Over.'

'Wheel; Earth Mission. We copy your mark. Over.'

The shuttle was now five kilometres clear of the Wheel. Tyler and Brodnik were in their seats preparing for the series of rocket firings that would transfer the shuttle to an elliptical orbit, then to a low circular orbit, and then to re-entry. From the first to the third burn would take five and a half hours. It was the cheapest way of doing it. The shuttle carried only enough LOX and LH_2 for the most economical re-entry.

From the Mission Specialist's seat behind Tyler and Brodnik which Morgan had begged for the occasion he could see only stars. The other three wouldn't even see that much. They were below in the lower deck module.

'Wheel; Earth Mission. We have ignition. Over.'

'Earth Mission; Wheeldata. We copy. Over.'

The only sound was the subdued whine of the turbopumps transmitted through the ship's structure. The acceleration was barely noticeable.

'Wheel; Earth Mission, Burn ends at fifty-three seconds. Over,' murmured Tyler complacently.

'Earth Mission; Wheeldata. Your new orbit is 296 kilometres by 35,786 kilometres, orientation eighty degrees, inclination twenty-eight point five degrees . . . '

Morgan relaxed and prepared to be bored. For a passenger this was less exciting than he had anticipated. The brilliant rim of the Wheel appeared over the bottom frame of the right-hand windscreen panel. It inched slowly upward, diminishing gradually. There was no sensation of speed. Morgan watched it until it was a tiny disk that disappeared out of the top of the field of view. It seemed to be moving faster by then.

Four and half hours of sporadic s-band dialogue later, after the astronauts had removed their helmets and Morgan had played fifteen hands of poker in the lower deck module – realising for the first time that he had neither handled nor thought of cash for nine months – they strapped themselves in for the low circularisation burn. Fifty-five minutes after that came the de-orbit burn and Morgan caught his first sight of Earth as the shuttle flipped over for re-entry. He briefly saw the thick muddy haze that hid all but a glimpse of the Pacific directly below. Then the nose of the shuttle came up to the thirty-degree re-entry angle and he could see only the horizon three thousand miles away over the Atlantic. He watched the altimeter over Brodnik's shoulder. At a hundred and thirty thousand metres the airframe began to hum with the first hot touch of the atmosphere. This built up to a vibrating roar, and the ionised air glimmered in shock bands around the canopy. Morgan felt his neck and arms pulled forward, and the blood weighing down into his hands and feet. But retardation peaked at two and a half gees, and it wasn't as bad as he had expected. Gradually the nose of the shuttle angled down.

And then he could see the rugged lands of Arizona, New Mexico and western Texas brown and lifeless far below, and far out through the murk to port, Colorado where even now ten thousand were immured for a vigil of countless generations. As the shuttle bit deeper into the upper atmosphere Morgan could see how arid and parched were the fertile plains and valleys of the south-eastern states. There was no green. No life. No possibility of movement. The great Mississippi itself had ceased to be. It was a twisting channel of cracked mud. undifferentiated from the surrounding lands. He wanted nothing more than to withdraw his gaze, but he watched, fascinated. Wheel-data was repeating some monotonous thing but no one answered.

Primary guidance banked the shuttle south east, passing twenty miles to the west of Jacksonville. They crossed a railway line where a train was derailed.

'Wheel; this is Earth Mission. Abort guidance now has visual, and we see the runway. Over.'

There were neat avenues below, chequered off into holiday bungalows and the homes of NASA workers and their neatly squared lawns and amoeba-shaped swimming pools. The lawns were brown and the pools empty. Somehow a sprinkler was still working on one lawn below. The water drifted down wind in a plume of steam. The lawn was still brown. To starboard a plantation of trees was blazing fiercely.

'Earth Mission; Wheeldata. We acknowledge your abort guidance system visual acquisition of the runway threshold. You are go to complete descent on abort visual. Over.'

Now that the ground was so near you could see how fast the shuttle was descending. Brodnik sat inert with his hands in his lap. The robot eyes of the abort guidance system could take in more than his and react faster. But he watched the displays. He was lucky. The runway threshold rushed up, steady as a rock. Abort flared as the shuttle crossed the end of the runway, and, but for the shriek of the tyres, the touch-down was imperceptibly smooth. Abort curved the track of the shuttle neatly to avoid the desiccated carcass of a horse that had strayed on to the runway and died there. Brodnik took over manual control under Tyler's direction. His task now was to try to freewheel to the shutle maintenance area. The taxi-ing route had been worked out from orbit, But Brodnik wouldn't have made it without burning the dregs of the shuttle's LH_2 in one of the powerful turbofan launch engines.

'Wheel; this is Earth Mission at Kennedy. Over.'

'Go ahead, Earth Mission. What's your position and how does it look? Over.'

'Hullo, Fred. Nice to hear a human voice for a change. Over.'

'Don't say that too loud. You never know who's listening. Over.'

'I could make a shrewd guess. We're nicely placed for the refuelling gantry . . . .' The men on the flight deck peered anxiously through the windows. ' . . . Not a very pleasant sight, I'm afraid. Quite a few bodies around. Perhaps twenty. Looks as though there's been something of a pitched battle. Rifles, automatic weapons lying around on the concrete. Some evidence of small-arms damage and maybe grenade damage to buildings. We saw on the way in that at least one of the admin. blocks is burnt out. No evidence yet of damage to the refuelling system. Over.'

'How about transport? Over.'

'Couple of trucks, three cars, station wagon, a minibus. A bit shot up. Flat tyres and that sort of thing. The minibus might be OK. The vehicles that Surveillance mentioned as looking as though they're still fuelled are around the corner of Fuelling Control from here. We're going to hope that they're OK. By the way, I've got all engine arms off and throttles closed. All systems are down and we're on battery power. D'you want me to power up the auxiliary power unit so as to keep cabin temperature down?'

'Negative the APU until you've got some hydrogen on board. Go down to one battery and one fuel cell to prevent LOX boil-off. So you'll have to put on your PLSS packs, which gives you a time limit of four hours for the first stage of the mission. Over.'

Within ten minutes the four space-suited figures emerged clumsily from the shuttle's under-belly hatch. Tyler and Brodnik stayed behind to make sure that all was well with the shuttle. All four loped heavily towards the minibus.

'We've just got to have transport,' gasped Morgan. 'Getting around in these things is going to kill us.'

'Getting around without them would,' replied Waldon. 'They're OK on the Moon! What are you complaining about?'

If walking along a familiar corridor in vacuum had been a disturbing experience for Morgan, walking on Earth in a space suit – and having no choice in the matter – disturbed him more. It brought home to him more than anything else what had happened to his planet.

And it seemed odd to Tyler and Brodnik on the flight deck of the shuttle to watch three astronauts pushing a rusty and dilapidated minibus. A year ago each of their suits could have bought twenty new minibuses. The engine coughed and churned reluctantly into life. Waldon was having trouble in the driving seat. He couldn't feel the pedals through his boots and he couldn't hear the engine through his helmet.

'That won't have done our PLSS pack endurance much good,' gasped Hawkins.

The three of them scrambled into the back of the minibus and it lurched off round the corner. There they wasted ten minutes trying to start the second vehicle – a station wagon that Surveillance had claimed would be drivable – with the battery from the minibus. Both vehicles had deteriorated badly in the extreme weather. Morgan had to sit sideways in the driver's seat because his PLSS pack pushed him hard against the steering wheel. He was thankful that it was an automatic. Sarin had to sit in the back.

'All set? asked Waldon. 'Remember to keep in contact with me and with the shuttle all the time. So if you find yourselves getting masked by something, one of you try to stay clear.'

The two vehicles sped off in their different directions. Morgan had a photograph in front of him with his route marked on it. It repeatedly curled up in the heat. Once clear of the buildings he could orientate himself by means of familiar landmarks like the Vertical Assembly Building and the remaining handful of vertical launch complexes. Soon he could see his objective, a worthy landmark in its own right; jutting out into the lagoon behind the natural breakwater that parallels the Cape Canaveral coast, he could see the files upon files of microwave receptor dishes whose function had been – and would, he hoped, now again be for a while – to gather the energy beamed down to Earth from one of the Powersats. He picked out the powerhouse several hundred metres from the near edge of the four square kilometre array, and headed for it. It was well placed. Although only two storeys high it commanded a wide view of the low-lying Cape. Through the front observation windows Morgan and Sarin could look out over the whole of the receptor array, and over to the swelling seas beyond, for although the wind was gusting to no more than twenty knots they were dashing mightily against the shingle bar. From the rear windows they could make good s-band contact with Joe Waldon. Only from above did the steel roof block microwave radiation.

'Joe; Morgan here. Over.'

'Morgan; Joe. Receiving you clearly. Go ahead. Over.'

'We're at the power-house, and everything seems to be intact. Controls and instrumentation are as expected. How are you doing? Over.'

There were sounds of heavy breathing and a clanking noise. 'Fine. We're at the splitting plant. But we've got a few dozen manual valves to switch which we weren't expecting. Should be no problem. How're your life support readings? Over.'

'Two and a half hours remaining for me. Two hours forty for Bill. We've been drawing on them rather heavily. Over.'

'Right. Let's get on with it. Call me when you're ready to send power. I'll call you when we want it. Over.'

'Check.'

'Powerhouse team, Wheel here,' came Zeffert's voice. 'I gather from that that you're about ready. If you'll confirm all circuit breakers on, then we'll start sending the stuff down. Over.'

'OK, Fred, but what should I do with this three-position switch labelled GAIN? Over.'

'Switch it down to auto. That way as soon as there's some power for the servos they'll track toward peak reception. Over.'

'We've done that, and all main circuit-breakers are on. And I affirm we are not yet switched through to the grid. Over.'

'Morgan; Fred. Good. We don't want to electrocute Joe until he's ready for it –'

'*I heard that.*'

' – so we are switching on power from one satellite on my mark . . . three, two, one, MARK.' The VDU slowly lit up with graphs and digital read-outs in an appealing variety of colours. Outside, the ten thousand dish antennae began slowly, as one, to track across the sky. They reminded Morgan of a fast-motion Walt Disney sequence he'd once seen of a bunch of daisies in the grass slowly tracking the sun across the sky. Unerringly they pursued power. The power peaked as they found the satellite and gazed directly at it. Then they were still.

'Well done, you lot,' Morgan said to the antennae. 'Fred, we've got twenty megawatts here. Joe, you can have any amount of that whenever you want it.'

The cold liquid gas was pulsing along the insulated umbilicals into the shuttle's voluminous tanks. It was now late afternoon and the six tired astronauts were relaxing in the lower deck module. Normally you didn't hang around a refuelling spacecraft if you could help it, but they felt they needed a long break while their PLSS packs were being recharged. The cabin atmosphere was quite comfortable. Although Zeffert hadn't let them use the APU because of the fire risk, he was allowing them to use more battery power.

They were just settling down hungrily to an unappetising meal when he came on the air again. 'Earth Mission; Wheel here, a couple of items. One is that there's quite a storm brewing a thousand miles south of you, so we feel that as everything's going well you should refuel through the night without a break. This would allow you to launch through the next window at about ten hundred hours.

'The other thing is that there's a Soviet Backfire G or H, Surveillance isn't sure which it is, heading down the coast towards you. He's doing about five hundred knots – trying to stretch his fuel I should think, because he's at extreme range. Our guess is that he's probably just coming to look you over, but you know how these things are, so I think it's safest for you to get well clear of the shuttle until he's made his intentions clear. No point in stopping the refuelling though.'

'Fred; Joe here. Where is he?'

'Just coming up on Jacksonville. That gives you about half an hour. Don't leave it too long though. He might up his speed. Over.'

Waldon acknowledged the sighs and oaths of his colleagues, and replied, 'Wheel; Earth Mission. We acknowledge your EVA recommendation, and we think it stinks. However, we will comply. Keep us posted on the intruder. Over.'

'Thank you, Joe. Will do. I'm sorry about that, but we've got to cover the possibility. Give me a shout when you EVA. Over.'

The six space-suited men were taking cover behind a low blast-wall five hundred metres up wind of the shuttle when Zeffert told them that they should be able to see the Backfire. The lowering sun was hidden by the murk in the west and the sky was red. It was hard to see. The arrival of the Backfire was first apparent as a patch of black smoke against the haze to the north. The centre of the smoke developed a dark nucleus which resolved itself into a lean and hungry profile.

'If they use a nuke we've had it,' said Tyler, almost to himself.

If they use a hand grenade we've had it, thought Morgan.

The bomber was flying at about seven hundred feet and five hundred knots. It seemed to be taking the line of the runway, but it banked steeply and roared over the watching men.

'Doesn't look aggressive,' said Waldon. 'He's got his wings forward.'

'He's going to make another pass,' replied Brodnik. 'Don't count your chickens.' Sure enough the big bomber banked steeply, the sun sending a red gleam across its wings. Its turn took it out to sea.

'I don't think he's likely to attack,' said Morgan. 'His whole approach is too leisurely.'

'It can afford to be. There's nothing we can do to stop him.'

'He's dropping his undercarriage!'

'He's going to land!'

The Backfire banked again sharply across the wind and turned tightly into the approach. It was a good landing, right on the runway threshold. The bomber sank firmly on its wide-spread undercarriage and three braking parachutes streamed out behind it. But the heat was too much for the conventional aircraft tyres. As the nosewheel touched down there was a spark from the starboard main under-carriage bogie and a ribbon of red fire trailed after it down the runway.

'We're going to need a car!' snapped Morgan.

'We can't start one up. They're both in the refuelling area.'

'Then we'll have to push it clear!'

'Tyler, Brodnik, get to the shuttle airlock. Get oxygen bottles.'

Already the six men were running to the shuttle. The Backfire had slewed sharply off the runway. The whole area shook as the pilot brought up the thrust of the engines to keep it moving, to keep the flames from the mid-section wing tanks – to get that crucial bit nearer safety. It was agony pushing the minibus clear of the refuelling zone, for each man was carrying forty-five pounds on his back, and the space suits restricted movement.

The last tyre on the Backfire's starboard bogie exploded, and the undercarriage leg jabbed into the concrete. The engine revs sighted musically down toward silence. The minivan wouldn't start and the three men pushing it were fighting for breath. The trap under the Backfire's nose dropped open and a figure jumped down. He turned and helped the other crewman out. They started to run towards the minibus. The bus started, and it had to cover another kilometre of burning white concrete. Morgan managed to climb in. Sarin and Hawkins fell back, stooping and gasping for air. The two figures ran on. They'd been out in the searing air for fifteen seconds now. Waldon had his foot hard down. Twenty seconds, and the Russians were flagging, their legs buckling under them. One fell. The other stopped and went back. He tried to lift his fallen companion across his shoulders. He stood erect, staggered a few paces forwards and fell to his knees. Bravely he stood again, still carrying his companion. The minibus skidded round to a halt. The Russian stepped forward slowly and intensely and placed his fellow crewman in the bus. Morgan hauled him in as the bus started, handed him the oxygen bottle, and concentrated on the unconscious figure. Both were wearing Soviet issue partial pressure suits, but the rubber oxygen hoses hung loose under the faceplates. Morgan unplugged his 'buddy' oxygen line, turned up the supply and tried to connect it to the Russian's hose. There was no hope that they would fit. He held them together, trying to seal off the leaks with his hands. There was a movement behind him. The oxygen bottle had fallen from the other Russian's grasp. He too was unconscious.

'Step on it, will you?' shouted Morgan. 'These poor sods are dying.'

'I'm flat out. I'm going to take it right up to the shuttle. We can coast the last couple of hundred yards.'

The two Russians were laid out on bunks in the lower deck module. Morgan and Waldon had unlatched their visors and were feeding them pure oxygen. Morgan was attending to the stronger one, the man who had carried his companion so courageously.

'It must have fried their lungs, trying to run out there,' said Waldon. Morgan nodded. His patient's face was grey and beginning to blister. His eyelids quivered.

'This one's got a chance.'

The Russian's hand came up and pushed aside the oxygen mask. He opened his eyes. His dry tongue moved across his blistered lips. 'Thanks,' he said, painfully.

'It's OK. Take it easy,' smiled Morgan.

'You speak Russian then?'

'Yes,' said Morgan. 'Stay quiet for a bit, eh?'

The Russian nodded. 'Take us with you. Please.'

'Don't worry. That's our plan.'

The Russian nodded his gratitude and relief. He turned his head painfully to see his companion. 'Will you take me over there?'

'You'd do better to rest.'

The Russian shook his head. 'I don't think so.'

Morgan looked at him carefully and then turned to Waldon. 'Can you spare a hand?'

'Surely.'

'We're taking this one over there.'

'Don't be stupid.'

'We're doing it.'

They lifted him to his feet and carried him across to the other bunk, his inert legs trailing. They let him down to a kneeling position and supported him. Painfully he reached out and took the hand of his companion. He pressed it to his lips. Then the quivering muscular effort ceased. Morgan felt for the carotid pulse. 'He's gone,' he whispered.

'So's she,' said Waldon. Morgan looked at the face of the other Russian. Dark eyes, long lashes, smooth skin. A fringe of black hair showing in disarray under the helmet rim. A young and pretty face. The heat hadn't scorched it, for she had stopped breathing long before the man.

Morgan looked away. 'They go with us,' he said with difficulty. How could you mourn the deaths of six billion? Grief for these two strangers filled Morgan's heart to the brim.

The shuttle squatted, her sharp nose pointing down the five-thousand metre concrete ribbon of the Kennedy runway. Her fuel tanks and payload bay were gorged with hydrogen.

'Wheel; Earth Mission,' said Tyler. 'We're in fan mode with throttles at low idle. Fuel systems, power systems, guidance systems are go. All circuit breakers are checked, all lights are green and we're ready to go. Only problem is the weather. It's a little worse than marginal. Over.'

'Earth Mission; Wheel,' said Zeffert. 'Your transmission is breaking up badly. . . .' So was his. The earphones whistled and crackled frustratingly with atmospheric interference. ' . . . We copy your launch readiness. Also the weather. You're on the edge of a cyclonic disturbance that can only get worse in your area for the next twelve hours. You could sit it out for that period, but things might get pretty hairy down there. We think you'd have to shelter the shuttle, but it will be clear by the next launch window. Over.'

The wind was blowing across the runway at twenty knots, gusting to fifty. On the flight deck the rocking of the shuttle was noticeable. Sea spray was rattling against the windscreen, and the runway was visible for only half of its length. Occasional debris was blowing across the field of vision.

'Wheel; Earth Mission. We copy your options. I don't know how long this runway's going to stay usable if we don't go now. Also we'd have fuel boil-off problems. not to mention the corrosion we're letting ourselves in for. I'm going for launch now. Over.'

'Earth Mission; Wheel. We confirm your judgement. Confirm you are go for launch. I'm handing you over to Wheeldata. Over.'

'Wheel; Earth Mission. We're launching in abort guidance. There's no way we can go manually in this weather. The shuttle is now in abort guidance. Fan revs stabilising at ten thousand five, brakes coming off . . . rolling – rolling *now*. Over.'

The shuttle surged forward in a cloud of spray and steam. As it picked up speed the sharp senses of abort guidance eased it through turbulence, wind-shear and the streaming water on the runway with the minimum of deviation. The fan engines swallowed tons of sea water, but they kept burning. The shuttle lifted off and began its ever steepening climbing turn.

'Wheel; Earth Mission. Abort has switched to Primary guidance. Speed nine hundred kilometres per hour. Altitude ten thousand metres. Over.'

Blessedly, the Earth could not be seen. Morgan had had enough of it in its present state, though the idea that he'd just stepped on it for the last time depressed his already saddened mood.

'Wheel; Earth Mission. Speed two thousand one hundred kilometres per hour. Altitude seventeen thousand metres. Primary has completed staging to ram mode. Thrust is nominal. Over.'

Morgan thought of the dead couple in the module below. They had finished their struggle. but they had died, no matter how painfully, in a privileged state of action, love and hope. He fell to thinking of Stephanie, what they would be doing when they died, and whether those deaths were written into the program early. . . .

' . . . Speed thirteen thousand eight hundred kilometres per hour, altitude eighty-five thousand metres, still in Primary. Staging from ram to rocket mode. We have ignition . . . .'

Seventeen

FIVE AND a half hours later the shuttle was back in geosynchronous orbit, matching that of the Wheel, only five kilometres ahead of it. Barring the unlikely event of a docking accident the cargo of liquid hydrogen was safe. And on the Wheel they knew it. They could now start spending it. 'Earth Mission; Wheel. If you're interested you can see the lunar ferry beginning its TLI burn. It's about ten degrees out from Asisat. That's your cargo they're going to be burning. We've got to the state of spending it before we get it. Over.'

'Fred, we've got to watch out for that,' said Morgan seriously. 'We can't go living beyond our means. Over.'

'What means? Yeah, I know. We'll talk about it. Over.'

They crowded up on the flight deck and looked out of the windows. 'Go easy on the hydrazine,' said Morgan as Tyler yawed the craft with his sidestick so that they could get a better view. Tyler looked at him in surprise. 'Sorry, Captain.' He winked at Brodnik. Morgan didn't notice.

The lunar ferry looked remarkably akin to the lunar module that had first kicked up dust in the Sea of Tranquillity half a lifetime ago. It was squat, wide, leggy and cluttered. But it weighed two hundred tons. Its reactor propulsion system could power the craft in either of two ways. For lunar landing and take-off, where a lot of thrust was needed, liquid hydrogen would be pumped fast through the incandescent reactor core. It wasn't outstandingly efficient, but lunar gravity doesn't make great demands on propulsion. For the more casual matter of leaving Earth orbit the reactors generated electricity in a closed cycle which was then used to accelerate a stream of ionized hydrogen. It wasn't remarkably powerful but its tenfold efficiency conserved fuel.

'There she goes!'

Brodnik's cry seemed melodramatic for the lunar ferry went nowhere. There was a brief spark of white light from the honeycomb

nozzle area between its three landing engines, which then subsided to
a blue glow that was only faintly visible against the blackness of space.
The efflux itself couldn't be seen. The ferry appeared to remain
stationary. But after twenty minutes of acceleration at one-tenth gee
it had picked up a thousand metres per second of velocity and was
dwindling far out beyond the Wheel's orbit. It would accelerate for an
hour yet, spiralling out from the Earth on its way to the Moon.

'Earth Mission; Wheeldata. The docking gantry is now clear. You
are authorised to begin close rendezvous manoeuvre. Over.'

'Thank you, Wheeldata. We have an Acquisition and Docking
program. Over.'

Both Rathbone and Zeffert were in the reception area to meet the
returning astronauts – Rathbone making a serious display of
generous commendation, though it was still in the name of the Pluto
project that he congratulated them. He finished by giving them
twelve hours to recuperate before debriefing. At that point the
medical team came through from the docking gantry elevator airlock
carrying two stretchers shrouded in white plastic. Rathbone stood at
attention with his head slightly bowed until the stretchers had left
reception. The others followed suit. On the way out of reception
Zeffert caught Morgan's arm.

'Fancy a beer before you turn in?'

'Is it really that time? To tell you the truth I feel so damned shagged
I don't know if I can even hold a pint.'

'Oh, come on. It'll do you a world of good. You need to wind
down. Hell, *I* need to wind down.'

The rim bar seemed as much like home now as had almost any place
on Earth – almost; given the unequal balance between memory and
immediacy. Morgan sat trying to keep his eyes open, wondering if it
was worth reaching out for his beer, vaguely upset that Stephanie
hadn't shown up and thrown ticker-tape over him – or something . . . .

'I expect it was your idea to bring the bodies back?'

'Who told you that?'

'Just a lucky guess. For someone who's keen on survival it was a
pretty non-survival thing to do. I suppose you know how much
hydrogen that cost?'

'Yes: not much comparatively. Anyway, the hell with the

hydrogen.'

'That doesn't sound like the post-Bootstrap enthusiast I used to know. You used to care more than that.'

'I care more. But you've got to give some thought to what it is that's doing the surviving – an intelligent, sensitive species or a mindless resources-grabber.'

'Good. You've put my mind at rest. I was wondering if Stephanie and I were going to have to tackle the problem on our own.'

That was a strange thing to say. Especially after such a mission. Stephanie? 'Is this all leading up to something? I'm not stupid. I'm tired. You are going to say something about Stephanie.'

'She's on that lunar ferry.'

'No.'

'She is. I was trying to lead up to it subtly. Sorry – '

Morgan stood up, spilling his beer. 'What stupid prat let her do that?' he shouted. Then, more quietly. 'Don't you realise what that means? She's stuck there. We may never – !' He slumped into his seat, overpowered by the thought.

'You can do better than that, Dick.' Morgan looked up sharply. 'She's got more faith in you than you have yourself. D'you remember how it started? I was saying how we couldn't survive for long because we'd no supply of hydrogen, and you said *Do it anyway*. You seemed so confident that you persuaded me. And you persuaded her. She's gone to the Moon to work for your idea, to make sure they play their part! So, was that all bravado? Have you taken us in with a load of bullshit?'

'No, it wasn't bullshit.'

'Then what's all this about never seeing her again? That doesn't sound like survival.'

'I didn't say we'd survive. I said it was better to survive or die trying than to just give up. It's a different matter losing . . . '

'Yes, I know about that. I've seen you two together.'

'I didn't know it was obvious.'

'It wasn't. Well, not very. I'm not stupid either.'

'How did she manage to get on the ferry?'

'It wasn't fully loaded: a whole lunar mission just for one integrated circuit. Rathbone was worried about the fuel waste – as he should have been. Copernicus is having its morale problems too – obviously. Serious ones. And they've no psychologist of any calibre. Rathbone was impressed by her handling of the morale problem here. So . . . '

He shrugged. 'She left me with the problem of telling you. Some problem.'

'Sorry.'

'Don't. I know how it is. But you haven't really given up hope, have you? I got the impression you really thought we could make it – though I never saw the slightest reason why.'

Morgan again felt the weight of history on his words, and at the moment he particularly did not want it. 'We can make it. We keep at it.'

Somehow that seemed to satisfy Zeffert, and Morgan couldn't see why *that* was so. He supposed it difficult for a man of Zeffert's character to have no hope. He was turning a blind eye on logic because he too wanted to end on a brave note.

The day after the debriefing the funeral of the two Russians took place. Rathbone insisted on giving them a Christian burial – ' . . . we therefore commit their bodies to space . . . ' – and they were sent off in a single aluminium coffin bolted to a hydrazine reaction control motor scavenged from one of the Powersats. They would orbit the Sun alone together for five billion years yet . . . .

The commander of the space station Astrogorodok, Commodore Litvinov, was present – by TV from synchronous orbit on the far side of the Earth. Rathbone had called Morgan – with others – to observe when he had called up the Commodore on the hot line frequency.

'Of course we want to do the right thing about the funeral,' he had said, 'but that doesn't mean that at the same time we can't do a little discreet probing about Astrogorodok's status – particularly its resource status.'

He'd made a call from Command A because he first wanted to take a look at the Russian space station. It too had changed a great deal since Morgan had first seen it. At the moment there were three views on the surveillance screens: one telescopic view from an American geosynchronous spy satellite whose permanent job was to watch the Soviet ship; a closer panned view from another satellite in a high elliptical orbit that would pass within a hundred kilometres of it; and detailed shots pirated from a TV-controlled repair robot which the Russians were using themselves.

Yet more cylindrical modules had been attached to the intricately sculptured space station. Some more hydrogen tankage had been added, but it amounted to only a third of the Wheel's reserves. There were sixteen kosmolyots in attendance, two lunar ferries, and one of the two huge nuclear craft that they kept in perpetual cycle between Mars and the Earth. Morgan doubted that they had the fuel to launch just this one, and they had sixty men and women on Mars.

Commander Saunders made the connection through his opposite number on Astrogorodok, and Rathbone slid into the seat.

'Commodore Litvinov, this is Captain Rathbone of the United States Space Force Station S-101. Do you hear me?'

'Yes, I hear you Captain Rathbone. These are hard times to live in, are they not? Are you in any difficulty?'

'No, we're not in any difficulty, Commodore Litvinov. How fares it with you? Have you any problems?'

'No, Captain, we're in fine shape here.'

'How are your consumable reserves? Can you hold out for long?'

'Our consumables are good. We can survive for a very long time,' said the Russian, his face quite unreadable. 'How about you?'

'Yes, we are in very good shape here. We have no problems in the foreseeable future.'

'Is there any particular subject which you wish us to discuss?'

'Yes, there is. In the last couple of days we made an excursion to the Kennedy Space Flight Center.'

'We were aware of your Earth Mission.'

'Er, quite. During the mission we picked up two of your comrades, a Colonel Belayev and Natasha Belayev.'

'The, er, *crew*, I take it, of the Tupolev 26 aeroplane?'

'Those are they. Unfortunately we were not quick enough to save their lives. We mean to commit them to space at thirteen hundred hours tomorrow, your time. We invite you to take part in the ceremony by communication on this frequency.'

'You understand , Captain Rathbone, that Colonel Belayev was disloyal to the AV-MF in that action?'

'I understand that, Commodore. I also understand that his action occurred at the end of the World, when he wasn't blessed by our privilege of prolonged survival and the AV-MF had no more use for their Tu-26. Also that in the reports of my crewmen he was shown to have died bravely. It's enough for us.'

'I accept that, Captain. We will listen in on this frequency at thirteen hundred tomorrow.'

'Meanwhile, if there's anything at all we can . . ?'

'There is nothing. Goodbye and good luck, Captain Rathbone.'

'All the best, Commodore Litvinov.' He terminated the link.

'Poor lying sod,' said Rathbone. 'They haven't more than a month or six weeks' survival left. Too proud to say it.'

Zeffert and Morgan exchanged surprised glances. 'You weren't all that candid yourself, sir,' said Zeffert. 'We're not a great deal better off ourselves.'

Rathbone led him to one side as the Team drifted out of Command A. 'Listen, Fred, I was impressed by your work in putting together the Earth Mission – and by the performance of the crew. It's made me do some thinking. Now that we're through the bulk of the Pluto support programme and most of our other roles are no longer appropriate, I think we ought to be giving some consideration to extending our, er, life viability out here.'

'I'm very glad to hear that, sir.'

'I believe that there are some problems that we can't get over, like the lack of LH$_2$ resources, but I don't see why we shouldn't be able to extend our, er, stay-time by a couple of months or so. Don't mention it to anyone because I think the crew's accepted the position, and I don't want to raise anyone's hopes. Can you try to give me some sort of breakdown of our options in a couple of days?'

'I'll do my best, sir.'

'That's what I like to hear. It's what I expect to see everyone do as we, ah, approach the final, ah, situation. Get Morgan to help you.'

Eighteen

ABOUT A fortnight later they discovered how the Russians planned to replenish their hydrogen.

Morgan was becoming accustomed to surprise awakenings so he found himself out of bed and alert before he knew why. His cabin light had come on. From outside his door came the repetitive, insistent, nerve-racking howl of the Alert klaxon, and Wheeldata's broadcast voice. 'This is an amber alert. Red and Blue teams to duty stations . . . . This is an amber alert . . . ' Inside the cabin Wheel-data was delivering a more specific message. 'Mister Morgan, this is Wheeldata. There is a military threat probability alert. Please proceed quickly to Command A. Acknowledge.'

Within a minute Morgan was flying – almost literally – along the long upward-curving corridor. He was glad to be on the same floor as the operations room. There were long impatient queues at the two elevator doors that he passed. Rathbone was already there at the Command console, and the other Command A personnel from the Red and Blue teams were pouring in, still pulling at zips and rubbing the sleep from their faces. The threat level couldn't have been that high after all. The crew were reporting to their Team Commanders and then rushing to queue at the coffee machines. Morgan deftly short-circuited the process by reporting to the coffee machine first. That put him well ahead of the field. Holding two cups he walked over to Rathbone's console at the front of the auditorium.

'Coffee, Captain? What's the confidence factor?'

'Good man. No sugar I hope? The factor's at twenty-one point five at the moment. It doesn't amount to a certain attack by any means, but it's the highest I've ever seen it.'

'What's it based on?'

Rathbone gestured to the screens at the front of the auditorium. 'We're not getting any data from our satellites near Astrogorodok.'

'Malfunction?'

'Negative. They're the only ones affected. We're still getting signals from them, but nothing coherent.'

'They've been blinded.'

'Looks like it.'

'Then an attack could be on its way already. Can you pick up anything from *their* satellites on the other side?'

'Negative. The cunning bastards have closed them down. We're blind. Bud reckons we goofed when I talked to Litvinov. We let them see we were intercepting their TV transmission.'

'Have we made any response?'

'No. I don't want to over-react. And in defence you've got to keep your options open until you know what you're dealing with.'

'Any point calling Litvinov on the hot line?'

'Not at the moment. I don't want him to know how little *we* know.'

Wheeldata was showing the confidence factor as thirty-four per cent. 'That's on account of the lapse of time since we lost the satellites,' said Rathbone, nodding at the display.

Zbijowski called over the intercom. 'Zylka, Captain. We've got visual tracking for the beam system on their twenty nearest spy satellites. We can hit them all in one revolution on your instruction. Over.'

'Fine. Hold it at that. Compute second priority targets for a subsequent sweep. Over.'

'Have done, Captain. Meanwhile I've got birds here waiting to fly. If we leave our defensive missiles until they show over the horizon, by the time we get there they'll have deployed decoys and MIV'd their warheads. That's sure to take down our kill ratio. So how about we let them go now? Over.'

'Wheeldata says to hold on the ABMs, Zylka. They might go for a retrograde attack in which case we'll have put all our eggs in the wrong basket. They might even hold back their attack so that we blow all our defensive capability on empty space. He suggests we hold until we get radar confirmation of the attack through the atmospheric lense.'

'OK, Captain. Will do.'

Wheeldata stepped the confidence factor up to forty per cent. Rathbone leaned over his console. 'Docking and Movement Control: I want all operational shuttles scrambled and dispersed. I want them way out from the Wheel so that there's complete fifty kilometre separation all round. Over.' He turned to Morgan. 'That'll play hell with our LH$_2$ reserves.

'Security: I want Commander McMurdo here on the double. We need him.'

'If there is an attack, sir, how long will it take to get here?'

Rathbone pointed to a display. 'That's Wheeldata's projection of the most likely attack, based on Astrogorodok's estimated weapons capability. All the missiles approach on very elliptical orbits, just grazing the Earth's atmosphere. That's the quickest orbit and it keeps us guessing for longest because they stay hidden until their mid point. Now some of them stay in the equatorial plane, and they can make it in about six hours. They can spread them right up to polar orbit which takes more energy and increases the flight time by maybe half an hour. Just a few may come round the Earth in retrograde orbit – from the east: that uses a dickens of a lot of energy and takes an hour longer. Total: thirty launch vehicles, maybe a quarter of them retrograde.'

'Thirty doesn't sound too bad. Can we cope with that?'

'We can cope with thirty. But at some stage in their flight they split up into maybe ten warheads – MIVs – and decoys *each*. That makes it more difficult.'

'That's why Zylka wants to launch his ABMs?'

'That's right: to hit them before they MIV, or when the MIVs still have only a small dispersion.'

'Sounds like a good idea,' said Morgan, meaning *Why the hell don't you do it*?

When McMurdo was brought in by two guards Morgan drifted tactfully away. He fetched another coffee and sat watching the master displays, trading off in his mind the defensive strength of the Wheel against Astrogorodok's theoretical attack – and wondering unsuccessfully what the unexpected elements would be.

Sandra Crabtree slumped down beside him with an indignant sigh. 'OK, Mister smart-ass secret service.'

'Ah, hullo, Sandra. Nice to see you.'

'So you pilloried McMurdo, and he was right all along.'

'Just what I was saying to myself,' replied Morgan obligingly. 'It was his pulling a gun that put me on the wrong track. Now I realise he's been a jolly good chap all along.'

'If I remember correctly I outlined the strategic options to you, and explained which was the correct logical choice for each side.'

'And this looks like either option Two or option Four, depending on whether we just defend, or defend and counterstrike.'

'Precisely.'

'Quite so. It shows what a logical sort of person Commodore Litvinov is. But perhaps we could take the rest of that conversation as read. What bothers me is why they're doing it.'

'That is precisely the sort of question which reveals your logical ineptitude. The motivation is *in the logic*. They've launched an attack because it's the move dictated by survival criteria.'

'Which are?'

'Preventing us doing it first.'

'Do unto others etc. etc., only do it first. Yes. We'll overlook the fact that we weren't going to do it to them.' He held up his hand to forestall her irate response. 'Yes, I know. But I was thinking of different survival criteria. What if they're after our hydrogen?'

'After our hydrogen?' She appeared to be considering it. 'I don't know. I'd have to game it out.'

'I'm not asking for an in-depth blow-by-blow decision diagram. I'm just suggesting that they might want some of what we've got, and that they're setting about getting it.'

'They'd have to knock us out without knocking out the hydrogen tanks. And they'd have to be sure we wouldn't destroy the tanks to prevent them getting the hydrogen. And they'd have to be sure it would work because they're blowing a lot of their resources and capability in doing it. Right. So I don't really see it. It looks too chancy for them.'

'And yet,' murmured Morgan, 'I can't see them starting something so monolithically destructive to both sides without some positive survival aim – and some high probability of accomplishing it.'

'Unless it's a last effort in a desperate situation.'

'They might be desperate, but I'd still expect their actions to be cool.'

Rathbone had been right to take McMurdo out of cold storage. He knew the surveillance systems available to the Wheel better than anyone. He took a spy satellite in low orbit which was just passing over Earth's northern horizon, and spun it. Then he switched on its radar. Instead of probing Earth's clouds as it had been designed to do, it now swept its beam across the hidden wedge of space on the far side. By now the scene in Command A was more disciplined. The commanders and the full complement of their teams were at their consoles, and the room hummed with subdued activity. McMurdo's voice came over the address system.

'Surveillance. We're now getting a radar picture of the occulted space zone. I'm putting it on the master screen.'

A hundred pairs of eyes were raised anxiously to the screen. Wheeldata was building up the radar picture slowly, line by line. Once or twice in each line a trace was left, and the computer labelled it as a known satellite, or enclosed it in a red diamond to indicate a probable threat.

Halfway through the sweep the picture started to break up. There were no more clean returns, just meaningless variations in signal intensity.

'The Soviets are now on to our radar sweep, and they're putting out heavy electronic counter measures. I'll put all the power to the radar that the satellite's got, and run an enhancement program on the picture.'

The image had built itself up to half the screen height when it started to show an echo far brighter than all the others. When the computer enhancement caught up with that point on the scan the image was sharpened to show the linked but discrete shapes of a mass of separate cylinders. The satellite's beam had caught Astrogorodok. And the satellite had, in its turn, been caught. For an instant the moving trace bloomed into an intense white light and then the picture dissolved into a storm of dancing points.

'Beam weapon,' said McMurdo. 'They've fired down the radar vector. To be expected. We've lost our eye. I'm getting Wheeldata to display the battle information that we've got.'

The computer drew on the screen a model of the Earth, squared off by its coordinate system. From a point behind it – the computed location of Astrogorodok at the instant of firing – it drew a series of curves that marked the orbits of twenty-seven missiles. They spread out, petal-like, to graze the globe at all latitudes of both hemispheres. Then Wheeldata added a further twenty-seven that he reckoned the radar had missed.

'That's how it looks, Captain. We haven't plotted them all, but there's enough there to show they're going for a random spread around the terrestrial horizon. I recommend you now put out their satellites on this side and initiate the standard response.'

'Thank you very much, Mac. That was a smart piece of work. Any sign of a strike against Pluto?'

'Negative, Captain.'

'Bud, give Pluto a rundown on the attack. Tell them to keep their heads down. Tell them we can handle it.'

Morgan looked across at McMurdo. He looked happy to be busy, not pushing his vindication. Perhaps he'd gamed it out and opted for a low profile.

'Zylka, power up the beam weapon. Fire in your own time on your original primary and secondary targets. When we've taken out their eyes on this side we can launch some ABMs.' He was answered by the distant scream of the Wheel's power-generation turbines coming up to full emergency revolutions.

'Preparing to fire under computer guidance, Captain.'

There was a howl and an echoing bang as the tunnel of super-conducting magnets was slammed back against its mountings. On the target screen to the left of the battle display a point of light appeared in space and puffed into oblivion. Seven thousand kilometres away a surveillance satellite had been hit by a stream of protons with the energy of an artillery shell. The beam weapon fired thirty times within two revolutions of the Wheel.

'We've hit everything within range, Captain.'

'Good shooting. What's your recommendation on the ABMs, Zylka?'

'Best computed option, Captain, is that we fire to intercept them ten minutes *after* they come up round the horizon. If we fired earlier they could retrofire their own missiles, so that ours would be out of sight before theirs appeared. That way we couldn't control the interception. But if we fire later, as soon as theirs come up we can go into terminal manoeuvre and zap them quickly. We should send out a second wave maybe five minutes later to cover our failures and the incoming shots we haven't spotted.'

'So you'll be sending off twenty-seven in the first wave?'

'That's it, Captain. And another twenty-seven in the second. That'll leave us forty-six in reserve.'

'OK, Zylka, fire on Wheeldata's timing. Sandra, what is our capacity to change this spacecraft's position? Now that we've knocked out their spy satellites we don't want to be where their missiles are expecting us to be.'

'We have it computed in with the battle model, sir. Any LH_2 expenditure we can bear gives us a very poor orbital displacement. We've got to assume their missiles have active terminal guidance, so they're going to pick up any marginal shift in our position anyway. Zylka says that in the terminal battle phase it's easier for us to hit their warheads if they're coming straight for us than if they jink at the last moment. So we recommend that we limit our evasive manoeuvring to attitude control. That way we can present our smallest profile to their sensors.'

'Affirmative all that, Sandra.'

'Fred here, Captain. I've had Wheeldata working on the idea of manoeuvring three of the Powersats into decoy positions for the terminal phase. With their radar cross-section we can expect some of the incoming stuff to home on them in error. What d'you think?'

'As long as they don't interfere with our own sensors, and they've got to be far enough away so that we don't get hit by debris.'

'Wheeldata's worked out the tactical problems, Captain. It checks out in all those respects.'

'Affirmative that, then, Fred. Leave it with Sandra. I need you free.'

'Check.'

'Captain; Zylka. We've launched ABMs. Two duds, replaced from reserves. Can we have a decision on our counterstrike?'

'Hold that counterstrike, Zylka. I repeat, hold. An early launch gives us no advantage now, and I want to keep our options open on that one.'

'Captain, Colonel Schnieder from Copernicus Base on the s-band.'

'Put him through, Bud.'

'Captain Rathbone, Schnieder here. How do you read me?'

'Rathbone here; loud and clear, Colonel. Go ahead.'

'We're coming under heavy artillery fire from three points about five kilometres distance. A lot of infantry movement in between. Over.'

'How do you estimate your capacity to respond? Over.'

'We're managing to intercept their incoming shells. But if they come any closer we won't have the response time. We're taking small arms damage but the patch system's holding air leakage . . . I've just heard they've taken the mass driver. That means twenty men dead or captured. We've taken no casualties in the main base yet, but they're littering the ground out there. Every hit's a kill in that environment. Over.'

'Sorry to hear about the mass driver, Colonel. Sounds like you're handling things OK at the main base. Also sounds like you'd better take out those artillery units. We're going to have our hands full in about three hours, but it looks as though it's going to be a turkey shoot. We wish you luck. Over.'

'Thanks, Rathbone. Same to you. Copernicus, over and out.'

Morgan sat very still with the cold sweat trickling down inside his overall. *Stephanie was at Copernicus Base, way beyond his ability to help her*. He put himself through to Rathbone's console.

'Can't we give them fire support, Captain? They could do with our help out there.'

'I hear you, Dick. Our missiles would take two days to get there at the inside, and it's way out of beam range. Don't you worry about Lieutenant Honeywell. She'll be in one of the deep levels, and those guys can look after themselves. Now forget it. Get on with your job. I need you one hundred per cent here.'

Morgan carried on with his job of tracking the Wheel's outflow of resources as she deployed her strength for defence. But he did it with less than half his mind. The other half was with a pretty female psychologist with guts and a marked flair for individual action.

'McMurdo, Captain. We've got direct radar sighting of a second wave launch from Astrogorodok on a wide ellipse that should intercept us in about twelve hours – that's about eight *after* the missile attack terminal phase.'

'Any ideas, Mac?'

'Yeah. We've intercepted some Omni communcation. Darnedest thing. The second wave launch is shuttles.'

'What the hell.'

'Yeah. Six kosmolyots. D'you think they're hoping to come in with a manned attack after the missile strike?'

'Well, it certainly looks like it if they are kosmolyots. They *must* be desperate. The kosmolyot's a real soft target. We'll blow them clean out of the solar system. What do the damn fools think they're playing at?'

'Search me, Captain. We'll keep tracking and see what turns up.'

Morgan pondered. It was complex, this three-pronged attack. The Moon. The missiles. And now the kosmolyots. And all were apparently suicidal. But Litvinov was no more of a fool than Rathbone was. A doubt lodged fearfully in his mind and stayed there.

'McMurdo; Captain. The first wave's coming round the Earth now. We have the first warhead on radar direct, now. More coming up. I'm laying it over the battle display.'

The red tracks, dotted where the courses were projected, grew over the blue tracks of Wheeldata's model. It wasn't a bad match, though there were fifty-seven incoming missiles to Wheeldata's guess of fifty-four.

'Zylka; Captain. Our first wave ABMs are coming under terminal guidance. Holding the second wave back.'

The green lines of the first batch of defensive missiles moved forward faster now, giving a greater separation from the purple lines of the second wave.

'They're MIVing!'

Within five seconds each of the incoming missile traces starred into a cluster of ten warheads.

'Can you compute out the decoys, Zylka?'

'Negative, Captain. In free fall an empty trash-can reads like a full trash-can. Ours are MIVing now, locking on for one-on-one interception.'

Morgan worked it out. There were now not fifty-seven but five hundred and seventy incoming warheads. Anything between sixty and one hundred per cent of them would be carrying five-hundred kiloton warheads – any one of which could blow the Wheel into vapour and a few molten fragments. Closing rapidly with them now were a hundred and thirty-five defensive warheads, with another hundred and thirty-five just behind. Even if they all scored hits that would leave three hundred warheads to be dealt with by the reserve ABMs, and there were only forty-four of them, with two hundred and twenty warheads. The hit ratio would have to be very high indeed. There was no magical force field to save the Wheel from anything that got through.

'We now have heavy ECM, but there is video lock-on confirmed for one hundred and three of our warheads.'

Each green track was now superimposed on a red dotted track.

'The secondary wave is now MIVed and targetted on remaining targets. We are getting video countermeasures. Warheads are now correlating radar and visual returns. Ten seconds to first interception.'

Morgan looked up at the left-hand display. It showed a real image of the haze-shrouded Earth. At a range of thirty-five thousand kilometres nothing could be seen of the precision manoeuvring that was taking place above the fringes of its atmosphere. Then a glaring arc-light flared over its western horizon, paled into a small expanding moon, and was gone. Then two more in quick succession. Within the space of two minutes the rim of the Earth's atmosphere was incandescent with nuclear flame, and the hazy limb of its night side was stage-lit by a lurid light. Each burst scrambled the Wheel's radar screens for the two seconds which it took for the hot radioactive debris to cool and dissipate in endless vacuum.

'Eighty-five targets are now off the screen. Too early to evaluate damage on the near misses.'

Ten seconds later and a thousand kilometres closer to the Wheel than the first interception, the second wave of warheads began to blaze.

And that was the end of the turkey-shoot. There were now three hours before the first Russian warheads could arrive: the two waves of ABMs had wiped a hundred and sixty-three from the screens. There were four hundred and seven still on their way. Of these Wheeldata was able to compute that fifty-two had been knocked so far off course that, even if undamaged, they would be unable to complete their terminal manoeuvres. Thirty of the remainder had been subjected to near misses which should have damaged their guidance systems, but it would be impossible to be sure until they malfunctioned at the terminal stage. That would involve the perilous expedient of waiting until the very last moment – and then still perhaps having to attempt interception. That left three hundred and twenty-five attacking warheads that were most likely to function, with two hundred and ten defending warheads to counter them. Zbijowski had to fire his remaining missiles soon, otherwise they wouldn't have time to spread their MIVs to the increasingly dispersed targets. But he placed his shots carefully. He released a few at a time, making sure that each warhead would count, trying, where he could, to make each count twice, so that a direct hit on one warhead was a near miss on another. Now he was saying nothing about *capability*.

With half an hour to go another bulletin came in from Copernicus Base. Schnieder was space-suited, grasping an automatic weapon and speaking hurriedly.

'We've lost forty-three as far as I can tell, though things are pretty chaotic here. We've lost north dome three. Hit by a shell. We're not sure whether they've taken it. Communications are down with the eastern complex, but there's still firing there. They're taking two or three times our casualties, but they keep coming. We think they're positioning to fire down sun. Our radar won't handle that. We're getting low on Whiplash missiles, and when we're out they take the domes. Then we go underground. We've got plenty of small arms ammo. We can hold out there for weeks, and I can't see them supporting the operation for that long. This may be our last transmission for some time. See you later. Over and out.'

Rathbone looked grim at that. He didn't look at Morgan, who had to force himself against blind fear to get on with his job.

'Stand by that counterstrike, Zylka,' growled Rathbone. 'Authorise Wheeldata to let go the lot if he comes through with a certain hit prediction against the Wheel. Then – instantly.'

'Count it as done, Captain.'

'And I want three assigned to their Tycho Base. If we take it I want that Russian Moon Base plastered.'

'You've got them, Captain.'

Morgan was working on an analysis of the Russian resources position. He was surprised. Their missile strike was costing them nothing. The missiles were solid fuelled. Their propellant couldn't be used for anything else anyway. It might just as well be spent. The six shuttles had used very little energy to get into their new orbit. And that was it. He didn't like it.

'Anything on their kosmolyots, Mac?'

'Nothing new, Captain. They'll apogee at our position in about eight and a half hours. No more Omni transmissions. They're holding a loose defensive formation.'

'Green Team take over battle stations. Red and Blue Teams suit up – PLSS packs – then relieve Green Team.

'Zylka, are we in beam range?'

'It's worth a try, Captain. We've got a lot of shooting to do, and not much time to do it in. But these are going to be hardened targets, so we're in pretty unknown territory. We're going to have to plug away until we've burnt off their ablative shields.'

'Give it a go then, Zylka. You might try for asymmetric hits to push them off course. Make sure you've got laser coverage one on one for when they pop out their TV eyes. I want them deaf and blind.

'Green Team suit up as soon as Red and Blue are back at your stations. Make sure your PLSS packs are fully charged.'

Wheeldata was displaying the incoming warheads under two codes now. Those that were probably live were marked by red diamonds. Periodically a red diamond would wink off the display as a warhead was intercepted by one of the few remaining ABMs. The glare of the fireball would momentarily occult the Earth and stars as the Wheel's windows polarised. Then the shutters came down. It was the last defensive gesture, like pulling up the drawbridge. The particle beam weapon was firing constantly with a monotonous grind and concussion that was as sapping to the nerves as the incessant operation of an aircraft carrier's steam catapult. There were fifteen red diamonds now.

'Full countermeasures,' said Rathbone. The warheads were relatively at the slowest point in their orbits now, but one by one the red diamonds began to pulse. They had begun their terminal phase, powering through the defences, changing course rapidly. The vast aluminium squares of the three Powersats were spaced out across the flightpath, two hundred kilometres up-range.

'Wheeldata, seal off all doors. Retract the crows'-nests.'

On the screens could be seen an occasional flare as an attacking or a hunting warhead adjusted its orbit abruptly. The instantaneous brilliant suns were closer now – the last one only two hundred and fifty kilometres away. There were five pulsing diamonds left.

A sun shone far more brightly than all the rest. Ten thousand tons of aluminium and steel had just been reduced to a brilliantly expanding globe of white-hot vapour by a direct hit. There were now only two Powersats on the screens.

'One down and four to go,' said Rathbone.

That could have been us, thought Morgan. He had never before felt so thoroughly exposed in space. He had an instinctive interest in the location of the cellar door, and of course there wasn't one.

A jet of blue flame lanced from the centre of one of the remaining Powersats. It left a little black hole behind it.

'Status on that one. Zylka?'

'Dead.'

The beam weapon caught a third with a glancing strike. It carried on, spinning too fast for its manoeuvring jets to cope. The last of the Powersat decoys was outlined in black against a blinding light. It crinkled, and the light spilled through. Then it broke up into sheets of aluminium and spars of steel, some of them kilometres long, that tumbled ponderously away from the zero point of the explosion. In the screens they grew fast.

'Where the hell's number five?'

'We're not tracking fast enough!' shouted Zylka at the sights of the beam weapon. He was tied to the spin of the Wheel. 'Take cover, everyone.' It was an instinctive but pointless cry.

The red diamond blinked again. '*Twenty kilometres*,' said McMurdo. 'It's outside the beam's sweep rate. And we've got a debris wavefront from the Powersat at thirty kilometres.'

'The hell with the debris,' said Sandra Crabtree, who had accidentally left her microphone on. 'We're going to be fried before it gets here.'

Morgan was counting off the kilometres. *Seventeen*.

'Switch off all non-essential systems . . . .'

Sixteen.

'Secure circuit-breakers for shock overload . . . .'

Fifteen.

'Fasten your seat restraints . . . .'

Fourteen.

'We're getting a probable hit reading from Wheeldata, sir. Do we let go our pigeons?'

Thirteen.
'At five seconds on my mark, Zylka . . . MARK.'
Twelve kilometres.
'One . . . two . . . three . . . '
Eleven kilometres. Morgan took a last look around Command A.
Again the feeling of unreality as he saw the fully-suited figures, their
faces unrecognisable behind the reflection-shot glass of their helmets,
in a room accustomed to shirt sleeves.
'Four . . . '
The screens bloomed, then darkened. The hammer blow of
thermal shock against the hull slammed Morgan's head against the
inside of his helmet. Flame tracked along the wiring conduits. The
lights went out.
'Keep your seats,' said Rathbone in the echoing silence. There
seemed little else to do.
'Captain, we'll be entering the debris front from the Powersat!'
shouted McMurdo.
'Right. Wheeldata, how about some emergency circuits round
here.' Wheeldata couldn't hear him. But Wheeldata was busy.
Morgan watched the seconds ticking away on his c-unit. The sensitive
crystalline circuitry hadn't been overloaded by the neutron burst.
Then there was some hope for his own delicate mechanism . . .
A staccato of bangs echoed through the space station. Morgan hit
his quick-release buckle and stood warily. A bolt of lightning smote
through Command A from floor to ceiling. It lit the room brilliantly
for a microsecond.
'Get back in your seat, that man!' shouted Rathbone. Morgan
wished to comply, but the shock had tumbled him uncontrollably in
the low gee of the operations room. The atmosphere was howling
through the breach in the sealed room. 'We've taken a debris strike,
Wheeldata. Where the hell are those standby circuits?' This time the
lights came on. Morgan looked first at his suit radiation tab. It was
red. He couldn't see his personal radiation read-out. It was inside his
suit.
Now that Wheeldata had brought up emergency power a bubble
generator started up, but the two punctures were too wide for it to
cope with. The balloons were sucked outside before they could
harden. Rathbone didn't appear too concerned by that: the whole of
the ship's company was space-suited. But when Morgan told him of
the oxygen loss-rate he directed engineering teams to the task, taking

the trouble to tell them precisely what sort of patch and sealant to use. Then he left them to it.

'Bud, get me Copernicus Base.'

'I've been trying, Captain. Nothing direct. We were picking up battlefield communcations from both sides when we were hit, but I think we lost our high-gain aerial then.'

'Keep trying. Joe? Have you got damage reports in?'

'Wheeldata has, Captain. I'm putting it on the master screen. You can see there that we lost all our sensors on the exposed side. Cameras and radar dishes are burnt out. All the internal circuits – sensor, communication, lighting, docking control – with cable runs on the exposed side have suffered surge overload, but we've maintained full capability with emergency circuits – except for the sensors them-selves. Hull leakage is now tolerable and should be nominal within five minutes. Some of our window shutters have welded closed, and so have some of the airlocks, but we've still got plenty of egress capability.'

'Sensors are OK on the other side of the Wheel, are they?'

'Yes, sir.'

'Fine. Sandra, I don't care what it costs, but I want you to flip the Wheel over so that sensors on the second disk side can be brought to bear on the quadrant enclosing the Earth and the kosmolyots.'

'I'm giving it to Wheeldata now, sir.'

'Good girl,' said Rathbone mischievously. Morgan couldn't see her reaction inside her space suit – but he would have liked to. 'Nothing up to date on the kosmolyots I suppose, Mac?'

'No, sir, but I don't expect any change from my last report. There's no profit for them in trying to shift their orbit now. It doesn't compute with any reasonable fuel reserve. Expect rendezvous in seven and three-quarter hours.'

'Right. Bud, anything from Copernicus?'

'No, sir. Picking up battle transmissions from the Soviets.'

'Not from our boys?'

'No, sir. Could be underground.'

'But they're still fighting?'

'Far as I can make out, sir.'

'Joe, assemble EVA teams to assess and repair outside damage.'

'Assembling at the airlock reception points now, sir.'

'Bud, patch me through for Wheel to shuttle transmission.'

'You're on, sir.'

'Rathbone, Wheel, to all shuttles. Stay off the air unless you have severe damage. Report by numbers if you're disabled . . . Good. Report by number if your damage is critical.'

'010 . . . 032 . . . 014 . . .'

'Damage 010?'

'Fuel leakage from a wing tank, sir. We took debris from the Powersat. We can make it back.'

'Damage 032?'

'Radar acquisition and docking system's out, sir. Laser ranging and docking out. We'll have to come in on passive voice control mode.'

'Do that, 032. Damage 014?'

There was a rustle of static and 014 came through faintly. 'All avionics are out, sir. We've no thrust control. Windscreens are pitted over. We can't see out. Batteries are low, fuel cells out, we're on emergency radio – '

'What's your physiological state, 014?'

'We've taken a lethal dose, sir. Otherwise not too bad. We feel fairly fit at the moment.'

Morgan heard Rathbone taking a couple of deep breaths. 'Bruner, Mylovitch, have I got the right crew?'

'That's us, sir.'

'What's your dosage?'

'Eight twenty-four Rems, sir.'

'OK, Bruner, we're going to get you out of there straight away.'

'We'd rather you didn't use the effort in that way, sir. We know the position. We'd like to see you use the effort on the Soviets. We hear they're murdering Copernicus.'

'We'll do that, Bruner. But you're coming back here for medication. You are not exempt from military orders. Whichever shuttle is nearest to 014, report.'

'027, sir. We're right alongside. She's rolling badly, but we think we can grapple her. No chance of docking.'

'Then I'll leave it with you, Mallory. Bring 'em back. Don't try to dock with the Wheel. Let the shuttles go if you have to. We'll have a Torc standing by or an EVA team at the tunnel, depending on conditions outside. Away you go.'

'Captain; Zylka. Now how about that counterstrike? We still have full capability.'

'Zylka, I know exactly now you feel. But they've eaten all their omelettes now, and we've still got our eggs. We can serve them up when and how we like, and there's no point hurrying. We've got the time to cook it right.'

'How about refreshing the Tycho crater?'

'It wouldn't help Copernicus. They'd take two days to get there. We'll have to hope our boys fight their way out of trouble.'

'Captain, you and I know they're not going to.'

'It may be, but our strike would still be too late to help. I want full data on the outcome at Copernicus before we throw the ball back over their fence.'

'Captain, Medical here.'

'Tell us the worst, Doc.'

'Well, Wheeldata's given me a radiation dosage analysis from personnel telemetry correlated with position at the time of the explosion.'

'And.'

'Typical readings are eighty to a hundred Rems, with fifty in Command A, which is well shielded and was facing away from the zero point.'

'So where does that leave us? Are we going to have any fatalities?'

'Not likely within that range if we all take our Interferon D jabs. It was a little more critical for people in A quadrant, which was opposite point zero. Fortunately there was no one in the rim bar at the time.'

'So what's the picture in quadrant A?'

'I'm switching to discreet channel.'

'Copy.'

And that was all Morgan heard for the moment of the state of the men and women in quadrant A – thirty-two of whom were to die lingering deaths in the time ahead.

A quarter of an hour later, with the atmosphere restored, the crew fully active, and the medical teams patrolling their reluctant practice with sharpened needles, Rathbone brought the alert status down to amber.

'Green Team stand down. Get some sleep. I want to tell you all that you did everything I could have expected. If you hadn't been on the ball we wouldn't be here now. Wheeldata,' he added wrily, 'we would all like to thank you for your infallible back-up.'

'Captain Rathbone; Wheeldata. I acknowledge. And I record your efficiency during the red alert duration as sixty-four per cent.' Rathbone reddened, and thought about it before replying.

'Thanks, Wheeldata.'

Morgan handed him a coffee. 'Forget sixty-four per cent. You did bloody well.' He said it without a smile. His mind was on the struggle at Copernicus Base.

For the next three hours the activity of the Wheel's crew was undiminished. McMurdo tracked the steady course of the six kosmolyots. They were due to intercept the Wheel in four hours. Nothing was heard from Copernicus Base – other than that the Russians were bringing in reinforcements from holding bases that they had set up discreetly outside the crater.

Crews leaving the Wheel to work on its hull and sensors were shocked by what they saw. The gleaming white paint was now charred, blistered, completely scorched away in places. Some of the thick milled-aluminium cladding was warped and buckled. The electrical components and wiring of exposed equipment – cameras, radar dishes, lights, docking grapples – had failed explosively, ripping gashes in the access covers. All the equipment would have to be replaced. There could be no thought of repair. The solar arrays on the exposed side were destroyed. The docking mast was askew . . .

'Captain; Bud. We have contact with Copernicus. Colonel Schnieder is on visual. I suggest you take it in the conference room.' Rathbone looked up at Saunders. He gazed impassively at him for five seconds, then walked rapidly toward the door of the conference room, speaking into his c-unit.

Morgan's c-unit spoke to him. 'Command Team to the conference room immediately. If you can drop what you're doing come instantly. Joe, stick to your EVA. We'll keep you informed.' Morgan lost no time in following Rathbone. He wanted to know what was happening at Copernicus. 'And Fred, I need you here – whatever you're doing.'

Nineteen

COLONEL SCHNIEDER was wearing a space suit with the helmet ring sagging around his neck. The chest instrument panel was smashed. The left arm-piece was ripped from shoulder to elbow. Frayed ends of carbon-fibre cloth and steel silk were hanging out of the gash. It would have taken high-velocity bullets to do that. The colonel's blond hair stuck spikily out of the top of a new bandage that bound his forehead and came down to his eyes. There was blood around his nose and mouth. His head was slightly bowed. His eyes were cast down. He raised his gaze slowly to a point just below the camera, and held it there. Then, with an effort, he lifted his eyes to look at his audience. He tilted his head back. His voice was clipped, but he was forcing it.

'Captain Rathbone, this is Colonel Schnieder. Do you read me? Over.'

'Rathbone here. I read you, Colonel. Over.' He spoke efficiently, betraying no unwelcome sympathy.

'Captain, I have to inform you that in my office as Commander of Copernicus Base military sector I have surrendered the base to Colonel Gurevich of the Red Army.' He paused. He obviously struggled with a desire to say no more. 'I believe that you know I would only take such a course in the last resort. We had been driven under ground and they were blasting their way down, level by level. Much longer and there would have been no Moon base at Copernicus. I couldn't go on fighting without taking heavy civilian casualties.'

'I sympathise with your position, Colonel. We all do here. Tell me, are they observing the Geneva Convention? You look as though you've been messed around a little.'

Schnieder brushed away the irrelevancy of his own condition with a wave of the hand. 'No, I'm all right. Just decompressed. Their behaviour is good. They're intelligent and well-trained men. And they took heavier cas –'

The muzzle of a Kaleshnikova appeared in the corner of the picture with a jerk.

' – That's a subject on which I'm not permitted to speak.'

'Please, Colonel, don't take any personal risk to give us information.'

Schnieder shook his head, and then winced, 'I'm permitted to say that we lost thirty per cent of our combat force, that we're being treated well, and have access to medical aid and supplies. They're discussing with me plans to restore the base to working condition, which I'm going along with.'

'I think you're wise, Colonel. Loss of Copernicus Base would harm the survivors – of whatever race they might be.'

'Captain Rathbone, that's not all. What I've been saying has been leading up to the thing that the Soviets have told me to tell you. They thought it would be more persuasive coming from me.'

'Go on, Colonel.' *Persuasive*. It didn't sound good to Morgan. He could see it coming: total Soviet victory. Totalitarian domination of the last few weeks of history. An unwieldy discipline that would end all intelligent efforts to survive. It had been no turkey-shoot. The Russians had executed a finely balanced plan.

'Colonel Gurevich tells me that you have withstood a heavy missile attack, and that you have held your counterstrike.'

'That is true.'

'It was a fine and humane effort, Captain. I applaud it. But the colonel says, and these are his words, that your crowing about it is over. There are six kosmolyot shuttles on course to intercept you in three and three-quarter hours: is that right?'

'That's right, Colonel.' Rathbone's voice was very smooth for a man who had seen what was coming.

'He says they will rendezvous with you. You will let them. You will take on board a team of Russian supervisors. You will do what they say.'

'Or.'

'Or they will lock the six hundred surviving members of my command in what remains of my base, and they will blow up the airlocks.'

'Received and understood, Colonel.'

'My advice is that we're ready to face that. You can blow them to hell and – ' The picture broke up.

'Someone's pulled the plug,' said Saunders. Rathbone nodded. The picture cleared. It showed a different space-suited figure, his condition not much better than Schnieder's. But his suit ornamentation included the Hammer and Sickle, the CCCP identification, and a cyrillic name tab.

'Are you still there, Captain Rathbone?'

'I am.'

The two men exchanged pleasantries, stonily on Rathbone's part, patronisingly on the Russian's.

'What Colonel Schnieder told you is correct. But I wish you to ignore his last little speech. He has suffered a shock. He does not really wish you to signal the destruction of half of the remaining

American population –'

'And the whole Russian population.' Interruption does not work well when there is a two and a half second communications lag. The discussion became scrambled at this point.

'You could not destroy our colony on Mars.'

'*Colony*! They can't survive without your support.'

'None of us will live for ever, Captain Rathbone.'

'Then why did you start this suicidal exchange?'

'Two reasons. One: because we intend to ensure that the means of survival do not remain solely in capitalist hands.'

'In other words you want something we've got.'

'Two: we will win. It is not suicide for us.'

'I wouldn't be too sure of that, Gurevich.'

The Russian smiled. 'Oh, but of course. Now, while I'm being unsure, which choice will you make? Do you wish to say goodbye to your six hundred friends? Or will you accept the instructions of a supervisory crew?'

'I need time to discuss the options with my Command Team.'

'*The options*,' mimicked the Russian in a creditable accent. 'What *options* have you?'

'You have defined them, Colonel Gurevich. The kosmolyots won't rendezvous for three and a half hours. You can give us until then to make our choice.'

'History makes the choices, Captain.' Then he contradicted himself. 'I haven't the time. I also have decisions to make. What is yours? It's one way or the other. Now.'

Rathbone froze the console and looked up at his hastily assembled team. 'Recommendations?'

'Give in,' said Morgan unashamedly. Rathbone nodded in a way that didn't necessarily signify agreement.

'He wouldn't do it,' said McMurdo. 'He's a military man.'

'Can I quote you on that?' asked Rathbone. 'There are precedents, you know.' McMurdo looked away. The rest were silent. Rathbone reactivated the console. There was Gurevich, one eyebrow still raised interrogatively. 'We accept, with counter-conditions. That the people you've got there continue to be treated well.' Gurevich nodded his head once. 'And that these supervisors leave the routine running of the Wheel to us. She's a complex ship.'

'Agreed – within practical limits. Now I'm sure we both have work to do. Your next instruction will come from Lieutenant-Colonel

Sidorenko in the lead kosmolyot on your customary shuttle operations waveband. That will be at about half an hour before rendezvous. We may speak again. Until then – goodbye.'

Rathbone walked to the window and leaned there, bowed, his hands gripping the guide-rail. A hundred metres out, a space-suited figure drifted past, wheeling with a puff of mist from his manoeuvring jets. The business of the Wheel was being carried on by a crew still elated by almost total victory. Rathbone's spirits were making the steep transition to total defeat. No one wished to interrupt his reverie, but it was pointless to prolong it.

'They've got us by the short and curlies,' said McMurdo.

'Ladies, gentlemen, there's no way out of this. I'm prepared to face military discipline if you wish to convene a Board of Inquiry.'

'If we had grounds for one it would mean there was an alternative to what you've just done. You said it: there isn't. You've just saved the lives of six hundred people. We all support you.' The rest nodded. Zeffert had spoken for all of them.

'Thanks.'

Again the Command Team was crushed by its thoughts. *There was no way out.* Soon there would be a Russian Command Team in the operations room, and a valiant tradition would be finished. A nation would be finished . . . . The silence was disturbed by the intricate noises of a maintenance robot working on the steel window shutters.

'Let's look at this logically,' said Sandra Crabtree, characteristically. 'We've got this three-hour hiatus. The very least we can do is use it to discuss our options.'

'What options? We've already capitulated. We've received our first orders. We're just waiting for the rest.'

'That's not exactly the case. Think of it as a game situation. I know that's not exactly popular with all of you. I've pushed it too much at times. But it does help clarify the situation – er, position. So sweep the board. Forget that we're committed. Sure, I know the *words* have been spoken to Gurevich, but let's look at all their implications. Anything can still happen.

'What we've achieved so far is to persuade them that they know what we're going to do. That's the one thing they're sure of. That puts us in a strong position. We can do it if we want to, or we can do something else, and catch them *really* flat-footed. All we've got to do is think what that something else might be.'

'Quite,' said Zeffert.

'Remembering we're talking in game situation terms,' added McMurdo, 'which means we're not looking at value criteria for the moment, we've still got the option of zapping the shit out of the whole Soviet space set-up. OK, so that leaves Copernicus at risk, but it also leaves us undoubtedly in complete control.'

'Don't gloss over it, Mac. It leaves Copernicus Base dead. There's no way we could land a party there inside three days. We'd have to count on losing six hundred.'

'So it's still a viable game-play – in strictly gaming terms, you understand.'

It was still defeat, but the Command Team were fingering the odds again.

'Of your two options so far, I'm not sure that the first isn't far more acceptable,' said Morgan tentatively. 'We accept Soviet domination and survive. We try – under that domination – to exert what influence we've got over the survival chances of the whole space community. There'll be more of us than of them. A thousand Americans with probably superior resources can't help but exert a powerful influence.'

'You don't know the Soviets like I do,' said McMurdo. Morgan doubted the truth of that. 'Their system's too unwieldy, too conservative. They'd push us around till us *and* them were all dead. Look at what they've done so far: started a total war. Does that look good for anyone's survival?'

'It may for them,' said Zeffert. 'What they're doing is in no way going to increase total human resources. That's obvious. But it's going to increase Soviet resources. They'd be wasting their attack if they shared out what's left with us. They're going to milk us dry. They'll survive longer and we'll die sooner. Dick, that option of going along with them may be the one we're left with, but it offers no hope whatsoever for our survival.' He looked closely at Morgan and promptly said, 'Have you got anything particular to say on the survival theme?' Morgan acknowledged the allusion.

'I may have, but I haven't finished what I was saying. Neither of the options we've discussed appears attractive, so let's look at the others.'

He was greeted by a chorus of '*What others?*'

'None as yet, but since we're talking gamespeak, let's just model some best possible outcomes. I'm pissed off with your worst ones. I can think of a good one.'

'Like what?'

'We relieve Mafeking.'

'Say again?'

'We relieve Copernicus Base. We mount a dawn raid. We come over the hill with flags flying. We set them free.'

'We'd be seen coming a mile off.' That was an understatement.

'It would take a day to set it up. Do we get the Red supervisors to help us, or do they stand back and watch?'

'We nobble them.'

'And they radio the Moon, then there are six hundred less Americans.'

'We stop them radioing the Moon.'

'They'll have a communications schedule. When they *don't* call the Moon there'll be six hundred less Americans.'

'Anyway, you're talking about a three-day mission, even after it's been set up. There's no way we can do that under their beady eyes.'

Morgan nodded equably. 'Now you're talking about details. Options within options. We can discuss them. But now we've got three ways of playing this game. We play it Gurevich's way: total Soviet domination. The result? Inevitable extinction for us. I agree. We do what Mac and Sandra have suggested –'

'Not *suggested* –'

' – indicated as options. Result, the deaths of six hundred Americans and all the remaining Russians. At the end of the World you just can't afford that many human beings. You do it my way, however chancy the process, however unlikely the outcome, and you're in with a fighting chance – and at least you're not setting out to kill your friends – or exterminate your enemies.'

'Nice sales talk, Dick,' said Rathbone tiredly, rubbing his face, 'but you're forgetting one thing. Whichever way we do it we die soon. Three days, three weeks, three months, what's the difference? I know you and Fred have been working out some fancy conservation schemes on the quiet. I'm not totally blind to what's going on on my own ship. I even gave them my approval: they seemed to be keeping a number of you happy. But they only put off the end by three months. I should know. Wheeldata and I are old friends.

'In view of our impending and inevitable demise I regret to say that we're discussing options so limited that we're wasting our time. We might as well let ourselves be dictated to by fate, since fate will shortly be decreeing our deaths anyway.' Morgan saw in the faces of his friends the recognition that Rathbone had spoken the truth. There was no fight, no dominant logic, left in them. Zeffert looked away. If he was disappointed he tried not to show it. Morgan rode out the silence. He waited while the psychological thread of the Command Team, so long in its superbly capable winding, frayed.

'You're forgetting about Callisto.'

'You don't have to remind us about Callisto now!' snapped Rathbone. 'There's nothing that can be done for them, as we've agreed. They're a write-off. Like the man said, it's a decision that's been taken by history.'

'I'm talking about what they can do for us.'

Rathbone was so long in replying that he seemed barely troubled to answer. 'Longbow won't solve anyone's problems now. It would take twenty years to complete, if the NASA and ESA teams were to live that long. It would take fifty years to fly if it worked – which privately I've always doubted. It would take hundreds of years to get a response, if any – which I also privately doubt. The universe is as empty as a bell, with us the clapper. It's about to lose that, and then you'll know what silence is – or rather you won't.'

The silence stretched out again. It looked as though Rathbone was preparing to dismiss his Team for the last time: a speech of gratitude and regret perhaps.

'You may have forgotten the Milk-run,' said Morgan. 'It makes its circumterrestrial pass in four days. I suppose we were going to let it pass without meeting it.'

'We've got nothing to send,' Rathbone grunted.

'No, I agree, But we've got something to receive. There are one thousand tons of liquid hydrogen on board.'

Twenty

THEY TURNED and looked at him. Zeffert winked. 'I was beginning to doubt you, my boy.'

'A *thousand tons*! You fixed *that*?'

Morgan shook his head modestly. 'Dave, Bill, Eurodefence,

Callisto.'

'Why the hell all this secret agent stuff?' shouted Rathbone. 'I should have known.'

'If you'd known when I set it up, you'd have stopped it. At that time nothing mattered but Pluto.'

'Possibly,' conceded Rathbone, becoming calmer.

'Then I hung on for a time when it would make all the difference. I may have been wrong. It can't be mended now.'

'All right. Forget that. How would it affect our logistics?'

'The logistics check out. Given a major effort on other resources we could survive indefinitely.'

Rathbone turned to Zeffert, who nodded. 'It's the *sine qua non*. It makes all the difference.'

'Or none at all,' said Rathbone. 'We can't touch it. If anyone gets it, it'll be the Russians.'

'It still makes a difference,' insisted Morgan. 'It puts long-term survival into our original three options: survival under the Russians *if* we can persuade them to set up a workable economy and *if* they reckon there's a place for us in it; survival after killing off the bulk of the remaining population including six hundred of our own people; survival as a reward for a high-risk venture that avoids both of those options if it succeeds, but leaves us with the possibility of getting both if it fails.'

'OK, so you're still putting top spin on option three. Run it through again.' Morgan did so, adding the necessity of mounting a ten-shuttle rendezvous with the Milk Train under the noses of the Russian supervisors in the Wheel. It looked impossible. The sudden hope deflated noticeably. Rathbone looked at his c-unit.

'We've only got an hour. What are our resources?'

Morgan listed them. 'One. Only the crew have anything like complete knowledge of the Wheel's systems. The Russians can't attempt to equal it in the time we're thinking of. And the most powerful of those systems is Wheeldata. Two. Only we know about the Milk Train resource; we'll have our eyes on survival and they'll be facing death at arm's length. So they won't know of our hope. Three. In their eyes we've no military option but to accept defeat. We keep them thinking that way.'

'We haven't a hope in hell,' said Rathbone. 'But we go in for it. The options stink. Let's relieve Mafeking.' He typed a code on his terminal. 'Surveillance? I want high data-rate input to Wheeldata from the Lunar Orbiter Net. I want a fall update on all Soviet strengths and movements on the Lunar surface and in orbit – vehicle by vehicle and man by man. You have literally one half-hour. I repeat: one half-hour. Understand?'

'Yes, sir, I understand.'

'Then get to it.' He broke the connection and looked up. 'OK, that's a start. What next?'

'Message to the shuttles,' said Morgan.

'Wheeldata, I want contact with all shuttles on the s-band in Most Secret Code –'

'Make that laser,' said Morgan.

'Wheeldata, reset on that. I want laser communication with all shuttles in Most Secret . . .'

Twenty-One

USSF SCC 101 was, for the next three-quarters of an hour, a theatre of intense activity.

Then at 1530 hours Rathbone made a short final address to the crew. At 1535 the grapples eased the first kosmolyot on to its padded bed on the docking raft. Twenty minutes later the prize crew of twelve men filed, in two batches, from the docking mast airlock. One man stepped aside to cover the reception area with an AK-58 that was slung from his suit harness. Two ran forward, brushing heedlessly past the waiting Command Team, and covered the reception area door and outer corridor. Rathbone was pale and dazed. Morgan averted his eyes, waiting for the pantomime of capitulation, humiliating even when the forms are observed.

A tall figure strode through the waiting group of Russians, handed his helmet to one, took a bulky document case from another, singled out Rathbone and walked forward without pause. He took in the cowed reception group with quick glances from keen grey eyes.

'Captain Rathbone?' he enquired, quite conversationally.

'Yes.'

'Sidorenko.' He closed on Rathbone with his hand outstretched, and gripped him by the upper arm. Looking down at the older man he spoke very quietly and intensely. Morgan barely picked up what he said. 'We'll neglect the submissive farce. There's much to do. You're aware that though we are few any resistance would bring horrible consequences to your lunar colleagues?'

Rathbone nodded.

'Then we won't dwell on it.' He was already walking Rathbone toward the door. 'We go first to your operations room. Bring your aides.'

Fred Zeffert, Sandra Crabtree, Joe Waldon, Bud Saunders, Doc Bardelli, Zylka Zbijowski, Mac McMurdo, and Dick Morgan milled in pursuit. Sidorenko and his team set a fast pace – and they knew where they were going. That was the first and least palatable thing that defeat meant: where you had led, you followed. Occasionally Sidorenko would briefly raise his hand and point. Then one of his men would fall out of the procession and stand at guard, feet apart, AK-58 covering a corridor intersection, the armoury, an elevator access. Morgan watched the Russian colonel closely. He was surprised: he had expected more pomp, less certainty, a measure of culture shock on first contact with the Wheel. But Sidorenko was a man in command – of himself, of his men, and already he had quite naturally assumed command of the Wheel. It would be difficult to undermine that command.

There was also a thought that he didn't want to recognise. What if the Soviet hammer-lock couldn't be shifted? The destiny of the human race would then be created by a few men and the forbidding constraints of space. Would the old terrestrial monolith of communism be any more real or to be feared than that of capitalism? By now they had both become myths; for this was a turning-point in history which made negligible any human revolution . . . .

They had reached Command A. Any one of Astrogorodok's modules would have fitted inside it with room to spare. Sidorenko strode to the Command console and wheeled to face the auditorium.

'Captain Rathbone, which is the communications station? Good . . . and your Communications officer?'

Rathbone nodded to Saunders, who, after a questioning glance at the captain, stepped forward.

'Commander . . . Bud Saunders, be so kind as to call Tycho Base on your s-band.' He looked round at one of his five remaining men.

'Boris. Look after it.' Boris caught up with Saunders at the communications terminal.

'Next. I want the kosmolyot raft manoeuvred to close formation with your liquid hydrogen tanks. Can it be done?'

'Yes, Colonel. Commander Crabtree's our Movement Control officer.'

'And a man to look after the transference of propellant to our tanks.'

'Commander Waldon: Engineering. Commander Morgan: Logistics.'

'Good.'

Morgan retreated to his terminal, with a man who had been addressed as Feodor in close attendance. From the second rank of the auditorium he could follow the conversation as he went through his automatic routines.

'Also ten of your shuttles. They are to fill up their propulsion and payload tanks, and take all the hydrogen they can carry to Astrogorodok.'

'We have only six serviceable.' This was not strictly true.

'*Six*? Out of thirty?'

'Mainly electronic failures. We took a near miss from one of your warheads.'

'I saw the damage. How near?'

'Six kilometres.'

'That near! Casualties?'

'About a hundred severe overdose cases. Some of the men here now will die . . . Morgan, Zeffert.' He pointed. 'They were doing emergency repairs outside when the warhead detonated. There are quite a few others.' Morgan saw Feodor glance at him under his brows. He hoped his pallid make-up wouldn't run. He tried to look subtly ill.

'I'm sorry.' There was no doubt from his manner that Sidorenko meant it, but he paused and filed his sorrow for future reference. 'By god, your air smells good.' He stretched luxuriantly. 'You must have good oxygen supply.'

'Not really. We recycle it all.'

'Not *all*, Captain Rathbone. I'm sure we'll find some.'

'Why not push us out of the airlocks and have done with it?'

'Don't be melodramatic, Captain. We're not pirates. This is war. It is survival. It is the final confrontation of our cultures on the edge of chaos. Ours will outlive yours, that is all. It is our vindication. We will leave you what we can, but you are well off compared with us. The air is making them sick on Astrogorodok.'

Then he added, 'Why are your windows shuttered?' This man *was* quick.

'The shutters were welded closed by the fireball.'

'Have Commander Waldon's team cut them open. I wish for an uninterrupted view of extra-vehicular work.'

'They're working on them, but cutting operations are dangerous in the window areas. However, we've got most of the external sensors working again.'

'Show me how to use them.'

Rathbone typed quickly on the console keyboard. 'Here's a schematic of the Wheel with the sensor fields of view coloured in: video in orange, radar in violet, infra-red in yellow and so on.'

'Whoever chose those colours should have been shot.'

'So we can choose say, video six with the keyboard, and pan the camera with the stick. Camera function's automatic.'

'Why can't I call them up by voice? My information is that your on-board computer is voice-operable.'

Rathbone pulled a face and shook his head slowly. 'We tend to use the keyboard. There is some voice function for simple switching, communications relay and so forth, but it's very unreliable. We tend to use the keyboard for everything except voicident and internal communications switching, where the spoken numbers are easily stored.'

'Really?' Sidorenko looked at him closely. 'My information is that you have rather greater computer flexibility than that.'

'I'm afraid you've been had by our propaganda. We were hoping to upgrade the system. We've had trials. But they're . . . they *were* still trying to debug the software. IBM, you see,' he added, as though that were an explanation.

Sidorenko was still looking at him closely. Finally his frown of concentration relaxed. 'The bureaucracies we rely on, eh? . . . relied on, rather.' He deftly typed out camera selections, and six screens lit up at the front of the auditorium. 'That's better. I like to know what's going on.' He looked carefully again at Rathbone as he said that. Morgan let out a slow breath, pretending that he hadn't been holding it. *As long as Wheeldata can keep his mouth shut.*

Sidorenko had panned the cameras to his satisfaction. They

showed the docking raft drifting with infinite caution past the Wheel, the free-jetting teams working on the transfer hoses out at the hydrogen tank cluster, and a couple of USSF shuttles homing on the same target. They also showed Waldon's teams labouring on the window shuttering with oxy-hydrogen torches. Soon all those shutters not welded into place by the thermonuclear blast would be welded into place by their work.

Within another five minutes Sidorenko had succeeded in calling up Wheeldata's directory file on display, and was using it freely. Morgan watched him minutely as he interrogated the state of the shuttles that were orbiting with the Wheel, because as Logistics officer he might be called to account for any discrepancy. But the computer supported Rathbone's fictitious report. Only six registered as serviceable.

'All but two of your unserviceable shuttles are crewed. Why is that?'

'We haven't been able to transfer their crews since your attack.'

'Why not? That was eight hours ago.'

'We've been unable to launch our Torc transfer craft until half an hour ago.'

'I want all the crews out of those shuttles. I want to see them leave their craft and I want to identify them coming in through the airlocks.'

'OK,' said Rathbone, with just the right shade of reluctance. He typed a number on the keyboard. 'Movement Control . . . '

Sidorenko waited for him to finish.

'Now I want eveyone out of this operations room except for my men and one of yours at each essential station. The rest will return to their cabins – each to his own cabin. Exercise periods will be arranged if it becomes necessary.'

Rathbone gave the orders.

The Russian colonel was irrepressibly active. He gave orders for two of his men to search the Wheel, room by room, and to ensure that they missed nothing he persuaded Wheeldata to give him hard copies of the ship's plan. He checked the identities of forty-four shuttle crewmen as they left their craft, and again as they entered the Wheel's airlocks – using, ironically, Wheeldata's voicident facility. He watched over the intricate rendezvous between the docking raft and the hydrogen tanks, and goaded the engineering teams who were trying to link up the incompatible transfer systems of the kosmolyots and the propellant store. By TV he watched impatiently over the shoulders of the crews who were putting on a convincing show of freeing the window shuttering. Punctually, every hour, he spoke to Tycho, making a brief report and signing off. Only once did Morgan catch a note of despair in his voice.

The last thing that Morgan saw Rathbone do that evening was hand over the secret access codes to Sidorenko, including his own that gave access to every last bit of secure information in the computer's profound memory. The codes had been up to date at 1445 hours that afternoon. Since then Wheeldata had been given an unusual batch of protocol instructions.

Morgan was tired when he went to his room; he had been working hard for twenty hours. He would have no rest for a while yet. Feodor went with him to check that his communication terminal was inoperative. Morgan indicated the charred gashes where the wiring had been blown during the nuclear strike. Feodor pointed at the screen with his AK-58. It was intact. Morgan shrugged, flicking the ON/OFFswitch to show that it didn't work. Feodor cocked the weapon and pointed it at the screen.

'Don't! The outer skin's only aluminium.'

'You speak Russian then?'

'A bit,' replied Morgan unidiomatically. 'I learnt some at school. Only I'm ashamed of my accent.'

'So you should be.' Feodor left.

Twenty-Two

MORGAN FLOPPED on to his bunk and relaxed for two minutes, breathing deeply and slowly. They he got up, opened his door manually, and looked out. The long curve of the corridor was empty. He resealed the door carefully, knelt under the terminal and started twisting loose wires together. He didn't follow the colour code, but a non-matching code that he – and others – had memorised. Then he switched it on and breathed into his c-unit. He used a new randomly-constructed twenty-four digit access number. It had been hell to remember, but it was hardly likely that the Russians would stumble on it by accident, or that they would be able to synthesise it intentionally.

'Wheeldata? Morgan.'

'Mister Morgan, this is Wheeldata.'

'Can anyone else hear this?'

'You have sole access to this data.'

'Are all of the Command Team alone?'

'All are alone but for Captain Rathbone. He is with Colonel Sidorenko in the rim bar.'

'What are they doing?'

'They are talking and drinking. Do you wish to hear their conversation? You now have equal access with the captain and the Command Team to my data-handling facilities.'

'No, thank you. I want you to warn me if any of the Russian supervisors approaches this room within fifty metres. I am going to ask you to set up a conference link with those members of the Command Team who are on their own. Similarly I would like you to warn them if any of the Russians gets within fifty metres of them. Understand?'

'I understand. Do you want me to call up the others now?'

'Yes. Go ahead.' Morgan had been the first to recommission his terminal, but within a quarter of an hour the faces of the whole of the Command Team but Rathbone were patched across Morgan's display. Zeffert was last.

'Sorry about that! I forgot the wiring sequence. Could never wire a plug, let alone one of these things.'

'Right, let's get on with it. First: Sidorenko intends to stay on after he's taken our hydrogen. That means that plan A is blown. We go for plan B. Other than that, does anyone report any glitches so far?' They shook their heads, with the exception of McMurdo.

'Yeah. Sidorenko. He's too on the ball by half. That's one hell of a smart guy. The thought of trying to put one over on him gives me a major credibility crisis.' This time the rest of the team had to agree.

Zeffert responded reasonably. 'Yes, there's no denying he's very much in control. But in a way that's what we want. He's got to keep thinking he's in control –'

' – No problem. He *is*.'

' – and if he has any doubts then it's our job to allay them. Remember we didn't set this up for congenital idiots. We're relying on a normal intelligent response from them at every stage. Any other doubts?'

'Some,' said Zbijowski. 'His men. They're not just space crew. They're trained fighting men.' There was a selfconscious stir among the Command Team, most of whom were 'just' space crew. 'If it ever comes to us having to hit them, a lot of our people are going to get hurt – and I mean quite badly.'

'Another reason to make them feel that they're absolutely in command. A few days of that and we can catch them napping.'

'No. You've missed the point. If we do have to take them out it will be because they've seen through us. That way we aren't going to catch them napping.'

'Then we just have to push them over slightly before they rumble us. Anyway it shouldn't happen. It's a second line of defence.'

'But it's got to work if we need it.' said Morgan. 'The moment we take on Sidorenko and his men, our people at Copernicus have got an hour to live – at the outside. With your permission, Fred, I think we should look again at the feasibility of the communication resource.'

'Suits me, Dick. I had it next anyway. Bud? Any progress?'

'Yes, I think we've got something put together here. But Sidorenko's just calling Tycho and I think it would help our analysis if we listened in.' Saunders further split the screen. It now showed Sidorenko's face and that of a young and tired-looking Russian lieutenant. Both were still space-suited but without their helmets.

'*This is Colonel Sidorenko at the Wheel outpost. Our hold on the Wheel is still secure, though my men are tired. They have paired up at their posts with one sleeping. The Americans are giving us reasonable co-operation. We have had detailed discussions with their industrial satellite. They're fabricating new refuelling couplings for us. In that way the surrender seems to be complete. It is, rationally, their only choice, but I don't trust it. I would expect incidents, a little more resentment. Oh, and their ignorance of the liquid hydrogen consignment from Callisto appears to be genuine. I can find no record of it. It's possible that the spy Morgan intended to use the information for some purpose of his own. If so, it's too late now. I'm keeping my mind open on the subject, and my men are watchful. How go things at Copernicus?'*

'*More what you would expect. Two minor bids for freedom. We've taken no casualties . . .*'

They listened to the four-minute exchange, Morgan, with his fluent Russian, puzzling over the Soviet knowledge of the Callisto consignment, the others in happy ignorance. Morgan didn't tell them of the other news. 'It looks as if they know about the Callisto hydrogen. Fred, we're going to have to find a way of making your rendezvous with *Minerva* earlier than the optimum time. I'm sure they're going to be there too.'

'OK, more on that later. Bud, what can you do with that transmission?'

'Wheely and I have been working quite hard. It's already there in his synthetic display programming, but I've had to increase his authority to call up data in real time from his holographic base – relying on his semantic net to carry the software.'

'Yes, quite.'

'Well, all right, we'll skip the radio-shack-speak. What I'd like to do is run a trial with Dick as the Tycho operator and Wheeldata standing in for Sidorenko.'

'Fine,' said Morgan. 'Whenever you're ready.'

'OK, we'll build it up in layers. *Wheeldata, will you screen your synthetic image of Sidorenko?*' The colonel's face appeared on Morgan's display. 'Now that image is not real. Wheeldata has put it together out of his store of TV data on the subject. *Wheeldata, run through the mobility test for us.* Now you see the figure going through Sidorenko's full repertoire of muscular movements. *Speed it up, Wheely, we haven't got all night.*' The figure became a blur, its lips and eyes moving rapidly. 'OK, so next we put in Wheeldata's speech synthesis and a translation program. That's correlated with a set of rules on what he may or may not talk about, and a prioritised list of topics he might introduce. *Switch them in, Wheely.* Now we're ready to go. Don't forget, Dick, he initiates the exchange, though he can do it the other way round if they call him up.'

Morgan allowed Wheeldata to lead him through a three and a half minutes dialogue, and he acted out, as well as he could, the role of the Russian lieutenant. He was accustomed to speaking with the computer. but not in Russian, and not with the Soviet colonel apparently speaking the words.

'Cut.'

'Right. Comments?' said Saunders – sounding rather smug.

'Picture and dubbing's spot on,' replied Morgan. 'I could only see two problems. One. He kicked off with exactly the same intro. that the colonel used last time. I think Tycho would spot that. You've got to get round it even if you write an intro. for him. After that the different Tycho responses will lead him on to new ground. Two. He's not reproducing Sidorenko's idiom. It doesn't show too much because he's pretty terse anyway, but you might try compiling a special language bank to be used whenever possible?'

'A systems man's work is never done. Yeah, can do. We've got the stored material.'

'Can you do it right away?'

'Yes, if you like. Why?'

'Because I think we ought to try this out on the next transmission.'

'Why take the risk this early?'

'So that if anyone's suspicious they can be reassured by the real Sidorenko on the next-but-one transmission. That means we can use it confidently when we need to.'

Zeffert vetoed the idea. 'No, it's too risky. If the real Tycho is talking to the synthetic Sidorenko, then the real Sidorenko would have to be talking to a synthetic Tycho, and we just haven't got that much TV data on Tycho. Also I don't want to try to con two people at the same time this early on. They might get wise to it when they talk to each other for real the next time. We'll just have to trust that it will work well on the night. It does, however, increase my confidence in the other con.'

Morgan had to agree.

'So we'll skip that item if it's OK with you, Bud?'

'Sure.'

'The next problem area, then, that I've had on my mind is the approach to Copernicus Base. Again, those people down there get shot the moment we show up on a radar screen. Now I don't know if you were listening at the time, but I heard Schnieder on one of his broadcasts saying that the Russians were trying to get in a position to shell the base from up sun. Right?'

'Yes, I heard that.'

'And shortly after that was when the base was overrun. In other words I think it worked. We know anyway that in space operations you've got a four or five degree blind spot around the sun – of late anyway.'

'So what are you suggesting?'

'That we do the lunar landing approach down the sun angle.'

'But how about previous orbits? We're not going to be up sun of their radar all the way around the Moon.'

'We don't go into orbit. We just go straight in. And further out in the flight we use active wave-inversion ECM. They won't know we're there. It's only close up to their radar that we can't jam it.'

'Does that affect our mission timing?'

'It *gives* us our mission timing. To approach from the sun angle all the way to ground cover we've got to land when the light-dark lunar terminator lies across Copernicus Base. That happens in four days. Are you still on to command that mission, Dick?'

'It's my mission.'

'Good. Then you die tomorrow night. And I've got to die midday tomorrow to make the Milk Train rendezvous – or rather I've got to be buried then. I'll have to die earlier.'

'Are the shuttles ready?' asked Morgan.

'We've no way of knowing. We've got to trust that they are. Sidorenko took two men out of each. That leaves two men in each, plus the heavy mob in 010. We've just got to trust that they're on the ball.'

'If they're not we really do die.'

'Don't think about it. Now that leaves us with two main areas. Dick, I've got to know what to do when I rendezvous with the Milk Train: IFF, docking, fuel transfer and so on. I'm assuming you've got all that?'

'Yes. I'll radio it to you when I'm on the lunar ferry.'

'Why not now?'

'Security.' Morgan hoped that he would be content with that. The real reason might not go down well.

'What if you don't make it to the lunar ferry?'

'Then Bill or Dave will contact you.'

'OK, I suppose. The other thing is the tactical plan when you get to Copernicus Base. Mac, what have you got on surveillance?'

The covert briefing continued into the early hours of the morning, with three breaks when guards passed the various rooms of the Command Team. By the end of it Morgan had been hard at work for twenty-four hours, so when he got up to join the Green Team in Command A he was convincing as a terminal radiation-sickness case without need of cosmetics. Feodor paid him the deference due to the nearly dead, although Sidorenko was not so generous. Morgan supposed that as a Russian he had had his fill of secret services.

Twenty-Three

COMMANDER FREDERIC Zeffert, USSF, died at 0827 hrs that morning, to the stoically subdued grief of his comrades in arms – though he did not strictly pass over to that bourne from which there is no returning until 1200 hrs. Then his bier was slid into the cylindrical aluminium coffin, the simple hydrazine propulsion unit was mated over the opening, Rathbone said the age-old words, and he was blown out of the missile launch tube by a charge of compressed nitrogen. The whole thing was watched over with suspicious forbearance by one of Sidorenko's men.

The colonel himself, restored to dynamic efficiency by five hours of sleep, chose to remain in Command A, where he required the presence of the majority of Rathbone's Command Team. From his console at the head of the auditorium he kept a watch on the funeral proceedings, but more particularly his brittle glance flickered over the grouped TV displays of the various activities outside the spacecraft. Morgan wished that he would find something else to do now of all times. And he too watched the displays: in particular he watched one shuttle – 027 – though he tried hard not to seem to. And as far as the TV camera was concerned – or rather the image from it that Wheeldata processed through to the screen – 027 kept its station a kilometre down-track of the Wheel, its reaction control jets blipping occasionally to correct some slight drift or rotation.

The time on Morgan's c-unit passed 1205 hrs. The shuttle was still apparently hanging there, occasional reflections from the Sun lancing from its narrow wings. If it hadn't moved by now Zeffert was truly dead. But whatever was happening it was beyond the scope of anyone on the Wheel to amend. Morgan brought his thumping heart under conscious control; Sidorenko was approaching him, casually negotiating the aisles between the consoles in the auditorium, still watching the displays.

'Is everything all right here, Feodor?'

'Yes, Colonel, as far as can be seen.'

'That is a point. I can't help feeling that the Engineering officer is taking too long to free the shuttering – too many tea breaks, eh, *Mister* Morgan?'

Morgan acknowledged that he had been addressed in Russian, and that he had been summarily demoted from his spurious rank of commander, with a smile that reflected none of his emotions. For he had just seen something that had disturbed him profoundly – just now when he was trapped by Sidorenko's penetrating glance.

'Coffee breaks, probably, Colonel. He'll do everything The Right Way – if you know what I mean.' What he had seen while too preoccupied with shuttle 027 was a row of six flashes on a different screen. The six flashes were sunlight, reflected from the glass canopies of the kosmolyots on the docking raft. The whole assembly of raft, shuttles and hydrogen tanks had been rolling slowly, by just a few degrees every hour. Where the human eye can be deceived by what it sees on a television screen it cannot so easily be deceived by what it perceives directly: and now the Russian shuttle pilots under those glass canopies were in a position to see with unaided sight all that was happening in the vicinity of the Wheel.

'I know what is meant by the term The Right Way, but I am quite certain that you do not.'

'If you would just excuse me for a moment, sir?' Morgan had to think quickly, under pressure from two directions. He typed through to Commander Crabtree's terminal and spoke into his headset microphone. 'Sandra, I have a Wheeldata alert on hydrogen temperature in the tanks.' He prayed that she would take *Wheeldata alert* as a hint. He looked across at her. She was doing something to her hair in a cosmetic mirror. Stupid woman: he knew she was going to refute the lie, so he carried on. 'In response to Wheeldata LH_2 temperature alert I recommend you put the raft-LH_2 complex into barbecue mode, starting with a positive ten-degree roll away from the sun angle.'

'I see no temperature warning,' said Sidorenko.

'There isn't yet.'

Sandra had pocketed the mirror, looked across at Morgan, paused, and started typing. *She had better be typing the right things.*

'There's a time lag. If we don't pre-empt the build-up then it starts to boil even when we've rolled away from the sun angle. If it's really bad we lose attitude control.'

Sandra was marvellous: he had known that she would understand. Wheeldata was now displaying a critical temperature increase and bubble formation in the tank most exposed to the sun.

'I thought *Wheeldata* was your voice-access code to the computer.'

'It is. It's also the designator for all data relating to movement of space vehicles – like a call sign.'

The attitude jets were now burning on the refuelling complex. The raft began its ponderous roll. The flashing canopies disappeared from sight. Morgan glanced at his c-unit as his hands moved over the keyboard. 1215 hrs. Zeffert's ten-shuttle flight should be moving out of matching orbit now. On the screens they hung there, inert. They were still displayed by Wheeldata as being unserviceable. He prayed that they had gone. There was no way of checking that wouldn't have been penetrated by Sidorenko or one of his men.

'We were speaking of doing things The Right Way, Mister Morgan. Your handling of the hydrogen shipment from Callisto does not seem to have followed that precept. I presume you had some selfish motive?'

'On the contrary, Colonel, I had hoped that the whole space community would benefit from the shipment. I suppose your use of it, on the other hand, won't be selfish?'

Sidorenko ignored the question. 'I'm surprised to find the British Secret Intelligence Service operating by such humane ideals.'

'The Service doesn't exist any more: it's just me. Nor for that matter does the Soviet Union. Likewise, what you do is up to you.'

'Each exists as long as one of its members survives, Morgan. The concept is one of loyalty. It is obviously unknown to you.'

'How did you find out about the Callisto shipment anyway? Our communications were secure.'

'But your institutions were not. We learnt from one of our agents in your Division Six. I don't interest myself in such concerns, but I believe his identity code was "C". The importance of that information is immaterial now, but I presume that means something to you?'

Morgan had no need to pretend at this stage that he was lost for words, for he knew now why the Head of Division Six had given him so ill-defined a mission. He'd been sent to spy for the Soviet Union. So C had already known about the CO_2 crisis, about Pluto. Morgan had not only given him the rest – he'd created some of it for him: the Callisto resource, at least. He felt sick. It was time to be ill anyway.

At 1856 hrs. Mr Richard James Morgan died, while serving with the USSF on an exchange posting from the British Meteorological Office, from radiation injuries suffered during combat – or so Wheeldata recorded it for public use. In his cabin he breathed deeply and slowly, and then slowly and shallowly, until his respiration was down to an imperceptible one a minute and his heart rate was down to the twenty-five a minute that a sleeping man reaches in weightless conditions. But Morgan wasn't asleep. His mind was at rest, its tranquil attention inward. He could hear movements in the room and see the subdued light through his eyelids, and the impressions were sharp. But they were distant, and not such as to register any demand on his consciousness. He took himself further away, luxuriating in this timeless peace. The idea of survival itself took on a different value.

Doc Bardelli examined the needle of his carefully-measured syringe of curare solution and looked at Morgan. Then he shrugged, emptied the syringe in a long glistening stream on to the carpet and returned it to its clip in his case. Morgan's way was just as good. Better in some ways. He sat down to keep vigil against any disturbance of the corpse.

An undifferentiated time later Morgan felt himself being shifted to a cold aluminium surface. The changes in pressure and temperature were distant and of nominal interest to him. He knew he was being carried along the corridor. He knew he was in one of the missile loading rooms.

There was a voice that he had not expected. He knew that it belonged to Colonel Sidorenko.

'You're making too much of an event of this. The man's a traitor. By dying he's only saving someone the trouble of shooting him – though for the life of me I can't decide which of his employers he's done most harm to.'

'We aim to give any man a decent burial, Colonel.' That was Rathbone's voice.

'Rather more elaborate that decent, I would have thought. Why the metalwork? It's a bit of a waste, isn't it?'

'It's a matter of belief. See the words we use? See what I mean? – *looking for the resurrection of the body, when space shall give up its dead.*'

'Yes, I see the words, though I didn't know you still took that stuff literally. But if you want his *body* preserved, I think we can assist you there. Here, Vladya – ' There was a rustle of clothing and a metallic click. ' – put a hole through that coffin for me. The vacuum of space will do your preserving for you.'

'I wouldn't advise it in here, Colonel,' said Rathbone's voice. 'The aluminium's not thick.'

'The walls of this room are of steel, Captain. I'm surprised you don't know that.' There was a reverberating concussion and a smell of cordite. 'Now carry on . . . . Well, go on then, he's got nothing to wait for.'

Morgan felt movement, and the light over his eyelids grew faint and vanished. There was a loud click just behind his head. It was interesting. He could hear Rathbone's voice mumbling outside. Then Sidorenko's. 'Well, go on then. We have other business to conduct.' There was something he had to do. He would think of it soon. He might open his eyes. They seemed far from his control; distant and unwieldy pieces of equipment. He had a go at it, and then the memory of how to work came back into them. They opened. They focused slowly on a small bright light. It was close to his face. It was a small hole in the coffin – about nine millimetres across. The light went out. He must be inside the launch tube. A sensation in his ears told him that the launch tube had been sealed. *But he shouldn't be able to feel that. The coffin was supposed to be airtight*! Then he thought again of the hole in front of his face and the sound of the pistol shot. He searched around in front of him with his hand. He found it and covered it with the end of his finger. That was all right. Seven pounds per square inch pressure difference. Hole about a quarter of a square inch. Less than two pounds on one finger . . . . Huh! thinking imperial again . . . .

He heard the pneumatic pumps.

Should be all right. One bullet hole's no problem. *One bullet hole? There must be an exit hole*! He screwed his other arm round behind his back. It was hard to find. *An ecstasy of fumbling*. It was a phrase that came into his mind. Someone suffocating. He found it, round the side.

Bang went the compressed nitrogen charge. The coffin was in space. For an instant Morgan was hunched up against the end of the cylinder, and his fingers lost the bullet holes. Then, weightless, he found them again, with the pressure in the coffin already halved. It didn't matter. There was no hydrazine in the motor unit – only oxygen which he could turn on by means of a simple little tap. He only had to reach it. He had almost moved his hand before he became fully awake and realised that it would be impossible to turn the tap on. Already he wanted to take great gasps, and he must not. Already he had to quell the impulse to shiver violently. Only fifteen seconds had elapsed, and he must conserve oxygen and body energy for long minutes yet. He sought the way back into his previous suspension, but it was hard with so many urgent calls on his pain centres . . . .

Twenty-Four

WHEN THEY emptied Morgan out of his coffin in the airlock of shuttle 010 twelve minutes later he was still conscious, feeling the want of clean oxygen, but deeply cold. He pushed aside the oxygen mask that Hawkins tried to hold over his mouth and nose, and the anxious faces of his two SOT comrades relaxed. He breathed the warm air deeply and worked his frozen and cramped joints. He interrupted their impatient questioning.

'Did Fred get off all right?'

'We saw 027 pick him up,' replied Hawkins. 'Took about five minutes.'

'Should be all right then. What kept you?'

'We looked on it as a training exercise for you. Didn't want to make it too easy.'

'Thanks, I really appreciate that. And the shuttles?'

'027 and nine other shuttles left parking orbit. They all burnt at the same time, and stayed together. We didn't dare to contact them.'

'Quite right.' 010 had drifted well clear of the Wheel, and a long burst on its reaction control system drew it away fast. 'All right, Bill, quit the massage act. You're breaking my back. What you can give me is food. Skip the lettuce; I want a beef sandwich – or six.'

'We've only got synthetic stuff, I'm afraid, but there's plenty of it.'

'Let's have it.' He unwrapped and ate disconsolately. 'I suppose no human being will set tooth into beef again – or duck or trout or bacon or eggs . . . . I sometimes wonder what the joy of survival is.'

'There are other creature comforts,' said Hawkins. That put Morgan in mind of Copernicus and Stephanie.

'If that lunar ferry's not ready I'm going down the pub to get pissed. Our time reference for landing is seventy-eight hours from now and it's usually a seventy-six hour mission. That gives us a very tight schedule at Asisat.'

'Can't we let it slip a bit?' asked Hawkins.

'No. We've got to approach down sun when Copernicus is dead on the terminator.'

'Radar blind-spot?' asked Hawkins.

Morgan nodded. 'They had ferry zero two – *Endymion* I think – on ready status at the time of the attack. We'll have to hope they haven't taken her down too far.'

The three of them drifted through the lower hatch into the payload bay. There were fifty Special Space Warfare Marines there whom Morgan wanted to meet – all those who could get out to 010 before the kosmolyots arrived. They were commanded by Captain Mitchell whom Morgan already knew to be a capable soldier. He had by now formed them into five combat units – the composition of each balanced for independent action on the lunar surface. The payload bay was chaotic. Some of the men were sleeping, their sleeping bags tied at random angles to any available hold. Those who were awake were all active: engaged in weapons drill or adjusting their rifle sights for lunar gravity, quizzing one another on the features from lunar orbiter photographs, practising signals drill (for they were not expecting to be able to use radio) and exercising against the insidious debilitation of existence in zero gee. Morgan, accompanied by Mitchell, drifted among them, sharing the problems and offering deferential advice where he usefully could. His purpose was to find out exactly what he could expect from these men – and exactly how to get it when he wanted it.

Tyler, the shuttle captain, called back from the flight deck and Mitchell relayed the order.

'OK, girls, we're due for rendezvous in about fifteen minutes. That means stow your kit for vacuum, don suits and round hats, strap into your seats and plug in to the oxygen and communications sockets. I want you ready in ten. Last man ready digs the latrines at Mare Imbrium. Now *move*!'

Morgan, Sarin and Hawkins glided hastily out of the ensuing maelstrom and strapped into the rear flight deck seats to watch Asisat approach. It grew large in the windscreens.

'No signals yet,' said Tyler. 'No docking lights, no beam, no radio.'

'Good,' said Morgan. 'They're responding to our silence. Let's hope they keep it that way.' The ECM panel was set to invert out any radio communication from Asisat that would give the game away to the Russians in the Wheel – but nothing could be done to jam docking lights and lasers if Asisat's crew chose to switch them on. The nose of the shuttle eased up until it was stationary, ten metres out from the centre of Asisat's main docking doors.

'Well, what do we do now?'

'Let's wait and see what they do.'

In a position that could be termed *above* the docking doors relative to the shuttle's attitude, several figures were clearly visible behind the well-lit windows of Docking Control. One of them waved tentatively.

'Let's have the cockpit lights.' Tyler switched them on. 'Take off your helmets. I want them to see who we are.'

The men on the shuttle's flight deck doffed their helmets. The figure who had waved before waved again, affirmatively. Ten minutes later two space-suited figures climbed out of a small airlock on one side of the Docking Control greenhouse and jetted cautiously across to the under-nose airlock of the shuttle. Tyler cycled them through into the lower deck module. They shrugged out of their manoeuvring harnesses, then Sarin and Hawkins helped them off with their helmets. The first to emerge was Chuck Lang. He grinned his greeting, white teeth against ebony face. Behind him Fulbrook, the ASI Space Operations manager, looked around him nervously. Lang nodded towards the lower hatch.

'You got Ruskies in there?'

Morgan shook his head.

'Well what the hell are you doing here? What the hell's going on? How long are we going to do what the Sidorenko bum says? Why –'

'OK, OK.' Morgan couldn't help smiling, but he was in a desperate hurry. 'We keep doing what Sidorenko says because otherwise all your friends die at Copernicus.'

'Yeah, yeah, we heard about that when he called us about the refuelling couplings. It was bad news. But what's he sent a shuttle across for?'

'He hasn't. He doesn't know we're here.'

'How d'you manage that?'

'More to the point,' put in Fulbrook, '*why* the hell did you manage it? The Russians have got us by the balls, and if you don't call the Wheel, grovel, and get back quick, you'll have six hundred corpses on your debit file. Does Rathbone know about this?'

Morgan didn't look at Fulbrook. He didn't have time to try liking him – anything like.

'You're pulling a sensor con, aren't you,' said Lang with conviction.

'That's right.'

'You mean,' pursued Fulbrook, 'there are Russians inside that space station who don't know you've just skated three hundred tons of shuttle over here?'

'That's right, Mister Fulbrook. This shuttle's on their screens now, and as far as they're concerned it's where it always was – in formation with the Wheel.'

'I like it. Just wait till they find out. They're going to be so mad–'

'We aim to delay that discovery, with your help, Mister Fulbrook,' said Morgan.

Fulbrook became resentfully sober. 'Don't worry, we're not fools here either. We saw you coming, we figured out how, and we haven't blown it yet.'

'Naturally. We're most grateful. Meanwhile we most urgently require that lunar ferry out there, and we need to leave orbit in an hour and a half.'

'You've got to be kidding. It takes days to check out a lunar mission, and that's at panic speed. It takes a week just to authorise one.'

Morgan seemed not to have heard him. 'I should imagine the most likely problem would be fuel boil-off, so perhaps you'd have that checked right away. Otherwise, as she was ready to go a couple of days ago, everything should be prepared, I would imagine?'

'You didn't seem to hear what I said. I said that it would take a week. We are not a military operation and we are not about to jump because you say jump. We have a serious resources problem here. We can't just go shooting off rockets like it was the fourth of July.'

Sarin interposed, looming respectfully over the Operations manager. 'So that's the deadline, Mister Fulbrook. We've got an hour and a half to get that ship ready to go, and we've got to get the fifty marines who are just on the other side of this bulkhead on board.' After a pause he thumped the bulkhead with a heavy hand to emphasise the presence of the fifty marines.

At that stage Fulbrook understood why he was not being understood. 'OK, I get you, I think. We'll have to see what we can do for you.'

'Not enough, Mister Fulbrook. We leave on the timeline. Now what are the problems?'

'The payload bay. It's fixed for cargo at the moment.'

'Then unfix it. Weigh in there yourself and help. That deadline stands. Now get going.' Fulbrook started to go, Chuck Lang assisting him.

'And no radio chat. Also you can get the ferry behind the space station to work on it. We don't want Sidorenko's hot breath on our necks.'

'We'll come and give you a hand,' said Morgan distrustfully. 'Bill, you stay and help Mike Tyler.'

The four men left through the airlock.

Twenty-Five

IN COMMAND A, Lieutenant Gorshkov looked up from his screen. 'Colonel, would you come and see this?'

Sidorenko was red-eyed and unshaven. The American overall which he had exchanged for his space suit was crumpled. He had been pacing the auditorium to keep himself awake, but even that was increasing the fatigue that was aching through his body. His single purpose now was to stay awake, to stay alive, to stay in command until the shipment of hydrogen from Callisto was safely in the tanks of his kosmolyots. He interrupted his pacing at Gorshkov's terminal, glad of the diversion from the wary monotony of the refuelling.

'What is it?'

'I've been watching the big industrial satellite through the small telescope. Ten minutes ago I saw two men come out of one of the airlocks near their docking doors. They drifted out a few metres and disappeared.'

'Behind what?'

'Behind nothing, sir. They just vanished. But the strange thing is that four men have just appeared in the same spot. Look, they're going back through the airlock now.' Sidorenko watched the display in silence for a while, as Gorshkov replayed the incident from Wheeldata's memory.

'Do they have many operations outside the spacecraft at the moment?'

'Usually one or two men on some maintenance task. The most I've counted until now is three.' Sidorenko considered the screen image of Asisat.

'It could be a trick of the light, Lieutenant. In that position two men might have passed from brilliant sunlight into complete shadow. The other two men might have come from another airlock and joined them in the shadowed area. We can hardly expect the Americans to have perfected the trick of becoming invisible, can we?'

'No, sir. It didn't look like a lighting effect though.' Sidorenko continued to watch the screen until it began to defocus before his tired gaze.

'Keep me informed.'

He strode back to his console. After a moment's thought he selected Waldon's access code through Wheeldata by voice. 'Commander Waldon, what progress are you making with those window shutters?'

'We're having a lot of problems out here – er, Colonel. We don't like to use enough flame to cut straight through, because we don't want to blow any windows out. The heat's dissipating quickly and we're getting through a lot of gas.'

'Commander Waldon, I find it hard to comprehend how a competent engineer can be defeated by a simple cutting problem. Is there no other way of approaching it?'

'Not without portable cutting and grinding gear. It has to be powerful thin-disk kit – which we haven't got.' Waldon saw the nature of the trap that was closing on him, but the lies he could tell were bounded by the limits of probability.

'Has your industrial satellite got this equipment?'

'No, we contacted them after the first attempts to repair the damage, but they couldn't help us.'

'Then I'll see if I can't get them moving. Boris, get me Fulbrook at Asisat on the s-band.' It took three minutes for Fulbrook to appear on the screen because he had to get out of his space suit, rush to Asisat's control centre, and look casual.

'Busy, Mister Fulbrook?'

'Not particularly, General, ah, Marshal –'

'Colonel.'

'Colonel, sir. If the truth be known I was asleep.'

'Another dynamic administrator, I see. What programmes have you in hand at the moment?'

'Well . . . er, *programmes* – none. It's hard to make any plans. We're just keeping the place ticking over.'

'Any EVAs?'

Fulbrook shook his head, caught the eye of Hawkins who was standing on the other side of the console, and continued, 'Not much. Just a few men outside on routine maintenance.'

Sidorenko quickly described the window shutter problem to him. 'So, Mister Fulbrook, I assume you've got the equipment to do the job?'

'Yes, we've certainly got portable cutting gear . . . .' Again Hawkins signalled frantically. ' . . . but it's not the sort of stuff you could use at the Wheel. It relies on anchorage points, and it's set up for our particular power supply and control systems. We could modify it for you.' Hawkins held up seven fingers. 'It would probably take about a week, going flat out, and we'd have to –'

'Do it in a day,' said Sidorenko, and cut the connection. *By God, we should have taken these Americans years ago. They're useless.*

'Gorshkov, is there any way our television cameras could be lying to us?'

'I'm not sure what you mean, Colonel.'

'Is there any way in which they could be hiding some activity from us, or showing us some activity that's not really happening?'

'I see what you mean.'

'Is it possible?'

'It's common for computer programs to generate screen images – like this one.' He pointed to one of Wheeldata's systems displays. 'But we can see things happening on those screens which we know to be happening – like the refuelling of our shuttles. So it would have to be a program that could mix the real and the synthetic. It would have to change the synthetic image constantly, and keep it consistent with the real. It would have to choose what to show and what to invent. That would require a very intelligent machine. From what we've seen the on-board computer is no more advanced than Astrogorodok's.'

'Can it be done?'

'It's possible, Colonel.'

'Prepare for EVA, Lieutenant. I want some flesh-and-blood eyes out there.'

'We're stretched thin here, sir. Are you sure . . . '

'I know, Lieutenant.' Sidorenko smiled. Another man might have come down on Gorshkov with the full weight of Soviet authority. 'We'll do our best without you. Go all the same.'

'Yes, sir.'

Behind its appearance of hopeless defeat the Wheel's remaining Command Team was suffering a genuine bafflement: this was a setback unforeseen simply because it was undesired.

And that bafflement was compounded. The six SC 3s which Sidorenko had liberated were already on their way to Astrogorodok with most of the Wheel's hydrogen reserves – and with the threat against the Copernicus hostages to keep them obedient.

The kosmolyots had completed their refuelling despite all possible technical hindrance, and were preparing to launch into an orbit that would rendezvous with *Minerva*; six kosmolyots wouldn't take all her hydrogen, but fully fuelled and facing a low-energy return to Astrogorodok they would be able to take more than half. More than that, their very presence would prevent Zeffert's rendezvous.

The hope of Rathbone's team was that the kosmolyot crews would be too busy to pay critical attention to errant space traffic in their vicinity. But they didn't equal the threat of the suspicious eyes of Lieutenant Groshkov.

Twenty-Six

A THOUSAND metres out from Asisat the lunar ferry *Endymion* stopped her drift. Her reaction control system quadrants twinkled, and she rolled purposefully to a new attitude.

Sidorenko was watching *Endymion* on the small telescope display in Command A. But as far as the display showed, the lunar ferry was still in close formation with Asisat – and was still inert. Groshkov, space-suited, was on the elevator to Docking Control at the centre of the Wheel's disk.

The squat cylinder of *Endymion's* flight deck afforded a three hundred and sixty degree panorama of the heavens from the top of the three-storey payload bay. That towered above the service module which carried the spherical fuel tanks, nuclear reactors and propulsion units and the fixed tripod landing gear. Morgan and Hawkins sat behind the two-man flight crew, conferring over the flight plans which the on-board computer was displaying. They were in comfortable fabric covered seats. The air was good, and the quiet busyness of the computer, evident in the muted tones of colour and sound with which it passed data to the crew, inspired confidence. They could see the whole of the Earth when *Endymion* had completed her attitude manoeuvre. It was beautiful now, a big unfathomable pearl of milk-white haze which seemed to burn internally with the scattered light of the Sun. The old swirled white and blue with its thin atmospheric glaze was finished. This new sterile Earth was so featureless, so perfectly turned, that it might have been man-made. But then, Morgan reflected, in a sense it was. He couldn't see the Moon. It was hidden by the Earth. But a few kilometres beyond Asisat he could see a satellite that weighed equally on his mind – the Wheel, attended by the tiny silver splinters of the parasitic fleet that swarmed around it. Sidorenko was there, unaware, he hoped, of the sleight of electronics that was taking place around him.

The four men on the flight deck quickly agreed with the computer on a trajectory. It would take *Endymion* close past the western limb of the Moon into a ten-degree orbit. Three-quarters of an orbit would bring the ferry round the farside for a first-pass landing down sun at Copernicus.

That was at T minus five minutes – time for the flight crew to check off the last few items on their list and for Captain Mitchell to see that all was secure in the payload bay.

The crew authorised the flight-control program. Now the on-board computer would be in command until *Endymion* touched down on the eastern rim of Copernicus in three days' time – although that command could be interrupted if it were necessary. Meanwhile there was little to do but watch the displays. Even that was not strictly necessary.

The computer marked off the zero moment and the event screen authorised the powering up of the ion propulsion system. The systems display confirmed ignition and quantified the thrust levels. On a TV monitor Morgan watched the honeycomb of nozzles flare to life, flicker and settle to the even, barely-perceptible violet of efficient running.

Long minutes passed before *Endymion* made any visible progress along the unwinding spiral of the trajectory display, or before the disposition of lunar ferry, the Earth, and nearby space traffic began slowly to change. It would be a relief to speed on, out of sight of the Wheel.

For months Morgan had watched night and day sweep across the same face of the Earth. Now, very slowly, for *Endymion* was accelerating at only one-twentieth of gee, he began to see the Earth revolve. Within half an hour the Wheel was out of sight.

The Command team on the Wheel had been able to delay Lieutenant Gorshkov that long. With the lunar ferry a barely discernible mote vanishing through the haze of the Earth's limb, he emerged from the Docking Control airlock. He crawled out on to the rail until he was on the face of the Wheel, and clipped his harness to the last rung. He turned to survey the hemisphere of space that was within his field of vision. He was more tired than he had ever been. He was one of a hopelessly small team fighting for the survival of his comrades. And now he had to fight the wearying battle against vertigo. Astrogorodok did not spin: the Russians did not simulate gravity. The great over-hanging face of the Wheel threatened to throw him off, and the vast Earth revolved ponderously about his bleared eyes. The Sun cast shadows that rotated, lengthening and shortening twice every minute. Ten minutes passed before he could begin to look around him at the vehicles that attended the Wheel. And they wouldn't stay still either, but seemed to revolve around his head with the Earth. It was almost impossible to pin any one of them down. He slowly set about memorising their relationship one to another. His lips moved in mnemonic repetition. He began to frown . . . .

'Lunar transfer injection burn ends at two hours three minutes and thirteen seconds,' said Tyler to no one in particular, for there was no mission control: *Endymion* was on its own. 'We're right on the time-line. Landing scheduled in seventy-four hours and twenty-two minutes.'

'Fine. Any radar warnings?'

Brodnik shook his head. 'There's nothing can pick us up against our wave-inversion – until we get near Copernicus, that is.'

'I hope so. Can you use the computer to maintain a position display? I'm thinking particularly of Commander Zeffert's rendezvous trajectory towards *Minerva*. And Sidorenko's shuttles: they'll have left an hour ago.'

'Can do. Take about ten minutes.'

'Thanks. I'll be with Mitchell in the payload bay.'

Mitchell and his men were poring over a three-dimensional display of the Copernicus area accessed from *Endymion's* holographic navigational store. The display's point of view was that of an imaginary vehicle roaming among the chasms and terraces of the crater rim. The men were matching the view with maps and orbiter photographs, and chanting off the landmarks together. Mitchell moved a cursor across the screen.

'Now that road down there is the first human artefact we meet – at least we'd better hope it is. It's called Highway East, and it gives access from the eastern edges of the Ocean of Storms, through this notch in the crater rim – which is Deep Cleft – down over the inner ramparts to Copernicus Base in the centre of the crater.'

'How far is that, sir?'

'From Deep Cleft it's forty kilometres. That's half an hour in the Rovers downhill with the Sun behind us.'

'What happens if we meet someone on Highway East, sir?'

'We send 'em to Hell,' said a deep matter-of-fact voice from the back.

'That's what we've got to avoid at this stage,' said Mitchell. 'The moment we make contact with the Soviets we can expect our people to get it in the neck within a short finite time. We run that risk particularly at and after Deep Cleft. Our data is that scheduled traffic on Highway East is light at this time. We choose our moment, and if we go by that route we have the Sun right behind us. If anyone comes we see them first. So we get off the road quick.'

'But, sir – '

'Can you hold that one for five minutes, Sam? I'll be right back with you. Lieutenant, take over. Run them down the highway.' He propelled himself over to where Morgan had just floated down the companion ladder from the flight deck, and took his arm. He spoke under the cover of a buzz of questions from the marines.

'They're not keen on this one, Dick. Not enough data. No clear plan. No dry runs. That's not the way we usually do things.'

'I know. But it's no use hanging around for safer options. We go or we're finished.' Mitchell looked doubtful. 'But we won't go in without a good working plan.' He wished he could think of one. How could you storm a hermetically-sealed base without letting anyone know? How did you detect five hundred people in a Pentagon-sized labyrinth without being detected yourself?'

'Any news from the Wheel?' asked Mitchell.

'No. If we hear from the Wheel it means that Sidorenko has managed to blow the TV simulation.'

'Then we go in fast and shooting.'

Morgan shook his head. 'If you think about it that's what we can't do. Imagine that Sidorenko got on to us now. He would give Gurevich three days' warning of our attack. Gurevich would deploy his forces to meet a·space attack and we'd be clobbered before we had a chance to land. Besides, he'd have three days to do what he liked with the hostages.'

'So what would we do?'

Morgan shrugged.

'Another Tehran?' said Mitchell. 'We sure wouldn't like that.'

'Nevertheless it would be our only choice. If Sidorenko finds out what we're doing we have to capitulate and go into an Earth-return trajectory. We'd have to switch off our ECM and apologise and promise to be good. And we'd have to mean it. There would a thousand American lives as surety.'

'If that happened it would be the end.'

Morgan smiled gloomily. 'It would be the end of the end of civilisation as we know it.'

Tyler spoke over the intercom. 'Dick, I have a position display for you.' Morgan arrowed up through the hatch to look at it. Tyler had produced a fine piece of computer graphics – a three-dimensional holograph in constrasting colours of spacecraft orbits against the revolving coordinates of the Earth-Moon system.

'Now, Dick, this red one is the Milk Train.' He pointed to a long thin loop that came in from the edge of the screen and hairpinned sharply around the Earth. 'That's coming in from Jupiter-wards at a hundred and fifty thousand kilometres per hour. The solar-fusion propulsion system is beginning to slow her down and she'll be at no more than Earth orbital velocity as she goes round the corner. That's where she's always met before she powers off again for the Jupiter transfer injection burn.'

'Have you ever done that?'

'I haven't personally handled the docking, but I've been on board a shuttle that's done it.'

'What's it like?'

'What can I say? In some ways very impressive. In some ways much like any ordinary docking, though there's more urgency than normal. You know that you're plugged into a beast that's going to go like hot shit for Jupiter in three hours' time whether you want it to or not. Sure as hell you don't want to go too.'

'Right. And we're this one?' He pointed to a green trace that curled out from Earth orbit, whipped back round the leading edge of the Moon, coiled once about the planet and slanted down to its nearside surface.

'Yes, that's us. Then the yellow one's Commander Zeffert's shuttle flight. You see he has to go out in a long ellipse away from Earth, and then back to rendezvous with the Milk Train as it comes tight round the Earth.'

'And these are the Russians?'

'Yes, the red trace. They started out later, so their ellipse is displaced. But the computer's projecting that they'll make two course corrections — here and here — so that they catch up with the Milk Train at its slowest phase.'

'So Zeffert and the Russians will rendezvous with Minerva at about the same time?'

'They will. I hadn't thought of that.'

'*We are in*, as you say out here, *a high negative desirability mode*.'

'You could say that.'

'How long before rendezvous will they be within observation range of one another?'

'With ECM?'

'Yes.'

'About twelve hours, if we've got their course corrections correctly guessed.'

'Mm. When Sidorenko's *Minerva* flight spots Zeffert, they'll alert Gurevich, so we'll have to hit Copernicus Base before they close to within observation range. That gives us another deadline. We've got to go in to the Base within twelve hours of landing, then?'

'Looks like it.'

'Right. There's no chance that the Russians will spot Fred's shuttles here, where the orbits cross on the way out?'

'No chance. They go through that cross-over at very different times.'

'Well, that's something. Are those present positions confirmed?'

'Only the Milk Train. Its solar reflectors show up on the telescope – or with the naked eye for that matter. But we can't use radar without giving our position away, so the others are dead reckoning.'

'Can you contact Fred on the laser system?'

Tyler looked at the position display. 'No reason why not. The Ruskies are way outside beam dispersion. It might take some time, though.'

The USSF's laser communication system could exchange information at a prodigious rate along its needle-like beams. Because they were so narrow they could not be tapped by anyone who was not directly in their path. But because they were so narrow you had to know precisely where to point them, and that, in secure times, was simplified by radar. The communication beam from *Endymion* was three metres across at the forty thousand kilometre range of Zeffert's shuttles. It couldn't be broadened because that would reduce its brightness. The on-board computer had to scan the beam methodically across Zeffert's track for ten hours before it picked up a reply and called for Tyler's attention.

Twenty-Seven

BY THAT time Gorshkov was on his fourth EVA, and had been at the docking bay airlock for a total of eight hours. His mind swam with revolving shuttles and the hypnotic sweep of the Sun's light. His eyes were gummed and weeping, and he wanted to wipe his nose. He was suffering, but he had guts to go with his family's illustrious military tradition, and in a cool rational room in his mind spacecraft were being checked off and labelled.

In the twelve hours since he had clipped his harness to the rail for the first time, the Wheel had completed half an orbit of the Earth, and so had all the vehicles which matched its path. And all the subtly different ellipses of the spacecraft had changed their orientations by exactly one hundred and eighty degrees in relation to the Wheel. The shuttles that he had first seen were out of sight behind the space station. Now he could see those that had originally been hidden. He was still able to count. And he had counted only thirteen shuttles, the docking raft (now empty), the hydrogen tanks (also empty), Asisat, whose attendant lunar ferry must still be hidden behind it somewhere, and NASA's Astronomy and Scientific Research satellite. The engineering teams were nowhere to be seen. The last set of cutting equipment had become unserviceable an hour ago.

'Colonel; Lieutenant Gorshkov here. Have there been any shuttle movements since I first EVAd?'

'No, Anatole. I was just going to call you in. Seminov can take over.'

'Thank you, Colonel, but I can only count — ' He said more, but a pair of wire-cutters, delicately wielded, rendered him audienceless by cutting his communication cable where it snaked from his helmet to his PLSS pack.

Joe Waldon, the man with the wire-cutters, continued the transmission on a different frequency. He spoke clearly and quietly.

'Waldon, Engineering. We have an external Wheeldata aerial failure — I suspect in the docking gantry array. Russell, Meyer, get to Command A and track it down.'

That was the Alert signal. After a pause of exactly ten seconds two men bearing the Engineering flash and the name-tabs of Russell and Meyer entered each of the corridor sections guarded by Sidorenko's men. Two more hurried officiously into Command A.

'Waldon! Sidorenko. I want Gorshkov back through that airlock in one minute. We have no indication of communication failure in Command A. What . . . '

After exactly twenty seconds Waldon added, 'Come on, hurry it up, you two. I want action.'

The seven pairs of men labelled Russell and Meyer had timed their movements carefully. The word *action* snapped over the intercom when each was within three metres of a Russuan guard. There was action. A burst of rapid fire echoed through the corridors.

Twenty-Eight

MORGAN SLIPPED on a headset. 'Skunk, this is Possum; how do you
read me? Over.'

'Possum; Skunk, five by five.' Zeffert's features clarified on the
communication screen. 'Glad to see you got away. What's your
situation? Over.'

'It's good, Fred,' said Morgan, barely able to restrain himself from
crossing his fingers. 'We got away intact and – as far as we know –
undetected. Over.'

'I don't believe it. What's your mission timing? Over.'

Morgan glanced at the event screen. 'We land at the eastern rim of
the target at sixty-three hours fifty-two minutes on my mark –
three . . . two . . . one . . . MARK. And you? Over.'

'We rendezvous with *Minerva* about twenty-four hours after that.
So you've got time to put plenty of planning into your relief of
Copernicus. Over.'

'Not so, Fred. Our information is that you'll be observed by
Sidorenko's shuttles twelve hours before you rendezvous.'

'So they've launched. I was hoping they wouldn't make it. By
Christ, I'd give a lot to know how they found out about the shipment.'

'They launched about twelve hours after you. And they were
planning to milk *Minerva* before they ever attacked the Wheel.' He
avoided mentioning the sieve-like discretion of Division Six. 'We'll
send you through our estimate of their flight plan on the high rate.
Ready? Over.'

The computers chatted happily to one another for five seconds.

'That doesn't look so good,' said Zeffert. 'We might have to fight
our way in to *Minerva*. And we haven't got a lot of fire power out
here.'

'Nor have they for that matter. Can you change your orbit and stay
out of their way until rendezvous?'

'Negative, Dick. We haven't got the energy to make that much
difference.'

'That's going to cut it fine for us at Copernicus.'

'Yeah, I can see that. How are you planning on going in?'

Morgan told him and added, 'Not much of a plan yet I'm afraid, but we've got a couple of days to work on it.'

'Have you got the data to send me on the *Minerva* docking system?'

'D'you mind if I don't send it to you yet, Fred?'

'Well, I'm not offended, if that's what you mean. But why? I've got to know some time.'

'Fred, that information is fundamental to survival – for the Russians or us. I want to make sure that it's we who use it. So logically I ought to send it on your successful rendezvous with *Minerva*.'

'Uh-huh. So you mean we might not rendezvous with *Minerva*? The Russians might take us and use the docking information themselves?'

'We've got to consider it.'

'Well, whilst we're on bad endings, what if you fail to retake Copernicus? Who's going to send me that data?'

'It makes no difference. If we fail at Copernicus this becomes a Soviet solar system. Then they get the hydrogen either way – even if you collect it for them.'

'OK. I accept that.'

Morgan felt bad about the conversation. His arguments were specious.

'Dick, I want you to know I have a lot of confidence in the outcome at Copernicus. You've got the guts and the imagination and the realism – plus the toughest team in the solar system.'

'Thanks, Fred. We're very optimistic here too.' They looked at each other candidly.

'Well OK,' conceded Zeffert, 'it's a lousy set-up – hostages rescuing hostages – but we're committed now.'

'Not all the way. We pull out if things go badly at the Wheel. And we pull out if the odds don't look good at Copernicus. Both of us. We save lives that way.'

'In the short term.'

'Agreed. But at least the people at Copernicus would live to see the short term.'

The half-Moon could be seen through the flight-deck windows now, with the ragged division between night and day lying notched across the Appenines. Tycho, in the south, was picked out like a halo in the lunar dawn. But Copernicus was still in shadow, a ghostly glimmer in the insubstantial Earthlight. Hurrying through despair of meeting her again, Morgan allowed himself the luxury of recalling the feathers of raven-dark hair against soft white skin, as it had been in the glimmering moonlight of Stephanie's cabin that night on the Wheel. The Moon was larger now, every hour, and he was going to her as fast as celestial dynamics would allow – but . . . he didn't allow himself to think of her in the hands of the Russians, or in the pitiless aftermath of a rescue attempt all too likely to fail. It surprised him when the likelihood of his own imminent death added itself to his thoughts.

The near future was strewn with imponderables and unthinkable outcomes, so as to inhibit thought and paralyse action. He was dragged out of his long reverie by a heavy hand on his shoulder and Sarin's blunt tones. 'Thinking about the girl, Dick?'

'Yes,' he admitted. Sarin seldom saw him that vulnerable.

'I'm bloody sorry we never got you and her spliced, old son. It would have been good to see that.' There was an unusual fatalistic concession in Sarin's voice. Morgan looked at him in surprise. He carried on. 'Face it, Dick, we've done a few of these things together in the past, the three of us, and we've hacked success out of bloody impossibility. But this is a different bloody kettle of fish.'

'*A whole new ball-park*, you should say. Bill, how did you feel when you heard I'd been working for the Americans all along?'

'It gave me a new respect for Americans. Seriously though, Dick, you seemed to be giving your little all to SOT. You're not telling me that wasn't real?'

'No. It was real. I was a friendly double if you like. We weren't out to thwart Division Six.'

'Well, that's how I took it. So what was the point?'

'The *Enemy Within* syndrome. American Intelligence has been shit-scared of KGB infiltration of the British Services – ever since Philby's Cambridge cell was prised out. Working so closely with the British they were afraid of infection – sorry, I still can't help calling them *they*. Anyway, *their* nightmare was of a complete KGB *coup* within Divisions Five and Six – from the top. Funny thing is, they seem to have been justified. Not that it matters.

'There was nothing they could do openly. The British were far too touchy about it. So the Department seeded both Divisions with its own agents, as a long-term precaution. Their job was to lie low, keep a friendly watch – and be ready.

'I was one of them. A Sleeper. As it happens I was woken up for an entirely different reason. So in effect I've never been anything other than what I've seemed. Will it pass?'

''*Course*. I was only curious. So what do we do now? I'm getting that pissed off with watching those blokes clean their rifles. I've seen one M-45 come apart a dozen times. I'll be buggered if any of them still shoot by the time we get there.'

'What we do now is hammer out a working plan, Bill. We're going in on the assumption that we're going to succeed. We split the mission up in the usual way and dismantle each problem until we see how to fix it.'

'And that's how we make it look to the marines?'

'That's how we make it look to *us*, Bill. We've got no choice.'

But there were always choices. Barely had Morgan, Sarin, Hawkins, Mitchell and Tyler sat down in front of the VDUs in the upper payload bay when the communication alarm buzzed on the flight deck. Reflexively Morgan pushed himself out of his seat, thrust with one hand against the companion ladder, and cleared the hatch. As he fended himself off from the flight-deck ceiling Brodnik announced, 'Laser contact. Space Force code. Addressed to us.' Morgan steadied himself in front of the screen, hoping that it was Zeffert but guessing that it wasn't. And it wasn't. It was Rathbone.

'Don't reply!' He felt physically weak.

'Possum; Wheel. Are you receiving me? Over.' It was Rathbone all right. But who else was with him?

'Possum; Wheel. Do you read me? Over.' There could be a gun pointing at Rathbone's head – Sidorenko probing for the truth. Or Rathbone could be taking a risk, with Sidorenko listening elsewhere in the Wheel. But that would be unlike Rathbone.

'Possum; this is the Wheel. It is OK to reply. We are back in control. Over.' But then if Sidorenko knew the direction of *Endymion* and the code word Possum, there was nothing left to lose anyway. Then Rathbone started reciting the twenty-four digit cipher which the Command Team alone was supposed to know. Morgan made up his mind. It wasn't necessary for the mission that Rathbone be acknowledged; but it didn't look as though Rathbone was going to impart his information unless acknowledged. That information could very easily be vital. Particularly it might mean that the mission had already failed.

'Beam to the Wheel,' said Morgan. Brodnik quickly established contact down the track of the Wheel's incoming beam. Morgan looked round. The other four men had crowded silently behind him.

'Possum; Go ahead, Wheel. Over,' he said cautiously.

'Possum, I am advising you that we have taken back control from the Soviets on board the Wheel. That was ten minutes ago.' Morgan glanced at his c-unit. 'Sidorenko sent a man outside. We hit them just as he realised what was going on. They didn't have time to get a message out. We lost seven. They lost three. The Russians are now locked up under heavy guard –'

'But wasn't Sidorenko due to contact Gurevich at Copernicus? Over.'

'Yes. Just now. Wheeldata made the contact as we had planned for this contingency. It worked – as far as we could tell.'

'Who answered? Over.'

'A lieutenant. We haven't seen him before. They're taking it in eight-hour shifts. Over.'

'So in another eight hours we might get someone who's more used to the real Sidorenko. You'll have to watch out for that. What did Wheely talk about? Over.'

'The usual stuff about everything being OK. Work on the shutters. Lieutenant Gorshkov's EVA – that's the man they sent outside – progress on the *Minerva* intercept. State of the crew. We fed him that. Over.'

'Your recommendation? Over.'

'Well, the way we see it is that you touch down in about sixty-three hours and make your attempt in anything up to seventy-five hours. Correct? Over.'

'That's correct. We have to go in before Fred makes contact with the kosmolyots on the transfer to *Minerva*'s orbit. Over.'

'So Wheeldata has to make a total of up to seventy-five contacts with Gurevich's men. Now Wheely's bright – but he's also naïve. There's always the possibility of errors in modular programming. It only needs one of the Russians to ask the wrong question – and he'll come up with the right answer.'

'Or else he'll start some dumb conversation about the oddities of Russian semantics.'

'Right. It's a possibility. We're trying to cover it.'

'In short, we've got a decision to make?'

'I'm afraid so. Over.'

'I suppose there's no choice really.' Morgan glanced at his team, wondering which of the possible choices was no choice. They looked pointedly elsewhere. 'Well, Captain, I think you ought to stay in close contact with us. Particularly beam us the Wheely-Gurevich dialogues, so that we can respond immediately if anything goes wrong.'

'How?'

'By turning the solar system over to the Russians unconditionally.' Rathbone nodded his agreement. 'So, your decision?'

'We go.'

Twenty-Nine

AT SEVENTY-four hours into the mission the ion propulsion system flickered to life for the second time. Its gently sustained thrust re-established a sense of floor and ceiling in *Endymion*. And it slowed the spacecraft and aimed it for low orbit insertion at the pale western limb of the Moon.

To be in planetary orbit is a remote experience. If you are two hundred kilometres or two thousand kilometres above the Earth, looking down on its continents and oceans, and on the shallow froth of clouds that used to hang a tiny distance, apparently, above its surface, nothing moves or changes in your eight kilometre-a-second timescale. Only the planet revolves ponderously, once every ninety minutes, and you may notice that a hurricane has moved a hair's breadth between successive orbits. On the Moon where nothing moves the remoteness is greater. It can make you feel that you are a profound philosopher, just to be there – and perhaps you can't help but become one under that awful detachment.

But if you are skimming the Moon, as Morgan was, at an altitutde of a mere sixteen kilometres, with an orbital velocity of nearly two and a half kilometres per second, detachment is not the only sensation. There is an exultation which is not entirely beyond previous experience. To fly a fast strike aeroplane low over rugged snowblown desert at twilight was something like it. But there all was noise and jarring vibration. Here was serene and infinite silence. Even the cockpit lights were turned off to avoid detection. Only the displays glimmered, and beyond them the scrolling landscape, dim but clear in the starlight, for *Endymion* had curved beyond the light of Sun and Earth.

The farside terrain over which they now flew was unfamiliar and cruel. It was a battlefield of overlapping craters and high rock, lacking the dark maria with their beautiful bays and promontories to relieve it. The walls of a large crater grew on the pocked horizon. It tilted toward Morgan until he could see the wide depression that it cut out of the notched landscape. In thirty seconds it was right underneath. Its ramparts became the horizon. But in a minute it was lost from view.

'That's Schrödinger,' said Tyler. Most of the landscapes that he pointed out were named after famous Russians of whom no one had heard. They lacked the classical lyricism of the nearside features.

For a few minutes the flight deck had been bathed in the cold nacreous light of bright filamental fans that spread out of the advancing horizon. Tyler nodded towards them.

'That's the solar corona. That old Sun's really pumping the hot stuff out this year.'

Then the auroral display was banished by the glare of the Sun itself as it blazed through the rugged valleys on the horizon. The up sun windows instantly silvered over and little could be seen of the dark landscape below. Within one hour *Endymion* would land at Copernicus. Mitchell called Morgan to the payload bay for a final briefing.

Two high-resolution photographs were on display: one of the whole of the Copernicus crater and another of the clustered domes, landing pad and roads of Copernicus Base. One feature figured large on both photographs – the mass driver electromagnetic acceleration system which extended from the Base to the rim of the crater forty kilometres away. Mitchell was building up a flow chart of the mission check list.

'OK, so we come down here, tucked nicely in on the outside of the crater wall. Time: zero. Then what?'

'Team Alpha, sir. At zero to M plus five minutes we provide observation and covering fire for the space ship. Captain Tyler, Lieutenant Brodnik and Mister Hawkins remain on board to secure the ship and provide communication with the Wheel. Anyone, but anyone who gets a peep at the ship gets eased out of existence by us.'

'Next?'

'Beacon, sir. We take Rover One with Team Condor as high as we can up the crater wall – which should be here.' He moved the cursor over the crater display from a handset. 'On foot we set up Beacon Base at the highest point on the wall between the ship and Highway East. We set up laser link between Team Alpha and the teams who'll be going into Copernicus crater – not later than M plus one hour thirty. In that position we're visible to Soviet radar at Copernicus Base, so we keep our heads down.'

'Condor?'

'We part from Beacon Team here, sir, and set up the Starfire battery two hundred metres south of Beacon on the wall overlooking Copernicus Base, also by M plus one hour thirty. We launch our missiles on the designated targets at M plus five hours unless Teams Delta or Echo countermand that. Like Beacon we keep our heads down until the shooting starts.'

'Right. We maintain radio silence until we've hit Copernicus Base. While Beacon and Condor are deploying, Delta and Echo, commanded by myself and Mister Morgan respectively, continue round the rim wall to the end of Highway East in Rovers Two and Three. Team Echo crosses Highway East, scales the wall at this point.' He indicated the spot where the mass driver intersected the crater wall. 'They conceal Rover Three in this trench in the wall. They then move down the Mass-driver unit on foot, using it as cover, to the point where it ends. That's two hundred metres short of the Main Dome. From then on they've got no cover until they get to secondary dome B, so they stop there. Any questions on Echo?'

'You said *on foot*, sir. That's forty kilometres. How long's that supposed to take?'

'Don't forget we'll be on the Moon, Corporal. We reckon on your keeping up eighteen kilometres per hour with ease. The point to watch is not falling over, so don't overdo it.'

'When Team Echo gets to this point here, Delta starts off again in Rover Two, so as to synchronise arrival times. We'll be coming down Highway East right out of the Sun, so we're not reckoning on being vulnerable to detection until we're within five to ten kilometres of Copernicus Base. At that point we hide the Rover behind boulders and proceed on foot under the cover of roadside rubble. Any questions so far?'

'Just supposing we are spotted, sir?'

'The moment we are spotted Mister Morgan's Team, Echo, goes in to the Base. We then reinforce them if and when we can.'

'That's what's bothering me, sir, the going in to the Base bit. Say in the best possible case we've got absolute synchronisation between Teams Delta and Echo. We get the covering fire from Team Beacon. Echo gets in and fixes the Base communication system – though that sounds tricky to me. We get in an airlock without having to blow it and open the Base to vacuum – which also sounds chancy. We know we've got a limited time before the Soviets start taking it out on the hostages: maybe ten seconds, maybe half a minute. But we still don't know where the hostages are, or how many Russians there are and how they are deployed. It worries me that it could be a massacre.'

'That's what we're trained for, Skinner. We can't sew everything up beforehand. We move fast and react quick and hit hard. You know our motto.'

'Yes, sir.'

'Any other questions?'

'Yes, sir. How about their orbiters? We've got these pictures from our surveillance satellites. How do we know they won't be pinpointing *us* from orbit?'

'Because we knew where to point our cameras. They don't. Yes, Wheeler?'

'Can we expect any help from the hostages d'you think, sir?'

'No. We know this from other hijacks. The period of inactivity and the sense of defeat will have dulled their ability to respond. Our only concern will be to get them to lie down and stay put. That's what the loud-hailers are for. First the stun grenades, then the order to lie down – repeated until they've done it – while you go in. Don't worry about their finer feelings at that stage. It's their lives we're concerned with. Any more questions? Right. We're at M minus thirty-five minutes. Suit up at minus ten, and make one last check that your weapons are oil-free. Now rehearse the fine detail in your combat teams and refer problems as you require. Let's move.'

Morgan intercepted Mitchell quickly. He spared neither time nor the other's feelings.

'Skinner's right. The very most we've got after we hit the Base is thirty seconds. After that we start to lose hostages, or the Russians start to use them as bargaining counters and we lose the initiative.'

'I know this game too, Morgan. But we've got some advantages that can't usually be counted on. The last thing in the world that the

Ruskies will be expecting is a rescue attempt. After all, they've got positive information that we're still on the Wheel.'

'I'll grant you that. But the moment we go in we'll lose that advantage – by simple virtue of the fact that we're there.'

'Not immediately. There's always some confusion. There's also the instinctive reaction to deploy against us rather than threaten the hostages. Those two factors will reinforce one another. I'm banking on buying a good two minutes that way.'

'Two minutes won't do it – not when we might have to search the whole Base.'

'The other point is that we've no choice. Either we go in or we sit out here and fritter away the only initiative that's left for American survival. You've said it yourself.'

'I wasn't considering that alternative: this chance has been dearly bought. I just think it's necessary to get some inside information.'

'You want to take a prisoner? First thing he'll do is scream over his radio, and we won't even know that he's done it. Besides, we haven't the time or the facilities for interrogation.'

'I was thinking more along the lines of making a polite request to Gurevich.'

'Don't piss me about, Morgan. We haven't got time for you to be smart.'

There followed a brief discussion on hierarchy. It had to be done. An unresolved command conflict meant failure.

Endymion had now passed round the eastern limb of the near side of the Moon. The clear white hemisphere of the Earth, half day and half night, had risen above the horizon. It was an unwelcome reminder of the fragility of human life in the solar system, for those few remaining men and women were about to be plunged for the second time into war. The sterile land over which *Endymion* skimmed was lit by the harsh and direct rays of a Sun that stood in the summit of the heavens. There was no shadow to be seen, other than the tiny insect shadow of *Endymion* itself.

At M minus thirty minutes contact was made with the Wheel over the laser communication system. Morgan rapidly made his requirements clear, and brooked no discussion: there was little time before the next faked contact between Sidorenko and the Russians in Copernicus Base. At M minus twenty-six minutes the synthesised face of Sidorenko appeared on the screen.

'Colonel Sidorenko, Wheel, calling Copernicus Base. Are you receiving me? . . . This is Colonel Sidorenko. Are you receiving me, Copernicus Base?' Wheeldata's modulations on the essential theme were quite subtly done. Bud Saunders had clearly been working hard. The reply came, garbled into the Wheel's next transmission by three seconds of delay.

'Copernicus Base reading you loud and clear.' The video was of one of Gurevich's communication staff – the same one who had made the last two contacts before *Endymion* had lost the signal on its pass behind the Moon. 'We are doing well enough here, Colonel. How goes it with you? Over.'

'Well. We have at last got the missile damage repaired and the ship is running quite adequately. Over.'

'Colonel Gurevich has asked me to relay an order that you should get more sleep. You've made every transmission for three days now. Have you had any sleep at all?'

'As much as any of my men.' Wheeldata had obviously been primed for this one. 'In weightless conditions you can manage quite well with frequent short rest periods.'

The lieutenant appeared to be peering intently at his monitor. 'Are you perfectly sure that everything is all right on the Wheel, Colonel? Over.' Had he noticed, Morgan wondered, that the shading of stubble on Sidorenko's face had remained unchanged for three days? It would take intelligence to mark such a phenomenon, and a very rare insight indeed to deduce its significance. He crossed his fingers for Wheeldata's reply. It had been just that sort of question which would elicit an honest answer from the simple-minded machine.

'Reasonably so, Lieutenant. We are all tired, of course. That's the price to be paid when twelve men keep five hundred under vigilance. There are some minor problems. I have no worries about the morale of my men; but until we've decided what role the Wheel will now play in our plans, I do need the willing co-operation of the Americans. Thus the state of *their* morale has become my problem. They are anxious about their own future – and about the position of your captives. In fact I believe there's some doubt as to their condition. Over.'

'Does it matter? Over.'

'It's causing tension which makes our task harder. Over.'

'Is there anything we can do to alleviate their doubt, Colonel?

Over.'

'I believe there is. What I would like you to do is make a brief TV transmission from the rooms where you're keeping the prisoners. It would make my job here a lot easier without risking anything.' There was too much of Saunders' reasonable psychology in the request. Morgan wished that Wheeldata would make it a little more snappy.

'I'd have to clear that with Colonel Gurevich. Over.'

'Clear it then. I want it done now. Then I can get some sleep. Tell him that. Over.' And the synthetic face of Sidorenko grinned tiredly. *Well done, Wheeldata. Full marks for interpretation!*

The negotiations were brief. Gurevich must have his work cut out trying to arrange for the survival of the scattered Russians, let alone worrying about what to do with his subdued enemies.

At M minus seventeen minutes the shots started coming through. Morgan wanted very much to see the dishevelled clusters of figures who were sitting in groups, lying on improvised beds, playing cards, unaware that they were being watched by their compatriots, oblivious of the guards who covered them with weapons held negligently – but held all the same. The picture quality was poor, filtered as it was through three computer systems, transmitted over three-quarters of a million kilometres by radio and laser. But they barely noticed them on the flight deck of the lunar ferry; they were watching another display on which Wheeldata was marking his assessment of the film on plans of the Moonbase. The transmission lasted for no more than two minutes, but it was enough. Wheeldata identified five rooms off one of the main corridors on the second level down from the lunar surface – right in the heart of the Base. The hostages were split roughly equally, a hundred to a room, with half a dozen guards in each room: few guards for so many prisoners it might be thought, but each had an automatic weapon in his hands, and they were grouped so as to maintain an uninterrupted field of fire.

Wheeldata continued to make himself useful by estimating the total numbers and dispositions of the Soviet troops at Copernicus, and by advising Marshall's combat teams on the best routes to take once inside the Moonbase and the best means of coordinating their assault. The men themselves milled in every available space, helping one another into their space suits, still discussing battle tactics in an excited hubbub of sound. By M minus seven minutes all were strapped in – or in some case strap-hanging: Fulbrook had not worked miracles with the payload bay conversion.

*   *   *

When *Endymion* began its computer controlled de-orbit burn it was already over the lava plain of Mare Imbrium with its descent engines pointing forward along the orbital path and the flight deck facing down toward the tumbled boulders that had been flung out two billion years ago when Copernicus was born. The crater itself was still beyond the horizon. Silence had descended, and with it the tension that comes before action. Each mind was matching its sinew against the ordained task, and wondering . . . Tyler and Brodnik were cool but watchful; *Endymion* was making the descent without radar lest a stray reflection should be detected. The Primary Navigation and Guidance System was operating in inertial mode. Abort Guidance was checking the landscape visually against maps in the on-board computer's memory, with an occasional stab from the doppler laser system as an altitude and descent check.

The Wheel remained in close touch, still sifting the attack plan, ready to abort the mission instantly at any sign that the Moonbase had been alerted to the approach of the lunar ferry.

The eastern wall of Copernicus humped over the flat lava horizon. The reaction control system brought *Endymion* upright by discrete intervals as her orbital speed dropped. The eastern crater ramparts were visible from rim to root now, soaring two thousand metres above the Mare Imbrium, though much higher above the unseen bowl within. They were formidable, although their slope appeared to grow more gentle as *Endymion* sank towards them. Morgan could see how they were notched by radial ravines, and thought he could discern which of the ravines had been deepened to carry Highway East.

'Twelve hundred metres . . . ' Brodnik was saying. 'West at three hundred . . . down at two.' Not once had they glimpsed the central promontory of the crater with its cyclopean phased-array radar system. Correspondingly, neither should it have glimpsed them; Tyler had made a good job of keeping the approach low. But crabbing along under the shelter of the rampart on the thrust of the descent engines was expensive on fuel. 'Six hundred metres . . . bring her up by five . . . west at two-thirty . . . fuel at two minutes . . . ' The Mare beneath *Endymion* was swelling up toward the crater walls now, and Tyler was having to increase altitude to head for a sheltered plateau north of the Highway East ravine. He was sharing control with the computer, letting it do the hard work of maintaining stability but instructing it where to take the spacecraft.

'Thirty metres . . . west at twenty-five . . . fuel at fifteen seconds . . . up three, we're over boulders, west at fifteen . . . fuel at minus five . . . ' That was the point of no return. Morgan shivered. *The low approach had cost too much. Endymion* had now started to use her take-off reserve. Now they were committed by the mechanics of space flight to make the attack or stay there and die. 'Cut drift . . . ' The ferry heeled sharply as the computer balanced the descent thrust against her westward motion. 'Down at one . . . down at one. Keep her on that setting . . . . Ten metres . . . fuel minus thirty . . . dust . . . contact light!'

Tyler took over the commentary with his landing check-list. 'Throttles closed . . . position stable . . . engines stopped . . . engine arm off . . . Wheel, this is *Endymion* reporting down at position Alpha . . . . Personnel ladder deploying from lower payload bay . . . '

'We copy you down at point Alpha, *Endymion*. Well done . . . .'

The five men of Team Alpha, having made the descent with the discomfort of wearing the PLSS packs, were already heading down the companion ladder to the lower decks, sealing their helmets, scooping weapons from the racks.

'Airlock cycling . . . once . . . twice . . . '

Morgan looked out of the window. Sixty feet below the flight deck the pads at the end of the ladder sent up dust and grit in slow sprays that settled lazily. Within seconds the men of Team Alpha were spreading out with long strides over the lunar surface.

'The unloading ramp is now deploying . . . .'

Three of them carried M-45s, modified for the use of thick gloves. Two carried Bright-eye missile launchers. No orders were given. Each knew where he was going and why. Within a minute they were invisible.

'Team Alpha deployed at M plus two minutes. Alpha Base is now secure.' That rather depended on how you looked at it. Morgan slid down the ladder into the upper payload bay to don his PLSS pack. He found himself next to Captain Mitchell.

'I liked that,' said Mitchell. 'Polite request to Gurevich. Say, what outfit are you from – originally?'

'Several. None of them exist any more. I was in the SAS for a time if that comforts you.'

'It does. Let's keep it like that. The SAS goes into action with the Special Space Warfare Unit for the first time.'

'And the last.'
'Let it be glorious.'
'Let's just win.' Morgan locked his helmet solemnly.

Within ten minutes Hawkins, Tyler and Brodnik were alone in the lunar ferry, still in touch with the Wheel and Team Alpha, but out of touch with Teams Beacon, Condor, Delta and Echo.

Strictly, Morgan had not yet set foot on the Moon, but that was not one of the many things he was concerned about. He was in the observation blister of one of three twelve-man Rovers that were skirting the outer wall of Copernicus in a long straggling convoy. Mitchell's Team Delta was five hundred metres ahead in Rover Two. Or rather he and eleven other marines were in the Rover: eight more, bristling with weaponry, clung to the top of the vehicle, plumbed into external life-support adaptors to conserve their PLSS packs. The surface grit sifted gracefully down from the Rover's eight bulbous wheels, but the vehicle raised no dust cloud as it sped over the airless surface. Five hundred metres behind were the five men of Teams Beacon and Condor in Rover One. The vehicle's spare capacity was taken up with their signalling and missile gear. At M plus seventeen minutes their laser twinkled briefly at Morgan's Rover. The message came through on his headset.

'This is where we wish you goodbye and good luck, Echo. Over.'

Morgan replied equally briefly. 'I'll buy you a beer in six house. Stay out of trouble. Over.'

The trailing Rover swung away from the tracks of the leaders and headed up the inclined terrace that, viewed from orbit, had seemed to give smooth access to the lip of the crater wall. From down on the surface it looked rugged and not perfectly continuous. Teams Beacon and Condor were soon taken out of laser contact by the lie of the land.

Rovers Two and Three continued, with ten kilometres to go before Highway East. They made good speed; the fierce horizontal rays of the Sun maintained their batteries at full charge. And yet they seemed to creep around the crater wall for they were reduced to insignificance by the towering lunar relief and the endless plain of Imbrium. Features that seemed from orbit like mere imperfections in the smooth lava now meant long detours and laborious ascents. Mitchell reported back with five kilometres to go.

'We're crossing a lot of tracks here. They head in our general direction – between Highway East and the vicinity of Alpha Base. They look fresh to me . . . .'

'Probably nothing to worry about,' replied Morgan. 'They'll still be looking fresh in a million years. We won't blink though.'

Deep Cleft, Highway East's access point into the crater, widened ahead. Five years previously the natural chasm, formed by local crust tensions in the aftermath of the meteor strike that had created Copernicus, had been further deepened by the marginally legal use of nuclear explosives. Now it could be negotiated by a steep but smooth gradient whose brink was the threshold of the forty-kilometre ramp that dropped four thousand metres to the grouped domes of Copernicus Base in the centre of the crater. Mitchell's Rover was rounding the northern flank of the Cleft and starting on the last three hundred metres of the incline. The communication lasers fenced to and fro again.

'Rover Three, this is Rover Two. Dick, I'm going to take a peep over the top of the rise here to cover your traverse of the Cleft. Recommend you stop where you are until I clear you. Over.'

'I copy that. Go carefully at the top.'

'You bet . . . . There's a hell of a lot of tracks here. Looks like a ski slope after a busy day. Makes a very compact surface though . . . . Easing off speed now . . . . Easy, Corporal . . . .Another two metres . . . . One more metre. Hold it there. Right. We're tucked down below the top of the rise and I'm in the observation blister just peeping over the top. I see it all there, very clear, just like a model. The central peaks and the far rim are in sunlight. I can see the radar dome on peak Zero One and the solar array on Zero Two. We should be right on the solar phase of their radar, so they'll be getting nothing but solar radiation from our direction. I'm getting their transmissions though. Millimetric. Very strong. A mouse couldn't move in that bowl without being seen.'

'But we've got to do it.'

'Yeah . . . . The Main Dome's completely illuminated. I can see some internal detail. The others are picked out by their window lights. Hydroponics is OK. Transport is dark: damaged I think, but there are lights moving in it. The Russians must be using it for their vehicles. North Three is gone completely. I can't see any trace of it. It strikes me it might be a good idea . . . .'

'Yes?'

'I don't know how it works out astronomically, but it might be a good idea to hold off our attack until the domes are lit by the Sun but the foreground is still dark . . . . '

'What's your depression angle between the edge of the sunlight and the base of the domes?'

'Oh, about two or three degrees . . . . .'

'Then that should work out at about the right time. Let's have that more accurately.'

'OK, let's see – *hold it. I'm getting something on s-band from the Base*. I'll patch it through to you.'

The dialogue was in Russian. ' . . . *loud and clear, Major. We're at the thirty-six kilometre marker. Over.*'

'*Good. Report again as you go through the Cleft. Over.*'

'*Will do. Over.*'

'Back!' snapped Mitchell.

'Rover Two, get back round this buttress at full speed. Stick to the tracks until you have to leave them.'

'Am doing. It's a Rover. Routine patrol – I hope. He's just come up over the next ridge on Highway East. No more than three thousand metres and making about forty kph. That gives us about three or four minutes before he comes through here.'

Morgan's driver reversed as far as he could into the cover of massive boulders at the foot of the crater wall without cutting the laser link with Mitchell. Rover Two scurried across the Cleft like a cockroach on a concrete highway.

Mitchell signalled. 'This could blow the whole thing. We're going to have to extrapolate those guys into some future existence.'

'Not yet! Not while they're still in radio contact. Anyway, Russians don't have a future existence.'

Rover Two slewed round behind a small hillock, showering grit. The Russian Rover lurched fast over the rise, pitching in its speed. Its commander was talking to control again. Zeffert's laser blinked.

'Then how about we stick him up when he's into the radio shadow. We might be able to learn something – even use their Rover to get into the Base.'

'We might use some of that, but negative on the stick-up. It gives them too much time. They might raise Copernicus by orbiter link. Then the vindaloo really hits the fan.'

'What do we do, then?' The Russian Rover was half-way through the chasm and moving fast.

'I think they're out to patrol the crater wall. That means that something's made them suspicious – perhaps Wheeldata's act. If they turn south we let them go. It would be the best outcome to set the Russians' minds at rest. If they turn north they're likely to spot *Endymion* before we complete the assault; so we hit them hard as soon as they're out of radio contact with Copernicus Base. Deploy your men back across the north trail and we'll do the same. No radio. I'll fire a red flare; then they've got to be plastered instantaneously with everything we've got.'

With that the men riding on the two Rovers dropped to the ground and spread out in four loosely-knit groups. For a moment they could be seen dispersing, then they were gone as they made the best use of cover in their grey suits. Although Morgan couldn't see them his battle-conditioned mind could chart their progress closely.

The Russian patrol paused at the highest point of the pass. The vehicle was American, pressed into service, the same model that Mitchell's marines were using. Morgan noted the number, 08, stencilled on its side and the rather less symmetrical red star, with one of its corners peeling, that signified its change of ownership. He could see the twelve men inside. They were in white space suits but they weren't wearing their helmets. He could see which of them, in the observation bubble, was reporting to control before passing into the radio shadow of the crater wall. He made a note of the end of the message. ' . . . *our next report will be through Orbiter Three at twelve hundred hours. Over.*'

'*That is correct. Have fun. Over and out.*' Twelve hundred hours? By whose clock? Copernicus or Tyhco? It mattered.

Now the Russians must choose to drive north or south around the crater. If south, they might live for some time yet: if north – their lives would be measured in seconds. The Rover turned decisively north. Morgan sighed in exasperation. The mission could have done without the complication. He could have done without killing twelve men – and possibly women – who counted in a human population of no more than two thousand. He armed a red flare on the weapon panel at his elbow. Twelve dead would be twelve fewer to cope with at Copernicus Base. That was worth it when you were fifty against – according to Wheeldata's assessment – at least a hundred.

The Russian had switched off his transmitter. The twelve heads inside the Rover were swaying rhythmically with its motion. They looked as though they were singing. This wasn't like combat in the past where you could be made to forget the infinite preciousness of life; now life was both rare and delicate.

The Rover had passed the place where Team Delta was hidden and was half-way to Morgan's Rover. One of the Russians stood up in the observation blister, pointing at the tracks on the surface. Morgan triggered the redflare. There were puffs of smoke and little darts of flame among the boulders. The windows of the Rover glowed for an instant before it ripped apart. The oxygen tanks ruptured and the vehicle became the centre of a brilliant expanding dome that vanished even while torn sheets of metal were glittering starward in elegant parabolae. And the whole thing had happened in perfect silence. Not even through the soles of their boots did the marines feel the slightest echo of the dazzling explosion. Morgan pressed his transmit button.

'Steve, this is Morgan. We must get going. Echo has a lot of work to do. Meanwhile, when you head down Highway East in two hours' time, I suggest you go in the guise of that Russian Rover.'

'How are we going to pull that off?'

'Your Russian's excellent. You'll have no problem. Say you've had a system malfunction – like your batteries aren't recharging from your solar panels, so you're coming back on reduced power and you're not going to make any more transmissions. That'll save you having to kid them along too much. How about that?'

'How about it? I don't like it.'

'Well none of this mission's going to be exactly relaxing. You're going to have to breeze down that highway anyway.'

'Well I'll tell you what, Dick, if it doesn't make any odds to you I'll save my chat with Copernicus until we get inside detection range. Then you'll be in a position to go in there if I goof. It seems a bit risky to try being clever that early.'

'OK. You're right. Also you'll need to change your serial number to zero eight and patch together some red stars. There's black and red tape in the repair kits.'

'We'll do that.'

Morgan's Team Echo was already speeding southward across Deep Cleft. 'We'll be in laser contact with Beacon when we get to the top of the mass driver, and so will you when you're about five kilometres down the highway. We'll exchange gossip through Beacon then. Until then . . . .'

'So long . . . .'

Thirty

ROVER THREE passed out of laser contact beyond the southern buttress of Deep Cleft. Team Echo was on its own. The mission had been on the Moon for an hour and twenty minutes. Sitting up in the observation blister, checking off landmarks, studying the map display and returning swift experienced answers to the questions of his men, Morgan provided a deep calm well of authority and confidence.

Inside him the well was at its lowest level. All the Teams but Beacon and Condor, who should be within sight of one another, were now isolated. They were held together only by the digits on the c-units that raced them towards a bloody meeting in the unclear future, and by a mission plan that was far from complete. The modified task of Mitchell's Team Delta, to drive undetected in the rays of the Sun down Highway East, and yet to simulate a Soviet patrol, bothered him. It was ambiguous. The task of his own Team Echo, to zigzag up the crater wall and find the top of the mass driver – then to canter down it to Copernicus Base – had seemed plausible in the electronically cocooned flight deck of *Endymion*. Now it was made foolish by the scale of the Moon, and there was only an hour left to get to the top of the rim.

He didn't think of Stephanie. He had tried not to think of her. That was to invite utter despair.

Yet we are what we speak. Our words and our looks of encouragement become us, and Morgan knew how to command himself, and thus his men until the bitter end. And slowly the Rover wound its minute way up the concentric ridges of the eastern wall of Copernicus. Much of the time it climbed at a precariously steep angle, its passengers gazing up into the infinite black depths. Not all the movement was upwards; on one particularly steep slope the Rover slid sideways three times on the loose regolith while its occupants feared that it would overturn. On the fourth occasion it started a scree slide which took it down two hundred metres before it could drive out to one side and make a detour around the troublesome slope. But from the top it became clear, as they had expected, that this was the penultimate ridge.

A steep two hundred metres above their heads, mirror-gold in the sun, was the thirty-metre square final course sensor of the mass driver. Had Morgan's marines been in their present position a week ago they would have observed a rapid fire of truck-sized aluminium containers flashing through the square sensor at the lunar escape velocity of 2.38 kilometres per second. The containers, almost impossible to perceive at that speed, containing metal ingots, crystalline minerals and lunar-manufactured components, would have been picked up three days later in high Earth orbit by the magnetic grapples of the Hopper ships. The Russians had no facilities for that particular celestial ball-game, which was fortunate because Team Echo had to continue its journey down the forty-kilometre ramp of the mass driver. But whatever the outcome of this mission it was essential for human survival that the machine should come back into operation within a month. Life in space demanded not only the hydrogen which Callisto alone could provide but also those mundane materials which were waiting on the surface of the Moon.

Morgan, Sarin and the twenty Special Space Warfare Marines of Team Echo left the Rover, and, having topped up their PLSS packs, tackled the final steep slope on foot. The bulky packs – light as they might be in one-sixth of Earth's gravity – and the uncertain surface, made balancing difficult, so they made use of careful rope techniques. Thus they were seven minutes behind schedule when they stood on the lip of the crater looking down the long magnetic ski jump at Copernicus Base. The Sun had risen slightly since Mitchell's report. Morgan could see not only the radar dome and the solar array on two of the central peaks, but the top of the control tower and a brilliant elliptical slice of the Main Dome. Next to him Sarin shaded his eyes against the sun-bright rock. He had depolarised his visor, the better to see the Earth-lit crater floor. He pulled Morgan down behind the summit of the rim to mask their radios.

'It's better than I thought. I was expecting smooth ground. You could hide a division down there.'

'Pity we haven't got one.'

Sarin half turned, tilting his head towards the rest of the Team. 'What do you think?'

Morgan had liked their response in Deep Cleft. 'Not at all bad.'

Sarin nodded firmly. Morgan waved forward the man with the

communications pack and pointed along the ridge. Without unslinging his pack the corporal quickly made the laser link to Beacon. From then on the pack's gyros would keep the link open.

'Beacon; this is Echo at point Echo One. Over.'

'Echo; Beacon. Five by. Over.'

'All set up?'

'Affirmative, Condor also. I'm afraid we rolled the Rover.'

Damn. 'Any casualties?'

'No. And we got our stores out. Condor reports ready to fire on time or command. We're in touch with Alpha. Their main problem is they want some of the action.'

'Tell them to stay put. I'd give a lot to be bored with them.'

'Nothing from Delta yet.'

'You won't until they come out of the Cleft at M plus three-fifty. Update on Delta: they'll be simulating a Soviet patrol that we knocked over, but they'll maintain silence till the five kilo marker.'

'We copy that, Echo.'

'Good hunting.'

Morgan personally checked the radio controls of Team Echo. Then he led them in file over the crater rim.

The slope of the mass-driver ramp was gentle. It cut straight through the inner crater ridges and soared across the chasms on flimsy looking spider-work of titanium that gleamed in the Earth-light without its customary film of oxide. The ramp was uniformly ten metres wide, ribbed for firm footing, but without the protection of hand rails. They started the long-striding lope that counts for running on the Moon, Morgan in the lead and Sarin at the tail depending on the bulky aluminium levitator rails on their right to shield them from the powerful millimetric radar array on peak Zero One.

Morgan reined in his pace cautiously. You might be able to take a twelve metre stride when running on the Moon, but at the end of that stride it's just as likely to be your head as your heel which hits the ground. Morgan had already found that as an athlete he was designed for one gee. His running speed was governed by the rate at which he could move his legs, and that was little different on the Moon from what it had been on Earth. The benefit was that a fast lope was easier to maintain on the Moon.

Not all the marines accommodated easily to the task. After two hundred metres the tenth man in the line kicked off too exuberantly from the ramp with his right foot. He soared along a metre from the ground, turning slowly to his left. His next step was sideways and uncontrolled. With his third he hit the man in front, hard, and they were both carried along by the inertia of their packs in a desperate flail of limbs. The man who had tripped first tried to save the other, but their comrades saw them both tumble in a slow cartwheel of disaster over the edge of the ramp.

The supporting struts were a hundred metres high here. No one dared to stop or to slow his pace. Even to look to one side in a space suit you have to turn your body, and no one cared to try it. Sarin calculated swiftly as he passed, last of the line, that the two men would hit the ground eleven seconds after they fell, at seventeen metres per second. Their suits were very tough, and would give good protection to the fragile bodies within. The men might just live. He had to leave it at that.

The first nine men knew nothing of the disaster until, after an hour, Morgan slowed cautiously to a halt. The others were by now more than ready for a mid-point rest, and they managed to stop without further incident. There was a quick silent check of PLSS instrumentation. Although they had been running for only an hour, Sarin, the heaviest of the Team, had used oxygen that should have sustained him through an hour and three-quarters of normal work. At that rate he had another two hours' supply. There was no helping it.

Morgan hurried to make his communications check, plugging his radio umbilical into Corporal Decker's laser pack.

'Delta; Echo. Morgan. Over.'

'Echo; Delta. Clear. We're at the forty-kilometre marker. We can make the five-kilometre marker in fifty minutes. That's M plus three hours fifty. You?'

'Copy. M plus three hours fifty is OK. That means we'll need Condor's covering fire at M plus three fifty-seven. Do you agree?'

'Affirmative; covering fire at M three fifty-seven. We'll advise Condor. Over. Out.'

Team Echo started on the second half of its ramp journey. The marines unslung their weapons and ran with vigilance, for they were well down in the crater bowl. From the cover of the levitator rails they could not see the domes of the Base, but they could see the long sheds of the mass-driver loading plant ahead. Also invisible to their right, now only five kilometres away, was Highway East. Driving boldly down it Team Delta would soon be overhauling them fast. Morgan looked at his c-unit and increased his speed slightly. The months at reduced gravity were telling on him. His legs ached, he had a stitch in his right side, and his oxygen consumption was well up on the first half of the journey. He worked scientifically on relaxing each muscle until it came into play.

The senseless monotony of prolonged running dulled him. He became reluctant to arrive. No one else need die until they arrived at the Base. He wasn't quite clear how he had got himself into the position of having to kill increasingly rare people; it was the last thing he wanted. It was infuriatingly stupid. But the plan was in motion. *Endymion* was stranded on the Moon . Contact had already been made with the enemy. There was no possibility of retreat.

The wide black opening, the size of hangar doors, where the rails entered the long shed, drew imperceptibly nearer, then quickly nearer. Judgement of distance is tricky on the Moon; you have to get used to the different cues. Two hundred metres short, Sarin and the rear half of Team Echo dropped the short distance to the ground and ran forward to take up station on either side of the opening, covering overlapping arcs of the dimly-lit interior. Morgan's group ran in without checking their pace, aiming forward and down to either side of the rails. The first cavernous shed appeared to be empty – though its many side doors and catwalks offered plenty of room for conceal-ment. Sarin's group followed, staying low, checking the access point to the reception and packing sheds, the machine shops and refineries. At M plus three hours forty they were a kilometre into the complex. It was utterly deserted, and, of course, utterly silent.

The second shed also was deserted. Team Echo passed quickly through into the third and last shed – Loading and Control. This was smaller, and it was not deserted. High on the left was a glass-fronted observation balcony. Three space-suited engineers were in it, work-ing on an access panel in the ceiling. Two hundred and fifty metres ahead, to the left of the railed marshalling area, four more figures were grouped around a console. Two of them, if they were to raise their eyes, would have an oblique view of Team Echo.

Morgan's group, having the better angle of fire, took on the three men in the balcony. The concentrated fire of ten M-45s hammered a section out of the tempered glass. It fell in glittering fragments among Sarin's group who were running below. One of Morgan's men followed up with a grenade. His confidence was remarkable: if he missed, the grenade would fall down among his own comrades. It went neatly through the hole. The three men were still toppling from their working platform under the access hatch. Morgan's team turned to cover Sarin. Little cubes of flying glass hailed against their suits. They didn't need to look back to know that the balcony had been taken care of.

The three deaths, the fusillade of shots and the grenade explosion had not intruded so much as a whisper into the total silence of the shed. Morgan was a hundred metres from the second group now, and Sarin was nearer. Still none of them had looked up. Three of them bore the insignia of Red Army engineers.

The fourth was an American NASA engineer. With his gloved hand he was pointing to the display on the terminal. As he pointed a hole appeared in the aluminium of the console, and then five more, all together. He watched, puzzled, flicking a switch. A panel peeled back in a shower of sparks. He half turned. The three Russians were still sinking to the ground, soundlessly, their helmets shattered. He opened his mouth. Someone crashed into him, slamming him against the console, turning him. His assailant held in his gloved hand a mangled radio aerial. It looked like his own. He cleared his throat, and from the dead sound he knew that his radio was dead. Sarin pulled the engineer's helmet face-plate against his own with a sharp rap. He shouted, so that the American could hear him through the glass. '*Stay here! Stay here until we fetch you! Don't move!*' Sarin frog-marched him to a space between two containers and pushed him to the ground. The man stayed, face down. In five seconds he was alone.

Team Echo came to a halt at the end of the third shed, just two minutes short of M plus three hours fifty. Two hundred metres beyond the aluminium wall would be the first dome of Copernicus Base. Half of Morgan's group had joined Sarin, so that he now had fifteen men. They guarded the head of the spiral stair that led down from the mass-driver complex to the grid of corridors below the domes of Copernicus Base. Although far from the hostages the staircase provided a route, exposed to discovery but just feasible, to the Base's Communications and Control room. That would be Sarin's target - if Team Delta had survived its journey down Highway East.

Morgan urgently needed to know the progress of Team Delta. He led his four men to the postern at the north-west extremity of the shed, and slid it open a few centimetres. He could see out across the shadowed floor of the crater to Highway East, half a kilometre away, and he could see part of the nearest dome, brilliant white in the sunlight. Nothing moved. He opened the door further. Now he could see the radar dome on peak Zero One clearly, and the lights of the control tower on Zero Three. He hung back in the shadow of the door and turned to look along the highway. Immediately his visor polarisation increased to maximum. The white on black of the lunar panorama vanished. He was looking directly at the Sun. It was some consolation that the Russians would also have difficulty in seeing Rover Two, but the mission would surely fail unless he could track their position.

Morgan beckoned Corporal Decker into the doorway and established the laser link with Beacon.

'Beacon; Echo. Point Echo Three. Over.'

'Echo; Beacon. We're tracking Delta, sir. They're just short of the five-k. marker.' Morgan felt a surge of relief. It quickly gave way to new tensions. He glanced round at Sarin's group. They were ready to go, with seven minutes to do their work. And yet he was reluctant to send them. Once Sarin went in the Soviets would be in no more doubt. Combat would be joined and the position of the hostages would be perilous. He felt himself immobilised while the seconds hurried by. Sarin was alert for his signal.

'Beacon; Echo. Give me contact with Delta. Over.'

'Echo, we're out of contact with Delta. They're talking to the Russians and we don't want to risk breaking in on that. Over.'

'I want to hear their dialogue.'

'Copy. Here it comes . . . ' The laser link echoed with the hollow static-filled space of the s-band wavelength. The first voice was Russian, from the Base.

'*Patrol Zero Eight, I say again, you are ordered to give your mission code.*' That sounded none too complacent. Morgan looked at his c-unit. Six minutes.

Mitchell came on the air slurring his rather theoretical Russian as well as he could: Morgan hadn't been quite candid with him about that. '*The fire's still burning . . . . At least three dead back there . . . . a lot of smoke . . . .*'

'*You are instructed to identify yourselves.*'

'*. . . . Don't know if we can make it . . . . Lot of smoke . . . .Can't see.*'

'*Evacuate the Rover.*'

'*Can't. Some suits damaged. You've got to get us through the Main Dome airlock. Fast. Don't know if I can hold on . . . .*' Then the radio cut out. Morgan understood the ploy. Mitchell was trying to keep the Russians intent on the wrong problem for as long as possible – and to achieve rapid access to the Main Dome. He saw the Rover. It had come out of the zero phase and was crossing in front of him. Mitchell was jinking and skidding the vehicle theatrically. Now there were no men on top. They would have rolled off two kilometres back and should now be following in the cover of the rubble on the far side of the highway. He couldn't see them, which was as it should be. Of course it didn't mean that they were there . . . . He turned quickly to Sarin, holding up four fingers; four minutes was as fine as he dared to cut it. He waved 'GO'. Sarin acknowledged, signalled to his men, and led them down the staircase. In a moment there was just one man left covering the head of the stairwell.

Morgan could feel the pulsing of his heartbeat through every limb. The desire to break the tension, to fight his way through to wherever they were holding Stephanie on the second level, was compelling. He turned to watch the erratic course of the Rover towards the broken surface-vehicle dome. The timing appeared to be about right. If there were no hitches it should be through into the Main Dome by the time Sarin hit the Communications room. He turned back to the guard, who waved once. Sarin's team was through the airlock.

The Rover's radio was still silent, and there was little contact from the Russians. They, as far as Morgan could hear, were directing emergency services to the Main Dome ready to receive their incoming patrol. That was good. It would add to the confusion. It would draw vital men and resources up from the second level. And yet it was bitter. Eighteen Russians out of a hundred or so were dead. The next batch of casualties would be among the rescue and medical teams. He could visualise them converging on the Rover to offer aid – and being scythed down. Team Delta would have no opportunity for ethical decisions. Morgan blinked the thought aside. It was that sort of mission. And he was a specialist in breaking the rules – or in taking full advantage of the knowledge that in truth there were none. The Rover was skewing into the surface-vehicle dome, spilling dust. One minute and thirty seconds.

'Condor; Echo. Ready on the timeline. First hit – the observation tower. Second – the radar. One minute twenty-five. Over.'

'Copy, Echo. After that? Over.'

'Hold further fire unless we call it – or if you decide that our position is irretrievable without support. Then with discretion. Over.'

They knew it. He was feeding his nerves. He looked back at the stairs. The guard waved twice: Sarin had crossed the first main corridor intersection. The meant he was down to ten men: one was left at the top of the stairs, one on either side of the airlock, and two at the staggered intersection with the main corridor. It was the only way to stay in contact with Morgan, and it established a zone of superiority. *Five men! Superiority!*

The Rover was out of sight now. Still there was no panic on the s-band. The stair guard waved three times: Sarin had crossed the second main corridor. With eight men he would be approaching the Communications room in – twenty seconds. Still no movement from the Main Dome or the surface-vehicle dome. Ten seconds. Sarin should be down there, poised outside the Communications room, looking at his c-unit. Either that or even now he was fighting a desperate pitched battle with his dwindling few against a company. There was no way of knowing. The thin line of signallers might so easily be severed . . . .

The four zeros lined up on Morgan's c-unit. The first combat exchange was over more swiftly than eye or thought could comprehend it. It happened only in Morgan's memory. On the Zero cue a line of pale fire printed itself across the black sky as the first Starfire missile slanted down from Condor's position on the rim of the crater wall. And something happened up there a couple of kilometres short of the Base: either there was a systems malfunction or the harsh highlights of the sunlit Base threw the missile's single-minded purpose. The pale light of the rocket exhaust brightened as a manoeuvring jet lit up viciously. The downward slant became a dipping curve. It wasn't a process that could be followed, just a sloping line of light with a tight arc at its end, and then the glare in the inter-dome way between the surface-vehicle dome and the Main Dome, the flying aluminium cladding, the flame front from the explosion dissipating into the Main Dome . . . . And the Rover of Team Delta outlined in black and searing white in the heart of the fireball. And that was before the first second had passed. In the next the control tower on peak Zero Three erupted in a tower of flame to leave only cratered dust, and then five seconds passed before the thousand microwave eyes of the radar array fountained out across the crater bowl.

For those seven seconds Morgan was paralysed. For what could he do? He was a spectator only. He had seen Mitchell killed and Delta One destroyed in an instant of flame. The attack plan was in disarray and the attacking force had been reduced by a quarter in the worst possible unthinkable balls-up; even at full strength it would have been stretched to meet its objectives.

The seconds were racing away and the hostages were *now* in peril. There were no choices. There was no retreat and defeat would be utter. It was time to break radio silence. He called up the remnant of Mitchell's men who were on foot.

'Delta Two; Echo. What's your position?'

'Lieutenant Van Den Burg here. We're in position and intact. What do you suggest?'

'You'll have to proceed as planned without Delta One. Go straight in through the Main Dome. Keep moving. Take and hold the corridor.'

'Will do.'

'Now *move*.'

Morgan glimpsed the group, loosely strung out, racing across the bare space before the Main Dome. They were coming under fire: dust was spurting up in lazy sprays. Morgan turned with his men to the head of the staircase, gathering up Sarin's guard in his wake. With the addition of Sarin's signal chain he had seven men by the time they had cycled impatiently through the airlock. They didn't slacken their pace there. Morgan unlocked his visor as he ran, anxious for the first time about the noise made by his heavily armed and suited team. At each junction a door was slightly ajar: Morgan beckoned and out of each came a wary marine. At two points on the regulation green carpet were the dark patches where unwitting interlopers had been coldly knifed.

He detached ten men at the first main corridor intersection. They ran on towards the ramp from the Main Dome airlock to rendezvous with Van Den Burg's Delta Two remnant.

Morgan, gathering the last of Sarin's signallers with him, headed for the Communications room. A clamour of alarm bells rose, repeated from corridor to corridor. From the direction of the Main Dome ramp a few bursts of shots echoed. It paused, and then continued as an unrelieved roar. The crash of grenades was followed by short silences, then the firing continued.

There was a frustrating halt at the second main corridor as ten heavily armed Russians ran towards the main stairwell, and as another six ran in the opposite direction. Two minutes after the beginning of the battle Morgan and his four remaining men passed

Sarin's door guards at the Communications room. Five Americans sat at the consoles for communications, life support, airlock control, power and remote surveillance. Six Russians were lined up on their faces with their legs splayed and their hands on their heads. Sarin was covering them with professional detachment. He glanced at Morgan, grinning gleefully. 'Under control here, sir. Main Dome airlock's open. Six men came through and they've got their teeth into the Russian defence. When Mitchell gets there we should be able to stroll down to the second level.'

'You can seal the airlock now. Mitchell won't be coming through. We've got to go *now*. We'll have to leave two here with two to guard.'

'How about our friends?' Sarin toed the nearest Russian.

'The guards will have to keep an eye on them.'

'There's no way two can defend this room and watch six prisoners. You know that.'

Morgan knew. He turned away, hiding his sickness by giving orders for airlock control in the rooms where the hostages were held. By the time he and Sarin ran from the room with seven men, the six Russians were no longer a problem.

They reached the main stairwell three minutes and fifteen seconds after the loss of Delta One. The ramp up to the Main Dome was littered with dead. Four of them wore space suits. The air was lethal with automatic-weapon fire that spat stone-dust from the walls and steps, and ran the steel hand-rail like a demented bell. The attack had spent its force. The hostages were a level and a corridor away, and they might be dying now.

An amplified voice echoed metallically up the stairs with the ricocheting bullets. *'Hold your fire or we will start to shoot hostages. Cease firing and throw down your weapons . . . .'*

Morgan and Sarin exchanged glances. They had bought time and it was gone. But the technique was second nature. You press them so hard that they must defend themselves. You drive the hostages from their minds. A stagnated attack was suicide.

They threw their grenades in unison – two anti-personnel and two smoke. Then they vaulted the rail together. Delta Two renewed its firing rate. The drop was ten metres, and although this was the Moon, some men baulked at it. Morgan and Sarin hit the floor together and rolled to their feet, firing from a crouch straight down the smoke-filled corridor. More space-suited figures thudded down behind them and others leapt down the stairs. The Russians, hastily armed and ill-prepared, gave back slowly, seeking cover; then, finding the side doors locked against them by remote control from the Communications room, they conceded the ground, taking up sniping positions at intersections.

Twenty men won through to the corridor and held it until Morgan signalled to a remote TV camera and the five doors hissed open.

He had to banish the other four rooms from his mind and concentrate on the one in front of him. He glimpsed scattered huddles of white-overalled figures, immobilised with schock. As he hurled his stun grenades he heard his own voice shrieking *'Get down! Lie down! Get down!.'* as though the dead themselves must comply. He didn't wait for the concussion of the grenades but followed them in, dropping his faceplate against the blast, sensing his three companions behind him as he hit the floor and rolled to his feet in the billowing smoke.

Since the mission had been born in the minds of the Wheel's Command Team four days ago he had focused on this moment, grey with confusion and sharp with death, when he must discern between friend and foe, and shoot whether certain or not.

His first glimpse had told him that the guards had made the instinctive error of separating themselves from their captives, herding them at the far end of the room. Shots had snapped at him as he came in. They must be flanking the door. This much he thought as he came up to a crouch. He turned, diving to the prone position again, already firing at those muzzle flashes which were wrongly angled to be from his own men. One by one they ceased, but the deaths were not heard above the thunder of firing. There was silence, then a distant hammering of shots from along the corridor. Then silence again. His buzzing ears could now hear the lesser sound of people coughing. The smoke dispersed, sucked in tendrils towards the environmental control system vents. There was a burst of rather pathetic cheering, but it didn't spread far. Morgan stood up tiredly and staggered under a thump on the back from one of the men who had come in with him. He didn't even know his name. He lifted his faceplate which had been starred by a glancing shot. Figures were advancing on him. He held up his hand.

'Please. You must stay there and stay down. We're not finished yet.'

One figure, though, continued to pick its way through the huddled groups on the floor. Morgan recognised Schnieder, looking pale but otherwise fit. He grasped Morgan's hand.

'Don't take this amiss, soldier, but you know, we never expected this. We thought the Soviets had everything nicely sewn up.'

Morgan paid him little attention. He was searching the faces in the room. But she was not there. He was disappointed. He had wanted to rescue her himself. It would have been a good private joke between them, and besides . . .

'So did they. That's how we got away with it – so far: we still have to establish control of the Base. I hope you won't take it amiss either, but I'll have to ask you to stay here until we're clear what the picture is.' Morgan was reluctant to relinquish command of events. He didn't relish that command, but neither did he wish to see the uncertain future handed back unchecked to traditional and inflexible control. There were certain problems outstanding which that wouldn't solve.

'Now wait a bit, soldier, as your ranking officer –'

'My rank is Mister. I'm not subject to your authority and, for the moment, you are to mine. Now I intend to see that your command is returned to you in good shape. Leave it at that and await instructions here. I'm already wasting time.' He pre-empted Schnieder's answer by striding rapidly back into the corridor where Sarin was redeploying the remnant of the assault force.

Within twenty minutes most of the key points had been secured. The demoralised Soviet force had been stretched very thin at its best. Sarin estimated that some ten or twenty men were stell holding out, but not where it would matter. Morgan had slowed the pace of the operation: the casualty rate had alarmed him – on both sides. Fighting had moved down to the sixth level and Morgan was keeping in loose contact, leaving the real-time decision to Lieutenant Van Den Burg.

Relieving Beacon and Condor Teams and organising searches for marines injured or lost outside the Base pressed hard on his time and resources. The two who had fallen from the mass-driver would, if they were alive, be near the end of their space-suit endurance. He lost no time in sparing a Rover and two men to search for them.

And there was still the enemy to consider – reinforcements from Tycho who were deployed at holding points in the Mare Imbrium. He needed satellite data on them immediately. That meant contact with the Wheel. It was the task whose outcome should define his next moves, so he delegated the rest to Sarin, briefing him quickly in the main corridor.

He still hadn't seen Stephanie. The hostages were discouraged from leaving their rooms. Now he hesitated. He had urgent business in the Communications room. This was hardly a moment for private pleasure. Much still depended on his actions, and it would take several minutes to find her. Better to choose a moment which they could savour . . . .

'Corridors to the Communications room are reported clean, sir.'

'OK, Decker.' He turned to Sarin. 'Shouldn't be more than half an hour, Bill. I think if you organise some of the locals into platoons and give them Russian weapons we could have a bit more freedom now?'

'Right you are, Dick. I was thinking that myself.'

Morgan started along the corridor with Decker. He heard running feet behind him, and turned, half expecting to see Stephanie. But it was just one the Base's medical orderlies reporting to Sarin. He continued, but Sarin called him.

'Dick?'

'Yes, Bill?'

'Something needs your attention here.'

Morgan walked back. 'What is it?'

'We've got a slight problem here . . . ' Sarin took his arm and steered him to an open door.

'Well?' He already knew.

'Let's go in.'

There were a hundred people in the room, but it was utterly silent. A few watched him enter – almost in fear it seemed – but most carefully did not. It wasn't difficult to see where he must go. A prone figure lay on a mattress, carefully guarded by a circle of chairs. Two peope in white coats, a doctor and a nurse, were bending over the figure. They stood as Morgan approached and the doctor met him. He had blue eyes that looked sternly at Morgan.

Thirty-One

'SHE'S GOING to die, I'm afraid. Caught a stray burst across the stomach. There was too much damage for us to deal with. She's waiting to see you.'

Morgan felt himself turn pale. He saw nothing but the bed as he walked to it. She looked very fine still – her cheeks with the smooth firmness of youth and her dark hair waving on the pillow. Her eyes were wide and dark and clear against skin as white as paper. When he looked down she smiled slightly, dimpling. He knelt and kissed her softly on the forehead, studying her face intently as though it were a transient thing. Her lips parted and she still smiled as she spoke very quietly.

'You did so well. I'm proud.'

'Thank you. I'm glad it turned out – ' He clenched his teeth. She still smiled. They were silent for a while.

'Never mind,' she said, 'you can't win 'em all.'

'But you were all I wanted to win.'

'You mustn't be uncharitable. There's nothing wrong with the others.'

'That being just like you wouldn't remedy!'

She was quiet again for a while, and then she said, as though she had been saving it up, 'I was looking forward to our next debriefing.'

'So was I.'

Then she died.

Morgan gave himself up to looking at her, still planning what might have been. The people around him didn't exist, and he didn't trouble to stop the tears that dropped on to her white sheet.

It seemed like a long time, but it could have been only a few minutes later when he felt the grip of a big hand on his shoulder.

'I'm sorry, Dick, but it's not over yet. We need you in the Communications room.'

'Handle it.' *She was the only hostage to die. That was impossible.*

'I can't. It's too big. We might lose control.' Not until they were hurrying along the corridor did Morgan question him further.

'We've found Gurevich. We've got him bottled up.'

'Alone?'

'He's still got half a dozen of his best men.'

'Where?'

'In the reactor room. He's threatening to blow up the Base.' Morgan was beyond dismay. He considered Sarin's report with little interest. 'There are two means of access to the room: a big hatch in the ceiling for heavy plant and a small access door to the corridor. Both heavy steel. Gurevich has cut all the control system cables to the outside, so we can't open the doors or instruct the reactor control system.'

'Gas them through the ventilation system?'

'They're wearing suits.'

'Then that rather puts a time limit on their occupation.'

'The other way round, Dick. They're putting the time limit on us.'

They brushed past the guards outside the Communications room at a trot. The six Russians were still there, lying in their blood by the wall. Marines sat intently at the five consoles. Sarin ushered Morgan to the remote surveillance console at the end of the line. He passed the communications screen. He saw the face on the screen with a shock of recognition. It was Rathbone's, and he could pick out the captain's hectoring tones from the medley of sounds in the room. He paused, but Sarin thrust him on. The man at the console vacated his seat and Morgan took it.

'Colonel Gurevich? My name is Morgan. I hear you have something to say. Can you hear me?'

'Morgan. Your rank? What authority do you have to make concessions?'

'I have no rank, Colonel Gurevich. That doesn't mean I'm an out-of-work potato farmer, though. I led the attack on Copernicus Base, and the marines are obeying my orders.' Morgan crossed his fingers at that. Whether or not it was true was going to matter. 'That is my authority, such as it is.'

'An ingeniously conceived exercise, carried out with spirit. I should like to know where you came from, and how you got here. Your arrival was entirely unexpected.' Morgan couldn't see the colonel's face in the remote screen, just the distorted reflection of the TV camera in his tinted visor. He sensed a strong bargaining disadvantage there.

'I'd like to discuss the whole thing with you – on some future occasion.' It was necessary thus to lengthen the stride of Gurevich's thinking. 'Meanwhile many have died – '

'Because of your adventure, Mister Morgan. I have lost half my men here. You will find that the more of us you kill, the stiffer will be our resistance.'

'Be reasonable, Gurevich. We didn't ask you to take Copernicus Base. I too have lost many men. And innocent people have died for whom I . . . we care greatly.' He gritted his teeth to mask his thoughts.

'There are no "innocent people". This is the last fight for survival. History will smile on those who survive. History doesn't deal with "innocence".'

At that, Morgan was within an ace of giving in to personal rage – and survival be damned. You can outface the end of the world if you see a world – even of only two people – still to create. But that was over now. Yet this barbaric reflex of killing among the last few human beings had brought a more detached fury to his motives, even though – or rather *especially because* – he himself had played a part in that killing. He felt a deep resentment against the scarcely hidden ape reflexes that could send the human tribe squabbling and gibbering to extinction. It humiliated him. He needed no noble emotion.

'But as you say, history deals at the very least with what survives. Let us look at survival, Colonel Gurevich. The killing has to stop now. Please come out of there. You will be treated with respect and your wounded will be attended to.'

'Your emphasis is mistaken, Mister Morgan. History deals with *what* survives. The nature of that "what" is all-important. There will be no survival under capitalism. It will not maintain its cynical grip out here.'

'What do you propose?'

'It's what I instruct that counts. You will return the control of this base to my men.'

'And if I don't?'

'I will blow the base off the face of the Moon.'

'Hardly possible with a fusion reactor. The plasma can't be sustained once the containing field breaks down. You wouldn't even succeed in blowing yourself up.'

'Not the reactor. The breeder jacket. There's enough plutonium in it to melt down and blow through every level. It only requires the damper rods to be withdrawn. We've bypassed the control circuitry and my good lieutenant here has his hand on the lever. If there's any attempt to take this room, or to activate any of its systems, he will pull the lever. He will pull the lever also if you don't follow my instructions. You need not doubt my sincerity, Mister Morgan. We've got nothing to lose.'

'On the contrary, you've got a lot to lose. I don't believe you give a tinker's cuss for Communism. You care for your country, but you've never exchanged three words with a genuine proletarian. I know that most of you were only too willing to exchange lunar basalt for Russian soil. You couldn't get into space fast enough. It entitled you to a great deal of privilege. Now for God's sake let's not quibble about what people ought to *call* themselves. Just get on up here and play your part in human survival.'

'Ah. I see you're coming round to my point of view. We'll do exactly that. And if the Soviet military presence in space is best suited by aptitude and training to supervise that survival I'm sure you won't quibble if we *choose to call* that supervision Soviet. It's only a name after all, as you say.'

The argument had reached a depth of rhetoric which Morgan no longer felt capable of handling. He wasn't even sure if he was right. After all, both he and Gurevich were talking about power. He needed time. He was sapped by grief. He wanted other shoulders to bear the decisions. The kitchen was too hot for him.

'There's a lot in what you say. Obviously you've got us by the – er, balls. But you'll have to give me time. I haven't the authority to do as you ask. I'll have to consult with my superior on the Wheel. You must have – what – three and a half hours' oxygen left? Give me that time and I'll present your case as well as I can.'

'So much for your authority, Mister Morgan. I should stick to potato farming if I were you. My case does not need skilful presentation. It is very simple.' He shrugged. 'All right. You're a small man. I see you must consult. But I want to hear the consultations, and I want Commodore Litvinov at Astrogorodok, Marshal Petrovski at Tycho, and Colonel Sidorenko at your Big Wheel to hear and take part in the consultations. If you do not comply with these conditions, or if there is any attempt to exclude us from your deliberations – then . . . ' He made the motion of pulling a lever.

Morgan could see that the conflict that he had grasped and held over the past few days was falling into other hands, and that those hands, tossing it to and fro, would surely slip.

'I accept.'

And yet he must still try. His influence might be small, so he must place it carefully. Alas, he felt incompetent to do so. He was no politician.

'Good. You have one hour.'

'But – '

'Don't try my patience. Call me when the radio links are complete.' Gurevich leaned forward and masked the TV camera.

Morgan turned to the corporal at the communications console.

'Can you do that?' Decker nodded. 'Then do it fast, please. You'll need to raise Tycho over the orbiter net, and Astrogorodok via Comsat link and the Wheel –'

'It's all right, Mister Morgan, I know what to do.'

'Of course. I've seen what you can do today.' He needed the loyalty of these men still. 'Call Commander Zeffert up on the laser system as well. I want him to be part of this. Also I want to keep full-time contact with Alpha, Beacon and Condor. Get someone to help you with that.'

He turned to Lieutenant Van Den Burg, who had returned to the second level. 'We've done well, Van. You and your men have done well. But what follows is going to be harder.'

'Gurevich? I don't see us cracking that one.' Morgan looked candidly, critically, at Van Den Burg. To win this man's allegiance, even for only the next few hours, was an absolute requirement. And yet allegiance is won or lost in action, and not coerced or cajoled. How could one seal it? Van Den Burg was a quiet man, without the tough talk of the other Special Space Warfare marines like Mitchell. He was tall, pale-skinned, grey-eyed, scholarly rather than aggressive. Yet he was a good officer. In action he had been fast and decisive. His men had responded instantly to his terse commands. He had dovetailed finely with Morgan's assault. A sympathy formed in battle is a fine sympathy, but could this one be projected beyond the action?

'Van, I need your help still. That was a good mission. Even though some fine men died I'll always remember it as the finest action I saw. It gave half the human race the possibility of a future. At this moment the solar system is at peace.' Van Den Burg was watching him speak, nodding in some perplexity. What he wanted was to be told something he didn't already know.

'That's true, but Gurevich threatens to take it away again.'

'Gurevich initially, but it's soon going to be opened up to the people on Tycho, the Wheel, Astrogorodok, the Minerva rendezvous missions – and the rest of the military here on Copernicus Base. It's going to be threat against threat. What have we got left really? The armed forces of the United States and the Soviet Union. Everyone else is too far away, or they're inaccessible. They have the habit of war. Only now there's no one to put the brake on. There are no political constraints, no tax payers to hobble them, no civilian casualties to worry about –'

'They're not that stupid.'

'No, they're very capable. But the capability is channelled by the old necessities of defence. The military machine has unstoppable inertia.'

'You're trying to tell me that we fight out of habit. But we're fighting for resources.'

'You make it sound as though there are achievable objectives. Well, think of Gurevich. How do we fight him now? Van, we all lose.' Decker signalled from the communications desk. 'Anyway, we've no time now. Look, I've got to ask you to bring Colonel Schnieder here for the conference. During that conference I've got to do some . . . *unconventional* things. This is not a conventional world. I believe our mission hasn't yet finished, Lieutenant, and I want you to use your men to maintain the security of this room during the conference – under my command. I know I've no formal authority over you, but I need your trust for a while longer. After that you can do what you want with me.'

Van Den Burg looked doubtful. 'I'll do what I can. But if I receive a direct order from a superior officer I'll have to think again.'

'That suits me well.'

Thirty-Two

THE BANK of screens in front of Morgan was dark. On his right sat Schnieder, facing him. They had exchanged few words. He now regretted not having made time to gain Schnieder as an ally: rather, he had achieved the opposite. On his left Van Den Burg stood stiffly, still in his space suit. The flap of his thigh-mounted automatic was unbuttoned and tucked back. His serious eyes offered no commitment. Sarin leaned lazily against the wall beside the door, his folded arms cradling an M-45. Sarin would buy five minutes with his life if it came to it. Since Stephanie's death he would have bought five minutes for Morgan with his immortal soul. But it wouldn't be enough. Morgan nodded to Decker who leaned in front of him and threw a switch.

'Colonel Gurevich? Morgan here. I'm now ready to begin my

consultation.'

'Go ahead, Morgan. My monitor is switched on.'

Morgan nodded again to Decker who threw another switch. The faces of the six military commanders appeared in sharp colour. They were blank faces that betrayed nothing but impassivity. They were grey-faced, tired-skinned, but for the younger Zeffert and Sidorenko.

'Gentlemen, please test for eight-on-eight communication.' The six men leaned forward at their keyboards, muttering their assent.

'Gentlemen, if you agree I'll make clear the purpose of this communication.' Morgan paused briefly, though not for quite long enough to receive their agreement. 'Less than an hour ago Copernicus Base was relieved by a commando force from the Wheel.' Gurevich in his deep sanctuary in the reactor room, Litvinov on Astrogorodok and Petrovski at Tycho each turned his gaze to the top right of his screen – to the face of Sidorenko: he looked on indifferently, but for the slight twitch of an eyebrow.

'This was not done with Colonel Sidorenko's knowledge,' Morgan added. 'He's no traitor.

'I regret that there were deaths. As far as we can make out forty men of the Red Army were killed. We lost eighteen of our commandos. One civilian was killed. We regret all of those deaths.'

Litvinov hummed sarcastically. 'Your high moral tone is noted and admired. Don't you Americans ever have anything else to talk about but the ethical values you would *like* to maintain?'

Morgan felt his throat constricting. In this league he was not going to be able to inspire the respect he needed. The fear of defeat was strong in him. He hurried on. 'We now have control of the Base.'

Gurevich laughed, the sound coming tinnily from his helmet microphone. 'Now surely that is a slight exaggeration, Mister Morgan. Remember the purpose of this discussion. Don't let –'

Morgan snatched the initiative back hurriedly. 'I'm sorry, Colonel. I was just coming to that. Colonel Gurevich has control of the Base reactor room. He has the ability to use fuel breeding rods there to destroy this Base, and we do not have the means to prevent him. He demands that Soviet control be restored here. I have explained that I haven't the authority to do that, and that is why we're having this discussion.'

Rathbone could be seen leaning to one side, talking to someone beyond the range of his camera.

'Code message from the Wheel, sir,' whispered Decker. He pushed a sheet of paper over to Morgan, who read it without turning his head.

Gurevich glanced to one side, holding his arm up.

'What was that?' he snapped. Death was very close then.

'A coded message from Captain Rathbone,' said Morgan immediately. 'It says *Lead him on. Get him out. Trick him. Reply.* OK?'

'You'd better tell your captain the rules,' said Gurevich.

But Rathbone didn't wait. At the least, he had been humiliated. 'If there's any loyal American there on Copernicus, I want that man Morgan under arrest. I want to talk to someone I can trust. Who else is there?'

Schnieder came to his feet. Van Den Burg crossed quickly behind Morgan and spoke close to the colonel's ear. 'Hold it a moment, sir. There's a reason for this. We've got to play it cool.' Sarin had swayed forward. Morgan saw him lean back against the wall. Schnieder glared contemptuously at Van Den Burg's restraining hand. Clearly his defeat and captivity had left scars.

'We're letting him explain himself, Rathbone. But don't worry. I'll confirm that arrest.'

Morgan continued. 'He'll pull the handle if he suspects that we're not playing it straight. He nearly did just then. As far as deception is concerned, I don't think we've got a hope. Gurevich isn't a fool. We've already caught him napping once. He's not letting it happen again.' Gurevich was listening to all this with a slight smile. 'Also we've got to have a permanent solution here.'

'What are you suggesting, Morgan?' asked Rathbone.

'Nothing. I'm asking all of you.'

'We are not discussing *suggestions*,' interposed Gurevich. 'You are meant to be obtaining authority to hand over the Base to me.'

'That does seem to be the point, Captain Rathbone,' said Litvinov. 'And it is fully endorsed by the colonel's comrades. We are not here to listen to your perpetual internal squabbles. We will first observe the unconditional surrender of Copernicus Base to Colonel Gurevich. Then we will consider your position. With or without your assent I am instructing the spy Morgan to submit.'

While Litvinov spoke, Rathbone had been busily studying displays and exchanging whispered comments with more than one person out of the range of his TV camera. Morgan remembered the cantankerous ingenuity of the Command Team with nostalgia. Those comfortable days seemed so long ago – before, that is, the stroke that had severed him from his past. Doubtless Sandra Crabtree was gaming the situation out, Zbijowski was, as ever, assessing military capabilities, and McMurdo flipping human life into an abstract balance.

'OK Litvinov,' drawled Rathbone with some display, at least, of assurance, 'we copy your ultimatum, and the answer is *nix*. We have three multiple warhead buses homing on Tycho as of this moment. They've been on their way for fifty hours and they'll impact in ten unless we self-destruct them. If Morgan submits or if Gurevich spills any plutonium, Tycho crater will take on a new depth. Lest we have any trivial debate let me assure you that you have no means of intercepting those missiles. Let me add that when you attacked the Wheel you shot your nuclear bolt. *We've still got ours*. After we've excavated Tycho, for each American who is harmed at Copernicus we will delete another Soviet base, and you'd better remember you haven't got many. I await your unconditional surrender. Message ends.' Rathbone sat back and folded his arms.

Morgan watched, fascinated, while the Russians leaned phlegmatically this way and that, listening to the comments of advisers. Petrovski at Tycho listened the longest, sourly getting the bad news from his radar team. He confirmed it to his comrades.

'It is true. Though I will not confirm the captain's assessment of our inability to defend ourselves.'

'Crap.'

'We will consider this in private. Meanwhile, Colonel Gurevich, we will ask that you be patient and that you do not yet carry out your threat against the Americans.'

'Then you must be brief. My suit's oxygen capacity determines the duration of my threat.'

The silently speeding warheads and Gurevich's immovable deadline hastened the Russians' debate. They returned to the screens fourteen minutes later.

'Well?' said Rathbone in confident anticipation.

'Your counter-ploy is interesting, Captain,' said Litvinov, 'but it neglects some of the more subtle points. You see, not only does it leave us with hostages at Copernicus, but with your shuttle crewmen dispatched to us at Astrogorodok from the Wheel. Your threats of overwhelming force will not improve their lot. Rather the reverse in fact.'

'Wrong,' replied Rathbone genially. 'For the dozen Americans on Astrogorodok we have Colonel Sidorenko and his eight remaining minions on the Wheel. I think they effectively cancel one another out.'

'Not exactly. If you destroy Astrogorodok your men die in that destruction. Ours still live on the Wheel. You might, of course, resort to selective violence, but that can't be helped. We know that the colonel and his men, like all staunch comrades, are able to bear suffering with fortitude.'

'We are honoured by your confidence,' said Sidorenko without expression. Litvinov glanced at him sharply.

'Good try, Litvinov,' said Rathbone, still looking confident, 'but our stance remains. Either Gurevich backs down or Tycho gets transmogrified.'

'Then you also lose your people on Copernicus.'

'Only if Gurevich blows up his own men too. I doubt that his remaining forces at Copernicus could retain control over five hundred – even if he were to be allowed to acquire it. But I repeat – for every American that's harmed there you lose a base. We can even take out Mars, given time; that is if they haven't choked out by then anyway.'

'So,' replied Litvinov, 'in twelve hours from now the Wheel might be the only secure outpost of human life remaining. Do you honestly see yourself doing that?'

'If necessary. If the alternative is to share space with people we can never trust, or to accept their domination, I'll do that. It's the price of total victory.'

'And do you think the Wheel could then survive alone, Captain?' asked Petrovski. 'How about the resources we command here and on Mars? Can you manage without them?' The faces of the Russians were as hard as ever, but Morgan could trace a defensive tone. They no longer spoke from strength. Their arguments were now in a posthumous mode.

'You bet,' replied Rathbone. 'We'll go out and get them. Don't forget, we'll have hydrogen to burn.'

Gurevich and Sidorenko were clearly now looking to Litvinov and Petrovski for leadership. Petrovski nodded slowly at Rathbone's logic. Litvinov raised his dark eyebrows and then brought them down again in a slow frown. Their arguments had run dry. It looked bad for them.

'That's not *quite* true, Captain,' said Morgan. He had been quiet for several minutes. The military leaders looked in surprise – Rathbone with obvious irritation – at this inerruption. 'You can't *necessarily* count on getting the hydrogen.'

'Meaning?' said Rathbone coldly.

Morgan appeared to change the subject. 'Fred, it's good to see you again.'

Zeffert smiled broadly. 'And you, Dick.'

'Tell the assembled personages about the *Minerva* docking, Fred.'

'My pleasure. My task-force, codenamed Possum would you believe, matches orbits with Minerva in about eleven hours. So, I believe, do six kosmolyots originally from Astrogorodok.'

'Possibly,' said Litvinov.

'No problem there,' said Rathbone. 'It fits the scenario. The kosmolyots éase off or we blow the whole works. Or better, they take on hydrogen under Commander Zeffert's control and bring it back here. That way we're all better off.'

'That's not the problem Dick's thinking of. You see, he's got the IFF codes and docking procedures.' *He knows*, thought Morgan.

'Still no problem,' said Rathbone evenly. 'He can give them to you now – over the laser link if you want to keep it discreet.'

Zeffert smiled slightly. 'Over to you, Dick.'

'The problem, Captain Rathbone, is that I'm not going to give Fred the codes.'

'So he goes in without them. He'll get that hydrogen somehow.'

'He won't. If anything approaches *Minerva* without the correct IFF, then the whole shipment blows apart.'

'Then give him the codes and stop trying to be smart. Without that hydrogen we're all finished.'

'I intend to – when you've withdrawn your ultimatum against the Russians.'

'You've got to be kidding. This changes nothing. Our nuclear threat still stands. Your arrest still stands. Van Den Burg, remove that treacherous son of a commie worm from the screen and put him in with your Russian prisoners where he'll feel more at home.'

'Do it!' snapped Schnieder. Van Den Burg put his hand to his automatic, to find himself looking down the barrel of Sarin's M-45. He glanced towards the corridor.

'Say hullo to the nice angels,' murmured Sarin.

Surprisingly, it was Sidorenko who resolved the tension.

'I think you'd better delay that arrest, Captain Rathbone. This does in fact change everything. You now no longer have assured survival. Without that hydrogen shipment the Wheel will last only twenty days.'

Van Den Burg still refrained from touching his automatic.

'So your ultimatum is removed,' said Litvinov. 'Colonel Gurevich's stands. You will now hand over control of Copernicus Base. Let us waste no more time.'

'I'm afraid you still don't understand,' said Morgan, his tone world-weary. 'You don't get the hydrogen either, Commodore. Not under threat.'

'Colonel Gurevich will get the codes from you.'

'Possibly. But you won't be sure they're the right codes – until it's too late, that is.'

Again it was Sidorenko who gave him the space to speak.

'I think the ingenious Mister Morgan may have a scenario of his own – as he has successfully refuted the other two.'

He was given total silence. The commanders had no choice but to listen. He spoke haltingly, choosing his words with care, for a moment in history may not be repealed.

Thirty-Three

'IN SPACE there are about two thousand people left alive,' began Morgan, 'and that's including Mars and the NASA/ESA team on Callisto. We represent the seed of the human race, and we can survive. On their own the people in the Pluto shelter and at Chelyabinsk are powerless to shape their future. It is up to us, and we are few.

'Any plan to kill any of these remaining people is plainly unsatisfactory – not to put too fine a point on it. National alignments are insignificant. Look at the Earth. Where are the boundaries now?

'It's obvious why we've been thinking the way we have: space has been colonised by military people. It's just an oversight. You might as well forget it.'

'Warriors today, saints tomorrow,' sneered Petrovski. 'Very likely.'

'It has been known. But I'm not expecting it. I'm only expecting what's inevitable. Look, we're bound together by need. None of us survives without hydrogen. That comes from Callisto. But on Callisto they can't make out without metals and plastics. Unless we supply them we won't get the hydrogen. We need oxygen and light metals from lunar rock – and especially the oxygen, all that can be produced. So we need the mining capacity of Tycho and Copernicus, and the mass-driver to transport the materials. But then we need heavy metals, and there aren't enough on the Moon. In the long term we will depend for them on the Russian bases on Mars: it's the only source that's anything like exploitable at the moment. And if we're to use all these resources we need supreme technical and industrial back-up. The Americans have that in Earth orbit, and it exists nowhere else.'

'You've got to give it to him. The man's right,' said Zeffert, helping where he could.

Morgan continued. 'We need each of these resources, and each is a unique link in the space economy. If just one of these links fails, if the colonel pulls his lever, or if the captain doesn't disarm those three warheads, then the whole fabric comes apart and the human race ends here, now.'

'And if we give in,' said Litvinov, 'how do we know that the captain won't betray us with the rest of his missiles?'

'Because if there's any betrayal the betrayer is also lost.'

'Who is to command this *Utopia* of yours? D'you think Rathbone will take orders from me, or I from him? Not for long, Mister Morgan. It's a nice thought, but you're up against a consistent history of human conflict. Under whose rules will we operate? Communist? Rathbone doesn't think so. Supposed capitalist democracy? I don't think so.'

'I suggest you curb your ambition for command, because *no one's* going to get a chance for that. It's no Utopia. Be realistic. We *are* commanded by the needs of survival. Requirements for materials and energy will provide ample rules.' At least they were listening. The threats were in abeyance. Rathbone had given no verdict yet. He broke his silence now, but he surprised the meeting with a shift of emphasis.

'I lost my wife down there on Earth. I know – we all lost everything. That's why I always questioned Bootstrap.'

'Bootstrap?'

Rathbone waved the question aside. 'So we survive. In space? What for, Dick? We survive – and then what?'

'What more has anyone ever done? We survive and then we die, and others survive. There's never been a way out, and should there be now? And do we break the cycle now because there isn't?

'Life is fulfilled by life and nothing more. We don't have to just sit up there in those tin cans and wait for death, any more that we just sat and waited for death on Earth. Have you forgotten Pluto and Chelyabinsk? I doubt that they'll forget us. There's a vast human reservoir down there condemned to slow death. Fred gives them twenty years, but whether it's twenty or a hundred they're going to need our help. We can do it. We can build up an ability in space that will think nothing of going down there and fishing them up, given a decade or two's work.'

'There are no people at Chelyabinsk,' said Litvinov. 'It's a museum of frozen seeds and embryos.'

'Good. The oak tree in the Main Dome here is in vacuum now. Perhaps we can replant it some day. We keep forgetting Callisto, too. That's a space operation with a purpose. They're building the first interstellar probe out there. We're not planet-bound now.'

'You're thinking of outside help?'

'I wouldn't bank on it. It's worth a thought though – or even the combined efforts of a few generations. It would keep the weapons experts off the streets at least.' Morgan sensed that he was casting his net too wide. He didn't want to overdo it. He waved the argument aside, as though in deprecation. 'The economy that's within our reach is a plentiful one. We can't hide poverty away as we did on Earth; you've got to be well-provided to survive out here. Nor can we be idle. Survival will demand our efforts, yet those efforts need not be unrewarding in other ways. The point is that we will obey those demands. The alternative is universal death.'

He waited long, fighting to keep his breathing even. This was the time. There was no more he could say. Again it was Sidorenko who lent his aid.

'The argument is compelling. There are no alternatives. I give my support to Colonel Gurevich if he will come out of the reactor room.'

'I have listened to the arguments. But if I come out, still how do I know what the Americans will do?'

Morgan looked at the screen. 'It's up to you. You'd better convince him.'

'We'll destruct the warheads,' said Rathbone. 'Marshal Petrovski can give radar confirmation.'

'We'll call off our reinforcements in the Mare Imbrium,' added

Petrovski, '*when* the warheads are destroyed.'

'Colonel Schnieder?' He remained indecisive.

'This has to be all or nothing, Colonel,' prompted Rathbone. 'May I suggest all? It beats radiation poisoning by a significant margin.'

'OK, Colonel Gurevich. I'll have your men released here.'

'Good man.'

'But you must also give them back their weapons.'

'I don't think I can do that. It wouldn't be prudent.'

'I will order them to be peaceful.'

'I don't place that much reliance on their discipline.'

'*Wait*! I have an alternative,' said Petrovski. 'I think you had better make the weapons secure on *both* sides. I won't say disarm: lock them up and let Colonel Gurevich *see* them locked up.'

Schnieder sat looking at his feet, steeling himself to overcome the honourable motives of half a lifetime's military service. 'I will do that.'

Twenty minutes later only Rathbone's face was still on the communications screen. Men were busy at the other stations. Sarin stood beside Morgan. Otherwise they were alone. The discussion was stilted. There had been moments during the last hour when Rathbone had threatened eternity in general, and had threatened Morgan in particular. It was impossible to forget those moments.

'I don't think we'd have reached this agreement without Sidorenko,' said Morgan. 'He came through decisively when his pals were still in Politburo mode.'

'You have an essential truth there.'

'He showed courage. Whereas . . . ' Rathbone's attitude had wounded him, and he wanted him to know it. ' . . . I'm sorry you couldn't have found it more – natural – to support me. We've faced a great deal together.' Rathbone didn't answer, and smiled uncertainly. Morgan continued. 'In your book I'm still under arrest. I should have liked to come back to the Wheel. I worked very happily with your Command Team.'

'It might be arranged. I could use you.'

'Thank you.'

'For one thing you could help me pacify Sidorenko.'

'How do you mean? What's the matter with him?'

'I'm talking about the *real* Sidorenko. He's still fuming in the dungeon.'

'Since when? Morgan made a swift and massive readjustment. 'You seem to imply . . . '

'Of course I do. Do you think the Soviets would have accepted your plan if I'd been wholeheartedly for it? They'd have been suspicious as hell! Why d'you think they bought it? *Because they believed Sidorenko had bought it*. We had to convert one of them or the others would never have come round. We tried talking to Sidorenko, but he was still pretty angry with us for conning him.'

'So you used Wheeldata instead?'

'We did.'

'I think I'd better get back to the Wheel.'

'I wish you would.'

MOUNTED SEARCH
by Jerry Ahern

Sarah twisted involuntarily in her saddle, her eyes drifting to the AR-15 rifle she had taken off one of the dead bodies the morning after the War. Her spine shivered.

As she and Jenkins rode deeper into the mountains, she felt less despair. She knew that her husband's survival retreat was somewhere in these mountains and that it was only a matter of time before she and John would reunite.

Each time Jenkins and Sarah turned a corner, every time they cleared a bluff, they searched for a sign of life. And through the dimness of dusk they found it. Looking down into the shallow valley below, they viewed a town, its people rushing in the streets. They heard sounds of smashing glass from the shop windows. They heard shots as well.

Jenkins rode up beside Sarah and pointed straight ahead. 'Those people were fools to stay in their town,' he observed.

'Can't we do something, Jenkins?'

Jenkins shrugged. 'I'm no weapons expert like your husband was.'

'You mean, like he *is*,' she corrected.

'I'm afraid you're wrong Mrs. Rourke. Atlanta is just one big crater by now, and you said yourself that your husband landed there.'

'But he can't be dead,' she insisted. 'Not my husband. Not John Rourke. Not THE SURVIVALIST.'

NEW ENGLISH LIBRARY

THE SHINING
by Stephen King

Danny was only five years old but in the words of old Mr Halloran he was a 'shiner', aglow with psychic voltage. When his father became caretaker of the Overlook Hotel his visions grew frighteningly out of control.

For as winter closed in and a blizzard cut them off completely, the hotel seemed to develop a life of its own. It was meant to be empty, but who was the lady in Room 217, and who were the masked guests going up and down in the elevator? And why did the hedges shaped like animals seem so alive?

Somwhere, somehow, there was an evil force in the hotel — and that too had begun to shine.

A Royal Mail service in association with the Book Marketing Council & The Booksellers Association.

Post-A-Book is a Post Office trademark.

Book
Tokens

NEL BESTSELLERS

All The Rivers Run	Nancy Cato	£1.95
Brown Sugar	Nancy Cato	£1.50
Forefathers	Nancy Cato	£2.50
North-West By South	Nancy Cato	£1.75
Adventures in Two Worlds	A.J. Cronin	£1.75
The Citadel	A.J. Cronin	£1.95
Grand Canary	A.J. Cronin	£1.75
Hatter's Castle	A.J. Cronin	£2.25
Keys of the Kingdom	A.J. Cronin	£1.95
Shannon's Way	A.J. Cronin	£1.75
The Stars Look Down	A.J. Cronin	£2.25
Women's Work	Anne Tolstoi Wallach	£1.95
Acts of Kindness	Charlotte Vale Allen	£1.50
Believing In Giants	Charlotte Vale Allen	£1.75
Daddy's Girl	Charlotte Vale Allen	£1.75
Hidden Meanings	Charlotte Vale Allen	£1.75
Love Life	Charlotte Vale Allen	£1.50
Meet Me In Time	Charlotte Vale Allen	£1.25
Moments of Meaning	Charlotte Vale Allen	£1.50
Perfect Fools	Charlotte Vale Allen	£1.50
Times of Triumph	Charlotte Vale Allen	£1.25
Almonds and Raisins	Maisie Mosco	£1.95
Children's Children	Maisie Mosco	£1.95
Scattered Seed	Maisie Moscoe	£1.95

NEL P.O. BOX 11, FALMOUTH TR10 9EN, CORNWALL

Postage Charge:

U.K. Customers 45p for the first book plus 20p for the second book and 14p for each additional book ordered to a maximum charge of £1.63.

B.F.P.O. & EIRE Customers 45p for the first book plus 20p for the second book and 14p for the next 7 books; thereafter 8p per book.

Overseas Customers 75p for the first book and 21p per copy for each additional book.

Please send cheque or postal order (no currency).

Name ....

Address ....

....

Title ....

While every effort is made to keep prices steady, it is sometimes necessary to increase prices at short notice. New English Library reserve the right to show on covers and charge new retail prices which may differ from those advertised in the text or elsewhere. (8)